# BLACK ROSE QUEEN

## BLACK ROSE SORCERESS, BOOK 3

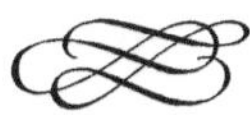

## CONNIE SUTTLE

SUBTLEDEMON PUBLISHING, LLC

*To Walter, Joe, Larry, Sarah, Lee, Dianne, and Mark*
*Thank you*


*And for those who waited patiently for this book, even when it was long over-due. You are my heroes*

# CHAPTER 1

*N*y-nes
  *North*

"I'm not hungry, but thank you for the offer of food," I told the woman.

"Your name—North? Really? Like ah," she couldn't recall the word *direction*.

"Yes. Like the direction," I smiled at her. She appeared nervous. They all did. I couldn't blame them; I was a relative newcomer to this part of Ny-nes. In the past two months, I'd made my way toward the largest city from the swamp country far to the south.

The time had come, after all. Time to bring my message to the regular people of Ny-nes—that the god they feared was a false one, and not to be believed. That the Prophet lying in a glass coffin wasn't the same Prophet their leader said he was.

I'd been born with power. I'd survived for many years in Ny-nes, until the time came to deliver the messages I bore—the truths the people needed to know.

"You come from—south?" The woman's husband asked. "Named North?" He chuckled.

"It's funny, I know," I agreed with him. Their lack of education made them no less human in my eyes—that could be remedied. What couldn't be remedied so easily was the pervasion of Ny-nes' national religion.

*Or the ever-present fear of it.*

"We thank for the healing," the woman stroked her daughter's hair as the child hugged her mother's legs.

"No healer been here for a while," the man added.

I wondered how they'd feel if they knew their daughter had a slight bit of power within her. I'd suppressed it, so she could live her life without that fear dogging her steps. Instead, I nodded to both adults, gave the girl a smile and walked out of their home, which was little more than a hovel.

Kaakos thought his people would never know how many lies they'd been told.

I would increase my power; I felt it. Soon, it would flow more easily through me as I allowed it to grow. *Then* I would inform Ny-nes' citizens of their leader's cruel duplicity. The time had come for Kaakos to account for his many sins.

~

*KING'S CITY*

*Kerok*

"I'm surprised Drenn was willing to come this far—it's filled with cobwebs." I ducked to avoid yet another low-hanging web.

"It should have been a deterrent, yet your brother found the way to your ancestor's resting place anyway." Adahi walked ahead of me, allowing the cobwebs to pass through his ephemeral body.

I wasn't ephemeral and was forced to either step aside to avoid the dusty, white webs, or brush the larger ones away as we traveled deeper into the catacombs.

Today was supposed to be a lesson day with Adahi, but instead, he'd chosen to lead me into the catacombs to see the ancestor I was named after. Sherra was spending the day at Doret's training camp, helping the younglings with their lessons.

In two days, the trial for Merrin would be held. Garkus' trial would be held two days after the conclusion of Merrin's. Hunter and I decided to do it this way, as their crimes involved the murders of civilians and weren't strictly a military matter.

The surviving members of Merrin's crew had already been put to death, as they were military deserters. Kage had dispatched them efficiently and as painlessly as he could.

*Not that they deserved such consideration.*

Things were changing, but the gears moved slowly to effect those changes.

"Just down this way," Adahi took a left turn, leading me into a side-tunnel.

"Half the lights are out," I complained. My words were useless—Adahi could see it as easily as I. With only a light on here and there along that tunnel, it became an eerie trip down a monster's gullet. The walls narrowed quickly, and became a gauntlet that could devour you whenever the darkness stretched too far.

Adahi turned another corner, disappearing into one of the darker areas. I almost had to feel my way to follow, until I turned the corner, too.

There, illuminated like the sun breaking through clouds, lay King Thorn I's body. For someone who'd been dead for centuries, he was amazingly intact.

"Did you do that? Keep him whole?" I breathed as I approached the dais where his body lay.

"I had nothing to do with it," Adahi replied, his voice a low rumble. "Thorn did that himself."

Increasingly, I'd come to realize just how much power the first King Thorn held. A spell that could hold long after his death? That was something far beyond my previous imaginings.

"We assume that death ends everything for us," Adahi pointed out, as if reading my mind. "In his later years, Thorn turned his thoughts to what could be maintained beyond that."

"He has calluses on his hands," I pointed out. "Like I do." Calluses like those were a side-effect of lobbing continuous fireblasts at the enemy—any seasoned warrior had them.

"Because he was also the ultimate Commander of the army," Adahi struggled to hide a smile. "Doret is currently writing a history of the times when all those things changed—when it became forbidden for the Crown Prince to serve the army in any capacity. You can thank Ruarke for that—and for many other changes, too."

"Why was Ruarke such a bastard?" I asked.

"Ah, you have managed to put your finger on it with a rhetorical question," Adahi chuckled.

"I think you'll have to explain that to me," I said. "He had to be of royal blood to use the book."

"Very true—an astute observation," Adahi nodded as he studied Thorn's body beside me. "You should know, however, that his father's first wife was also of royal blood—Wulf I married his second cousin."

"Fuck," I breathed.

"Yes, Ruarke was of royal blood; he merely wasn't the King's son. He was the Queen's son."

"What happened to her? I know Doret married Wulf before Ruarke went crazy and murdered her sister."

"Let's say the Queen continued her affair," Adahi shrugged. "The King eventually discovered it. To save Ruarke's position as the King's son, she claimed it was a recent thing. She and her lover were put to death—according to the laws governing the royal family. Ruarke maintained his title of Prince Commander of the army, as he was believed to be the King's eldest child."

"You're saying that Ruarke wanted revenge for his mother's death?"

"Ruarke was always a bit twisted," Adahi said. "Remember, too, that the King put both Ruarke's parents to death, not just the one. In my mind, Ruarke was angry with his mother for carrying on with another man—he didn't know at the time that the King wasn't his father. His hatred for women grew from that moment, and when the King took Doret for his wife, it blossomed into a deadly flower."

"At least he's dead, now," I mumbled.

"Yes, but that is only a lesser evil. Kaakos—he is the greater threat of those two. As much power as Ruarke held, Kaakos' is far stronger."

"Where was Thorn's Book?" I asked, focusing on the body again while struggling to put Kaakos out of my mind for a moment. "I don't see any evidence of it around his body."

"Because it was floating above it," Adahi explained. "All Drenn had to do was pull it away."

"And run out of here, no doubt," I said.

"Like hounds were after him, I'm sure."

"I should have been more curious," I admitted. "I should have been here before my brother. So many things could have been avoided."

"Don't blame yourself too much," Adahi said. "This one was more at fault for laying a flawed spell," he jerked his head toward the body. "This isn't why I brought you here, either, as much of a pleasure as it is to revisit past mistakes."

Adahi's sarcasm made me turn in his direction. "Why did you bring me, then?"

"Look at his left hand—it's lying at his side away from anyone casually perusing his body—or taking away the book floating above his chest."

That meant leaning over the body to look at the left hand, and could bring me into contact with the body itself.

"Don't worry, he won't be angry that you touched him," Adahi smiled. "Lift his left hand, if that will make things easier."

That's what I ended up doing—reaching over the body with my right hand to capture his left hand and lift it up so I could see it in better light.

King Thorn wore a ring. My eyes went to it immediately, once I lifted his hand. I attempted to put out of my mind how supple the body remained—the arm and hand lifted easily and showed no signs of decay.

"Take the ring," Adahi sounded reverent. "It belongs to you, now."

It took both hands and my leaning over the body to do it, but I managed to work the ring off the finger. I laid the hand and arm down again, as gently as I could before drawing away to examine the crest on the ring.

The ring was gold, with a large square of onyx forming the base of the crest. Atop that, in delicately carved detail, was a tangle of golden thorns surrounding a rose made of tiny rubies.

"Put it on," Adahi said softly beside me.

"What if it doesn't fit?"

"Put it on," he repeated.

Like the previous owner, I slipped it onto the third finger of my left hand. It glowed for a moment, before adjusting itself to fit my finger.

"Step back," Adahi grasped my elbow to pull me away from the body.

He was wise to do so—the body decayed and transformed before our eyes, turning flesh to dust and leaving only rotted clothing and a skeleton behind. I think I held my breath during the entire process.

~

*South Camp*

*Sherra*

"Those two are troublemakers," Pottles said as we watched the group play with shield balls on the training field.

I knew the ones she meant without having them pointed out.

On a nearby field, Caral, Misten, Wend and a few others were training a group of girls to make their first shield balls. Eventually, those trainees would be playing the games, too, to increase their agility and the strength of their shields.

In the game Pottles and I supervised, some of the shield balls—the strongest ones—were destroying the weaker ones thrown against them.

Each student was allowed three shield balls of uniform size. Once their balls were destroyed, they were out of the game. It was incentive to make better, stronger shields.

Ferni and Jeen were the troublemakers; Pottles frowned at them more often than not. Those two would have been chosen as favorites by the Bulldog, had she still been alive.

They saw their fellow students as lesser beings, and I was considering how to deal with that—as was Pottles.

"This is what happens when their parents allow them to run wild, I suppose," Pottles breathed a troubled sigh. "No discipline, and no concern for others."

They were fourteen and fifteen; I was grateful the boys were being trained at West Camp or there'd be trouble for sure, unless I was badly mistaken.

"I think it may be time to tell them what the discipline used to be for flaunting the rules," Pottles grumbled, crossing her arms tightly over her chest and frowning.

"What was that?"

"Putting a damper on their power. The more serious the infraction, the more the power is dampened. If they don't learn from their mistakes, they could end up having their power burned out of them when they reach adulthood."

"That's how the laws used to be?"

"Yes. I'd say those laws could use some revisions, but there's a place —and a reason—for them now."

"I'll ask Kerok if there's a way to do that."

"Of course there's a way to do it—he's the Supreme Commander of the Army, and the King. He can put those laws into effect. I'd ask Hunter to write the final draft, first."

"Cole is working out as my advisor—with Caral, obviously. I'll ask Cole to help shape the law with input from Caral and me, then give it to Hunter and have him write it out. Kerok can decide whether he wants to sign it or not."

"Let Thorn know you'll be putting something together," Pottles advised. "It's never a good idea to spring something like this on anyone, especially the King."

Nobody called Kerok by his middle name except me. They either referred to him as the King, King Thorn or just Thorn, depending on their station and how well they knew him.

Usually he smiled when he heard me call him Kerok. Hunter told me not long ago that Kerok was the name he'd been called as a child, until he reached adulthood and took over the army.

The only time he went by Kerok after that was when he didn't wish to be recognized.

*Like at North Camp, when he was searching for a new escort.* I breathed a sigh at that thought. Until the end of our training, my fellow trainees and I had no idea the Prince Commander was in our midst, acting as a lesser officer in the Prince Commander's army.

Back then, I had no idea who he was, or how much I'd come to love him.

"Adahi told me two days ago to talk to you about the Bulldog," Pottles said, changing subjects and surprising me with the new topic.

"What about her?"

I understood that he, as the Phantom, had brought about the Bulldog's death. He'd ensured it by having her bitten by a poisonous snake. That's all I knew.

"Kyri, Adahi and I have known for a while that Ruarke and Kaakos have spies in Az-ca," Pottles began.

I shifted uncomfortably while absently keeping my eyes on the trainee game before us. I'd suspected there were spies, but hadn't found any—other than Merrin. That alliance had been made after Merrin's criminal acts. He'd committed high treason by allying himself with Ruarke to destroy Az-ca.

"Willing spies?" I asked, my voice a whisper.

"Most of them," Pottles nodded. "They prefer those who used to have power, and are angry or carry a grudge for some reason. Anyone who is disenchanted with Az-ca's leadership becomes a prime target. Those who are invisible are preferred, because they are easy to overlook and easily swayed by gold and promises. Ruarke never sought to restore their power, because it would make his spies simpler to find. It was far better to tap them for information, leaving them disgruntled by their limited capabilities. They were more pliable that way."

"What does that have to do with the Bulldog?" I asked.

"She was approached after she was dismissed as an instructor. Adahi was already keeping an eye on her—because I asked him to keep watch over you during your training."

I could tell she didn't like admitting to having me watched. "Adahi would never interfere with the Bulldog's favoritism or her lack of skill as an instructor—those were problems for the leadership of Az-ca to deal with. It was only when Thorn punished the Bulldog, sending her to the potato farms in the southern domes that he began to worry. She'd be close enough to the King to bring mischief, or act as a spy on occasion."

"What about the one who approached her?" I asked, still watching the trainees. They were down to four girls, now, all of them talented.

"He's dead, too; Adahi killed him first, then took the Bulldog from her sleeping quarters. I believe he questioned her at length before she died."

"I didn't hear about another death," I began.

"Because that one was invisible. An old servant, who washed out of warrior training long ago. He attached himself to one of the Council members, only taking a pittance for his pay, as he was rewarded by Ruarke or whomever held his reins. He approached the Bulldog when he learned of her punishment. We had no idea someone so close to the Council had been converted to Ruarke's cause. Adahi ensured that his death appeared natural—that the servant had died in his sleep."

"So Adahi doesn't know who the spies are—he must hunt for them, like anyone else?"

"Adahi isn't anyone else," Pottles snorted. "But yes, he must hunt for them. It's a self-appointed task, you understand."

"Does the enemy know he's doing this?"

"Kaakos knows now, I believe. That in itself is a blow to his ego. He believes he destroyed Adahi long ago. To find that he's still active? That will burn Kaakos' soul—what small, twisted remnant of it remains within him."

"You think Kaakos will increase his efforts, now that Ruarke is dead?" I asked, while a fear I hadn't known before crawled inside my mind.

"He will want revenge against Az-ca for the destruction of his army, both times. He'll want Adahi dead, too," Pottles' laugh was humorless. "He wants Adahi and Az-ca destroyed, however he can do it. I've worried about this ever since I learned that Kaakos was in control of Ruarke's mind—secretly, of course, until just before Ruarke's death. What Ruarke had done to his spies, Kaakos did to him. It would be fitting, if it weren't so terrifying."

"What are you holding back?" I asked, watching as one of the four trainees was eliminated from the game.

"Kaakos has abilities that Kyri and I have little knowledge of, and other talents we've only speculated about," Pottles said. "In Kyri's absence, I worry that Kaakos will work out a way to recruit more spies—willingly or not."

"How? I thought he'd have to be in close contact with the ones he controlled, to set the spell," I began.

"But hasn't he been? We don't know how many are still living, with whom Ruarke came in contact. If Kaakos was using Ruarke as a pair of eyes—secretly of course, how many of those could he have marked —also secretly? It takes a great deal of power to pull them into his web, but he's angry enough to expend that power."

"The villagers from Vale?" I turned to Pottles, then, forgetting the trainee contest before us. "Were any of those washouts?"

"Only the King or Hunter would have those records. We can't say for sure, Adahi and I. Without Kyri's assistance in this, we can only assume."

"And Kyri was foolish enough to go after him herself," I breathed.

"I haven't heard from her in several days." Pottles' admission contained a great deal of worry.

"At least you've heard from her," I began.

"I think she may be attempting to contact your dreamwalker, who may be avoiding her," Pottles said.

"Why would she do that?"

"To ask questions that only the dreamwalker might know."

"That bothers me."

"That Kyri won't contact you?"

"That—and that my dreamwalker has a mind of her own," I confessed.

"It's you—just a different you, buried in a part of your brain that isn't conscious when you are. You share memories, but only after the fact, according to Adahi."

"I vaguely recall what the dreamwalker has done and said," I agreed. "At first, I thought those things were only dreams."

"Do you remember if the dreamwalker had any other interactions before you came to us in Kyri's City?"

"I don't know. If she did, then I considered it a dream and forgot about it."

"Interesting. Two more out. We have a winner," she said, drawing my attention back to the game. With a sigh, I followed her onto the training field to congratulate the victor.

∿

"I HAVE SOMETHING TO TELL YOU," I said, at the precise moment Kerok informed me of the same as we sat down for dinner that evening.

"You go first," he said, a smile curving his mouth. Even with a deep scar, he was handsome, especially when he smiled.

"All right," I frowned at my plate, considering how to begin. "We have two students at the girl's training camp. They're what Pottles calls troublemakers. She and the others have to watch them every second."

"We get the same thing at the men's camps sometimes," Kerok agreed.

"What do you do about it?" I asked.

"Punishment. Demerits, too. If they still don't behave, they're washed out and their power is removed. If a crime is committed, then the appropriate punishment for that is also levied. Those are crimes against the King as well as against Az-ca."

"Pottles said that in the old times, the troublemaker's power was reduced if they continued to get into trouble, with a warning that it would be burned out of the offender if they still refused to behave according to the rules."

"I haven't heard of that," Kerok's brows drew together in a frown.

"She says it can be done, it just hasn't been done in a long time. She'd like to request your permission to reinstitute that rule."

"I'll need to see it in writing, and then determine who is talented enough to limit power rather than removing it. I can make a decision after that."

"Will you mind if Cole, Caral and I work on it?"

"Mind? Of course not. If what you say is true, it may be a good alternative to what we're doing now. With recent losses and dwindling numbers of those with the talent, we need every able body we can get for the army. I don't believe for a moment that Kaakos is done with us."

"That's something else Pottles said. She told me that all along, Ruarke had spies here in Az-ca. People you wouldn't notice, normally, because they were mostly invisible to the rest of us. One in particular was a warrior washout who went to work as a servant to a Councilman. When Adahi found him approaching the Bulldog to convert her to Ruarke's cause, he discovered the plot and killed both, as the Phantom. He made the servant's death appear to be from natural causes, so no questions would be asked.

"That's—interesting," Kerok lifted his fork cautiously, as if it would turn on him next, as some of Az-ca's citizens had already done.

"It frightens me. She said Kaakos was secretly in control of Ruarke, and my dreamwalker confirmed that. Anyone with power or who used to have it, that came into close contact with Ruarke, may be targeted by Kaakos now, because he knows who and what they are."

"Did Doret say anything about Veri's death? Was she approached, too?"

"I don't know," I replied. "I was so stunned by the other news, I forgot to ask."

"I think I'll have a conversation with Adahi the next time he's here," Kerok's frown became a grimace.

"What's your news?" I asked.

"It can wait," he said. "It's nothing important—not compared to yours. Write up the proposed law. Hunter and I will review it together."

~

*ARRESH*

I call myself by that name—Arresh—because it is the near-mirror image of Sherra's name. We are one and separate, at the same time. I stand at her bedside, watching her sleep, taking care to place a shield over her so she won't be wakened.

This time I had to be careful; if she awoke, she would argue with me. I disliked that idea—in this case.

I intended to break the law.

With a fleeting glance at Thorn's sleeping form, I *stepped* away from the royal suite and straight into the King's lockup, where Merrin and Garkus were held prisoner. One would be freed—the other would die. I had reasons for both, and those reasons would be kept from Sherra.

Once inside Merrin's cell, I cautiously approached his sleeping body, careful not to awaken him. His death would anger Kerok, but there were things Kerok didn't know and likely wouldn't, until it was far too late.

I only needed to enclose Merrin in a tight shield and remove the air from it, allowing him to suffocate. Reaching out a hand, I formed the shield.

Merrin's eyes flew opened as he gasped for breath.

Then, the worst happened—I struggled against the power that suddenly infused Merrin's body; his power had returned and he fought to *step* away. Merrin I could hold. What I wrestled with was the power *behind* Merrin.

In the end, Merrin didn't *step* away. Kaakos jerked him to Ny-nes, knocking down half the cell to do it before I could bring Merrin his death in another way. That's when Garkus, whose cell was nearby, began shouting for guards.

Hurriedly, I turned to perform the second portion of my plan, since the first had gone so spectacularly wrong.

With a heave and a great deal of expended power, I sent Garkus in the same direction Merrin had gone.

# CHAPTER 2

*K*erok

My angry shout brought Sherra into the sitting area of our suite immediately. Wrapped hastily in a dressing robe, she looked disheveled and terrified from being awakened so abruptly, but there was no help for it.

"Repeat that, please," my voice was a hiss as Kage stood in the doorway with Hunter and Barth.

Kage kept his voice steady as he repeated the message from the guards at the lockup. "Merrin and Garkus have escaped. Half of Merrin's cell was destroyed in the process. We still don't know how Garkus slipped away—his cell is intact and the door is still locked."

"I have done divination on the guards who were on duty at the time—none were involved in any way," Barth confirmed Kage's words.

"Adahi," I shouted.

He appeared beside me, looking concerned.

"Did you do this?" I demanded.

"Do what?"

"Set Merrin and Garkus free?"

"Why would I do that?" Adahi shook his head. "That defies reason."

"Have you determined anything from the divination of their cells?" I turned back to Barth.

"It was blocked," Barth confessed. "I couldn't determine anything from the walls or inanimate objects there."

"Bloody, fucking hell," I cursed. "Does it look like either regained their power? How is this possible?"

"I've never heard of anyone regaining power on their own," Barth said, his expression troubled. "If the power is removed, someone would have to give it back to them. I burned the power out of Garkus myself."

"I will take a look at the cell. Do you wish to come with me?" Adahi asked.

"Yes. Let me get dressed."

"I'll come, too," Sherra said and almost ran toward the bedchamber to find clothing other than her robe.

❧

*SHERRA*

"How?" I shook my head, just as Kerok did. Barth had done a second divination in both cells, while I maintained contact with him.

The mystery surrounding the escape was just as deep as it was before our attempt.

Nothing came from it. Even if someone had Merrin's talents gained through Thorn's Book, we should have sensed *something*.

*Do you suppose Kaakos is involved in this?* Kerok asked in mindspeak.

*I hope not.* The idea made me shiver in the dim, early-morning light inside Merrin's cell. The covers on his bed were rumpled, as if he'd awakened suddenly before disappearing through a broken wall. The trouble, however, was that beyond the wall lay the only escape from the lockup, and it was guarded. "We should have killed him when he was captured," I whispered.

"A let-down, isn't it?" Somehow, Pottles had received word and she'd *stepped* in, with Armon right behind her.

"I sent mindspeak to both," Adahi said as he gazed at Merrin's cell. "As they should be made aware of this."

"Do you think Garkus is a danger to the people?" Kerok turned to Barth.

"I didn't see that in him when I removed his power and had him locked up," Barth said. "But that was before he spent time here." He swept a hand to indicate the lockup.

"Nevertheless, we must inform the villages, so they will report to us if either are seen," Hunter advised.

"Write the message and order it carried to the villages," Kerok ordered.

"It will be done, my King."

*If Kaakos is involved, somehow,* Adahi warned Kerok and me.

I'd already thought that; his silent words merely confirmed my fears.

~

N*y-nes*

*Kyri*

"Why in the name of anything resembling sense would she send you to me?" I glared at Garkus, as if that would make him disappear as quickly as he'd appeared early that morning.

"She calls herself Arresh, when she's like that," Garkus looked troubled—by where Sherra's dreamwalker had sent him, and by my reluctance to accept his help.

She'd restored his power, too, before tossing him through the barrier to land in the poor lean-to I'd inhabited for a few weeks. It lay in a very small, incredibly poor village outside Kaakos' main city.

Long ago the city had another name, but for five centuries it had been called Mendacium. The people no longer knew the meaning of the word, and to the unenlightened, it was held as a holy name and one associated with their Prophet.

Years ago, I'd laughed about it—that the city itself stood upon the lies that held Ny-nes together.

I couldn't see Mendacium for the clouds of pollution surrounding it, and people choked on the soot and filth of it every day.

Garkus cleared his throat—he thought I was ignoring him. I wasn't, I'd merely been distracted for a moment. He and I were back to Arresh, and the thing she'd done that troubled me most of all. She'd changed Garkus' skin tone. His normally darker skin would have made him stand out in Ny-nes, and mark him as an intruder. After Sherra's dreamwalker was finished with him, he essentially looked like anyone else in this despot-ruled land, except for his well-fed appearance overall.

"Merrin disappeared—I was told that much before I landed here," Garkus sighed.

"I think he was inhabited by the one you call Kaakos. I heard him talking to himself at night—or so I thought. Until I heard him answering questions that sounded relatively sane," he shrugged.

I went still, staring at Garkus after his admission. It was more than possible that Kaakos had done just that.

"Tell me the answers he was giving," I snapped.

"He gave numbers—of Council members. Names, too, of those who'd attend his trial, and their rank or title."

"No wonder Sherra's dreamwalker intervened." I was beginning to see the sense in her actions, now. Sending Garkus to me with this information was helpful, too, in allowing me to see how sly and inventive Kaakos had become. Somehow, he'd pulled Merrin away—probably to serve his purposes in Ny-nes, or to teach him before sending him back to Az-ca, at the head of an army.

Kaakos likely had hidden spies in Az-ca—ones that Adahi hadn't located yet. With Ruarke dead, it was only a matter of time before Kaakos found a replacement, too—and Merrin could be a suitable fit, with his penchant for torturing before killing. Merrin also had sufficient information on how Az-ca's army fought. Kaakos would revel in that knowledge, before finding ways to destroy Az-ca, once and for all.

"We have a lot of work to do," I sighed. "Tread carefully here,

Garkus. Kaakos' spies could be anywhere. Unless I'm wrong, Merrin has joined the enemy, willingly or not."

"What are we doing here, then?" Garkus demanded. "We could be found and killed in the next few minutes, if what you say is true."

"We're looking for a way into Kaakos' palace," I said. "What else would we be doing?"

~

*KING'S PALACE*

*Sherra*

"Nobody knows where Garkus may have gone," I said. "Merrin—I worry that he's defected to the enemy."

Cole's brow furrowed as I spoke, but he didn't say anything. He and Caral had joined me in my study—the one Kerok had given me, suitably appointed for my needs.

My study wasn't far from his, actually; Kerok said it was in case he needed to confer with my advisors and me.

Cole and Caral had become regular attendees at advisory meetings with the King, Hunter (whose title of Crown Prince still befuddled him), Barth, Armon and Levi. Occasionally, Kage would join us in discussions regarding the King's guards, because he also served as their commander-in-chief.

It didn't hurt that Kage still held all his warrior's abilities in his position. He'd gone with Kerok and Hunter to relieve many former Council members of their positions, sending them home without retirement compensation.

They'd done nothing to deserve it.

The ones remaining had given at least a half-effort to represent their villages, although they'd been outnumbered during their tenure and any suggestions made were quickly voted down by their opponents and Crown Prince Drenn, Kerok's deceased brother.

"Word has been sent to the villages about Garkus and Merrin's escape, and a reward has been posted," I went on, coming back to the subject at hand. "Although I don't believe Merrin is still in Az-ca."

"How much?" Cole asked.

"Fifty gold pieces for Garkus, two hundred fifty for Merrin."

"That's quite the reward," Caral blinked.

"Kerok is that angry about it," I explained. "He swears if he finds that anyone participated in either escape, they'll be brought before him for swift judgment."

"What would the Queen's position be on that person?" Cole asked, his voice steady.

"I don't know—I trust Kerok in the matter," I waved a hand. "He has the most experience in this."

"Very well. You say you wish to rewrite the old law? Is there a written reference to the old one?" Cole was back to the business at hand.

"I—there may be one in Kyri's library," I said. "I can ask Pottles."

"I can send mindspeak to Doret," Cole offered. "If there is a copy of the old law, I'd like to see it before writing the new version."

"What if it's in the older writing?" I asked.

"Kyri taught me how to read it. I can write it, too, if necessary."

"That would be helpful," Caral ventured. "Armon says there are records in the King's library that nobody can read because they're written in an archaic fashion. Hunter told him so."

"Kyri has many copies of those things in her private library," Cole said. "She let me read some of them, but this particular set of laws wasn't included in that list. With your permission, my Queen, I'll visit Doret at the training camp to ask about those."

"Go ahead," I told him. "Caral and I can put a list of considerations together while you're gone, and we'll compare that to the old laws when you find and translate them for us."

"Good idea." Cole gave me a smile and left my study, heading for the side door of the palace. He'd *step* from there to the training camp for his conversation with Pottles.

"We need a list of possible infractions," Caral began after Cole left the room. "So they'll know exactly what they're doing when they break the rules."

"Good idea," I said, taking a seat at my desk and pulling a sheet of paper toward me to write.

~

*KEROK*

Absently, I reached for my mug of tea while going through the lists of supplies needed at Secondary Camp.

I realized something had happened only when the cup slid the short distance across the desk and slapped into my hand, slopping tea over the side and onto my fingers. Had the tea been hotter and I without my power, I could have been scalded. As a fire wielder, it couldn't burn me.

The fact that the mug had come at my unconscious command?

That was certainly new.

*And somewhat terrifying.*

"The ring is waking your latent power," Adahi appeared in a chair before my desk. "I thought this would happen."

"A warning would have been appreciated," I lifted a kerchief from a drawer to wipe tea off my hand.

"Where's the fun in that?"

"Did you come to taunt me, or give me advice?" I glared at him.

"Perhaps both. One can't be serious all the time. I also came to tell you that I know where Garkus is."

"Where?" I was on my feet in an instant, ready to send someone or go myself, if need be.

"Where you can't reach him," he shrugged. "I heard from Kyri. Garkus has joined her in Ny-nes."

"If he's allied with the enemy," I hissed.

"He has done nothing of the kind. He is in a position to watch Kyri's back, I believe, while she continues this foolish quest to defeat Kaakos."

"How in Hades did he get there?" I demanded. "He can't *step*."

"You can't say for sure whether that is true, and Kyri was less than forthcoming as to his method of arrival in the enemy's land."

"Then demand that she tell you," I slapped a hand on my desk.

"My dear King, why don't you tell her yourself, and see how far that gets you," Adahi's laugh was humorless. "She is there. We are here. Threaten all you want—Kyri has a mind of her own in this, and now she has a hulking guard at her back. I hope this works to her advantage, because before, I worried that she'd die alone there."

"Fucking hell." I sat again, keeping my eyes on Adahi. "How dangerous is Kaakos?" I asked. "To either or both?"

"You're asking me how dangerous he is? Do you know where my body lies?" Adahi snorted. "What you see here is my dreamwalker," he pointed to his chest.

I hesitated, but curiosity got the better of me. "Where is it?" I asked.

"It lies in Kaakos' palace," he replied, his voice feigning indifference. "He pretends it's the body of Ny-nes' Prophet, so he can keep an eye on it. I was a formidable foe to him, but you see where that got me. Now you ask me how dangerous Kaakos is? He is more than dangerous, King Thorn. He is the destroyer the real Prophet warned about so many years ago."

"How is your dreamwalker still here, then? I thought it would have died with your body."

"That would have been true, if not for your ancestor—the first King Thorn. He found a way to hold my dreamwalker away from my body, keeping the two separated. That is how I—in this ghostly state, still exist. If I ever go back to Ny-nes, however, the pull of my physical body will prove too great and I will rejoin it and die completely, you understand."

"I—don't understand," I shook my head. "I have to trust you in this, I suppose."

"Thank you. There's something else you must know. Kyri believes, after talking with Garkus, that Merrin was pulled to Kaakos' palace, to serve his purposes. That means you must continue your search for Garkus here in Az-ca," Adahi went on. "To keep Kaakos guessing. Neither he nor Merrin need to know that Garkus has joined Kyri in Ny-nes."

"Because he may have spies here." Sherra's words from the day before came back to me.

"Yes, and now he has an advisor in Merrin, who knows more about Az-ca and its military than Ruarke ever did. Everyone here knows the legends surrounding Garkus, whether true or not. Let Kaakos and Merrin believe that Garkus is outsmarting you here."

"I'll keep it to myself," I sighed, closing my eyes. "If he makes it back here, though," I blinked my eyes open and frowned at Adahi.

"If he survives, I hope you have the decency to hear him out, at the very least." Adahi dipped his head and disappeared.

"Bloody. Fucking. Hell," I growled at the empty chair.

*SHERRA*

"Tea, my Queen." Caral jerked her head up; she stood beside my chair as we went over the list of infractions we'd written down. Briar carried the tea tray into my study, her head down as usual.

She'd been the one to clean my suite that fateful day. She'd walked in, thinking nothing was amiss, as I was asleep and suspended inside my mirror shield. It was only when she'd walked straight into my invisible, suspended body that she'd shrieked and wakened me, bringing chaos and death to the battlefield.

I didn't blame her for any of that.

She blamed herself, however.

Many times over.

"Thank you, Briar," I told her gently.

"Is there anything else?" She still wasn't meeting my gaze.

"This is fine," I said.

Briar turned and walked quickly out of my study, while Caral and I exchanged glances. "Tea break," I sighed. Caral nodded and moved toward the tray to pour tea for herself.

"I love honey cakes," Caral sighed after consuming one of the treats provided with our tea. That's when Cole arrived, a sheaf of papers in his hand.

"I had to copy the law by hand; Doret wouldn't let me remove the book from Kyri's library," he reported. "She says the one belonging to the King's library was destroyed when Ruarke killed her sister and pretended to be dead. His father, the King, basically destroyed the red roses, creating the black roses in their stead. Doret also says that this was King Wulf I's way to take revenge on all roses, for what appeared to be a single rose's crime."

I set my teacup down carefully. Here was the reason Doret's rose was red on her wrist. Ruarke was responsible for destroying that, and who knew what else. "Did she give you anything else?" I asked, my words breathless. I wanted to know so many things about that time—when laws had changed so drastically that they were unrecognizable today.

"Only that her former husband wouldn't listen when she attempted to tell him the truth," Cole set the papers down and rubbed his wrist. No doubt he had writer's cramp from copying and translating the law so quickly.

"No wonder she faked her death," I grimaced. "He probably blamed her, too, for his son's death, when the bastard was alive the entire time and likely laughing at all of them."

"How long did it take for Ruarke to join the enemy in Ny-nes?" Caral asked. "After he caused so much trouble here?"

"No idea," I shook my head.

"Perhaps he was already in contact," Cole suggested. "Before he caused the trouble."

"That would explain a lot, I think," I said. "If the enemy were looking for high-ranking spies who were displeased about the way things were."

"I'd say Ruarke was more than displeased," Caral huffed. "I really want to hear the whole story, now that I know this was all a plot for revenge. What rights did the red roses have that the black roses didn't? I certainly want to hear that part."

"I want to hear it, too. I'll have a conversation with Pottles—Doret," I said. "I think it's imperative that she tells us what she knows."

"I believe," Cole began, before hesitating.

"Believe what?" I chewed my lower lip as I studied him.

"I think she's held back, to keep from causing a revolt," he admitted.

"Because the laws changed so much, didn't they?" I pressed.

"I worry that this is true," Cole admitted. "And when roses learn that the way things are has been nothing more than a sham for centuries, well, you see where that might lead."

"I feel a great deal of anger about it already, and I don't really know anything," Caral said.

"The truth is a double-edged sword. Kyri says that often enough," Cole nodded. "Too much truth too quickly can cause trouble. Let a fine mist of it soak parched ground slowly, or the flood of reaction will drown us all."

"Do you think there was a reaction then? When the King changed the laws?" Caral asked. It was a question I wanted answered, too.

"Can there not have been?" Cole said. "I only saw one such instance in Ny-nes, when things changed drastically. Those who protested were executed."

"What happened there?" Caral asked.

"All gold was removed from the hands of the people. They have worthless money chips to use, now, and no jewelry or such—it is forbidden. Marriage rings were taken, along with coins and other items. I still recall the headless bodies on display outside the market, because dissenters' heads were blasted to bits by Ruarke."

"That's sick," I breathed.

"All of Ny-nes is sick—with the disease Kaakos has brought to it, and those who came before him. They call themselves the Free Nation of Ny-nes. There is nothing free about any of it, except death. That is the only thing given freely by that poisoned country."

"It must have seemed that Az-ca was becoming like Ny-nes when the red roses became black roses," Caral observed.

"I believe that, too," Cole agreed. "When I turned fifteen and Kyri told me how the black roses were treated in Az-ca, I saw parallels between their condition and that of women in Ny-nes. Kyri also told me that since Doret served as Queen, no other Queen has worn a rose, red or black, until you, Sherra."

I turned my left wrist to study the tattoo there. "This is wearying, isn't it?" I pivoted my chair to point the question at Caral.

"More than you know," she said.

~

*KEROK*

"This can't go any further than you two," I told Barth and Hunter. "Everybody else has to believe that Garkus is on the loose in Az-ca."

"That part I have no problem with," Hunter sniffed. "What I have a problem with is Garkus somehow showing up in Ny-nes. How did that happen?"

"Adahi says Kyri wouldn't tell him, so we don't know," I said. "I could tell by Adahi's expression that he holds little hope that Kyri and Garkus will survive, so we may never know."

"What about Sherra and Armon?" Barth asked.

"I'm keeping it inside this room," I stated flatly. "I wish I could tell them, but I think it's too dangerous. Kaakos could be watching every move, and I can't trust anyone else to keep it from lovers, guards or servants. If there are reported sightings, without an immediate and appropriate response from the army or anyone else, that could be telling."

"I hadn't considered that," Hunter grumbled.

"We're playing a carefully guarded game with Ny-nes, now," I said. "Every move will be scrutinized and dissected."

"Kaakos will be hatching new plans to use Merrin, most likely," Barth said softly.

"Barth?" I turned toward him in shock.

"Yesterday, I did a divination on some of Merrin's belongings. The guards took them away from him after he'd been in the lockup for nearly three weeks," Barth admitted. "They discovered he was sharpening his wooden comb to attack a guard. And, until yesterday, those belongings were kept in the guardroom, under lock and key.

Merrin's comb was most revealing, as it held evidence that Merrin had been—commanded in some way. I almost couldn't stomach what I found."

"What did you find?" I demanded.

"Kaakos had plans to restore Merrin's power during his trial, and add to it with his own. We could have died in the Council chambers, my King. Whatever precipitated Merrin's disappearance, I can only call it a fortunate event."

I'd gone still; Barth's words chilled me. Kaakos could restore power from afar—and add to it? "Barth, I didn't think I could become more worried than I already was," I said. "But that no longer holds true."

"Can we be sure that Garkus wasn't under Kaakos' influence?" Hunter asked. My head jerked toward him—I hadn't considered that.

"Barth?" Hunter said.

"What?" Barth responded.

"Don't do divination on suspected spies in the future. If divination is required, let someone else do it from now on. We don't need Kaakos ensnaring the King's Chief Diviner."

"Hunter?" My worries were back and increased ten-fold.

"Thorn?" Hunter turned to me.

"You just scared me to death. Keep it up," I held up a hand to stop his half-formed apology. "Here's our newest concern," I went on. "The villagers of Vale came in contact with Ruarke. Did any of them once hold power? If so, how are we to decide whether any of them are now controlled by Kaakos?"

*ARMON?* I sent mindspeak after my meeting with Barth and Hunter.

*Thorn?* He sounded surprised to hear from me in the middle of the day. Usually we communicated early and late each day, unless there was an emergency.

*Are there any villagers from Vale still at Secondary Camp?*

*A few,* he replied. *Why?*

*Come for dinner tonight. Bring Levi, Marc and Wend with you. I'll ask Caral, Sherra and Cole to be there, too. I have a special assignment.*

*We'll be there,* Armon said.

Sherra knew through Doret that some of those villagers could be tainted by Kaakos. Now to decide what to do about it. Hunter had records of former power holders, since I'd taken command of the army. Before that, records hadn't been kept. Too many of those could still be alive and causing trouble for us.

*Doret?* I sent.

*Thorn?*

*Will you have dinner with us tonight? I'd like to discuss the villagers of Vale, if you don't mind.*

*I'll be there.*

*Thank you.*

～

"WE HAVEN'T KEPT track of them—some have gone to live with relatives in other villages," Wend reported. "I know that from the drudges at Secondary Camp. They usually have better information than the troops on things like that."

"Did we ever do a count of those who survived?" I asked.

"I believe there are records at Secondary Camp, but those are reports filed by survivors. If an entire family perished, we may not have reliable records for them," Armon answered my question.

"I'd like those records, if you don't mind," Hunter said. "I'll send copies back to you when I have them."

"The ones remaining—nothing out of the ordinary with any of them?" I went on.

"Hard to say," Levi replied. "Since we really didn't know them before they arrived at Secondary Camp after the attack."

"I hate to target people like this," Sherra said. "Especially after they've been through such trauma already."

"I understand that, up to a point," I turned to her. "But with the threat that Kaakos represents, he could be inside anyone. That can cause problems for the rest of us."

"Why not do divination?" Caral asked.

"Because if he chooses to expend the power necessary, Kaakos can invade a diviner as easily as he might invade a former power-holder," Doret sighed. "He can lie dormant within a victim, too, until he chooses to strike, as he did with Ruarke. Heavy shielding will help keep him out, but it isn't infallible. This is a horrible impasse."

"The entire problem would go away if Kaakos died," Armon pointed out.

Sherra's mouth tightened, but she didn't say anything. "We've never really considered an attack on Ny-nes, and we only have men and women to fight them; we don't have machines or bombs," I said.

"I'd prefer not to panic everyone in Az-ca, based solely upon supposition," Hunter offered. "Yes, we keep our guard up and remain watchful, but we don't need the country turning upon itself and tearing their neighbors apart, based on suspicion and rumor. Besides, Vale wasn't the only village that encountered Merrin and Ruarke. Remember Merrin's hostages?"

Hunter had drawn our attention to the largest flaw in our conversation. That Merrin or Ruarke could have been in contact with almost anyone who'd washed out or retired. That didn't include active members of the army, but we'd done divination on those recently. They'd passed our tests then. I hoped Kaakos hadn't turned his attention in that direction, for fear of detection.

"Kaakos is spreading his preliminary diseases of fear, suspicion and distrust," Doret muttered. "It's what he does best, you know."

"He's still trying to destroy us from the inside, isn't he?" Sherra turned dark, worried eyes in my direction.

"It looks that way," I nodded, dropping my eyes to stare at my plate. Food was half-eaten and congealing there; I was no longer hungry.

# CHAPTER 3

*Ny-nes*
*Kaakos*

My fury resulted in the deaths of two guards, whose bodies were hauled out of my quarters, dripping blood across the floor.

None questioned me; fear shone in eyes that never met mine as they removed bodies and cleaned spilled blood from the floor.

Someone had attempted to kill my mole in Az-ca, foiling my plans to destroy the new King and his Council. Merrin was asleep in his new quarters; I'd seen to that before venting my anger. He could still be of use to me, as he knew so many in and out of Az-ca's army. He was also familiar with the Commander's strategies, which could prove quite useful in the future. That worked to my advantage; I merely had to learn it to make my plans.

Now, to search for another in Az-ca to invade; someone capable of running my widespread spy network. I wanted real power at my command—power that I could augment from where I was to increase the damage, rather than wasting energy to restore what had once been. Eventually, I'd consider sending Merrin back, but he needed reprogramming before then.

Meanwhile, I wanted someone close to the King. Someone Merrin was familiar with. I searched the fragile memories I'd gleaned from Merrin already, hoping to find a suitable mind.

I needed someone prone to disagreement. One primed to accept the idea of a secret revolt. Merrin had been cooperative—he'd hoped to save his skin that way, and it fell in with his previous desire to kill the King and those around him.

Too bad the former Crown Prince was dead as well as powerless— that would have been ideal. Merrin's uncle wouldn't cooperate to my satisfaction, either. Hunter had seldom agreed with anything Merrin did.

This could take time, as I'd made the mistake of not going through Merrin's memories well enough to target another vessel. I'd be forced to search his mind again, paying closer attention to small details.

If all else failed, I'd target Hunter anyway. If I devised the proper spell and poured much of my power into the effort, there could be a small window where I might force him to kill the King and any others with him.

Before I resorted to that, however, I wanted to try other measures to accomplish the same thing. I merely had to get one of my minions close enough to do the deed. Perhaps I should contact the one spy I commanded who had mindspeak, to seek a suitable follower through him.

"Yes, just lay the rug over the blood stains. Those two displeased the Prophet and died for their sins," I waved a hand at the servants who'd brought a rolled-up rug to my quarters.

The work was done quickly and perfectly, lest they displease the Prophet as well. It made me smile for the first time all morning.

~

*Sherra*

"Kerok, I don't think he'll target just anybody," I said as I watched him toy with his breakfast. The dinner meeting we'd had the night before had ensured a restless night for both of us.

I'd had time to think, though, in those hours spent awake. "What makes you say that?" He absently scraped butter across his bread before biting into the roll.

"When you consider who his target is in this," I said. "He wants to kill you and the Council. I think he still wants that—more than anything. Why invade a villager who has no power left and no real reason to approach either of those targets? Your guards will kill anyone trying to get into the palace without your permission."

Kerok considered my words as he chewed. *You're right*, he admitted in mindspeak. "Invading and killing villagers only gains him so much, and brings Az-ca's army running if that happens," he conceded aloud.

"Right. He's much more devious than that. He'll look for someone with sufficient power and suitable access, unless I miss my guess. That way, he won't have to pour himself into some hapless washout or retiree to obtain his goals. That could leave him vulnerable where he is, I think."

"If it were me," Kerok said after considering the problem for a moment, "I'd invade a few villagers to frighten the population—just to make the entire country uneasy. Then, I'd search for a specific target to achieve my goals, but only after everyone else is distracted from the many uprisings, as citizens fight themselves based on suspicions alone."

"Neighbors who distrust one another will go to war if that happens," I pointed out. "Each believing the other could be a part of the enemy."

"Use it as an excuse to express their hatred, you mean?"

"Yes."

"This is untenable, and possibly the worst attack we've ever dealt with," Kerok shook his head. His eyes became unfocused as he considered a divided population, where suspicion and hatred would thrive unless a way were found to destroy those things.

How to do that, though? Once those thoughts invaded a mind, they may as well be controlled by the enemy. "I'm sure Kaakos is smiling, wherever he is."

"I wanted Merrin dead," Kerok snorted. "I should have delivered that death, rather than wait for a hearing before the Council."

"The only thing to be grateful for in all this is that we don't have an invading army tossing bombs or flying planes at us," I said.

"I worry about the plane part, though I don't understand that term, specifically." Kerok went back to his food. "If they can manage to fly longer distances, we're in trouble."

"I know." My weariness and lack of sleep came through in my voice.

"Ask Hunter for a marching draught if you need it," Kerok didn't look up from cutting into the ham on his plate.

"I don't like that stuff," I mumbled.

"I don't like it either," he admitted. "Sometimes it's necessary."

"I'll just have extra tea."

He reached across the table for my left hand, and leaning forward, kissed the black rose on my wrist. "I love you," I told him.

"I know." A smile curved his lips.

"Thorn, here are Armon's reports on the villagers from Vale," Hunter arrived to set a pile of papers at Kerok's elbow.

"Want tea, Hunter?" Kerok offered, turning toward him.

"I'd take tea," he pulled an extra chair from a window and sat at our table with us, while I poured a cup of tea for him from the pot.

"KAAKOS IS JUST as misogynistic as Ruarke ever was," Pottles informed me later, when I arrived at training camp. I'd told her about my conversation with Kerok at breakfast.

"Does this mean he'll look for a male to invade?" I asked.

"Or males. Thorn is correct, I think. If Kaakos hasn't arrived at that plan yet, he will, just to cause us trouble."

"And it will have to be someone who's been in contact with Ruarke or Merrin. We're back to those villagers from Vale, and any former hostages that Merrin took from other places."

"True enough."

"Pottles?"

"Yes?" She sat at her desk while we spoke, and had turned back to reading training reports before sending them to Hunter.

"What about those current trainees that Merrin knew? The ones who managed to escape from him?"

Pottles' head jerked up immediately and her eyes locked with mine.

Currently, Anari was helping teach the youngest girls. Kyal and Laren were doing the same for the young boys at the boys' camp. All three were far ahead of the others, having been trained by Pottles.

If anyone remained prominent in Merrin's memory, it would be those who'd thwarted his plans by getting away.

"Then we have villagers and trainees to be concerned about," Pottles went back to her reading with a decided grimace marring her face. "Fucking hell," she whispered.

"I'll let Kerok know when I go back to the palace," I said. "I hate to cast suspicion on those three."

"Because we love them," Pottles growled. "Fuck you, Kaakos," she whispered. "And fuck the whore who birthed you, too."

I wasn't sure a whore had birthed Kaakos, but Pottles sounded deadly serious, so I didn't argue. I knew nothing about Kaakos, other than he was the enemy of Az-ca. Who was I to argue with anyone about his birth, legitimate or otherwise?

"I'll write a letter to Thorn, if you'll deliver it," Pottles said, breaking me away from my thoughts.

"Of course," I said.

"Good. How's the writing of the law coming along?"

"Cole is working on it today. He says he should have something for me to look at tonight."

"Keep me informed. The sooner we can limit two troublemakers, the better off we'll be."

"I will. I have a question," I hedged.

"What's that?"

"How many laws changed regarding Az-ca's army when Ruarke ah, murdered your sister?"

Pottles stared at the papers in front of her for a long time. So long, I thought she'd refuse to answer.

"Nearly all of them," she whispered. "So many things happened, and none of it for the better."

~

*Secondary Camp*

*Armon*

"At least they're competent, now," Levi stood at my side as we watched roses and new warriors training side-by-side. "The warriors' blasts are better, too, once they understood they wouldn't kill themselves with the shield still up."

"If I hadn't seen Sherra do this from the beginning, I might have worried about the same thing," I confessed.

"Do you ever think that history is happening all around us?" Levi asked. "I think all this will be studied in the future—if there is a future for Az-ca."

"What we heard last night doesn't aim very far in that direction, does it?"

"It scares me that some of our own could become our worst enemies, because we can't point a finger at any of them and say with certainty that they belong to Kaakos."

"Kaakos and his perverted religion," I snorted. "The one that says we're evil and have to die."

"My father said that once there were many religions, but the religion in Ny-nes destroyed them with the End-War. He said their religion favors some people over others, to create zealots—fanatics to their cause. Add to that the drug given to their army, and they have more than enough hate for those of us they see as different or evil. He said that they mistrusted anyone who didn't look like them, too."

"What do you mean, didn't look like them?" I didn't understand.

"You've seen the enemy captives, Armon. They're all light-skinned under their tans. None of them are like this." He tapped his hand to indicate his darker skin.

"Did they ever have anyone with darker skin?"

"My father said so. He said that Ny-nes' religion dictated that those people be killed, too, just like the ones born with power, or the ones attracted to the same sex—or both."

"Is that information written somewhere?" I asked. I'd never heard Levi tell this tale before. How could anyone target their own citizenry over the color of their skin? It made no sense to me and I told Levi that.

"My father said he heard it from his grandfather, who heard it from his grandfather, and so on," Levi said. He looked troubled to me. I didn't reach out to touch him—we were on duty.

"I wish you could mindspeak," I sighed.

"That makes two of us," he replied.

∾

*KEROK*

"Doret says that Kaakos is a misogynist, like Ruarke was," Sherra said. She and I were having dinner with Barth and Hunter. "That makes me think that he'll stay away from invading a female mind, unless there's no other choice."

"I heard disturbing news from Armon this afternoon," I said after acknowledging Sherra's words. "He says that after having a conversation with Levi, he understands better why there were never any dark-skinned enemies seen or captured. Levi says that according to his family history, Ny-nes killed any dark-skinned citizens long ago, just as they continue to kill the ones born with power today."

"That makes no sense," Hunter said. "Are they not exactly the same? That's like killing the few spotted horses foaled, because they don't look like the usual black or brown ones. Those are people. How ignorant can they be in Ny-nes?" he huffed.

"Hunter, when was the last time anything about Ny-nes made sense?" Barth asked the rhetorical question.

"I find it disturbing, my friend," Hunter replied.

"As do we all," I agreed. "But like those born with power there, we don't have the ability to intervene. All we can do is attempt to push them back when they attack us."

"I have a question," Sherra said. "It's off-topic, but it just came to me."

"What's that?" I turned in her direction.

"We divine things from objects at times. Can we perhaps find those invaded by Kaakos that way?"

Barth sat up straighter at Sherra's words. "I would certainly be willing to try it. I've never heard of anyone invading an object to pass on malevolence. I have no idea whether it's even possible to place a part of yourself in something inanimate." Neither of us mentioned Barth's divination of the objects taken away from Merrin; that could lead to other tales we didn't wish to tell.

"If this works out, maybe we'll have some defense against Kaakos' terror. If we suspect someone, we divine their favorite belongings," Sherra's expression was thoughtful.

"I'm hoping we can use the same method to track down his spies," Hunter said. "It angers me that we've had this going on without our knowledge."

"Coordinate with Adahi," I suggested. "He knows more than anyone about that particular subject. He's probably still tracking them, unless I'm mistaken."

"Will he answer my mindspeak?" Hunter asked.

"As well as he'll answer anyone's, I suppose." At times, I found it disconcerting that there were no threats available to be used against a ghost, when he chose not to obey anyone's commands.

*Including the King's.*

I wanted to hear more about Adahi's death in Ny-nes, too, but Adahi appeared reluctant to discuss that subject.

*How did King Thorn separate the living body from the dreamwalker, and keep them apart?* That act must have required a great deal of talent and power.

I wore King Thorn's ring. I studied it on my finger while the others talked. How much would I give to be able to speak with my namesake, and ask questions?

*Shall I join you?* Adahi's mindspeak sounded in my head.

*Please*, I replied. *I think we have questions.*

~



How had I not seen the ring on Kerok's hand until now? I certainly hadn't noticed it before, so it was new, or new to him. Perhaps it belonged to his father, and he was only now wearing it.

I resolved to ask him about it later, when Adahi appeared and took a seat at the table.

"I have questions," Hunter told Adahi.

"I will answer if I can." Adahi dipped his head in a half nod.

"You've been hunting the spies in Az-ca?" Hunter began.

"Yes. They are not easy to find at times. Kyri helps upon occasion, but she is kept busy with other things, you see, and cannot spend her life tracking down this disgruntled one or that, to determine who they all are."

"You make it sound as if there are many," Barth began.

"I believe you may have discovered recently that one spy can recruit and infect others?" Adahi presented it as a question.

"We've heard that, yes," Kerok agreed. "It doesn't sit well, as you may imagine. I want to know what we can do about it."

"You've already made a start, but it may not go as quickly as you need it to go," Adahi replied.

"What start?"

"You've started mending the disconnect between the royal city and the outside villages. You understand that trust can only be built slowly between those two things, as the separation was building for more than two decades. So much can happen in that time, and the people from those villages will not trust easily again."

I could see Kerok's mouth tighten. He didn't wish to speak ill of his father, but his brother, Crown Prince Drenn, had been left in charge of the Council for nearly that long, and the trouble had mostly come of that.

"Let's speak the truth here, Thorn. Drenn didn't care that the villagers suffered, so long as he could pull the Council under his sway. Whether they'd started that way or not, they became greedy and grasping, just as Drenn did," Hunter pointed out.

"I wish to also point out that Thorn was busy with the army during that time, and wasn't available to do anything about it. It matters not that you feel guilt over not being involved—when would you have had the time?" Barth raised a hand as Kerok started to protest.

"Until now, the enemy hasn't let up long enough to allow Thorn to involve himself in that convoluted mess," Armon said. "The problem has now dropped inconveniently into his lap, after the deaths of his father and brother. Nobody complains about Drenn's death anymore. Even his former Council cronies don't miss him; they only miss their sources of income—legal or not, that Drenn allowed them to have."

"They're not fit for anything else," Levi pointed out. "They'll likely starve, unless someone takes pity on them."

"There's your first source of disgruntled citizens," Adahi advised. "I'd watch them carefully, Thorn, if I were you. Information—important information—can still be gleaned from that unholy gaggle, and may prove to be a treasure-find for any spy who listens."

"Will you be watching them for us?" Hunter asked.

"My dear Crown Prince," Adahi turned toward him. "You know their names, so they're easy enough for your own spies to watch. I search for those whose names you don't know."

"That's—that makes sense," Hunter sat back in his chair with a sigh. "Thank you, Adahi, for your continued efforts on our behalf."

"I promised a King named Thorn long ago that I would spend my efforts to help a future King named Thorn," Adahi said. "If you look at your records, word spread of the phantom after your birth. I may have done a few things before that time, but my efforts certainly increased once you were born."

"He also kept an eye on Sherra, because Kyri and I asked," Pottles admitted.

"Both are important to me," Adahi's eyes became slits as he dipped his head. His admission made me squirm in my seat—he'd known about the Bulldog and her pets. All three were now dead. One because of an outdated law and Merrin's actions, the other two dead because of Adahi.

*Not that they didn't deserve it,* I reminded myself.

*Don't feel guilty about those two deaths—they were inevitable, either then or shortly in their future,* Adahi informed me. *You have no blame in this. As for the first one, you and I know that law is unjust, and should never have been enforced—especially in that case.*

*I'll start working on an update,* I replied. *I hope Kerok sees things our way.*

*If you can't convince him, perhaps together we can.*

*I'm willing to work with you,* I said. *Anytime. Just don't, well.*

*Don't hit you again. I promise to never do that. I shouldn't have done it to begin with, but the situation with Ruarke went wrong and I needed you to stand with me against him—and Kaakos.*

*I understand the necessity, but I'd like to be better prepared next time. Surely there's a way to separate the dreamwalker from me if needed.*

*My dear, that only can occur during sleep or death.*

His words shouldn't have surprised me, but they did. *We will talk of that later,* he said. *Let us turn our attention to the subject at hand.*

"If we're to determine whether anyone has been recruited by Kaakos, or whether they're in his grasp already, what are we looking for?" Barth asked. I readied myself for the ensuing debate.

"Why didn't we think of this before?" Kerok tossed out a hand as I followed him toward our suite. "Handing out census papers is ideal, and we can keep them categorized by village, and ask that they be updated every few years—as we used to do. We can include the questions about former military training or service. That will pinpoint the ones to watch."

"It's still a great deal of work," I pointed out. "We need to recruit more diviners for this."

"Barth has the lists, so you can go through those if you want," he replied. "I'm exhausted. Let's get in bed." *No clothes—skin to skin,* he added in mindspeak. *I wish to hold my black rose against me. I'll do my best not to wake her, too.*

"I'll do my best not to wake," I said aloud, as he opened the door to our suite.

~

*Ny-nes*

*Merrin*

It took several hours before I realized I was in Ny-nes. Kaakos' mind control deserts me when he sleeps, and I am grateful to have my senses back in that time.

I imagined that no one could hate Thorn as much as I. That was before Kaakos' mind invaded my own.

His hatred was a blast furnace that could melt iron, and it terrified me in those lonely hours I was myself.

As much as he hated Thorn and Az-ca, however, his hatred for another—a woman named Kyri—was hottest of all.

As I couldn't read his memories, I didn't know why he hated Az-ca and desired its destruction. I'd learned that all along, Ruarke had played me for a fool. He'd never intended to hand the King's City to me.

I would have died with it, if his plans hadn't been thwarted.

What I failed to grasp was Sherra's continued existence—I'd seen her again, just before Kaakos pulled me out of my cell and forced me to *step* to his palace in Ny-nes. I had my power back, but he'd placed a lock on its use, somehow. I'd never known that was possible, until it had been done to me.

For now, I was a prisoner in his gilded cage, until he decided to do something with me. I worried about what that could be.

~

*Secondary Camp*

*Armon*

"Do you still have family?" I asked Levi. "Living?" He and I were getting ready for bed; I'd just stepped out of the shower and was toweling off while Levi shaved. He'd never had a beard problem as I did, and shaving the night before always got him through the following day.

I, on the other hand, shaved every morning, and had a shadow by the time dinner was served.

"I do—my parents are old but still alive, and I have a sister. She always wanted to go with me when I went for training."

"No power?" I asked, settling my arms around Levi's shoulders. I kissed his neck and smiled at his reflection in the mirror.

"No. Dad always told her she was lucky not to have it. At the time, he was right. If she'd had power, I'd want her trained by Sherra. I figure she's married now, with kids."

"My family is gone, except for a much younger brother, who was small when I left for training," I said, pulling away from Levi. "We don't know one another, but I ask about him now and then, when news comes from the villages."

"War keeps people apart," Levi leaned toward the mirror check his face before rinsing off soap. "It's an unwritten law that you won't contact your family, once the army takes you."

"Power keeps people apart, too," I pointed out. "We're different from the moment we learn to form fire."

"Face it—we scare them," Levi said. "They think we'll fry them if we get mad. People like Merrin only reinforce that belief. When we went to see that child's mother, she wouldn't come near us until the money bag appeared. If Caral hadn't been with me, her sister may have been reluctant to approach, too."

"Darissa's one of our biggest supporters, now," I grinned at Levi.

"Don't you know it," he agreed. "Come on, I'm exhausted, but I still want your arms around me so I can sleep."

"You can have that anytime," I said. "You don't even have to ask."

∾

N*Y-NES*

*Kyri*

*Because if you have gold on you, it's a death sentence,* I told Garkus, as I handed over base-metal money chips to pay for a few vegetables. Food was extremely scarce, and meat even scarcer within the general population.

Filth was everywhere, too, and to someone as fastidious as Garkus, it revolted him that black grime covered nearly everything, including most people.

The only thing worse than the grime covering the city, was the same grime when it rained. During those times, falling raindrops washed ash and soot from the air, which became a black sludge that would take repeated washings to remove.

*This makes no sense,* Garkus responded as we walked away from the rickety vegetable stand. I knew he wished to be anywhere but here, but there was no help for it. Arresh had sent him here; I hoped there was a true purpose in that act.

*We believe Merrin was pulled away from Az-ca by Kaakos,* Adahi's mindspeak came as Garkus and I made our way through narrow, junk-cluttered alleys toward our lean-to.

*We think the same,* I said. *What do you think Kaakos intends to do with that traitor?*

*I think Kaakos saw Arresh through Merrin's eyes and knew his plot to kill the King was uncovered. Kaakos likely restored Merrin's power and forced him to step to Ny-nes, or helped by pulling him away. He'll use Merrin as a replacement for Ruarke, now, unless I'm mistaken.*

*I think that's possible, too.*

*How is your plan going?*

*I still can't divine past the second wall,* I said. *He has a shield up that I can't get past.*

*Not good, but not unexpected, either. What is your next move?*

*I hear that several times each year, the palace requisitions replacement servants—drudges, cooks and such. Garkus and I may have to wait a few weeks until they search for recruits to serve. They're looking for able bodies, and we fit that description more than most around us.*

*Proceed carefully, Kyri. Come to his attention too soon and he'll kill you —and Garkus with you.*

*I know.*

Adahi cut off his mindspeak then; Garkus and I reached the lean-to shortly after. Lying against the base of the lean-to was a bundle wrapped in rags—which hadn't been there before we left.

"I'll check it; stand back," Garkus put out an arm to keep me from stepping closer.

Cautiously, he touched the bundle with one hand. Nothing happened. Lifting an edge of the roughly-woven rag, he released the scent of honey cakes.

Arresh had sent us a gift of food.

~

*KING'S PALACE*

*Kerok*

"How long will it take to print the census forms?" I asked Hunter.

"We can start with the number needed for Secondary Camp, then distribute to the outlying villages as the forms are delivered from the presses," Hunter replied. "This way, we won't overburden the diviners as the papers come back."

"Once we get Secondary Camp done, I want reliable troops to accompany the messengers when they deliver to the villages," I said. "To ensure that every adult completes a form."

"Good idea. We should give them full information on the complete purpose behind the census, before we send them," Hunter advised.

"Then we'll only send those above reproach," I agreed. "Those we can trust with sensitive information."

"Those who won't take it wrong that they were divined without their knowledge," Hunter sniffed.

"There's that," I agreed.

*Thorn, you need to come,* Armon's mindspeak reached me. *Two drudges were killed early this morning.*

# CHAPTER 4

*S*econdary Camp
   *Kerok*

Sherra and Barth came with me. Armon, Levi, Marc and their escorts waited for us in the physician's cabin. The physician had done a preliminary examination; both women died of stab wounds.

Logically, that would point to another drudge. With the current climate, logic went out the window. This could be a ploy to throw us off the scent of a perpetrator with power.

As for the stab wounds—Adahi would never employ that method, so it wasn't the Phantom, either.

"Found outside their cabin," Armon said. "Both dressed for work in the kitchen, so it was this morning, early."

Caral stood behind Armon, a grim expression on her face. She and her sister knew both victims. I made a mental note to speak with Caral's sister. If there were any disagreements or grudges going on, she'd know about it.

Barth and Sherra waited to examine the victims' belongings— Armon would take us to their cabin shortly.

*Is it safe to divine the dead?* Sherra asked Barth and me.

*I cannot say, as I don't know Kaakos' power,* Barth answered. *If this were done by anyone from Az-ca, I'd say yes. I don't trust anything that could be tainted by Kaakos.*

*Don't try it,* I warned both. *That's your King's command.*

Sherra's mouth tightened—I could see she wanted to get to the bottom of this gruesome crime and find the one—or ones—responsible.

"Will you remove some of the clothing—around a wound from each victim?" Sherra asked the physician.

He frowned, but when I jerked my head in a nod, he retrieved a pair of scissors to carefully cut bloodied cloth away from each uniform.

*What about the blood?* I shot at Barth as Sherra reached out for the scraps.

*I can't imagine something so small could be invaded by a rogue entity,* Barth said. *Although I obviously don't know everything.*

"Go ahead," I growled as Sherra hesitated and turned in my direction.

Releasing a sigh, she took the bloody scraps from the physician, and crumpled a piece of cloth in each hand.

~

*Sherra*

My indrawn breath frightened Kerok—his hands were on me immediately, with Barth's following close behind.

They saw what I did.

The drudges had found someone waiting for them outside their cabin. Two, actually. We'd thought them dead, and Merrin never said otherwise.

Willa and Narvin had somehow escaped death and were now murdering innocents.

"They wanted food and a shower," I opened my eyes and pulled away from Barth and Kerok. "I don't think they've been snared by Kaakos, yet, but that could be a matter of time."

"Let's go to the cabin," Kerok growled. "How did they get past the shields around the camp?"

"We've found that a tunnel works," Caral sounded ashamed.

"Bloody, fucking hell," Kerok cursed. "We'll *step* there."

∼

*KEROK*

It was as Sherra said—they hadn't ransacked the cabin, but they'd taken showers and stolen food and a few other things. We followed tracks after that, finding their tunnel beneath the western edge of the wall.

"I'll drive the shields farther into the ground," Sherra muttered, her body stiff with anger as we surveyed the sloppy tunnel. Narvin and Willa had burrowed deep, creating a hole large enough to crawl through beneath the existing shield. Scattered around the edge of the hole were a few stolen objects they'd left behind—larger items that wouldn't fit on the return trip.

"I sent mindspeak to Hunter, to notify the villages," I said. "Offering a reward, of course."

"Which will, in turn, let every spy under Kaakos' thumb know who to look for," Barth grumbled.

"Better that we know who we're looking for," I grimly observed. "Just put out the word that they're wanted for murder, all right? The rest of our suspicions must remain among those here, as your King decrees."

I'd used my position twice in less than half an hour, and it angered me to do so. What Willa and Narvin had done angered me more.

They were ripe targets for Kaakos, and I'm sure he'd recognize that the moment he received word. If he had Merrin as we suspected, he'd question him without mercy soon enough.

*Merrin, you fucked up your life yourself*, I sent to empty air.

∼

*Ny-nes*

*Kaakos*

As I was connected with Merrin at the time, through a spell I'd developed, I heard the message sent when the dolt couldn't do it for himself. Merrin didn't have the talent for mindspeak.

I would pay a great deal to know who'd sent the message, but to engage the sender would tell him I wasn't Merrin, since Merrin didn't have the natural ability to hear or reply.

"Fuck," I growled softly. Merrin's eyes blinked—I'd lost control of him momentarily, because of the interrupting mindspeak. Exerting power, I drew him under my control again, to further search his memory.

~

*Jubal Raime*

"I hear the military isn't what it once was," my neighbor, Stave, turned his head and spat on the dry ground just off my porch.

"Hmmph," I snorted my opinion of Az-ca's current military. "Give those roses too much rope and they'll hang the whole damn lot."

My time in the army had ended more than seventy years ago, because my first—and last—escort's shield broke during our first battle. It killed her and left me crippled and blind in one eye. It was all her fault. I'd been valuable to the army until then. After I lost my left eye and that side of my body was partially paralyzed, my aim was off when I fired blasts and they were too weak to reach the enemy.

I'd been forcibly retired and sent back to my home village, although I was one of the army's few mindspeakers.

It was *her* fault that I was stuck in the farthest northeast corner of Az-ca, where nobody officially came—unless a messenger showed up in the nearby village of Gaull with a few words from our new King. Faugh. No better than the old King, and probably worse, because he was in charge of the army.

I shifted my next-to-useless left leg into a more comfortable position, making the ancient wooden chair I occupied creak with its age. I should still be on the battlefield, working among those I'd trained with.

All. Her. Fault.

*Jubal?* His voice came while Stave was going on about something that didn't make a damn bit of difference to anybody. Stave was just talking to fill empty space.

*What can I do for you?* I asked, pretending amiability.

*I need more spies, although I'd prefer that they be able-bodied and have full power.*

*I'll send out messages and keep my eyes open,* I replied. I suppose the voice had gotten tired of the time it took for the network of spies in Az-ca to travel on foot between villages, until word finally reached me at the ass-end of the country. I'd send the information on, but it was often days or weeks old by the time I received it.

"I heard half the army died in the last battle," Stave continued. With a sigh, I turned back to the mostly one-sided conversation with him.

❀

*Sherra*

It took Armon, Levi, Kerok and several others to help me drive the shield around Secondary Camp farther into the ground, but we got it done before we left. A bolt of lightning would have been convenient, but there'd been no rain for days, and certainly no thunderstorms.

"The messengers were sent to the villages, and the Council has been informed," Hunter told us when Kerok and I returned to the palace. "Murder charges only, of course."

"Good. Let's hope we find them before the enemy does."

"We've ah, had some concern for the villages voiced by a few of the new Council members," Hunter said.

"That they'll be murdered, too?" Kerok's expression turned grim.

"Yes. Not in so many words, but yes."

"Schedule a Council meeting, then, and we'll decide what to do about that."

"Tomorrow morning?"

"Yes. Early."

"I'll send the notices." Hunter turned swiftly and strode out of Kerok's study. Kerok's eyes met mine briefly; I understood that meeting with Council members was the last thing he wanted to do.

"Why don't you let Hunter handle most of it?" I suggested.

"Are you saying Hunter may be more tactful in this situation?"

"Maybe."

"Point taken. What do you think should happen?"

"We need at least one warrior-escort pair in as many villages as we can place them. Larger villages, two pairs. I'm hoping that they'll realize their roles are as guards and ambassadors for the army, and act accordingly."

"I think we should arrange to have the messengers sent out regularly, to gather reports," Kerok said. "That the pairs will obviously write," he added.

"You can put them in charge of the census in their assigned village," I said. "Let them serve double duty. I wish we had more mindspeakers than we do—in case they find Narvin and Willa. Who knows if they'll be able to fight off that desperate pair."

"I was hoping for capture or a kill, but you're right—those two will be desperate. Not just for food and water, but for anything else they don't have."

"What about retired mindspeakers?" I asked. "Do we have records? Can we pull some of those into service?"

"Most of those are still serving in some capacity—the able-bodied ones work for the Crown because it means better pay. Only those who are far too old, or disabled in some way, are fully retired."

"It was a thought," I sighed.

"And a good one, just not practical," he said. "I'd like you to be with Hunter and me at the Council meeting."

"Perhaps you should bring Armon, too, so he can address issues brought up regarding housing and supplies for the troops in the villages."

"True. I hadn't thought about that."

"Would you like a table set for you in here, my King?" A servant walked through the door left open by Hunter.

"I'm hungry," Kerok turned to me.

"I'd love to have lunch—I don't care where it is," I agreed. Breakfast was long ago, and we'd expended power to deepen the shield at Secondary Camp.

"Bring it in here," Kerok told the man, who bowed and left quickly to alert the kitchen.

Briar and two others appeared not long after, one pushing a small, wheeled table, the other prepared to lay linens, plates and cups, while Briar carried a tray of food.

Briar's eyes were downcast.

*Briar,* I sent mindspeak. *You did nothing wrong. That is from your Queen—and your King.*

Her head jerked up when she heard my mental words, blinking in astonishment for several moments.

"Here, set that heavy tray on the desk." I smiled at her, now that I had her attention. She did as I asked, waiting until the table was set and the other two stepped back.

Filled plates were set out and their covers lifted away. The scent of roasted chicken reached my nose.

"That smells heavenly," I breathed.

"Is there anything else?" Briar still sounded timid.

"No. Thank you Briar," Kerok smiled at her.

You'd think the sun had risen for the first time in days, as the light appeared in Briar's eyes. *She was astounded that the King knew her name* —I could see that plainly. She and the others bowed and left us alone in Kerok's study.

~

*Northeast of the Village of Gaull*

*Jubal*

I've grown accustomed to hiding my emotions over the years.

When Stave arrived to tell me the latest news delivered by a messenger, he looked fearful.

"What is it this time?" My voice was gruff as usual.

"A rogue warrior and his escort committed murder at Secondary Camp," Stave said, shaking his head as if that would do any good. "Messenger said they were part of that murderer Merrin's bunch. Thought they were dead in the last big battle, until they showed up to steal food and kill drudges."

"Well, now," I said, taking my time to form a response. My mind was turning in circles, however.

These were the spies, perhaps, that were requested by *him*.

He'd never named himself, and lately, it sounded as if his mental voice had changed, but he still wanted the same things, so I responded to him.

In exchange, I received bits of gold, some of which I spent on better food, clothes and for paying someone to fix my porch and my roof, since I couldn't do those things for myself. The pittance paid by the army wouldn't cover everything—not to my satisfaction, anyway.

"What are the names?" I asked.

"Narvin and Willa. Said they came from villages farther south before they went into the army."

"What did they say to do about it—if they show up?"

"Report it. Says they're hoping to get troops out to the villages just in case, but that could take time. Said there's a reward, too."

"What if they show up with murder on their minds before then?" I huffed. It was the proper response to make, and had probably been made by most of Gaull's residents already. I hesitated to ask how much the reward was. Now wasn't the time to switch priorities—not if I wanted to stay alive.

"They say to give them whatever they want, just to get them gone. They can fry us, you know." Stave shook his head again. "If that happens, we have to make a report as soon as we can."

"And hope they don't kill us first," I snorted.

"Here lately, the army's more dangerous to us than the enemy,"

Stave grimaced. "I know you were in the army," he held up a hand when I started to speak. "But it ain't what it once was."

"You're right," I shifted in my chair. "It sure as hell ain't what it used to be." *I have two names for spies,* I sent while Stave considered what to say next.

*Good. Tell me.*

*Narvin and Willa,* I replied. *Used to be with Merrin's bunch.*

*All the better. Payment will be sent.*

"Well, I'd better go on," Stave said. "Garden needs the weeds pulled."

"At least you're able to pull 'em," I tapped my nearly-useless left leg. "I gotta pay somebody to do for me."

"I don't know which of us is the worst off, then," Stave joked.

I watched as he stepped off my porch and shambled toward his home a quarter mile away. His wife died of fever three years earlier; until then, she'd done the gardening. It was woman's work, like cooking and cleaning.

*Like shielding should have been.*

All. Her. Fault.

∾

N*Y-NES*

*Kyri*

*Those are the warrior-priests,* I told Garkus when he asked. Their long, dark robes swayed as six of them made their way through our narrow alley, the last in line banging a metal rod against the gathering bell.

The bell commanded all residents to come from their shabby homes and stand outside, waiting for them to pass. *Looking for suitable bodies to become Kaakos' servants,* I added.

Garkus dipped his chin and lowered his eyes—not out of respect, but because he didn't wish to start a fight here among the poorest of Kaakos' subjects. Neither of us wanted to draw Kaakos' attention that way, when we weren't prepared or in the proper place.

The first warrior-priest stopped in front of Garkus, just as I knew he would. We both dipped our heads, as was required.

"These two," the warrior-priest growled at the one behind him.

Chains with tags were placed around our left wrists, marking us as Kaakos' property. *Stay calm*, I told Garkus, whose breaths had become shallow and quick.

"You will report to the palace in three days," the warrior-priest snapped. "Do not attempt to remove the chains, or you will die. Sell your belongings; the High Lord will provide for you when you report for duty."

Garkus and I waited until they were past us; the bell resumed its clanking, the warrior-priests' robes swayed in unison, their steps became measured and even as they continued their mission.

"I hope you know what you're doing," Garkus hissed as those who lived nearby disappeared into their hovels, like mice scuttling through the walls. This time, the cat had passed them by and they were grateful.

∼

*Ny-nes*

*Kaakos*

"My Lord, Aspe is here to see you." The servant named one of the warrior-priests searching for new servants for my palace.

"Send him in." Reports were expected, if the priests saw or heard anything unusual in their search for suitable slaves.

Aspe went to his knees three steps inside the door to my audience room. "Rise," I waved a hand.

"My Lord." His head remained bowed as he approached.

"What do you have?" I toyed with a loose thread on the arm cushion of my ornate chair.

"I have received word that a healer has been among the people."

"Any show of the enemy's power?"

"It is doubtful. I think it is the belief of desperate people—that some charlatan has helped them in some way. I can find no residence for him, and they say he only appears at irregular times."

"I love how rumors start," I growled. "Did you find anyone who has been healed by this—man?"

"No, my Lord. They all say they know of someone, or someone's neighbor or such, but none have seen him directly."

"Then it's another tale and nothing more."

"What shall we do if the rumors persist?"

"Unless you can bring me the man in question, or one who has actually been healed, then pay it no mind."

"It will be as you say, my Lord."

❧

*SHERRA*

"I don't have any memories of my dreamwalker acting lately," I answered Hunter's question at dinner. The day had become a long one, with reports already coming in of sightings.

Kerok and I figured those were mostly from ones who wanted to collect the reward money, but Armon sent troops out anyway, to ask questions.

Nothing substantial came of it, and on several occasions, a warning was given regarding the crime of false reporting.

If I were Narvin or Willa, I'd go back to my hiding place and only venture out again when I ran out of supplies.

"I know I shouldn't say this, but I feel comforted by that," Hunter responded. He'd worry if my dreamwalker had been active, as that, to him, spelled trouble.

Kerok listened while he ate and nodded when I said I didn't recall my dreamwalker doing anything recently.

"I hope Adahi is looking for Narvin and Willa," Barth interjected. "It would relieve me greatly if he found them and delivered their deaths."

"While that would be ideal, I can't imagine it would happen as soon as we'd like," Hunter agreed.

"Unless they're unseeables," I pointed out, "then someone should be able to track them, somehow."

"Barth?" Kerok finally spoke.

"I divined the things they dropped at the shield line," Barth replied. "I didn't get anything from them, likely because they hadn't held them long enough."

"It is easier to tell things from objects they've handled for a long time," I said, recalling Pottles' shell. The bloodied cloth I'd handled belonged to the victims, and I'd only seen Narvin and Willa's images, before their victims died.

"Then we're at a standstill, divination-wise," Hunter grumped. I watched as a frown tugged at his mouth—the unnecessary deaths of two drudges angered him greatly. They'd had no power to fight back, and would have given Narvin and Willa anything they asked for, just to keep from being harmed.

Instead, the drudges were attacked with knives first, and then their things were stolen after they died. Caral and Darissa were both upset —the victims were their friends.

"We have a problem," Adahi appeared near Kerok's elbow; Kerok's battle reflexes brought his hands up to form a fireball at the sudden interruption. He dropped his hands the moment he realized it was Adahi.

Kerok was wound tighter than the rest of us expected, due to Azca's current dilemmas.

"What problem?" Kerok growled before offering an empty chair at the table to Adahi.

"I was tracking Narvin and Willa," Adahi said. "To take them down tonight as they slept. I had a reliable divination line on them, until it disappeared."

"How did that happen?" Barth asked.

"I assume that they are now protected by Kaakos' power, and that, my friend, is as unseeable as you can get."

"I think you should tell me how all this is possible," Kerok rumbled. This angered him greatly.

"Kaakos won't expend that power lightly," Adahi took the offered chair. "It requires a constant feed to maintain that shield."

"Does this mean that power is being pulled away from Kaakos while he sleeps, too?" Hunter asked.

"Yes. Kaakos is very strong, however, so this will only weaken him a little."

"How did he escape Ny-nes' death sentence so successfully, with so much power?" I pointed my question at Adahi. "How did he know as a child to hide it so well?"

"He is crafty. Sly. A genius at evil," Adahi shrugged. "As if he were born knowing it."

I felt Adahi's words were guarded and chosen carefully, so as not to give too much away. What could he be hiding, though? I shoved that worry to the back of my mind. Kyri had hidden things too—as had Pottles.

They were still hiding things, I think. *Perhaps*, I considered, *Kyri went to Ny-nes to avoid answering questions.*

I studied Adahi's face as he and Kerok talked about this latest threat. His eyes were little more than slits, but for him, that was normal. And, as he was a dreamwalking spirit, I imagined he didn't have to show any emotion unless he chose to do so.

"What are you thinking, child?" Adahi turned toward me, then.

"I was just thinking that when I was younger, I never imagined I'd be sitting at a table, having dinner and conversation with a ghost," I improvised.

Adahi ducked his head. I realized after a moment that he was laughing.

Kerok reached out to grip my hand in his, while a smile curved his mouth. It lightened the mood around the table, and I was grateful for the respite from grim circumstances.

~

*HUNTER*

"So. We're back to hunting Narvin and Willa the old way," Barth set his wineglass down with a thump.

He and I had retired to my study after dinner, while Sherra and Thorn went to bed and Adahi disappeared.

"Where do you think they were all this time—before they decided to murder for a shower and a loaf of bread?" I asked.

"Could have been any one of the places Merrin hid while they were together," Barth sighed. "Or somewhere else. Who knows? We had no idea they were still alive, or we'd have found them before this."

"How the hell did they get away?"

"A question you'll have to ask them, no doubt," Barth's words were dry as dust. "The convoy they traveled with was hit too hard for anyone to survive, unless they were able to *step* away."

"Ruarke got away. Adahi told us that. Merrin also escaped, as did a few others. It makes sense, I suppose."

"We assumed they'd all follow Merrin," Barth's mouth twisted into a frown. "That was the logical thing."

"Even Merrin assumed them dead," I offered.

"True. And yet here we are, faced with the folly of our assumptions." Barth poured more wine for himself. "If they are hidden and controlled by Kaakos, and now serve him, willingly or not, that spells terrible trouble for us, my friend." He lifted his glass in a silent toast before drinking.

~

*Ny-nes*

*Kaakos*

"I don't know Adahi," Merrin complained.

"You call him the Phantom, you dolt," I shouted. The fear that spread across Merrin's face almost made me laugh. He'd been terrified of Adahi.

Understandably so. Not many could stand against Adahi. Too bad he'd come after the strongest of those who could. I still couldn't fathom how his dreamwalker survived, long after his corporeal body had perished.

He'd had help; I had no doubt about that, and little doubt as to who'd provided that help. After all, I had Adahi's physical remains in my sanctuary. Too bad his phantom couldn't see the steady stream of worshippers who came to kiss the glass enclosure surrounding his rotting flesh.

"I see you won't be much help in this; I'd hoped for more information so I might find him again. I'm making plans, you see, to destroy what little he has left."

"Hmmph. Destroy that bitch, too. I saw her in my cell. She's not dead, like I thought."

"No woman has ever been a match for me," I reassured my new minion. "She and the new King will be targeted soon enough. Your friends, Narvin and Willa, will accomplish this for me."

 

*KEROK*

"Did you ever finish Thorn's Book?" Sherra yawned. She sat up in bed, watching me pace across the rug at the foot of our bedframe.

"Why are you asking me about that?" I stopped to frown at her.

"You told me once it was sort of boring, except for the instructional parts. I think you could use some boredom right about now."

"I'm not sure boredom can cure this worry," I sniped at her. "They could be killing right now, and we won't hear about it until afterward." It made me wish that Adahi had saved his troubling news for later—at least I could have slept some before it came.

"I know." She buried her face in her hands, while dark curls fell about her shoulders. Her hair was growing longer, and it looked good on her. It made me wish that our troubles were far away so we might enjoy our time together, instead of constantly fighting to keep Az-ca alive.

"My love," I moved to her side of the bed quickly, and sat beside her. Pulling her into my arms, I kissed her temple while rocking her body against mine.

"When will it stop?" She dropped hands away from her face to lock eyes with mine.

"I don't know," I said, my reply bitter on my tongue. Hunter was right—sometimes I was too honest for my own good. "Scoot over and I'll lie beside you while I hold you," I whispered against her hair.

Once I was beside her in bed, her arms stole around me. We held one another until we fell asleep.

~

*DORET*

"They were chained today," I informed Cole. "They're to report in three days."

"I hope she knows how dangerous this is," Cole whispered. I'd poured wine for both of us in my training camp study. He'd brought the news of Narvin and Willa; I'd given him what I'd received from Kyri.

Neither bit of news was good.

"Do you think Kyri understood—truly—how long her long game might turn out to be?" Cole asked.

"Or how abrupt the ending is likely to be?" I snorted.

"How terrifying it is, to watch someone you love walk into danger," Cole held up his glass in a toast.

"And that's for damn sure," I replied before drinking.

*a*rresh

Sherra fell asleep late, leaving me little time to work. I'd gotten a feel for Narvin and Willa; a minute amount of their blood had mingled with that of their victims—enough that I could set the shields around the villages to prevent those two from entering. I merely had to work quickly to get it done. It also required pounding those shields into the ground, and that took a great deal of energy to accomplish.

Doing it long distance was much faster; I bent my power in the direction needed, to recalibrate against the missing rogues.

As for Kaakos getting them past a shield; I knew his signature well enough to block him, too, unless he brought a great deal of power to bear against the shield.

Would he be angered enough by such a rejection to expend that power? I had no answer to that question.

It made me wonder, too, whether he'd protected any of his spies the same way.

*Not likely,* I decided. It would be too much to protect someone he saw as expendable. Adahi said that the shield around Narvin and Willa would be a continuous drain on Kaakos.

Too bad we couldn't turn that slow drain into a rushing river, to empty him of power long enough to defeat him.

It was something to consider, however, if a way could be found. After all, Garkus and Kyri were close enough to the palace and together, which also bore thinking about.

~

*SHERRA*

"I'm considering a marching draught," I admitted at breakfast. I felt weary, as if we'd done battle the whole day before.

"Short night," Kerok rumbled and stuffed scrambled eggs in his mouth. I doubted he'd ever move past the military necessity of eating as quickly and efficiently as possible. Moments later, Hunter appeared with two small, white envelopes.

"This is for you," he handed a small envelope to me and another to Kerok. "Thorn sent mindspeak to me, asking for marching draughts," he added.

With a sigh, I opened my envelope and added the marching draught to my tea, then stirred and drank. Today, extra tea wouldn't work if I wanted to stay awake during the Council meeting. Kerok wasn't looking forward to it either, but we couldn't cancel; we had to be there to ensure it ran smoothly and the information was disseminated properly.

The word *spy* wriggled its way into my mind. Would there be a spy in the Council meeting? Would Kaakos be a secret observer, through him?

I shuddered.

"What's wrong?" Kerok stopped stirring marching draught into his tea.

"Just—worried about Kaakos' spies," I mumbled.

"I know. I worry about that too."

~

I'D NEVER BEEN inside the Council chamber, and only now realized how massive it was. *How many are here?* I sent mindspeak to Hunter. He'd know better than anyone.

*Three hundred eighteen,* he replied. Kerok led us toward the dais, where chairs and a long table waited for the three of us; the King, the Crown Prince and the Queen.

Barth took a seat not far from the door, in a group of chairs reserved for the King's Diviner, the Commander of the Army and a few others.

Armon, Caral and Cole were already in their seats, waiting for the meeting to begin. The low rumble of hushed voices quieted, once the door guards thumped their staffs on the tiled floor and announced the entrance of the King.

"Rise for the King and the Crown Prince of Az-ca," someone shouted. Three hundred eighteen Council members rose as Kerok made his way to the King's chair, at the center of the long table.

*No acknowledgment of the Queen?* Caral's mindspeak reached me.

*It doesn't matter,* I returned.

*It does to me. They wouldn't be here except for the Queen.*

*We'll discuss that later,* I warned. We had other, more important things to consider at today's meeting.

Once Kerok, Hunter and I were seated, the same guards tapped their staffs to tell the crowd to sit.

"You've all received word regarding the rogue warrior and his escort by now," Hunter began. "They murdered two innocent drudges at Secondary Camp and stole food and supplies from their cabin. We are currently taking steps to protect the villages from the same fate."

"And what might that be?" Someone shouted at the back of the room.

"Stand, please, and identify yourself," Hunter said quickly. "Otherwise, you will not receive permission to speak in this hallowed chamber."

"Jerr, from Wildtree Village," he spoke.

"Very well, Jerr from Wildtree, you have the floor. What say you?" Hunter said. His voice contained the slightest amount of chiding—all

Council members were given the rules when they accepted a place in that governing body.

"I wish to know what it is, exactly, that the King is doing to protect the villages." Accusation—and a challenge—rang in his voice.

"The King is providing troops for your protection," Hunter said. The rest of his words became fuzzy, as if I'd fallen into a lake of near-unconsciousness and was attempting to hear through what felt like deep water.

My vision went dark, then, and that's all I remembered for a while.

～

*KEROK*

Hunter drew back the moment he realized that Sherra's dreamwalker was now in charge of her body—while she was still awake.

*Adahi*, I sent desperate mindspeak. *Sherra's dreamwalker has taken her over.* Hunter's hand slapped over my forearm as I moved to rise; Sherra had *stepped* to the end of the row where Jerr stood.

～

*ARRESH*

"I placed a shield to keep those two miscreants out of your village last night," I hissed at Jerr of Wildtree. "Unless they have a great deal of power at their disposal to get past that shield, you should be safe."

His eyes had grown round with fear as I accosted him. "All of your villages have the same shielding," I turned swiftly to address the crowd. "It will not prevent you from going in and out; it is set against those who would do you harm."

"Is that possible?" someone else shouted.

"Stand and identify yourself, or you will be sent back to the village of Baker and not allowed to return here," I snapped.

"I, ah," he stood, somewhere in the first three rows. "How did you know?" he gulped.

"I know many things," I said. "Tell everyone else who you are. I know your name already."

~

*KEROK*

All eyes were on Sherra when Adahi appeared at my side. "I know many things," she told a new Council member. "Tell everyone else who you are. I know your name already."

*I'll be damned*, Adahi sent mindspeak.

*Can you stop this?* I begged.

*Why would I? She appears to have their attention, and a little bit of fear is a healthy thing in this bunch.*

*At least sit with us; I'm worried this will turn into a debacle*, I admitted.

*Happy to.* Adahi moved to take Sherra's chair at the table. Crossing his arms over his chest, he leaned back and appeared to be enjoying the drama set before us.

~

*SHERRA*

I didn't regain control of myself until the last Council member exited the chamber. I was conscious for perhaps a count of ten, when I saw Kerok, Adahi and Barth coming toward me.

Once again, my vision failed me, and Kerok said later that I was unconscious when I dropped to the floor.

~

"I'M NOT sure how it was done." I woke to hear Adahi speaking to Kerok. "Somehow, her dreamwalker separated itself, without Sherra's consent or full unconsciousness," he added. "I've never heard of that before, but then I've only heard of three dreamwalkers in my life."

My eyes blinked open to find those two at the foot of the bed, where someone had laid me before covering me with a light blanket.

"You're saying there were three?" Kerok demanded.

"Two of those are dead," Adahi replied.

"So, your physical body is dead, another dreamwalker died and Sherra is the only living one you know about?"

"Yes. I believe it to be that rare a gift, too, if you consider it a gift."

"Water?" I croaked, causing Kerok to jump and Adahi to turn in my direction.

"There's some here," Kerok moved swiftly to my side of the bed to pour from a pitcher. I emptied the first glass and asked for another.

"Child, do you recall anything that your dreamwalker did or said?" Adahi asked as I slurped the second glassful.

"It's vague," I said, lowering the glass. "I sort of recall it, but it's like it happened in a dream."

"Why do you suppose your dreamwalker felt compelled to take over the meeting?" Adahi asked a second question.

"There isn't a single woman on the entire Council," I blurted. "They're all men." I wasn't looking at Kerok when I made my confession; I kept my eyes on Adahi instead. I didn't add that like Caral, my dreamwalker didn't like it that the Queen wasn't acknowledged, either.

The entire Council knew who the Queen was, now. They were also terrified of her. I had mixed feelings about that.

"Did she—you—really adjust the shields around those villages to keep Narvin and Willa out?" Kerok asked his first question.

"I—she did. I remember it now. That's why I was so tired this morning."

"Will it keep them away—truly?"

"Unless Kaakos pours himself into them," I said. "I doubt he'll want to do that, because it will make him vulnerable in Ny-nes."

"That's an interesting idea," Adahi said and disappeared.

"I wanted to ask him more questions," Kerok grumbled.

"Can I have something to eat?" I asked. "I'm starved."

～

*Secondary Camp*

*Armon*

"Caral, I know you're thinking about something; you've been silent since we left the Council meeting," I told her while we ate lunch with Levi and Misten.

"I saw something I never thought I'd see," she said, keeping her head down.

"What's that?"

She lifted her head and her eyes locked with mine. I didn't miss the light of excitement in them. "I saw a woman take control today," she whispered. "Of the King's Council."

"Caral," I sighed. I hated to destroy this happiness, but I'd seen the grim expressions of many Council members when they left the chamber.

They'd been far from pleased that a woman had taken charge. The looks they were casting at one another angered me. Everything Sherra had done was true, useful and powerful.

They had no reason to complain, other than she was female and not male, as they were. Too many times I'd experienced the same thing, for my attraction to the same sex.

"I know what you're about to say," Caral's eyes dropped to stare at her plate. "They don't think a woman should be in charge of anything."

"We know that's not true," Levi said gently. "A lot of people do. Sometimes, the ones who are bothered by it think it makes them look weak, or some other nonsense that doesn't matter. If they knew that it wasn't just the army who saved their skins the last two times the enemy attacked, maybe their minds would change."

"Doubt it," Misten said before setting her fork down. "I made really good marks in school. The boys were always praised for their work. The girls weren't."

"Because they're expected to cook, clean, garden and have babies," Caral huffed. "The only reason they get an education is because the Crown insists."

"I had no idea things were getting so bad," I said. "Of course, we wouldn't hear these things while Drenn was in charge of the Council."

"Sounds like he had a lot of sins to atone for," Caral grumbled.

"He paid for some of them with his life—when he attempted to kill Thorn and the King."

"I blame Merrin for putting that idea in his head," Levi said. "Along with the enemy's weapon. Too bad he had no idea what it could do if misused."

"Never had warrior training," I pointed out. "He might have learned a few things if that were the case."

"I hear that was Ruarke's doing—when he faked his death and turned his father against the roses in the army," Caral said. "I learned that from Cole. That's why the rose on the banner is red instead of black, too. The King decreed that the tattoos be of black roses from then on, because he believed a rose killed his son."

"That's not fair," Misten said.

"Hmmph. I think if we dig deep enough, we'll find out just how unfair things have been for the roses since that time."

"Caral, I hope I don't have to tell you to keep that to yourself. Information like that can divide us, at a time when we don't need to be divided," I warned.

"I know. Cole says the same thing."

"Cole may be in a unique position to know how dangerous it could be, coming from Ny-nes as he did," Levi said.

"He's mentioned a few things like that," Caral agreed. "It's terrifying. He said a lot of people died when they took all the gold away from their citizens, including marriage rings. Those who refused or complained were killed."

"That's so heartless," Misten breathed.

"That may be the least heartless thing about them," I huffed. "Killing children with power, or those attracted to the same sex? That's not just heartless. That's pure evil."

Levi didn't speak, but I noticed the tightening of his mouth. If his story were true, Ny-nes had killed their dark-skinned citizens—adults and children—long ago. We'd only seen the pale-skinned ones in the army. It made sense that the army came from the population, and extrapolating from it, there were no dark-skinned citizens left in Ny-nes.

Once again, I wished Levi had mindspeak. Where had such hatred come from? Was it written into the religion at the beginning? If so, why did it take so long to manifest itself? My teacher said long ago that there was a very long history of life on this world before the End-War.

What happened?

"You're the one thinking too much this time," Levi pointed his fork at me.

"I know." Forcing unsolved riddles from my mind, I turned back to my food.

~

*Ny-nes*

*Kaakos*

"The latest tests on the new solar battery show that it could last an hour or more, depending upon the load the plane is carrying," my chief of technical sciences reported. White-haired, now, his eyes weak enough to require thick lenses, Liam had served me for most of his life. His father before him had also served.

"How far will that take the plane?" I asked. "Is it possible to carry more than one battery, and switch from one to the next, when the power runs out?"

"We're working on making them small enough to carry three on board, but the plane won't have enough room to carry three batteries and more than a dozen troops, or perhaps three large bombs."

"Bombs will suffice," I said. "What about flying in darkness?"

"We're working on that difficulty now. I believe you'll be pleased with what we've accomplished so far."

"Very good. Keep me updated."

"Of course, sir."

~

*SHERRA*

Adahi asked for a private meeting the day after the Council met. I was still embarrassed about losing control, and felt even more confused by my dreamwalker and how it had taken over while I was essentially awake.

My dreamwalker hadn't separated from my physical body, and I found it uncomfortable to relinquish control like that.

"Adahi wishes to speak with you at the table in the garden," Hunter informed me. I sat in my study after breakfast, going over the law Cole had written. He, Caral and I still had to go over it together, and ask for Hunter's input before presenting it to Kerok.

"Thank you." My shoulders sagged as I walked toward Hunter, who stood in the doorway.

"I'll send tea down," he said, stepping out of my way.

"Thank you."

"Don't let this bother you too much," Hunter said. "Those bastards need their eyes opened now and then."

"But I wasn't in control, Hunter," I sighed. "That's what bothers me the most."

"You think of your dreamwalker as being a separate entity, instead of a deeper part of you?"

"I think she has less tact."

"Discuss it with Adahi, then. I have no advice to offer, because I've never been in that situation."

"From what I understand, nobody has ever experienced it, until now. I want to know how it's possible, and why she did that to me."

"Then this advice I will offer," Hunter said. "Don't go to war against yourself, Sherra. It's obvious we need both parts of you, if we're to survive Kaakos' attacks."

I wanted to complain about his lack of a usurping dreamwalker, but didn't. Hunter didn't deserve my anger. That should be reserved for the one who did the usurping, which, by all accounts, was a part of me.

I was back to Hunter's advice in this—not to go to war with myself. For now, I didn't know how to avoid it, my anger was so hot.

"Go to Adahi, he's waiting," Hunter said gently. I went.

~

*ADAHI*

She looked angry as she approached the table. I couldn't say I blamed her. She'd lost control—in her mind—for the first time.

"Sit, daughter, and we'll talk." I pushed out a chair with the power I held. Thorn was only beginning to see the same power within himself —through his namesake's ring. For now, I was content to let him explore that on his own.

"Can you show me how to do that?" Her words surprised me. I imagined she'd explode in anger at her dreamwalker. Instead, I'd distracted her with a simple trick.

"I can." I found myself smiling at her. She took the offered chair and turned to me with a hopeful expression on her face.

"We'll get to that," I promised. "I remember the first time I was angry—or my physical self was angry—with the dreamwalker," I began.

"When was that?" The anger was returning.

"Many centuries ago—before the End-War," I said.

Her indrawn breath revealed how shocked she was.

~

*SHERRA*

How old was Adahi? Was he telling me the truth? If he were, here was someone who could fill in so much history for me.

"I see you wish to ask questions. I cannot answer much of them— to preserve sanity in both of us," he said.

"Then tell me why you were angry with your dreamwalker." I turned my head away so I couldn't see his face. He looked weary and old when he made that statement, and I didn't want to know why.

Actually I did, but didn't think he'd tell me.

"My dreamwalker—well, I—took leave of my physical body for

three days. There was no reason for it, and had I not been where I was at the time, I could have died."

"What were you—your dreamwalker—doing?" I asked. My hands were folded in my lap, so I absently studied them while Adahi spoke.

"I was whispering words in the ears of those who eventually built the catacombs beneath this palace," he said. "Telling them that they needed to prepare themselves for the inevitable. I also told them to stock the catacombs with everything needed to build the King's City and the domes over it—after the bombs fell. The catacombs, as you may guess, are far larger than anyone now living suspects."

My eyes lifted and locked with his. His smile was wry. "You see," he went on, "I didn't think that advice was good advice at the time, because things hadn't gotten to the point where any of that was needed. I—my dreamwalker—knew that it would take a great deal of time to build the catacombs, and that's why I gave the warnings when I did."

"How long before the End-War did that happen?" My voice quavered.

"Nearly a century."

I forced my trembling breaths to even out before I spoke again. "I'm uh, grateful someone listened to you."

"I had to make my selections carefully, and was then forced to show them some of my power to get them to listen. Those I approached had to be very wealthy to build the catacombs, and the construction had to be done mostly in secret. That kind of wealth is no longer a part of this world's landscape."

His eyes lost focus, as if he were looking into his past. "Survival and sustenance became wealth for a very long time after the End-War, as you may imagine. Too many in the present still struggle with those needs."

"I know." I dropped my eyes again. I'd lived through that, as had the others in my village. Every day, it was a struggle to find enough to eat.

"It's a hard lesson to learn—that all the gold, silver or credits you've accumulated in your lifetime won't feed a single soul."

"Soul? Are you talking about the religion in Ny-nes?"

"No, daughter. What do you think your dreamwalker truly is? Most people's souls live within them all their lives, and never manifest. Only a few have ever had the separation that you and I have experienced. Until today, I'd never seen a dreamwalker manifest when the physical body is still awake. I feel it was necessary, and for a purpose we may never realize."

"It's terrifying."

"I know. Terrifying and wondrous at the same time."

"What should I tell Kerok?"

"If you would, please don't tell him about my part in building the catacombs, or any of the End-War information. I'd prefer to tell him myself—when the time is right."

"All right. I'll tell him we're studying the recent, ah, phenomenon of my dreamwalker manifesting to take control while I'm awake."

"That would be truth, daughter. Or as near as we can get to it."

"Adahi?"

"Yes?"

"Someday, I'd like to hear what it was like—before the End-War."

"I'll consider it," he said and *stepped* away.

"Tea?" A servant approached the table.

"I'll take some," I sighed. I needed to sit and ponder Adahi's words, and tea would help while I did it.

∿

*KEROK*

"I gave her some things to consider," Adahi said. He'd appeared in my study after leaving Sherra at the garden table outside. "I don't think she'll be angry with her dreamwalker for long."

"Good. We need her—both sides of her—I think."

"Hunter has already said the same thing," Adahi smiled. "Keep our girl together, all right? And, when you're not too busy, practice what the ring is showing you."

"You mean this?" I reached out a hand and a pen from my desk slapped into my palm.

"Yes. I suggest heavier items, however," he chuckled. "Go move a truck." He disappeared while my mouth was surely hanging open.

~

COLE

"Adahi?" He didn't often visit me at home. Usually he found me when I was wandering through the nearby forest. It served to exercise my legs and my mind at the same time.

"I'm sure you've heard by now that Sherra's dreamwalker took over while she was awake."

"I heard it from Caral."

"Good. We have a project, you and I."

"What's that?"

"We have to ensure that Kaakos never learns how Thorn separated my dreamwalker from my physical body."

"You're worried that he'll attempt to trap Sherra or her dreamwalker, aren't you?"

"Yes. Very much so. I have no illusions that the messages her dreamwalker delivered in that Council meeting will stay within the borders of Az-ca. Who knows how or when, but Kaakos' spies will eventually hear of it and he will know it shortly after."

"That is most unfortunate," I sighed. "The one talented enough, perhaps, to protect us is now in danger, too."

"I hope her dreamwalker realizes the danger she placed herself in by doing as she did."

"I hope that, too. If Kaakos captures either, terrible things will surely follow."

~

JUBAL

*They will come to you tonight*, the voice informed me. *Extra gold will also arrive.*

I sure as hell hoped extra gold would arrive. I'd be damned before spending my money on two more hungry mouths, and the village would surely notice the increase in purchases. I'd be forced to send my guests farther afield to buy food and supplies.

*Guests.* I snorted at the term. These weren't guests—they were leeches. Especially since one of them was an escort. I didn't want any female in my house, but the voice dictated my actions. I'd accommodate, but I wouldn't be civil—not unless I was commanded to do it.

*All her fault.*

*y-nes*
*Kyri*

Garkus was forced to hold back his temper; we were searched thoroughly outside a guardhouse at the gates to Kaakos' palace. Garkus wanted to blast the four guards standing outside as they went about their business—he didn't want their hands anywhere near him.

If the guards found anyone carrying weapons or other contraband, they'd be killed immediately. We were supposed to arrive with the clothes on our backs, the chains on our wrists and nothing more. Even shoes weren't permitted, but most of the population didn't have those to begin with. Callused bare feet were the norm; I convinced Garkus to cover his feet with dirt and cinders to appear normal to the guards.

Once inside the palace, uniforms and shoes would be issued after we were forced to bathe; Kaakos hated disorder and the obvious appearance of filth or poverty inside his home.

Garkus had improved his shields greatly since his arrival, too; we were shielded so tightly against our skin, it was almost uncomfortable. We'd had to leave our clothing outside the shields, so the guards could search it.

As for my appearance, I'd changed it dramatically since my arrival; even Kaakos wouldn't recognize me unless he were very focused, and he never paid attention to his servants.

I hoped that remained true.

After all, when Kaakos and I had fought before, it had been in Nynes and I'd called him out. That was a mistake I wouldn't make again. He thought he'd banished me for good, too.

Sherra had gotten around that piece of sorcery. I'd landed so hard on the ground when she tossed me through the barrier, I cursed her name for days as I limped toward Kaakos' city.

I learned later that her dreamwalker had been pressed for time. I wondered if she'd have given me a softer landing, had that not been the case.

"Follow that one," the guard who'd searched us pointed toward a servant waiting inside the gate. "He'll take you where you're supposed to go."

I didn't miss Garkus' angry exhale as we began our journey into Kaakos' stronghold.

～

*SHERRA*

"Kyri and ah, well, she's now a servant in Kaakos' palace," Pottles informed me when I arrived to hand her a rough draft of the law Cole, Caral and I were putting together.

She held something back; I didn't know what it could be, but reserved my unasked questions. If she wasn't comfortable telling me something, I wouldn't get it out of her.

"This looks good so far," she quickly read the opening paragraphs. "This can't happen soon enough, you know. The troublemakers are trying to bully the younger ones, and we have to watch them every second. Anari is helping with that; she sends mindspeak to me whenever she notices something. So far, those two haven't figured out who's telling the instructors about their misdeeds."

"What sort of punishment are they getting?" I asked.

"Demerits. Extra work and exercises. Reduced rations. What you'd normally expect. If they were adults, I'd burn their power away myself."

"How well can Anari shield?"

"Well enough."

"Tell her to keep a shield up all the time, if she can," I said. I still had bad memories of two instructors burned to death in their beds, because they no longer had the talents they'd been born with.

"I know where that's coming from," Pottles pointed a finger at me. "Still, it's a good idea."

"I'm worried they may target someone whose shields may not be so good," I added. "We don't need injuries—or worse."

"I concur. Those two—I worry they'll carry things to the extreme if they suspect anyone of telling on them, even though they've been warned multiple times."

"If it were possible, I'd remove their power temporarily and put them to work with the drudges," I blew out a frustrated breath. "So they'd get a taste of what their future could be."

"How about working on the farms, instead? I hate the thought that they could spit in classmates' food."

"Now there's a better idea," I agreed. "Do you think we could add that to the proposition?" I nodded toward the papers in Pottles' hands.

"I don't see why not."

"I'll ask Cole to write it in," I said, rising to go.

"I'll keep you posted on training sessions. It's nice to have Caral and the others working with us two days a week."

"I know. Don't let those two get out of hand. They worry me, for obvious reasons."

"I know what you've dealt with in the past, and what the outcome was for all involved. We're doing our best to stay on top of this."

"Are there any others who look to be following in Jeen and Ferni's footsteps?" I thought to ask before *stepping* away.

"Not to that extent. We get infractions, but most of the time, their punishment is enough to keep them from doing it again. How goes the search for Willa and Narvin?"

"No real sightings, and the false reports have dwindled to nothing. Wherever they are, they know we're searching for them."

"I'd appreciate regular reports," Pottles said. "I'll see you in a few days."

~

*J*UBAL

Keeping angry words behind my teeth whenever Willa came too close became a chore I greatly disliked. I ate the food she cooked and left the dishes and cleaning up to her, too. That was the extent of her usefulness, in my opinion.

Narvin wasn't saying much, either. On several occasions those first two days, I tried to start a conversation, only to have him cut me off.

They were in my home, eating my food and sleeping in my spare room, and already I wanted them gone.

They were instructed to *step* away for a few hours every night, to gather information and bring it to me so I could relay it to the voice. The most recent information wasn't important in my opinion—Narvin and Willa said that the Crown was taking a census, when it hadn't done that for decades. The voice paid me for the information, though, so it must have had some importance.

*The voice.* That's what I called him, since I'd never learned his name. It didn't matter that the voice had changed, either. No matter what, my messages were eagerly received and gold would appear on my table by the following day.

I hoped the amount of gold would increase; I had two extra mouths to feed, now, and they ate to keep up their strength.

Willa refused to look at me as she walked through my small sitting room, carrying clothing to the kitchen to wash. Too tall, she was. Scrawny, too, probably from being away from the regular army for so long and not knowing where the next meal would come from. A pile of mousy-brown curls topped her head. Hell, she was so tall, she could probably brush the cobwebs from the ceiling with her dust-mop hair.

Narvin should have left her behind. There were plenty of village girls he could bed if sex was a priority.

I didn't think for a moment that her shielding was as important as people made it out to be. Narvin was lucky to be alive. He'd never said how long he'd served in the army. Willa, if the average lifespan of an escort bore out, had only been with him in the army for less than five years.

"Hmmph." I caught myself making the noise aloud. The sound of scrubbing on the washboard came from the kitchen.

*Better her than me.*

*SHERRA*

"There's one more thing I'd like to add to the law," I told Cole and Caral that morning. "Pottles and I think that in some cases, the power should be completely repressed and the perpetrators sent to the farms or elsewhere, to perform menial tasks."

"Why not the kitchens?" Caral asked right away.

"That was my reaction, too, but if the infraction is serious enough, we don't want them to have contact with their former classmates while they're being punished, because they can still cause mischief if they're in charge of their food or cleaning their barracks."

"True," Cole nodded his agreement. "I'll begin writing that now."

"We need to work on eliminating another law while we're at it," I said.

"Which one?" Caral was curious.

"The one that hands a death sentence to any escort who has sex before she goes through the choosing. Eventually, I also want to eliminate the choosing and merely train troops to do a job. Pairings can come later; you and I know that we can shield anyone; it doesn't have to be the one you're paired with."

"That will allow teams to shield, while teams fire blasts," Cole looked up from his copy of the proposed law.

"That's just what I was thinking," I said.

"Do you think we might train the army on this—before the law takes effect?" Caral wanted to do this because she saw the possibilities, just as Cole and I did. I had no idea whether Kerok would ever consent to it, but the idea was too good not to give it a try.

"I think I'd like to take that training a step further," I said. "If we can get the teams trained successfully."

"How?" Cole was very interested.

"I'd like to see if we can combine the shields—and the fireblasts."

Cole went still, while a light appeared in his eyes. I knew then he was thinking the same as I—that we could use that method to attack Ny-nes.

"By the first warrior," Caral breathed. "Sherra, we need this. We need this now." She tapped a finger on my desk to emphasize her words.

"For now, I have to ask you to keep this secret," I said. "I don't want Kaakos' spies to hear the slightest whisper of it."

"I see the sense of it," Cole said. "We'll keep this to ourselves until we have the King's permission to attempt the training."

"I'm not sure all the troops may be suitable. If we try this, we'll select the ones who'd work best with one another," Caral said.

"Some will balk, and those are the ones we don't need," I concurred. "The unwilling ones can get the others killed if they're not careful."

"Armon and I can put a preliminary list together," Caral said. "I hope the King will let us try."

"Good. Tell Levi, Armon and Misten, then, and inform them that the Queen commands secrecy."

"I'll see to it," Caral vowed.

"Now," I said, "Where were we on the updates?"

～

*Anari*

*Ani?* Laren's mindspeak reached me during midday meal.

*Laren?* I replied while keeping my head down and moving vegetables on my plate. I didn't want the instructors guessing I was using mindspeak to talk with a male. They didn't want contact between the two while in training.

*I just wanted to say we miss you—Kyal and I. I wish we could train together again.*

*I know, but we must follow the King's rules.*

*Do you think we'll get to see one another sometime?*

My shoulders drooped and an involuntary sigh escaped my lips. *I don't know. I'd ask Doret, but I'm afraid what the answer may be.*

*Same here.*

*At least we can talk to each other this way. If we couldn't, it would be so much worse. Laren, the instructors are watching. I'll talk to you later—at bedtime.*

*All right.*

I pushed peas onto my fork and stuffed them in my mouth as the instructor walked past. She didn't have mindspeak. So many of them didn't. I doubted any of them wanted communication from their students that way, even if they did have the ability.

I missed Laren and Kyal so much. We'd become very close after escaping Merrin's clutches, and it was hard on us not to see each other and share lessons. Maybe if I sent mindspeak to Sherra, she'd let us see one another now and then.

~

*Secondary Camp*

*Armon*

Caral arrived from the palace in time for the evening meal. Taking her seat next to Misten and across from Levi and me, she smiled widely to let us know there was news.

Something good, I'd imagine, from the light in her eyes. "What is it?" I asked.

"I can't tell you here. We're sworn to secrecy by the Queen." She almost giggled when she said the word *Queen*.

Sherra never pushed her weight around by using her title. Her dreamwalker, on the other hand, had browbeaten a few Council members recently, but it hadn't been anything that didn't need to be said.

"Then we'll have a glass of wine in our cabin after dinner, and you can tell us," Levi grinned back at Caral.

"Is it exciting?" Misten asked, bumping shoulders with Caral.

"I think it is."

"Good. I can't wait to hear it."

Dinner was pot roast in gravy, something we all loved, with potatoes and carrots. We dug in and talked of other things while we ate.

~

"You know we're working on updating some of the laws," Caral began after Levi handed her a glass of wine. She and Misten sat together on the sofa, while Levi and I took the chairs on the opposite side of our small living area.

"How's that going?" I asked.

"We've had some good ideas—on the types of punishment to levy if the students break certain rules, or are repeat offenders. That's not the news I have."

"Well, let's hear it, then," Levi said before sipping his wine.

"Today, Cole, Sherra and I were talking about training, obviously, and she said that she'd really like to make it so the choosing was a thing of the past, and that people could be trained to do their jobs singularly or together, without a forced relationship tied to it. That's not the most exciting thing, though."

"Come on, you're keeping us waiting," Misten teased.

"Well, she said that she wanted to try combining shields, and combining blasts—at the same time. Do you know what we could accomplish if we could do that?" The light grew brighter in her eyes— she was enthralled with the prospect and the feasibility of it.

I set my wineglass down carefully on the small table between Levi's and my chair. Levi's eyes met mine as I did so.

"We could attack Ny-nes," we both whispered at the same moment.

"Sherra says she doesn't know how the King will react, so we have to keep this secret until she can present it to him at the proper time," Caral went on. "You know the Crown has always been against us going to Ny-nes, but it was because we didn't know anything about their leader's city, or how many bombs or war machines they have. Kyri is there now, and with information from her," Caral's words were so rushed she'd gone breathless.

"I wish this were reality. I'd be ready to go tomorrow," Levi breathed. "It's time we taught them not to come anywhere near Az-ca."

"This means a lot of training," I warned, holding up a hand. "Even if we have permission from Thorn, we'll have to train—possibly for weeks or months—to get this right. We also need Sherra's help, because all the escorts will have to be coordinated with all the warriors' power, so we won't be fried when we send out a combined blast."

"We'll need Sherra's help to understand how to combine blasts," Levi pointed out.

"True. I'd like to experiment with this—if she's willing," I told Caral. "Ask if the five of us can meet in a remote location to practice."

"I'll ask tomorrow—Cole is busy writing up changes, and adding another law as a suggestion. Maybe he could bring a few of his people that he trusts, and we could really work on this, just to make sure it's possible."

"I'd go for that. Ask Sherra first," I cautioned. "I realize Cole already knows, but she didn't give him permission to share it with his troops."

"I can't wait to try this," Misten bounced beside Caral. Caral laughed at her partner's excitement.

*Perhaps we should petition the Crown for a law permitting the bonding ceremony between women*, I sent to Caral.

Her face became serious as she blinked at me.

*I would very much appreciate your speaking on our behalf*, she replied. *I still remember Levi talking to our training class, when he said that a bonding between women wasn't allowed, according to law.*

*Things have changed,* I grinned at her. *I'm grateful for it—it's good to see you happy.*

*Instead of dead, you mean?* She lifted an eyebrow.

"Enough mindspeak," Misten scolded us. "You're leaving Levi and me out of it."

"True," I chuckled and went back to my wine.

SHERRA

I was surprised to receive mindspeak from Armon as I sat down for dinner with Kerok. Tonight, it was just the two of us—at his request. He and I felt as if our duties were pulling us apart, so he'd asked for a private meal.

*Caral and Misten would like a bonding ceremony,* Armon informed me. *But at the moment, that's not allowed—by law.*

*You're right. I'll work on that tomorrow,* I replied.

*Thank you. I intend to tell Thorn myself, but I feel it would be better if you approached him about it first.*

*I'll do that. I should have figured this out myself, but too many other things are getting my attention, nowadays.*

*Understood. Thank you, my Queen.*

*Armon, don't start that nonsense with me. You know better.*

*I do,* he sent a mental laugh. *I'll see you soon.*

"I think Caral and Misten would like a ceremony," I said casually as Kerok took a seat on the opposite side of our small table.

"You're in the middle of writing up proposed laws—I suggest you get on that," he said while reaching for his mug of beer. I wasn't fond of beer, so I'd asked for wine with my meal.

"I will," I said. "I think I'll take off my shoes."

"Why?" He frowned at my sudden change of subject.

"So I can tickle your legs with my toes," I sighed and concentrated on doing just that.

"You know where that may lead," he growled and drank more beer.

"Finish your beer, first," I said.

"And if I don't want to?"

"You're the King."

"Yes, I am."

We didn't eat for a while after that.

~

*Anari*

*We're just now getting to bed*, I told Laren. *Two students got into a fight at dinner, so all of us had to clean the kitchen and the dining hall.*

*That happens here, too*, he admitted. *Fights are frowned on. Did the ones who fought get extra punishment?*

*They did, but that didn't help the rest of us*, I said. *We were washing dishes and scrubbing the floor on our knees.*

*We never had to worry about that when we were in training at the palace*, he pointed out.

*We got along*, I said. *Here, there are so many who didn't know each other before, and things just happen. We have some bullies, too. Nobody likes them because of that, and it makes them act worse.*

*At least the youngest ones are still in Kyri's City. They weren't sent back.*

*Sometimes, I think they're the lucky ones.*

*It was cooler there*, Laren said. *And we got used to it being cooler under the domes of the King's City. Here, it's just hot.*

*Here, too. We have to shower every day, because we're covered in sweat and dust when training's over. The games they let us play to practice our shielding are the best parts of it.*

*I wish we could do that. Right now, they're so serious all the time. Like, if you don't do this, you'll die, or if you don't learn that, you'll die.*

That's when I decided to send mindspeak to Sherra the following morning, rather than putting it off. Some things needed to change—for Laren and so many others.

*I wish I were there—we could sit together, you, Kyal and I, and read together at bedtime.*

*I miss that too. Look, the lights just went out. I have to go.*

*All right.*

~

*SHERRA*

*Sherra? It's Anari.* The mindspeak came at breakfast.

*Ani?* I was worried immediately.

*I uh, it sounds silly, now.*

*No, what is it?* I asked.

*Laren, Kyal and I—we really miss each other. I was hoping that I could see them now and then. Laren told me that the boys don't get to play games like we do. Can you do something about that? He says their instructors just tell them if they don't learn their lessons, they'll die.*

*That sounds depressing,* I soothed, because the longer she'd spoken, the more upset she sounded. *Look, why don't you let me talk to the King, and maybe we can work something out, all right?*

*Will you let me know? This is so—upsetting.*

*I know. Look, I'll let you know what he says. I'll talk to Doret and Colonel Armon, too. Maybe they'll have suggestions.*

*Thank you. I'm just so worried.*

*I know. Those are your friends. Of course you're worried. I'll start working on this right away.*

*I have to go—we're going to breakfast, now.*

*Enjoy your meal.* I leaned back in my chair with a sigh.

"Something wrong?" Kerok walked into our sitting room, where the breakfast table was laid. He'd just come out of the shower, his hair still damp and ruffled.

"Anari misses her friends," I said. "And the boys aren't allowed to learn by playing games. Their instructors are always telling them they'll die if they don't learn something. Now, I don't know about you, but telling an eight-year-old that he's going to die doesn't sound like the proper way to teach anything."

"Damn." Kerok pinched the bridge of his nose after sitting across from me. "That's the old school method of instruction, and it works for the most part with the older ones going for training at twenty. You're right—this isn't the way to teach the younger ones. We need different instructors for them."

"The girls are being trained using Pottles' methods, so they're doing better," I said. "Still, it doesn't address the issue of Anari, Laren and Kyal. They were being trained together, and it worked for them. None of the others are trained to Anari's level, so she's having to go backward so the others can catch up."

"I would imagine it's the same for Laren and Kyal," Kerok frowned. "What do you think we can do about it, though?"

"Well, I don't know—wait. Cole's people train the boys and girls together," I said. "They don't get many students, and don't have any at the moment. Would you be opposed if I sent those three to him? They could probably pick up where they left off with their instructors, instead of having to wait a long time for the others to catch up."

Kerok frowned again, which wasn't a good sign. "I dislike the idea of them going outside Az-ca for training," he began.

"But," I said.

"I know. These are special circumstances, and those three had distinctive talents from the beginning. It's a shame to hold them back, now. If you'll oversee the training they get, then I'll allow it."

"I'll be happy to." I couldn't help smiling at Kerok.

"I haven't forgotten that you're in charge of Cole's troops," he pointed out. "They were more than helpful last time."

"They coordinated well with Armon and the others," I said.

"They did." Kerok busied himself with his plate. I poured tea for him and didn't mention that we'd been classified as deserters at the time.

*Ani,* I sent to her, *I'll take you, Kyal and Laren to train with Cole, and we're working on getting new instructors for the boys.*

Her mental shriek of joy scorched a few brain cells, I think. I wasn't sure what Pottles would think about this, but I hoped she'd accept it.

～

*J*UBAL

"I tried walking into the village last night," Narvin complained. "Something held me back—a shield or such."

"A shield?" I sniped. "Can't be."

"It's true," Willa countered. I was furious that she had the temerity to speak directly to me, and question my opinion at the same time. "We have to meet the spies outside their villages to get information," she huffed. I wanted to spit on her for her impertinence.

"Then it's a damn good thing I live outside the village, isn't it?" I snapped at her.

"Willa, go to our room. I'll handle this," Narvin growled. Just as well he did that—I was ready to blast her. I still had power left, by the first warrior, and I'd show her what I could do from a few feet away.

"Fine. He's a bastard," she threw up her hands and stalked toward the spare room.

"It was a shield, put up by that witch," Narvin hissed at me. "I'd bet on it."

"What witch?" I demanded.

"The one who's Queen, now. Haven't you heard about her?"

"That's all bullshit, to scare us," I dismissed his claim with a wave of my hand. Narvin's voice changed, then. Became rougher. More menacing. "Fear her, puny worm," the voice commanded, while a terrifying, reddish light appeared in his eyes. "She is formidable, and her life is mine to take. Obey me in this, or I'll kill you now and find another servant to convey messages. I've already taken steps to protect my spies from the King's meddling census," he added. "Don't think I can't destroy you if it pleases me."

Dropping to my knees, I quaked at the fire burning deep within Narvin's eyes. Before pain and unconsciousness claimed me, I cursed my existence.

~

*SHERRA*

"Written permission from the King to take Laren and Kyal with me," I set the sealed paper on the camp commander's desk.

Lifting his head, he studied me for a moment, as if deciding whether I was worthy of a reply. No wonder the boys were threatened with death every day; under his command, I didn't see how it could be otherwise. I'd ask Kerok about this one the moment I returned to the palace.

"Was it signed by Thorn himself?"

"Yes."

"I'll have a look." His movements were deliberately slow as he took the paper from me.

"Ah, Queen Sherra," Hunter suddenly appeared at my side. "I ah, forgot to give you important information, earlier," he added. "Captain Mort," Hunter addressed the camp commander politely afterward.

"Crown Prince Hunter?" Mort lifted an eyebrow at Hunter before rising and dipping his head.

"What information was that?" I asked Hunter, puzzled.

"Information from King Thorn," he said. "That if Mort fails to be respectful to the Queen, he can clean out his desk and I'll find something else for him to do."

Mort almost choked at Hunter's words.

~

*HUNTER*

"The ass was still sitting while the Queen stood in front of his desk," I complained to Thorn.

"Where's Sherra now?" Thorn asked, steepling his fingers and studying me from behind his desk.

"She took Kyal and Laren to the girls' camp, to get Anari. I believe Cole already knows they're on the way."

"Good. Did Mort's attitude improve? Father put him where he is, training the men, because he was too surly to work with an escort."

"I believe it only improved because I was there," Hunter snorted. "He has no place teaching boys."

"Then I'll make sure he only trains the twenty-year-olds from now on."

"Did it upset Sherra?"

"She told me she's used to it."

"There hasn't been a queen in Az-ca for a long while, and certainly not one who's been in the army," Thorn grumbled. "They have no respect—most of them. If she's not upset, I'm upset on her behalf."

"As am I. Without her, we'd likely both be dead. Mort hasn't learned that lesson, yet, and will probably be ungrateful when he does."

"Too bad her dreamwalker chose not to interfere with that one."

"That is a weapon best left sheathed until it's needed, my King."

"You're right, as usual. Do we have new sightings of Narvin and Willa to go over?"

"I have three reports," I said. "One is—shall we say strange, at best?"

# CHAPTER 7

*erok*

"All this is about a neighbor who takes long walks at night?" I handed the report back to Hunter.

"I said it was strange, and probably one disgruntled neighbor pointing a finger at another," Hunter said. "He hasn't followed the neighbor, or if he has, decided that a long walk was all it was with nothing else to report about it."

"Do you think we should investigate?"

"If we go during the day, it may make the night-walking one suspicious enough to curtail his activities—if he's doing something wrong."

"Then pull in the messenger. Let's ask him questions," I sighed.

"I'll send for him," Hunter promised and walked out of my study.

～

*Sherra*

"I have to supervise the training," I shrugged at Cole. "Teach them everything. Anari can fire blasts—I just know it. You train your people to do the same—and to shield. Those three," I studied the tea in my cup for a moment, "I think they will be the future of our army."

"It will be a pleasure." Cole smiled at me over the edge of his tea mug. "How often might we expect you here to supervise?"

"At least two days a week. Three, if I have my way. I can bring Caral with me, and we can work on the laws here, too, if you'd like. It's nice to be surrounded by trees, with a view of the ocean in the distance."

"It does make a nice backdrop to work," he agreed. "Very well, three days per week it will be. The young ones will be assigned separate sleeping quarters, of course, and they can train together during the days."

"I know he's much older, but I think it would have been fun to train next to Kerok," I sighed.

Cole only smiled at my wistfulness. Anari, Laren and Kyal were being given a gift that they would appreciate their entire lives, I think.

"I'd like you to provide training on the more recently developed lessons—you and Caral," Cole said. "You're most familiar with those things, and it helps at times to go straight to the source."

"Have you heard from Kyri?" I asked, causing Cole's eyebrows to rise.

"She is now working as a servant in Kaakos' palace," he grimaced and set his mug down. "To Kaakos, his servants are invisible, unless they displease him. Keep your hopes alive that she will continue to escape his notice, until a way can be found to destroy him forever."

"That's something else I'd like to talk to you about," I said. "Remember the idea of combining shields and blasts?"

"I do. It would be wondrous, if we can accomplish that feat."

"I think we should begin training here—with your people—three days a week. I can arrange to bring Caral, Misten and Levi, I think, and perhaps trade off with Armon and Levi, just so they can both get some training. I can't leave Secondary Camp without one or the other."

A light appeared in Cole's eyes as I spoke—he was hoping for this; I could see it clearly. "It will be done," he breathed. "When shall we inform our army?"

"I'd say let's do it two days from now—when I'm back to supervise the young ones' training."

"Well enough," he slapped a hand on his small table. "Well enough."

～

*Anari*

Laren, Kyal and I were allowed to sit on Cole's front porch to drink our tea and talk, while Sherra and Cole discussed things inside. In the distance, we could see sunlight shining over so much water it was almost blinding.

"This is so amazing," Kyal grinned as he squinted at the water. "I never thought I'd get to see the ocean like this."

"Doret wasn't happy about me leaving, but she didn't say anything," I said. "She asked me weeks ago to keep an eye on the troublemakers and let her know what they were doing, but I hated being the one telling on them every ten minutes."

"Not fair," Laren agreed. "I'd hate that, too."

"I just hope they don't cause more trouble, now that I'm gone."

"Let the instructors worry about that," Laren said. "Come on— we're here. We're together. That's behind us."

"I know."

"I never felt like I fit in," Kyal sighed. "I already knew what they were teaching, and it was boring. Then they kept telling us we'd die if we didn't pay attention. Like we didn't think we were going to die when Merrin took our village."

"They say he escaped from the lockup," Laren said. "That's terrible. He could hurt other villages, like he did ours."

"Who was that other man who escaped with him?" I asked. "I don't remember hearing about him, before."

"Garkus. He's the one who fired on the supply camp, with the people still inside it. Burned it down, too. That's what I overheard at the training camp," Kyal grumbled. "He was supposed to go on trial a few days after he escaped."

"Merrin, too. They got away just in time, I think," Laren grumbled. "What do you think they'll do, if they're together?"

"I don't think that will happen," I said. "Doret said that Garkus wanted to kill Merrin; that's why he blasted the camp."

"I wish they'd just come out and tell us what's going on," Kyal said. "I hate having to sneak around to get information."

"Maybe Cole will tell us," I said. "I hope so, anyway. He seems nice enough."

"I hope they'll train us to shield and fire blasts, like Doret was doing before we got separated," Laren said. "I think we're good at all those things."

"I like shielding," Kyal agreed. "It irked me that they weren't training us on it when we moved to the boy's training camp."

"Irked? Good word," Laren bumped Kyal's shoulder with his. "I'm stealing it."

"Words are free, man. Did you not get that message?" Kyal teased.

"Do you think Cole has a library? I really want to read stories," I said. "There weren't any books at training camp."

"I miss that, too. It was nice to choose books from the King's library," Laren agreed.

"Kyri has a library," Kyal pointed out. "Maybe Cole will let us read some of those books."

"I don't know," I said. "Doret only let us see a few of those, before we left."

"We wouldn't damage them, if that's what they're worried about," Kyal huffed. "We know to take care of things like that."

"Well, nobody's there, now," Laren pointed out. "Those books are just sitting there, getting dusty with nobody to read them."

He was right, and a plan began forming in my mind, then, if Cole didn't have books for us to read.

~

*SHERRA*

*Keep an eye on them,* I told Cole in mindspeak. *We worry that they may come to Kaakos' attention.*

*I've already considered that;* his expression became grim. *I'll be watching. I hope Kaakos stays far, far away from these. He has killed so many children already.*

*I'm worried he'll use them to attack us, and force us to kill them,* I voiced my biggest fear.

*That would indeed be a tragedy,* Cole agreed. *Terrible. Is that one of the factors you considered when you brought them here?*

*Yes,* I confessed. *I can depend on you to call me for help, when that fool in charge of the boys' camp would just blast first and ask questions afterward. Plus, I can lay a special shield around your village, to keep them from being pulled away. They can only leave if someone else is with them,* I added.

*I understand your concerns, and appreciate the shield. I will most certainly send mindspeak if I see or hear anything out of the ordinary.*

*Thank you. I'll let Adahi know, too, in case we need help.*

*Good.* "I'm almost finished with the current revisions on the laws," he said aloud.

"I'll take copies with me to read, then, and ask Hunter to do the same."

~



*Secondary Camp*

*Armon*

"Our schedules just got busier," I told Levi, as he and I supervised a training class. Today, Caral and Misten were helping Doret train younglings. I'd already gotten mindspeak from Caral; Doret wasn't particularly happy that Sherra had taken Anari, Laren and Kyal to Cole for training together, but I thought it a good idea.

"How's that?" Levi stood beneath a tree with me, his arms crossed over his chest while we watched training exercises.

"Sherra wants us to go with her to Cole's village, to train on the new method one or two days a week."

"You could have said that to begin with; I was worried we'd have to do stuff we didn't like."

I bit back a laugh. "I wanted to go together, but that's not possible—one of us has to be here," I said. "I suggest I go with Misten, while Caral stays here with you and vice-versa, so somebody can send mindspeak if the camp explodes while we're gone."

"Good plan," Levi nodded. "I suppose we'll get to practice with Cole's bunch?"

"That's what I hear."

"Good."

"I'm looking forward to this," I went on. "I really want to take down Ny-nes."

"We have to convince Thorn, first."

"I know."

~

*Ny-nes*

*Kyri*

I washed dishes in the massive palace kitchen, next to a woman with three teeth missing. "Soobi," she introduced herself as she lifted a pan to dry it. "I'm—new."

"I'm new, too," I told her.

"Healer reason I'm here."

I frowned at her words—at times I had difficulty sorting meaning from those on the outside.

"He make better—then they chain me," she shrugged.

"Someone made you better? How?" I hadn't heard of a healer when I'd been among those outside Kaakos' palace. Besides, trained medical skills weren't found on the outside, either. Kaakos didn't care whether the people died or not; only that they continued to have babies they could barely feed—if at all.

"I pulled teeth," she grinned, showing me the gaps near the front. "But went bad in mouth. Tasted bad. Sick after that. Healer made better."

I blinked at her for a moment. In the past, there'd been a few healers with power, but I hadn't seen one born in a while. I had some talent in that area, and what I had I'd used to help Sherra. Kaakos would be watching for someone like that—because it was an indication of power.

"When?" I thought to ask as thoughts raced through my mind.

"Don't know. Days."

"I'm glad you're better."

"Me, too." She lifted another pan to dry.

*Garkus, did you hear anything about a power healer out in the city?* I sent mindspeak. He was working at another station in the kitchen, chopping vegetables for the evening meal.

*No,* he replied. *Have you heard something?*

*Maybe. I'll keep listening for more. If that's the case, Kaakos will start looking for him—he can't stand for anyone to be left alive who has power in Ny-nes.*

*You're not making me feel better about my future,* he pointed out.

*Keep your shield up, then,* I told him.

*You think I wouldn't? This place is giving me a rash.*

I almost laughed at his statement. Instead, I ducked my head so Soobi wouldn't see and kept washing dishes.

*North*

My hands dangled in front of me while I sat on a large stone near the main roadway. Power was trickling in—I could feel it.

Had anyone guessed for centuries that the rock I sat upon had once been part of a massive structure?

"You there."

They'd found me, as I hoped they would.

"You look sound enough. Lower your hood so we can see your face." A bell clanked as the warrior-priest made his way toward me.

Rising to my feet, I let the hood fall. I grinned at the warrior-priest who approached while he studied me. I did look quite sound to him, and would be an ideal addition for Kaakos' stable of servants.

Except I only came here to announce my existence to him.

The warrior-priest held out a hand, so an underling could give him a chain for my wrist. "Not today, bastards," I grinned and disappeared right in front of them.

*KEROK*

"This is the messenger," Hunter brought the man into my study.

"I remember you," I said. I did—I'd recognize that gap-toothed grin anywhere. "Claude, how are you?"

"I'm fine," Claude kept grinning. "Never thought to see the Commander in the King's chair."

"That makes two of us," I agreed. "Have a seat. Hunter, will you have tea brought?" Hunter left the study to order tea, while I considered what to ask Claude.

"You want to know about the report, don't you?"

"I do. What do you think about it?"

"I'd say the one who told me sounded worried," Claude shifted on his chair. "Didn't say anything else about his neighbor, either—not like it might be if he had a grudge against the man."

"Has he witnessed this behavior before? In the past?"

"I asked him about it. He says he's usually in bed before then, but his wife is sick, now. He's gone outside to think a few times after she's in bed. That's when he noticed."

"So it could be someone out for a stroll."

"I don't think so," Claude shook his head. "It's safer there to stay within bounds of the village—plenty of hungry predators are outside at night. He'd be asking for trouble—unless somebody waited outside who could make sure there wouldn't be any."

"How dangerous is it to walk away from the village at night?"

"Most wouldn't do it more than once or twice, and not by choice, if you understand my meaning."

"What predators?"

"It's hilly around there—wildcats, coyotes, that sort of thing."

"Here's my next question," I said. "Being that remote, what would this man have to offer to the enemy?"

"Well, some of his relatives live in a village about twenty miles away. It's not as dangerous to go outside the town there. There's flat land around them, and fewer predators, you see. Relatives have been to visit a couple of times in the past month, and that's more often than usual."

"So, the relatives are in a valley of sorts, while the one who takes night walks lives in a hillier area. I have no idea what that means, if anything."

"I was only thinking from an attack position, Commander. That's all."

Claude's observation shook me. The old army sergeant he'd been hadn't left him. An attack position—could it be possible?

"I'll look into it," I said, as Hunter returned with a servant right behind him. "We'll have tea, now."

*Get the coordinates from him before he leaves—we need to pay a visit to two villages*, I told Hunter.

*I'll see to it*, he replied.

"Claude," I said, "You used to be a mindspeaker. Is that no longer true?"

"Oh, it's still true, but there's not many to talk to that way, and as for talking to you or anyone else in the palace, that just seems —presumptuous."

"Understood," I chuckled.

~

*SHERRA*

"I know you're upset," I told Pottles. She'd ignored me for several seconds inside the camp commander's office, shuffling papers about. I stood before her desk, feeling as if I were eight years old again, after I'd done something Pottles didn't like.

"I needed her here."

She meant Anari—we both understood that. I wanted to point out that she'd used Anari to tattle on fellow students, and it made Anari uncomfortable. I would have felt the same, as my instruction hadn't been that long ago.

"I know that's what you wanted." I sighed. "But what Anari wanted —needed—was something else."

"You didn't discuss it with me, first."

"I know. I apologize. I just felt it was important to get the boys away from that—man who calls himself a training commander. I think Kerok may have him removed from the boys' training camp, because of his attitude. Not only was he scaring those boys to death, but he was rude to me. Probably to every other woman he's met, too."

"Hmmph."

"What do you want me to do?" I flung out my hands in a helpless gesture. "Clean floors? Make beds? Cook your dinner?"

"Settle down—I just want to be miffed for a while, all right?"

"You *want* to be miffed? I never knew that about you," I countered.

"I assume you asked Cole to keep a close eye on the boys?"

"I did. They'll all be looking for signs, now."

"Good. I worried about them where they were, and you're right to get them away from the others."

"Well, then. I think I'd like tea," I said, taking a seat.

Pottles' eyes unfocused as she sent mindspeak. "Someone will be here soon with a tray for the Queen." She followed her words with a reluctant grin.

~

Ny-*nes*

*Kaakos*

Aspe had returned. This time, the news wasn't to my liking. "You say he disappeared in front of you? What, exactly, did he say before that happened?"

"I told him he was being conscripted for work in the palace. He told me, 'Not today, bastards.' Then he vanished."

"Anything else?"

"His smile—was evil, my Lord."

"Can you expect anything else from the enemy?" I lifted an eyebrow at Aspe.

"What do you wish us to do, my Lord?" Aspe was terrified I'd send him after the devil power wielder he'd reported. I had other plans.

"Come back tomorrow," I said. "I'll have someone selected by then to send after this menace. You'll describe the enemy carefully to my servant, who will then find and destroy this evil."

"Thank you, my Lord." Aspe's head dropped in reverence and gratitude.

"It is the Prophet's will," I waved a hand, dismissing the warrior-priest from my audience chamber. Let Aspe think that one of the enemy had invaded Ny-nes. I knew that was impossible; Ny-nes had spawned this evil and we'd missed it until now. Nevertheless, I had plans to make and Merrin to control, to do the Prophet's will in this. The healer would be dead soon enough, and the threat eliminated.

Smiling at my own thoughts, I watched Aspe scuttle backward, until he was past the guards at the door. Then he turned and walked as quickly as he could out of my sight. I love how people fear the Prophet.

Through *me*.

*North*

Soon enough, Kaakos would send out his hounds. Time to step up my game. I stopped walking along a narrow, filthy path between hovels when a hand tugged on my cloak.

"Yes?" I turned to ask of the one who'd come.

"Baby come," the man whimpered. "Except—stuck."

"Lead the way," I said, turning to follow the man, who took off at a near-run.

~

*King's Palace*

*Hunter*

"I'm working on the rewrite on one of the laws," I told Thorn. "It's good—what they've done. It makes sense, and only needs clarification in a few places. I think you'll approve," I added.

"This is the one about limiting trainees' power if they have too many infractions?"

"That's it," I agreed, setting the pile of papers down on the garden table where Thorn sat, having afternoon tea. "Where's Sherra?"

"Having tea with Doret, and trying to placate her for taking Anari away, I imagine," Thorn grumbled. "Tonight, Armon, Caral and I are going to visit the village with Claude. I'll take Sherra, too, if she returns in time."

"Perhaps you should stay here, my King," I pointed out as diplomatically as I could. "The ah, presence of the King himself may be—somewhat intimidating to a common citizen."

"And staying here is safer, too, no doubt, for the King," Thorn replied dryly.

"I was getting around to that one," I said. He bit back a laugh.

"I know you want to go," I sighed. "I would, too, if I were in your place. It's hard to place those limits upon yourself. Your father found it difficult, too, at times."

"Then would you allow Sherra to go?"

"I think so. I'd also ask Adahi to go."

"You know, this is like that old game of strategy—I can't recall its name," Thorn blew out a breath. "The one where the Queen has almost unlimited power to move about on the board, while the King is very limited in his movements."

"I never learned that game."

"I barely recall it—from an early lesson in strategy."

"Was the King unimportant in this game?" I asked.

"No—the King is the most important piece. If he is successfully attacked, then the game is over and the King falls."

"Then he's the most powerful piece."

"No, actually, the Queen is given the most power in that game."

"Strange game, then."

"At the time, I considered that it wasn't reflective of real life, or real battle."

"Now has your opinion changed?"

"You see that I'm allowing my Queen to visit a village, while I'd prefer to go myself, don't you?"

"I do see your point," I agreed.

"I want her protected, too," Thorn grumbled. "That's why I want Adahi to go as well."

"Because he's already accepted a role as a guardian of sorts? In the past?"

"Yes. For both of us."

"He and Sherra were able to stand against Ruarke," I recalled. "It's a sound request."

"Glad to have your approval, Hunt."

"Glad to be of service, Thorn."

"Did you speak to my father like that?"

"As often as possible."

This time, Thorn didn't hold the laughter back.

"So, tell me what you came to talk to me about," Thorn said after the laughter died down.

"The census," he said. "We have forms printed and ready to send out. I only need to give the word to have them delivered. Secondary Camp's should be back in our hands in two days."

"Then I'll ask Levi and Misten to coordinate troops to go to villages afterward. Tell them to send people to their home villages if possible, so there won't be so much mistrust. I'm hoping that will relieve villagers' fears in most cases—if they recognize at least one of the warriors or escorts we're sending."

"Good idea. I'll send mindspeak to Caral, so she can inform Levi and Misten."

"How long do you think this will take?" Thorn asked. "Have you arranged for enough diviners to go through the papers afterward?"

"Barth and I have been working on that. He's sending out commands now, under the King's seal."

"It's so nice to delegate," Thorn grinned. "Even when I don't know I'm delegating."

"That's the way this thing works," I said. "You say handle it, so we do. Barth will collect the ones that draw the others' attention, for another confirming divination," I went on. "Before bringing the final information to you."

"Sounds good. I assume you'll be collecting the information to give numbers to the King?"

"Of course. It will also be recorded in the archives—for the official records. It's about damn time, too."

"Do you have someone engaged to hand out census papers in the King's City?"

"I ah," I sputtered. It hadn't occurred to me until then that we'd need one, too. "I'll put that together this afternoon."

"Good."

∼

*Kerok*

*Armon,* I sent mindspeak as Hunter hurried away from the garden table.

*Thorn?*

*I have a special project in mind for you, Caral and Sherra tonight,* I responded. *You'll be traveling to a small village to investigate a report of unusual activity.*

*We can handle that. Will you be available for a briefing?*

*Come for dinner; I'll tell you what I know.*

*We'll be there.*

*My love?* I sent to Sherra.

*Kerok?*

*I have a mission for you tonight, with Armon, Caral and Adahi,* I sent. *There's a report from a village that needs confirmation.*

*I can do that.*

*I know you can. I need discretion in this, my rose.*

*I'll be as discreet as possible.*

*They're coming for dinner. I'll give you details then. Don't be late, my love.*

*I won't. I'm almost done here with Pottles.*

*Adahi?* I sent next.

*Thorn?*

*Will you come for dinner tonight? I have a mission for you, Sherra, Armon and Caral,* I said.

*Of course I will come. You don't have to bother with a plate or drink,* he added.

*I know. Have you heard anything from Kyri, lately?*

*Nothing, other than she and Garkus are working in Kaakos' kitchen.*

*I assume you'll inform me if there is anything worthy to report?*

*I promise to do my best.*

*Thank you.*

⁓

NY-NES

*Merrin*

The moment the lock clicked and Kaakos walked in, I understood my mind wouldn't be under my control for much longer.

There was an unholy glee shining in his eyes, and that didn't bode well for Merrin, former Captain and warrior from Az-ca.

CHAPTER 8

*N*y-nes
    *Kyri*

Rumors ran quietly through Kaakos' palace, just as they did in any other. Soobi's head leaned to the side, her forehead wrinkled in concentration as she strained to capture every word whispered to her by another, newer kitchen helper.

"The healer helps all," the man breathed in her ear. "Any who ask."

Rumors came from others, also, that the healer had been discovered by Kaakos' warrior-priests, although there were differing opinions on how he'd avoided capture.

*Wouldn't be hard to get away if he could* step, Garkus expressed his opinion in mindspeak.

*I hope Kaakos gets distracted by this new development,* I lifted a bowl to wash. *Enough that we'll have an easier path to killing him when the time comes.*

*Keep dreaming,* Garkus' mental voice growled. *You saw those bloody rugs, same as I did.*

No wonder the warrior-priests were continuing their search for new servants—Kaakos was killing them off at an alarming rate. At

107

least he'd focused mostly on guards and upstairs servants so far. He seldom wandered into the kitchens, I think.

As for the bloody rugs, I wanted to shudder; we'd watched as that dripping mess was carried past the kitchens and out the back door.

Bodies of two hapless guards were enclosed by the thick fabric, and still the blood had dripped. Other servants followed close behind, cleaning up blood as if a cyclone were behind them.

Kaakos hated mess. He didn't mind creating it; he merely disliked it afterward. Why did servants or slaves exist, other than to swiftly serve his whims?

*I curse your name and the dirt beneath your bones, mother of Kaakos,* I swore mentally. She was long dead and immune to my curse, no matter how much feeling or power I put behind it.

As for cursing the father of Kaakos, well, that one had cursed himself, so there was no need for me to add to it. And, since he was also dead, it didn't matter anyway.

My desire to curse Kaakos?

I waited to do that in person, even if it killed me.

~

*Sherra*

"This is Claude," Kerok introduced the messenger and former warrior to us at dinner. He'd be the fifth member of our team during this investigation run. He'd brought reports of unusual activity to the Crown, and Kerok obviously thought the report bore enough credence to do further research.

"I feel I can trust the source—in my gut," Claude said as a plate of food was set in front of him.

"The source of the information will be more cooperative if Claude goes with you," Kerok said, lifting his fork and nodding for all of us to eat.

"You say it's the source's neighbor who goes out at night, past the town's boundaries?" Armon asked.

"Yes, that's right, Colonel. It's too dangerous to make a habit of it in those parts, too."

"Could be carrying messages," Armon shrugged. "No reason to risk your life like that, otherwise."

"He's had visits from relatives, who live twenty miles away," Kerok added. "When that's not a habit, either. The terrain from that village is flatter, according to Claude. It may have some significance, but I don't know what that might be."

"We may not know, unless we can crawl inside Kaakos' mind," Barth pointed out.

"I dislike that idea," Kerok gruffed. "Besides, we're already assuming that this is related to the enemy. We don't know that for certain."

"What do you think, Claude?" Hunter asked.

"I think there's something to this," he replied. "He's not walking outside the town at night for his fucking health, I know that."

Caral stifled a snicker; Claude was a former sergeant and not accustomed to mincing words. I appreciated his candor, just as Caral did.

"If you'll do the mirror shield, I'll do the regular shield," Caral turned to me.

"I was just thinking that," I said.

"Mirror shield?" Claude asked.

"They'll never know we're there," Caral reassured him.

～

*ARMON*

I was grateful Claude could transport us to the village; I wasn't familiar with it, so it would have been shields and guessing if I'd done it.

Regardless, Claude set us down on the informant's front porch before knocking lightly. Sherra allowed him to stand outside the mirror shield, but Caral kept him shielded anyway.

No reason to take chances, since we could be walking into a trap.

I'd had that conversation with Thorn before we left; to stay on guard the entire time, in case we weren't reading the situation properly.

The village of Sa'wann was quiet around us, with barely a sliver of moon overhead to cast its light upon the small town. Claude tapped the door again; there'd been no answer to his first knock.

*Armon, I'm not feeling good about this,* Sherra sent.

*Caral, keep your strongest shield up while I try the door,* I barked in mindspeak.

*It's up,* she replied.

Taking two steps forward until I could reach the door, I tried the ancient knob. The door swung open.

The stench reached us before we could adjust our vision to the darkness. Someone had murdered the informant and his family.

When I turned to ask Claude who the headman of the village was so we could make the report, enemy weapons fired at us. Projectiles from pistols and larger rifles were slamming into Caral's shield before ricocheting away with a terrifying whine.

*I'm leaving my shields around you—they still can't see you and they're firing blind,* Sherra shouted mentally.

*Wait,* I shouted back. *Where are you going?*

She'd *stepped* outside Caral's shield; I could see that much, but I had no idea what her intentions were. As for our shooters, the bullets were coming from several directions, so I couldn't pinpoint a particular location to fire a blast at them.

Besides, the entire town was tinder dry, and one house burning could mean the destruction of the entire village.

～

*Sherra*

*My shields are holding—with yours,* Caral reported as I kept a heavy, mirrored shield about myself to hide from the shooters.

*Move them off the porch—that's where they're firing,* I told her. *They won't see where you go, and you'll be safer away from there.*

*Moving now,* Caral replied. *Armon isn't happy, but he'll have to accept it for the moment.*

*I can see the light when the guns fire,* I said, gathering myself to *step* toward the first shooter I could see.

*Sherra, what the fuck are you doing?* Armon demanded.

*Armon, shut up and help me,* I retorted. *Make a mirror shield,* step away from Caral and go looking for the brief flashes of light when the guns fire. You'll find an enemy there.*

*Dammit,* he cursed. *Fuck. Why is it you thought of this first? I'm making shields, now.*

Squaring my shoulders, I considered *stepping* to my selected target, when he cried out in pain and fell; I could hear it clearly during a lull in firing.

*One down,* Adahi's voice sounded in my head.

He was ahead of me in this, and didn't need a shield to protect himself. The bullets would fly through him, unless he decided to block them.

*Choosing another target now,* I told him and went about my business. It was nothing, after all, once I could see an enemy clearly enough to form the blast tube and direct my fire into a vital point in their body.

Across the street, I understood that Armon was having success doing the same. As for Adahi, he took down most of our shooters that night, and we counted seventeen bodies when the sun peeked over the eastern mountains.

*KEROK*

*Seventeen with enemy weapons—pistols and rifles,* Armon reported. *The rest of the village is dead inside their homes. Uncooperative is my guess.*

*Was the suspect one of the dead?*

*He was one of the shooters, along with his wife and son,* Armon replied. *All dead, of course, so we can't ask questions.*

*What about divining their belongings?*

*I believe Sherra is gathering things now, to bring to you and Barth.*

*Good.* I wanted to grind my teeth at this turn of events. While I'd spoken with Claude about the reports from Sa'wann, the spy had killed most of the village before lying in wait for the ones I'd send.

He thought we wouldn't be prepared enough to survive his gunfire. Or, he'd been led to believe that, anyway. I didn't discount the idea that he'd become a liability to the enemy, and this was a way to destroy evidence and witnesses, along with an unwary warrior or two.

*Does Claude know the relatives from twenty miles away? I want to ask them questions, if they're still around.*

*He says most of them died last night—they were firing at us, too.*

*I still want this investigated.*

*Understood. We'll get to that when we're done here.*

~

*SHERRA*

Caral carried the small crate, while Adahi fished personal items from pockets or bits of clothing from dead shooters, including a woman and a thirteen-year-old boy.

I didn't want to touch them; not now, anyway. I was too tired, I think, to withstand what I might find in those things.

"Claude, we have to go to the other village when we're done here, King's command," Armon said behind me.

"That's everything, except something from the other victims," Adahi settled a wood comb in the crate.

The entire time we'd searched bodies, I'd castigated myself. Yes, I'd placed shields around this village, too. It didn't do a damn thing to keep out its own residents or those from other villages. It had done nothing to prevent them from carrying mundane weapons inside with them, either.

Fuck.

*Stop blaming yourself,* Caral told me.

*How do you know I'm doing it?* I didn't look at her when I sent mindspeak.

*Your body language says a lot,* she informed me. *You and I know we're not perfect, or even close to that. Neither of us can read minds, or see this kind of mischief coming. We did the best we could when the enemy attacked. It's all anyone can expect.*

*What if we find a second village dead, when we go there?* I replied caustically.

"That's not our doing," Caral said aloud. "That's on the enemy, not us. Don't take that burden of guilt for yourself; you know where it belongs."

"Daughter, stop punishing yourself," Adahi appeared in front of me. "Caral is correct—this is not your burden. That goes to Kaakos—he killed this village. You had nothing to do with it."

"What about the weapons?" I asked as tears threatened.

"I've sent the guns to the King," Adahi said quietly. "The decision on what to do with them is his."

"All right." I wiped moisture away from my cheeks with a sleeve.

"We're ready to go to Balsom, now," Armon strode into our midst. "Claude, will you take us?"

Claude nodded. We gathered closer together, before Claude *stepped* us away.

~

WE FOUND ourselves inside the headman's home, having tea with him while Armon and Claude questioned him. Armon, unless I missed my guess, was in mental contact with Kerok the entire time.

At least Balsom was intact, and its residents alive—except for those related to the spy in Sa'wann.

"Left yesterday," the headman explained. "Early. Would have taken most of the day to get from here to there, walking."

"Unless someone *stepped* them," Adahi growled.

More and more, the evidence was piling up against Narvin and Willa. If they'd *stepped* the spy's relations away from Balsom, they'd have plenty of time to kill everyone in Sa'wann, allowing bodies to decompose in the heat of the day before lying in wait for us to knock on a neighbor's door.

*Why was Kaakos interested in this remote village?* I kept asking myself. My mind and body were exhausted, however, so an answer wasn't coming. Here, the land was so flat you could see for miles, unlike the hilly region surrounding Sa'wann.

From an attack perspective, Sa'wann would be much more defensible. *Where do you think Narvin and Willa are holed up?* Caral sent while Armon asked more questions of the headman.

*They could be anywhere.* My weariness came through in my sending. *He can* step *from one end of Az-ca to the other, you know.*

*Damn, I'm tired,* Caral responded. *I know you are, too.*

*We'll have to answer the King's questions when we get back. I really need a marching draught right now,* I complained.

*Agreed.*

*Kerok?* I sent.

*My rose?*

*Will you have a marching draft ready for Caral and me when we get there?*

*I'll order it now. I've already had one. I hate when our days extend into the following days,* he added. *I wish I could just let you sleep, but there are reports to write and questions to answer.*

*I know.*

*I've had word from Doret,* he went on.

*What did she say?*

*She was forced to implement the law before it was signed,* he told me. *Those two—you called them troublemakers? They tried to burn down the mess hall last night. Doret has suppressed all their power, and is waiting on me to pass judgment in the matter. Hunter is writing his hand off, trying to get the law into a final version for me to sign.*

*Oh, no. Why did they do that? Did she tell you?*

*One of the other instructors told them to be quiet, and to put their shield balls away during the meal. Attempting to burn the building was their response, later, when the place was empty.*

*They were forming shield balls during a meal? That's insane,* I said. As weary as I'd been before contacting Kerok, I felt even more so now.

*Before they were stopped, they'd already lobbed several shield balls at other trainees, who had to be sent to the infirmary. Now, I've seen warrior trainees form fire balls during a meal and toss them at others. That infraction carries a heavy penalty. Their power is removed and they're sentenced to farm labor. Another infraction after that will result in banishment to the poison lands.*

*They sent other students to the infirmary?*

*Yes. That's why the law needs to be signed today, so I can ponder a punishment.*

*I think they need to spend time in the lockup,* I blurted without thinking.

*That will be one of my options,* Kerok responded.

*Wait, I think Armon and Adahi are done with their questioning,* I reported.

*Good. I'll be waiting for your return.*

❧

"Adahi killed eleven; Sherra and I took the others down," Armon reported. Caral and I sat together in Kerok's study, while Armon sat nearby, a half-drained cup of tea laced with marching draft clutched in his fingers.

Caral and I'd already drank ours, both of us hoping for a respite from our weariness.

Adahi stood behind Armon's chair, as if he felt as fresh as a flowering weed after a heavy rain. With arms crossed over his chest and eyes narrowed to their usual slits, he nodded now and then as Armon made his report to Kerok and Hunter.

Even with the marching draft, I began to feel light-headed. "More tea, my King?" a servant entered Kerok's study without knocking.

My dreamwalker roared to the surface as the explosive was tossed into our midst. This time, my dreamwalker didn't bother hiding any of her actions from me; I felt like a helpless bystander as she formed a shield about the small, round bomb, then made the shield larger, to include the servant who'd delivered it.

Blood and bits of bone and flesh bloomed inside the shield, with the accompanying percussive boom of detonation rattling the window behind us.

We watched as streaks of fresh blood stained the inner walls of the shield as they coursed down the sides, with bits of skin and organs floating within the deep red rivulets.

Had the sound of the explosion not been dampened by the strength of the shield surrounding it, the window would have shattered and the rest of us could have been pelted by flying glass.

$\sim$

*KEROK*

"I have no idea whether my shield would have withstood something so powerful and so close," Hunter sounded shaken.

My silent nod confirmed my agreement. Kaakos was now attacking us with weapons made in Ny-nes, and pointed at us by our own people.

"The name of the servant?" I asked.

"I'm still working on that," Barth said. He hadn't been in the meeting, and a part of me was grateful for it. His voice and hands were steady, at least, as he poured whiskey for Hunter and me.

"Sherra's dreamwalker," Hunter began.

"I know that," I grunted. "For now, Sherra's asleep in our bed. At least she was the one to return, once the dreamwalker *stepped* away to dispose of the ah, remains."

"I almost wish Kaakos had witnessed what happened," Hunter hissed. "The fucker."

"I sent Armon and Caral back to Secondary Camp," Barth said. "They need the support of their mates, I think. That was a very close call, Thorn. Ny-nes has improved their bombs, it appears."

"We'd be deaf, even if our shields held, if Sherra hadn't," Hunter said.

"Say dreamwalker," I sighed. "That's who showed up for this."

"For the second time, while Sherra was awake," Barth pointed out. "I've sent three diviners to collect personal items from every servant in the palace. If there are others waiting to lob bombs, I want to know about it."

Barth was thinking—even if I wasn't at the moment. "Give me those reports the moment they're available," I said.

"Thorn," Hunter said, "go lie next to your lady Queen. I'm going to bed as fast as I can get there. Let Kage and his guards watch the palace for now. I'm sure Sherra has placed extra shields already."

I wanted to argue with Hunter, but didn't have the energy. "You're right," I admitted. "Going to bed, now."

~

*SECONDARY CAMP*

*Levi*

Armon, even asleep, looked as if he'd aged ten years in a single night. *A bomb tossed by a palace servant?*

Kaakos' reach had grown longer than we'd expected, and faster than anticipated. In the cabin next door, I figured Misten watched Caral sleep, as I watched Armon.

*An entire village destroyed by enemy weapons.*

The King could have died, or sustained injuries, at the least.

Caral said Sherra's dreamwalker arrived in time. Uncanny. Terrifying, too, if I bothered to dissect the event in question.

Sherra—how did she feel about this? I wouldn't like being taken over, even if it were by another, hidden part of myself.

The result was the best outcome, however; I couldn't deny that. Armon was alive, as were the others.

"My brain is addled," I whispered to myself. Armon stirred in his sleep. I smoothed a lock of hair away from his brow.

~

*J*UBAL

Failure. That's the message I received from the voice. He was angry, too. The weapons he'd sent—and the small bomb, hadn't killed any of the targets specified. An entire village lay dead, but that was nothing to the voice.

Narvin and his bitch lay sleeping in my spare room while I was castigated for their shortcomings.

How I longed for the day when the other voice only demanded that messages be passed along. That was easy enough, and drew no attention to me.

This—I worried that Narvin and Willa would lead the infernal King and his army straight to my door. They'd managed to place a mole in the palace, and given him a weapon and instructions to kill the King. As for how that attempt on the King's life had been foiled—I hadn't heard that story, and neither had the voice.

*Do better next time,* the voice hissed.

*As you say, my Lord.* My promise, as usual, was insincere.

~

*N*Y-*NES*

*Kaakos*

"Fools." I wanted to break something. Kill something. Merrin's subjugation wasn't complete yet and this—they'd botched everything I'd planned in Az-ca.

"My Lord?" A quiet voice spoke outside my open door.

"What is it?" I hissed through clenched teeth, keeping my back turned toward this unexpected intrusion.

"Ah, Aspe's body has been delivered to the back gate, my Lord. With a piece of paper, which the guards cannot read."

"What?" I whirled in the guard's direction, finding him bowed and ready for my wrath to fall upon him.

"Come," I snapped at him. "Bring other guards. I shall read this note that my underlings cannot decipher."

"Of course, my Lord."

~

*KYRI*

Every kitchen worker shrank away from the door as Kaakos and his guards strode past. I had no idea what troubled him enough to walk out of his palace, but something had him so angry I could see the power glow about his body.

This made him more than dangerous—to anyone who crossed his path. I'd gotten mindspeak from Doret the night before—an attempt on Thorn's life had been made, and only Sherra's dreamwalker had thwarted the attempt, as it was so unexpected. Garkus' eyes had widened when I told him the news—no doubt, Kaakos was furious about this failure.

Now, something else had drawn Kaakos' attention, and two such blows against him likely meant people would die. Across the kitchen, Garkus rose slightly from his squatting position to watch the unholy parade outside the kitchen door.

*Stay down,* I hissed mindspeak at him. *We can't take Kaakos on like this. It's suicide.*

*You don't have to tell me twice.* He'd hunkered down behind a prep table across the kitchen, and lowered himself again after my warning. He'd either seen or felt the power wrapped about Kaakos for himself, and I was grateful I didn't have to convince him.

Other kitchen workers had knelt behind the nearest cabinet or table, to make smaller targets of themselves. Anyone with the tiniest amount of sense wouldn't approach Kaakos in this mood, unless they wished to die a painful death.

A kitchen worker scurried in, once Kaakos and his guards exited the palace. "Body dumped—back gate," he panted, as if he'd run to get away from Kaakos' wrath. "Aspe, me thinks."

Aspe. The one who'd chained Garkus and me. One of Kaakos' highly-placed warrior-priests.

Damn. Who'd bait Kaakos like that?

"Get down," someone hissed at the new arrival. He joined them behind a sturdy table. We heard the roar of anger outside the palace, and the disturbing sound of blasts being fired. *How many had Kaakos killed this time, and why?*

~

*KAAKOS*

The note dangled from my fingers as I stalked toward the palace. Behind me, six guards were dead, their bodies added to that of Aspe, whose face was the only recognizable part of him.

The rest had been burned to a crisp.

As I'd burned the guards surrounding me.

Blowing the back door open with power, I stepped inside, neither glancing left nor right. I had an enemy to kill, and I needed the proper weapon to do it.

Merrin would become that weapon, and he would bear my merciless wrath when he killed.

The note was written in Az-ca's shorthand, developed through decades of scant supplies of paper and writing instruments. The guards couldn't read it, because they'd never been taught to read it.

Therefore, the message had been sent specifically to me, and it meant the sender knew more about me than I wanted them to know.

*You failed*, it read. *I succeeded.*

~

*MERRIN*

He was coming; I heard his footsteps on the flagstones outside my locked room. Little of myself was left to me—gradually, he was taking everything.

I wished I'd allowed Thorn to kill me. Or that I'd stayed in the poisoned lands. Those deaths would have been preferable to this one. I would exist and not exist—as Kaakos' puppet, once he was done with me.

The scrape of a key in the lock froze my thoughts and amplified my fears. Would this be the last time my thoughts were my own? I would not show him tears. I vowed never to do that.

Merrin would fall, and Kaakos' puppet would rise.

What would he ask me to destroy?

*Az-ca*, my mind whispered as his boots came to rest before my huddled body.

~

NORTH

"Hide," the woman hissed at me as she ducked inside the hovel where I sat, having a weak cup of tea with her husband, whom I'd just healed of a broken leg. "Aspe dead. Sent to palace gate. Lord Kaakos angry. Warrior-priests come."

"How killed?" I asked, setting down my cup of tea.

"Burned," she said. "Not face—to see who."

"Ah." They'd burned the body, leaving the face intact for Kaakos to recognize. A nasty ploy, but effective. Kaakos would be looking for revenge, now, and he cared not that innocents died with the guilty.

For a moment, I considered sending mindspeak to the one I suspected of accomplishing that feat.

No—better not to let them know of me.

Not yet. I had things to do before that time came—penance to serve and bodies to heal.

Soon, perhaps. I did and didn't look forward to that day.

~

ARMON

I still felt the ill-effects of a lengthy day when Levi and I passed out census papers at breakfast the following morning.

"Fill these out completely and return them to us by tomorrow," Levi instructed. "The towns and villages are also receiving papers, as there hasn't been a census taken in decades. If you have questions, come to Colonel Armon, Captain Caral or me. We'll find an answer for you."

Several warriors and escorts were already scrounging for writing instruments. We'd have some papers filled out before breakfast was over.

I considered sending mindspeak to Thorn, asking after Sherra, but held back. Levi and I—we loved the Sherra we'd first met. Now, there was another to contend with. One whom we didn't know and weren't familiar with.

One who was Sherra—and wasn't, at the same time.

That one seemed harder. Angry, too. I couldn't guess what she might be capable of. Sherra—the one I knew—I could gauge her reactions. The other? I had no idea.

Levi hadn't said it, but that part of Sherra frightened him.

Me, too.

Was Thorn having these feelings as well?

I worried our fears would alienate the Sherra we loved. What would we do if that happened? Were we all destined to be afraid of her?

*She will never mistreat you, no matter what,* a small voice told me.

I sighed and allowed an invisible burden to slide from my shoulders.

CHAPTER 9

*Ny-nes
Kaakos*

"The name Merrin is no longer a part of you," I informed the cloaked and bowed figure before me. "You will be my revenge; therefore, I name you Vengeance."

"Yes, my Lord." His head remained bowed as he spoke.

"My first assignment for you is to go out into the city and find this healer—North—who troubles me. Use whatever force is necessary to locate and destroy him."

"It will be as you say, my Lord."

"Of course it will. Reports will come to me daily of your progress, and ah, the numbers of citizens killed during your search."

"I understand."

"Good. I'm sending six warrior-priests with you. They'll be your guides through the city. Make sure they stay alive, as they are responsible for making the reports to me."

"Yes, my Lord."

"Take him to the back gate; the warrior-priests wait there," I commanded a guard. He bowed to me before leading Vengeance away.

123

~

*KYRI*

*Merrin*, Garkus' growl filled my head as the cloaked man, led by a guard, strode toward the palace's back door.

Kaakos had taken his mind; that was clear. Whatever Kaakos had commanded he do, that one would do or die in the attempt.

While I had no sympathy for Merrin in his right mind, nobody deserved this. *Two guesses who he's sending him after*, Garkus added.

Soobi stood beside me, her eyes round in fear. She understood what this meant as well as Garkus did. The healer was in Kaakos' sights, and neither would stop until North was dead.

Had the healer actually killed Aspe? I had my doubts. Only time would tell whether my feelings about the matter would hold, as I'd never met the one Soobi and the others spoke of with such reverence.

"City will burn," Soobi whispered as the back door swung shut with a nerve-wrenching clang.

She was right about that, too.

~

*NORTH*

Word spread faster than fire through the narrow streets and alleys. The Supreme Leader had released a raver against me.

Kaakos had expended a great deal of power to make one; I understood that. Aspe's murder had enraged him. It made me wonder what the note delivered with Aspe's body said, but as few could read, that information wouldn't come to me.

He imagined that I'd killed the warrior-priest and then sent the body to him, bearing a note. If I'd intended Aspe harm, I'd have killed him to start with.

If Kaakos had used sense, he might consider that nobody native to Ny-nes could read or write anything, without his permission to learn it in the first place.

He also thought I'd be simple enough to find, once he killed a few citizens. I didn't want that to happen, but true peace and freedom always bore a heavy price.

Nevertheless, I had work to do, to warn the population. After that, if they chose to stay in Kaakos' path, their safety—or lack of it—lay in their own hands.

"What think?" the woman whispered as I handed the healed infant back to her.

"I believe it is time to move away," I said. "From now on, nobody is safe, here."

"He Supreme Leader," she sighed and turned her head away.

"He may call himself that," I countered. "He is nothing more than a figurehead who likes to kill his own. You and your neighbors owe him nothing, as he is a false leader, who represents a false prophet. Why do you suppose he prevents you from learning to read the Prophet's book for yourself? The words written there are far different from the words and deeds he allows to reach you."

She had to think about that for a moment, before dipping her head in a slight nod. "Tell your neighbors it is no longer safe to stay in the city. Take what you can and move across the river."

"That far," she began.

"I know, but if people move and scatter, it will be more difficult to hunt them down. Keep your lives if you can. You were never meant to serve a false prophet. The book warns against such."

"He—false prophet? In palace?"

"Yes. That body belonged to someone else when he was alive—an enemy of the Supreme Leader. Kaakos keeps the body there, not only to gloat over his enemy's death, but to taunt the people of Ny-nes with the lie of it."

"I tell husband. Try to move."

"Good. Tell others you trust only—for their own safety. Tell them the healer has spoken."

"Why you come to us?" she whispered as I turned to leave.

"Because the real Prophet predicted it—in the book."

"I want—see that."

"Someday, if all comes right, you can learn to read if you want."

"That—be good day."

"Yes. If you leave the city, do it in hiding—and at night if you can."

~

*Az-ca*

*Kerok*

"I sent Claude to Balsom, so he can relay messages if anything unusual happens there," I said. I sat at my desk the following morning, after leaving Sherra still asleep in our bed.

"That's what I'd do," Hunter agreed. Barth nodded his agreement as he sipped tea. "If Kaakos has his eye on Balsom for any reason, we need to know. Claude can *step* away, too, if somebody starts killing Balsom's residents with enemy weapons."

"I'll ask him to send mindspeak and *step* to Secondary Camp if that happens, so Armon can send a squad to stop what they can. I don't want another village slaughtered," I growled.

"I'll prepare the message, and send mindspeak to Armon," Hunter agreed, scribbling notes on a slip of paper.

"Good. I've already asked him to send two warrior-escort pairs, to burn Sa'wann and place a shield around the burning, so the dry countryside won't go up with it. I dislike the idea of predators scavenging bodies."

"I dislike the fact that there will be none to mourn their passing in their own village." Barth's voice held anger. "Kaakos has much to atone for."

"The bastard needs to die," I snapped. "If I had a way to do it, he'd be dead already."

"Doret is here to see you," a guard tapped on the open door of my study.

"Send her in," I said.

Doret walked in; I didn't miss the angry set to her features or the stiff movements of her body. "I see you're as angry as we are," I indicated an empty chair. "Tell me what's wrong."

"I received mindspeak from Kyri earlier," Doret grumbled. "It's not good news, I'm afraid. She confirmed that Merrin is in Ny-nes, and now, Kaakos has turned Merrin into a raver. Once he's done with the troubles plaguing Ny-nes, I have no doubt Merrin will be sent back to Az-ca to cause trouble for all of us."

Silence reigned for several seconds as Barth, Hunter and I absorbed Doret's words. "What, dear lady, is a raver?" Hunter spoke first.

"Something Kaakos has complete control over. Merrin is no longer Merrin, as vile as he was. Now, he is Kaakos' right arm, commanded by Kaakos' evil desires. As much of a killing machine Merrin was before, multiply that by a thousand and you may get close to the mark."

"I assume Merrin's power is now Kaakos' to command?" Barth asked.

"Yes—and it can be enhanced by Kaakos whenever he determines it necessary. There are rumors of a healer running through his city, and recently, one of Kaakos' pet warrior-priests was killed and left at his gate. Kaakos is searching for the healer in their midst, convinced that he was the one to kill Aspe. Kyri doubts the veracity of it, but that leaves all in the city at Kaakos' mercy."

"Do we care what happens to those people?" Barth asked the simple question.

"Most are innocents," Doret snorted. "Just as most are innocents in Az-ca. They don't send the armies against you; Kaakos does that."

"It becomes easy to blame an entire race or country, for what only a few of them do," Adahi arrived to add his opinion.

"You received mindspeak, too?" Doret turned to him.

"Yes. These events in Ny-nes can be seen as convenient—and inconvenient—at the same time."

"Will she keep us updated on Merrin's ah, exploits, so we'll know when he might be sent back to trouble us?" Hunter asked.

"As much as she knows," Adahi shrugged. "What we haven't discussed is the healer. He must have power—Kyri says so. That means he has either fooled those around him for a very long while, or has recently arrived in Ny-nes, getting past Kaakos' barrier in some way. She only knows about him through the rumors she's heard, you understand."

"He won't last long, now that the raver has been sent after him," Doret snorted.

"One or the other will certainly die," Adahi confirmed. "Ravers have a single-mindedness instilled by their creator. They will achieve their goal or perish in the attempt."

"Why haven't we heard of this before?" I demanded.

"Because you can't read the old records," Adahi replied. "Ravers—were created and assigned to kill those with power in Ny-nes, those attracted to their own sex, and those of any color other than the color of the ones in power."

"That means that there has been power all along in Ny-nes," Hunter breathed.

"Now you begin to see," Adahi said. "But power—and wealth—were allowed only to those in charge. Those things were held away from the common people, and, as education was also withheld from them, they had no hope of attaining any of it. The ones in charge wanted it to stay that way, because someone with wealth or power on the outside could lead a revolt."

I understood that quite well. Armies required food, weapons and funding. Those were early lessons in my military training. It brought something else to mind, too. "The spies are paid, aren't they?" I asked.

"Yes." Adahi's answer was short and swift. "Either in gold or favors. Disgruntlement only takes you so far in that particular game."

*Armon*, I sent. *Before the attacker's house is burned in Sa'wann, I want it thoroughly searched for gold or other types of payment.*

*I'll see it done*, Armon replied.

"There's no need to search that house," Adahi said. "Normally, I give what I find to the very poor. This time I kept it, in case you asked." He pulled a small bag into his hand before leaning forward to place it in front of me.

Carefully loosening the tie around it, I found a small, neat pile of gold inside. To a villager, this would be a fortune and could be spent on many things. Drawing a heavy sigh, I retied the bag and handed it to Adahi. "Distribute this as you see fit," I told him. "It is enough to know he was paid."

"I'll add that to the official record," Hunter said, jotting words on his scrap of paper.

"Meeting without me?" Sherra, dressed in a working uniform, wandered into the study, a mug of tea in her hand. She'd told me today was a training supervision day with Cole, but I'd forgotten. She was late, too, but I wasn't about to tell her something she already knew.

"We're just discussing the latest in Ny-nes," Doret told her. "Merrin is now a raver, and I'll explain that to you later, if you'll drop by the training camp before dinner."

"I will," she nodded and stifled a yawn.

"Need a marching draught?" Hunter asked.

"No, thank you," she held up a hand. "I've had enough of that for a while."

"We'll talk at dinner tonight," I said. "After you've spoken with Doret."

"Good. Cole is waiting for me, so I'll go, now," she nodded in my direction. "See you at dinner."

~

*SHERRA*

Caral and Levi met me at Cole's house; they'd been there for half an hour, drinking tea and talking with Cole while they waited for me.

"Sorry I'm late; Kerok didn't wake me," I apologized.

"Don't worry—we've enjoyed the respite," Levi's grin was wide and welcoming.

"I think you'll be pleased with the young ones," Cole said, rising from his seat. "They're so happy to be working together; I think it will be second nature to them when you ask them to combine their blasts and shields."

"I was hoping for that," I said. "They're so comfortable with one another, and they have mindspeak, which will only help, I think."

"Maybe we should look at this when training the younger ones—they'll form friendships. It shouldn't be difficult to form fighting pods with that connection," Caral suggested.

"We can do that with the adults, too, you know," Levi pointed out.

"A workable solution, perhaps?" Cole smiled.

"Let's see how it goes with Anari and the boys, and then how it goes with the four of us," I said.

"A pod with the four of us, plus Armon and Misten? That sounds wonderful," Caral nodded.

"And powerful," Levi added. "Like taking down the enemy's palace powerful."

"Let's not get ahead of ourselves," I warned. "We have to see how well this works, first."

"I really want this to work," Caral breathed.

"Me, too."

~

*ANARI*

"They're here," Kyal said, bouncing on his heels as Sherra, Caral and the others walked toward us. Our instructor, Liri, had been testing our shield-making all morning. I was hoping to learn something new when Sherra and the others came.

I wanted to hug Sherra and Caral, but was afraid that wouldn't be allowed. Sometimes, I forgot that Sherra was the Queen and Caral was a Captain in the King's army.

It didn't matter, I guess. Everyone got hugs from Sherra and Caral when they got close enough. Laren was grinning like an idiot when Sherra hugged him. I thought about digging him in the ribs with an elbow, but held back.

"We're going to try something new, today," Cole announced. Laren turned to me with a huge grin—he and Kyal wanted it just as much as I did.

"What is it?" Kyal asked.

"We're going to ask you to combine your power—to build a shield, first, and then to form blasts."

"That—would be excellent," Kyal saw the possibilities while Laren and I were still thinking about them.

"How?" Laren asked.

"Well, I'm going to touch all three of you at the same time," Sherra said. "So you can feel the others' power, along with your own. Once we do that, then we'll work on putting all of it together."

I wasn't sure how that would happen, but I was willing to try. "Kyal, take Ani's hand. Laren, take her other hand. I'll take Laren's and Kyal's hands, to form a circle, all right?"

We joined hands as requested. Once our circle was formed, she asked us to close our eyes. Kyal gasped when the vision of our power appeared in our minds—I had no idea Sherra could do this.

*Now*, she instructed us in mindspeak, *see the others' power.*

I drew in a breath; Kyal's and Laren's power were white lights, like mine, but Sherra's was such a bright blue, it was nearly blinding.

*Ani, push your light toward Laren's. Kyal, once those two are joined, add yours to theirs. Don't touch mine—I'll disengage once the three of you are joined.*

It was so easy, I couldn't believe we hadn't tried it before. Kyal's slipped in right behind Laren's and mine, before it became a part of the whole.

*That's right*, Sherra encouraged. *Now, I'm going to pull away. Don't let anyone go—keep all three together. When I tell you in mindspeak, form a shield with the combined power.*

We watched as the blue light disappeared, leaving the combined white lights behind. It couldn't be my imagination; together, the white lights shone much brighter. Stronger, too.

*Form a shield*, Sherra said.

For a moment it was disorienting, as if Kyal, Laren and I had to make a slight adjustment before combining in reality to form a shield.

*Very good*, Sherra's voice breathed in our minds. *Open your eyes and see.*

We opened our eyes to find Captain Levi firing blasts at our combined shield. We hadn't even felt them hit, the shield was so strong.

"Can you feel that?" Sherra shouted as Levi's blasts became stronger.

*We can't feel anything,* I sent mindspeak. I didn't know how well my voice would carry over the noise of fireblasts cracking against our outer shield.

*I'll ask Levi to do his worst, but gauge his blast so it won't hit any of you if the shield breaks. Strengthen it if you can,* Sherra sent.

*Laren? Kyal?* I sent.

*We're ready,* Kyal grinned. He was excited about this.

Levi hurled a blast at us, so hard and so big, the fireball was all we could see for several seconds before it burned away to nothing. We barely felt it as it burst against our shield.

The combined shield had held. Dimly, I could hear Cole, Caral and Sherra whooping and hugging one another. The experiment had worked, and the three of us—just trainees, after all, had held our shield against a seasoned warrior's fireblasts.

~

*SHERRA*

"That's right, don't worry about destroying it; concentrate on making your blasts stronger," I told Anari.

Cole had set up a lean-to on a beach far below his village, where sparks and stray flames from fireblasts would be washed away by an encroaching tide.

Anari was getting her first lessons on fireblasts. The boys, who'd already done preliminary training for it, stood on the sidelines with Caral and me, shouting encouragement to Anari.

Levi stood nearby, arms crossed over his chest and beaming, as if these were his children who were doing so well.

Once Ani was at a level with the boys on fireblasts, we could do the same experiment. Their shield had performed above expectations. Those three could hold off a powerful warrior—perhaps two warriors. Caral's eyes were shining; she couldn't wait for us to try this together. She and Levi would carry good news back to Armon tonight, at the very least.

I waited to see how it went with fireblasts before mentioning anything to Kerok. Fireblast lessons would take another two training days with Anari, even though she was learning quickly.

Then, the adults would try it. If it weren't so late in the day, we'd try it now, but the sun was falling toward the horizon, and Kerok would be waiting.

"Well done, Anari," Cole said, calling a halt after she blasted the lean-to to kindling. "Time to wash up for dinner."

Kyal shouted his approval and ran toward the narrow trail leading to the village above, with Laren close behind.

Anari came to me, first, before following those two.

"You did so well," I hugged her against me. "I couldn't have asked for better."

"It was fun," she looked up at me with a smile. "I'm really hungry, though."

"I'll *step* you back," I said, squeezing her shoulders. "You may even get there before the others."

～

*KEROK*

Sherra's hair was still damp when she arrived in the small dining room, where Barth, Hunter and I waited. With a nod, Hunter let the servants know to set out food.

"What's the word on the servant who ah," I began after the servants left the dining room.

"A newer hire," Barth said. "His name was Alun. Came from a village not far from Balsom, which is no real surprise, given other events surrounding that area."

"What about the divination on the others?" Hunter asked.

"Nothing. I did a divination on Alun's personal items, and there was evidence that he'd sold himself to the enemy for a bit of gold."

Barth's mouth straightened into a grim line; he hated that this one had been so close to us, without our knowing.

"I'm concerned about the raver," Sherra frowned while helping herself to rolls and butter. She'd spoken with Doret; that was obvious.

"So are we," I conceded. "Merrin, with Kaakos' power behind him? That's terrifying."

"Pottles says he has no mind left, other than Kaakos'. It makes me shudder to think that can happen."

"She told us it takes a great deal of power to make a raver," Barth observed.

"She said that to me, too. Still, it's horrible that it can be done in the first place. How crazy has Ny-nes been all this time?"

"Who knows. It's disheartening to hear that they've had power among the elite all along, and unwilling to let it manifest in the common people," I said.

"Power often corrupts those who possess it," Hunter sighed. "The laws must be observed, to hold it in check."

"The laws must be fair in the beginning," Sherra said, pointing her fork at Hunter.

"Yes. I agree," he acknowledged. "We're working on that. Thorn signed the law you wrote with Cole and Caral." He smiled when he said that.

"Thank you—for straightening out the language and making it workable," Sherra told him. "I don't say that to you enough, Hunter."

I'm not sure I'd ever seen Hunter nonplussed before. Honestly, I couldn't recall the last time I'd paid him a compliment for his work, which was exceptional. Always.

"Here's to the keeper of the laws," I raised my glass to him. "And to the changer as well," I gave a sly wink to Sherra.

"To King Thorn," Barth raised his glass, "Who recognizes the need for both those things."

*I love you*, Sherra sent to me, her eyes catching mine over the rim of her wineglass. I shamelessly winked at her again.

~

*Ny-nes*

*Kaakos*

I wasn't stupid enough to rely solely on reports sent to me by Vengeance and the warrior-priests. Beels, a trusted spy among the warrior-priests, was one of the six I'd sent with him. He had orders to kill my raver, should he show signs of unraveling my spells.

It hadn't happened with any of mine before, but there were records in my personal library, telling of the few times it had happened to others in the past.

Weaklings, with weak skills, in my opinion. None of them had a proper education, as far as their power and talent went.

Beels had power, but I'd suppressed it—except for his mindspeak. He thought it was a gift from the Prophet and kept it secret, as I'd told him such gifts were not meant to be shared with others.

I, being Supreme Leader, was the voice of the Prophet in Ny-nes. Nobody questioned my authority, lest the Prophet's wrath fall heavy upon them. Every time I recalled that fact, I smiled.

As for the fools in Az-ca, I considered how to attack them next time. They were still no closer to finding my spies, although my last attack had only killed civilians instead of the powerful.

Narvin and Willa had somehow been prevented from entering the villages themselves, or I'd instruct Narvin to burn as many of them as he could.

Time to use a bit of gold to turn more civilians into disposable instruments, perhaps.

~

*Secondary Camp*

*Armon*

Caral and Levi were bursting with news; I asked them to wait on their report until after the evening meal.

We'd barely walked into Levi's and my cabin, before Caral lifted Misten in her arms and swung her around while laughing.

"I take it the experiment worked?" I turned to Levi. His grin was worth a pile of gold. "Better than we thought," he pulled my head down for a swift kiss. "We only saw it working with shielding, and with the young ones, but they took to it so fast, it was like a miracle. I threw everything I had at them afterward, and I couldn't crack their combined shield."

"The young ones did that?" It would take a very strong shield to withstand Levi's blasts, and no youngling trainee had ever stood up to his full blasts until Sherra came along.

"Yes. I can't wait to try this myself—Sherra says that our group—our four, plus her and Cole, will form a pod and try this together."

I considered those implications. With six of us working in tandem, if we were successful, we could destroy—I hesitated to say the Supreme Leader's city, but I was certainly thinking it.

"Please let this work," Misten had pulled away from Caral to bounce on her heels, her hands clasped together in a supplicating gesture.

I felt the same way—*please, let this work.*

~

*Sherra*

Caral and Cole sat in my study the following morning, while Briar set out cups of tea for us. I hadn't announced the day's agenda, yet, because I wanted to surprise Caral with the news. We were about to write up the law to allow escorts to have bonding ceremonies.

"Is there anything else?" Briar almost smiled when she asked the question.

"I think this will do us for an hour or two," I told her. "Thank you," I added. She did smile shyly, then, before stepping out the door, empty tray in hand.

"What are we working on today?" Caral asked.

"Recently, it came to my attention that it's unfair for the laws to allow bonding ceremonies between men, without having the same concessions available to the women," I said, waving an arm in an off-handed gesture.

Caral's hands went to her mouth, while tears shone in her eyes.

"I think she likes this idea," Cole grinned.

"It's almost a done deal," I told Caral. "When I asked Kerok about it, he told me to get on with it."

"I can't believe I get to be a part of this," Caral breathed.

"You get to be a part of it," I told her. I couldn't hold the wide grin back, either.

∼

*J*UBAL

*I need more servants—to replace those killed recently,* the voice demanded. *I'd prefer those who enjoy watching things burn.*

*I heard a rumor that two youngling trainees recently set the dining hall on fire at their training camp,* I replied. *Got their power taken away because of it.*

*Where are those boys now?*

*Not boys, more's the pity,* I replied.

*Ah. This—may bear consideration. Find out where they are and tell me the moment you find out. I'll have Narvin and Willa collect them. We'll see how well the enemy responds when they find themselves under attack from the least expected direction.*

I wanted to argue with the voice, to tell him it never paid to put a woman in charge of anything. I didn't.

*You'll receive word the moment I find their location,* I sent.

*Good. You will be well-rewarded for this information.*

You're damn right, I thought, although I didn't tell him so.

*Have Narvin and Willa on standby,* the voice added. *I expect information, if our targets are behind a shield they can't cross. We'll find someone else to do a bit of abduction, if necessary.*

*I understand.*

*Good.*

137

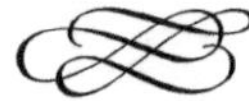

*nari*

We'd been too excited to sleep right away the night before. Kyal was the one to make the suggestion, but Laren and I fell in with his plans quickly.

We knew how to combine our shields, now, and I'd figured out how to make a mirror shield on my own. We used that information to get into Kyri's library. Whatever she'd done to allow us into her home to begin with was still in place, or someone could have been alerted.

As it is, we dropped our shields the moment we were inside her library, and spent an hour picking three books each to read before returning to our bedrooms in Cole's village.

Then, we'd stayed up longer to read for a while, and that meant we were all yawning at breakfast the next morning.

"Trouble sleeping?" Cole asked as I covered another yawn on the training ground later.

"Too excited," Kyal grinned. "We want to do more of what we did yesterday."

"You'll have to wait for Sherra's return tomorrow," Cole smiled. "Today, we'll practice fireblasts again, so we'll be prepared when she asks you to combine those."

Laren's eyes were wide as he turned toward me. *Yes,* his voice breathed into my mind.

"We really want to try that," I told Cole. "We'll do our best for you today."

"Very good. First, we'll build another structure—stronger, this time, and then we'll see how long it takes to blast it to bits."

~

*KEROK*

"We have census papers from Secondary Camp," Hunter walked into my study waving a sheaf of papers in his hand.

"Good. Have you alerted Barth?"

"He's going to meet me in his workroom, with two other diviners. I just wanted to put you on notice, because he'll be compiling a list of warriors and escorts to send to the villages with their papers."

"Good. How long will it take to get this done?"

"I don't know. A week—maybe two or more. We may have limited manpower to visit the villages, and then it'll take two days at least to hand out papers and get them back."

"And to make sure they're all handed in," I said. "Tell them to take counts of papers distributed, and make sure it matches the number returned."

"Already thought of that. I'm putting a list of rules together now."

"Good. Have the ones you send to the villages file a report every time."

"To determine if they've been compromised. Good thinking," Hunter nodded.

"We can't take any chances. To be honest, I see Kaakos behind every rock and cactus, now, and I don't even know what he looks like."

"Do you think Doret knows?"

"She does seem to know a lot about him, but that could be through Kyri. Somehow, I'm positive she knows what he looks like."

"After I drop these off with Barth, I have a few minutes," Hunter said. "Perhaps I'll visit Doret."

"I want to go, too," I said, rising from my chair.

"Then let's hand these to Barth and get going."

"I'm right behind you, my Crown Prince."

~

AN HOUR LATER, we were having tea in Doret's office while we waited for her to join us. The kitchen staff had gone to a great deal of trouble when they learned Hunter and I had come to see Doret.

We had honey cakes, tea, cheeses and crisp wafers in front of us while we waited.

"What's this about?" Doret asked. She'd come straight from the training grounds, sweat and all, to glare at Hunter and me.

"We ah, want to know what Kaakos looks like," I stammered.

"Oh. I thought you'd ask that question long before now."

"Do you know?" Hunter pleaded.

"I can show you," Doret's words were followed by a disdainful snort. "Give me a moment, I have to *step* to Kyri's home to find it."

I didn't know why her words made me freeze—she was going to show us? How?

I watched her disappear in front of us. She was gone perhaps ten minutes before she returned, placing a book in my hand. "They still made images in Ny-nes—when he first came to power there." Her words were gruff. Angry, too.

I opened the book. It was written in a strange language that I couldn't decipher. On the second page, an image jumped out at me and I almost gasped, it was so clear and realistic.

"They called them photographs," Doret snapped at my reaction. "Part of a technology that has been lost or fallen away without the proper equipment."

I stared at the image, taking in the dark hair, green eyes, fair complexion. A small scar marred a full, lower lip, which was bent in a twist of cruelty. Whatever technology had been used to form this image, it had been accurate in its depiction.

"I can see the evil in him," I told Doret while handing the book to Hunter.

"He doesn't bother to hide it," she shrugged. "From those who can see. Most people only see the fair image. Some think him handsome. He cultivates and encourages those views. They haven't learned that a fair face is never a worthy exchange for a heart filled with malevolence."

"Merrin was somewhat the same," Hunter offered the book to Doret.

"Keep it. Kyri may not be back for it, you know. This way, you can let your Queen and those you trust in the army know what they're fighting."

"Thank you," I said. "I wish I could read the words that go with this."

"Be grateful you can't. It's all a lie, glorifying a bastard who should have never been born."

"Then we'll be going," I said, rising from my seat. "Thank you again —for this and for the hospitality."

"Next time, send mindspeak. I'll clean up before the King and Crown Prince arrive, if that happens."

Hunter stifled a snicker as we *stepped* away from Doret's office.

"THIS IS WHAT WE'RE FIGHTING?" Barth examined the photograph with interest while he, Hunter and I had our midday meal together.

"Doret says the book is filled with words glorifying that one. She called him a bastard who shouldn't have been born," Hunter told him.

"I agree with Doret, then, as it would likely make our lives much easier," Barth said, closing the book with a heavy sigh.

"Tell me what you've found so far in the census papers," I said.

"We've found several pairs suitable to send out," Barth replied. "Some pairs and individuals are fence-sitters, who can't make up their minds about a good many things. This includes the new methods, who is now in charge of the army, and varied lists of other things. We've found nothing overt as yet, but we're still looking."

"We're also compiling lists of places the best candidates were from —so they might receive a warmer welcome on their arrival," Hunter added. "If we assign them to home villages and perhaps a few others close by, things should go much easier."

"I'm hoping for that, too, and the sooner we get the information, the better. I'm concerned that Kaakos won't take kindly to his most recent failure, here. What's the word on Narvin and Willa? Any leads?"

"Nothing since Claude's report," Hunter said. "He had the best lead and paid attention, when others may not have."

"Is it possible to put him in charge of a task force?" Barth asked.

"I think that idea has merit," I said. "Hunter, in your copious free time," I teased, "will you divide Az-ca into four quadrants, and find task force leaders for each? The messengers can send all information through them, no matter how unimportant it may seem, and let the leaders decide whether to bring it to our attention."

"I'll have it done by the end of the day," Hunter promised, scribbling on his usual scrap of paper.

"Good. Where is my Queen? I'm surprised she didn't bring her assistants to have a meal with us."

"I believe they're having ah, a working meal," Hunter said.

"What does that mean?"

"I think it means they're working on the bonding law, to allow Misten and Caral to have a ceremony," Barth lifted his tea to drink.

"Well, I see they have their priorities," I laughed.

"Yes, they do."

~

"My King, Colonel Armon has arrived," a guard announced later, as I went through audience requests from Council members. Hunter usually did this, but he had enough on his plate already.

"Send him in," I said.

Armon strode in seconds later, dipping his head to me as usual. "Have a chair, Armon," I said.

"You sent for me?" he asked, taking one of the chairs before my desk.

"I did. I'd like for you to tell me what it is my Queen has been so secretive about, recently. What is she hatching, Armon? This is your King speaking."

Armon had never looked so uncomfortable to me. "She's breaking the law again?" I queried. "Come on, man, out with it."

"You're asking me to betray a friend," he mumbled, staring at his hands. "And she's not breaking the law. Not that I know of, anyway. I think you should ask her yourself, my King."

His voice was stiff when he used my title.

"Very well." *Sherra,* I sent, *I'd like you to join Armon and me in my study, please. Just you. Leave your assistants behind.*

*I'm coming,* she replied. A few minutes later, she walked into my study, lifting an eyebrow at me after seeing Armon hunkered in his seat.

"Why are you browbeating Armon?" she demanded, crossing arms tightly over her chest.

"I'm not browbeating Armon. I asked him a question. He is reluctant to answer."

She studied me through hooded eyes for a moment, before speaking again. "We don't know that it'll work, it's still in the planning stages," she tossed out a hand. "Armon isn't keeping royal secrets from you, Kerok. I have no idea why you're so worried about that."

"Tell me." I steepled my fingers and frowned at her.

"We want to work on combining shields and fireblasts, if you must know, sir nosey King. Kaakos threatens our very existence, unless we can find a way to take him down. Now, I don't know whether you've noticed, but he's not personally coming to us so that can happen. He's more than happy to use our own people against us, and he's killing entire villages whenever it suits him. That means we need to go to him, and destroy him once and for all, in such a way that anybody who thinks to take his place will be too terrified to attack us again."

I leaned back in my chair, watching my Queen's hair crackle with anger. Her power was coming through her pores, it appeared, she was so angry.

My father told her once that we would never attack Ny-nes, because we didn't know the extent of their weapons, the layout of their cities and the enemy's overall strength.

Sherra was trying to compensate for all of that. "What do you know so far?" I asked gently. "Of this new method of yours?"

"It worked perfectly with those three young ones yesterday. They built a shield strong enough to withstand the worst of Levi's blasts. That's how well it worked."

"Have you combined fireblasts yet?"

"Not yet. We just started working on this yesterday." Her chest heaved with anger, still. I was working to calm her down, while the wonder of what she was attempting made my hopes rise unexpectedly.

"You're saying the three young ones did this? When do you plan to try it with seasoned warriors and escorts?"

"I was hoping to try it with Levi, Armon, Caral, Misten, Cole and me in a few days. We're all familiar with one another's power, so it may be easier to combine it." Her breaths were steadier and farther apart, now.

"That sounds like a workable plan, except I'd like to move up the date. I know you're excited about what you're currently working on, but take the afternoon off and return to Secondary Camp with Armon. I'd like to see what you can come up with by the end of the day."

"Are you serious?" The anger was almost gone, now.

"Yes, of course I am. It more than angers me that Kaakos can reach out his hand from thousands of miles away, to interfere with my country and its citizens. I'm eternally weary of it, in fact. Make this work, my love. Once we have an army trained in this, we will lay plans to move against Ny-nes. Until that time, however, this must remain our deepest secret. When we go to Ny-nes, they must be unaware that we are coming."

I wasn't sure how she'd gone from anger to tears, but Sherra now had a hand at her mouth to stifle a sob. "What is it, sweetheart?" I stood to go to her.

"I'm so—happy," she sobbed.

Armon, who'd sat silently listening to our exchange, burst into laughter.

～

*Sherra*

Caral hugged me so tightly, I couldn't breathe for a moment. "He really said that?" she asked. Neither she nor I could believe we'd received Kerok's permission.

Cole was beaming his approval, while Armon was content to watch Caral hug the air from my lungs.

"Come on, let's go to the garden so we can *step* to Secondary Camp," Armon cleared his throat. "We have work to do this afternoon."

I was still so happy, I wanted to cry again. I didn't like sneaking around behind Kerok's back. I should have known he'd notice something was up. The four of us practically ran through the palace and down stairs to get to the garden. We wanted to see if we could form a working pod.

～

*Doret*

*Kyri, those young ones have sneaked into your library to filch books,* I sent mindspeak.

*Did they take anything important?*

*No, just fiction, mostly.*

*Then it's nothing to worry about,* she told me. *Let them read as much as they like. You know the most important things there are indecipherable to them, anyway. Besides—the lure of getting away with this will only make them more insatiable for stories and learning.*

145

*I know. I just wanted to keep you apprised.*

*Thank you.*

*What's the word on the Raver?*

*Well, there's already a wide swath of killing through the city,* she complained. *I doubt they'll find what they're looking for, no matter how many civilians they kill.*

*Always the way,* I grumbled my reply. *The innocents die, because the powerful and evil among them want to take revenge against someone or something.*

*True. And there's no reasoning with it, either. When you point out that killing innocents gets them nowhere, they just step up their efforts.*

*This is his way of doing another purge, without calling it that,* Kyri's sending was sarcastic.

*No doubt,* I agreed. *He doesn't care who dies, as long as he isn't bodily harmed.*

*Always squeamish about his own pain, that one.*

*Can't take a punch,* I countered.

*Never could.*

*Never will.*

Kyri wouldn't go after Merrin. I understood that. Her quarry was the same one it had always been in Ny-nes; Kaakos, the bastard. I hoped she'd find a way to end him. More than anything, though, I worried he would end her, instead.

~



"I can't move," Misten complained. She and Caral lay flat on their backs on what little grass grew under an ancient pine tree.

Armon suggested getting away from Secondary Camp for our experiments, so the secret would remain secret.

We'd gone northward, to practice on the only solid ground south of where the land bridge once lay.

We'd exhausted ourselves, combining shields, blasts and anything else we could think of. "I'm in awe," Levi said, leaning his shoulder against Armon's. They sat on the grass not far away, tired and content with what we'd accomplished so far.

Only Cole and I were still on our feet, and Cole wore a very satisfied smile.

"We only have to find others who are comfortable working together, and convince them to keep the secret, too," Armon said. "We can't let the enemy catch even the slightest whiff of this."

"I wonder if King Thorn will be upset that we've carved away sections of Az-ca during practice," Caral joked. We'd done just that, knocking a great deal of land into the ocean while practicing our blasts.

"I don't think he keeps records of that stuff," I teased back. "He won't be worried."

"If we do this many more times, he could start worrying," Misten giggled.

"Who has enough energy to *step* us back?" Levi asked.

"I'll take you back, before going to the palace," I offered. "Cole needs to go home and get a meal and a bath."

"I think we all need that," Caral attempted to sit up.

"We won't smell good if we don't," Misten agreed.

"I hear that. Come on, then, I'll get you back. Cole, you go home, you've had a long day."

"I'll see you tomorrow in the north," he said before disappearing.

"Help," Caral held up an arm, begging for somebody to lift her to her feet. Armon laughed and went to do just that.

~

*KEROK*

*How did it go?* I sent mindspeak to Sherra during our evening meal. She looked weary and satisfied at the same time.

*It was amazing. I wish you'd been there to see it*, she responded. With power, I pushed the butter dish in her direction. Nodding her thanks, she buttered her roll and bit into it with a sigh of pleasure.

*What did you blast?*

*Well, Az-ca may be a bit smaller than it was. I told the others you don't keep track of that. Please say you don't keep track of that.*

I choked back a laugh.

*I ah, have a suggestion,* she went on.

*What's that, love?*

*I know Barth is going through the census papers for Secondary Camp.*

*He is,* I acknowledged.

*I'm sure he's separating the ones who are most trustworthy from the others.*

*He is—we'll be sending them out to the villages to take the census for me.*

*I'd like for Barth to go through those a second time, and find the ones most cooperative with the new methods, if that's possible.*

*You want to segregate the ones most likely to be successful in your new experiment, don't you?*

*Yes. Some of those in the army—I don't think they'll be suitable at all. We need to keep this from them, in case, well, I get itchy, thinking Kaakos' spies could be anywhere. I'd like to train the new ones at what used to be North Camp. There's nothing left there to damage, except rocks and hills, so we can pit groups against each other, to protect their territory.*

*You're assuming they'll be able to do this.*

*I think we can get them there. You need to impress on them, too, how serious this is, and to keep that secret, no matter what.*

*Agreed. I'll consider how to approach this with them, too, and let them know they can opt out before we get into the details of the experiment. They'll know first off that it will be dangerous, and it will be their choice to proceed.*

*I like that idea.*

*Good. That's settled. Eat your dinner, my love. You must be starved.*

"I am starved," she said aloud, stuffing the last bite of her roll in her mouth. "I have to be at Cole's early in the morning, too. Long day ahead."

I found myself wanting to go with her—to see the things she saw and work beside her again. I'd never been to the north, as she had.

*There is news, and it isn't good,* Hunter sent, causing my hands to still over my plate.

*What news?* I asked.

*Those two from Doret's camp with suppressed power?*
*Yes?*
*They've disappeared from the berry farms.*

"Fuck," I snapped and rose from my seat.

"What?" Sherra stood almost as quickly as I did.

"Those two young troublemakers have disappeared from the farms," I said. "Come with me. We'll get to the bottom of this if we can."

*Sherra*

Barth and Kage went with us, with Kerok *stepping* us to the farm in question. The overseer waited there for us, an angry scowl on his face.

"We have footprints leading to the outer gate, three sets," the overseer growled, slamming a fist into his palm. "We found one of our adult workers missing, too. It's no mystery who went with them, I think."

"When did this happen?" Kerok asked.

"We've done bed checks with those two since the beginning," he said. "They managed to get away between the evening meal and bed check. Alf, the missing worker, didn't turn up to help us search for them. Then, we found three sets of footprints next to the gate—two smaller ones, and an adult male's."

"What can you tell us about Alf?" Barth asked.

"Too quiet, most of the time."

"May I see his quarters?" Barth went on.

"Of course. And those two miscreants' as well."

"Good. Take us to Alf's first," Kerok said.

"Of course, my King."

"Alf has been slipping outside the domes regularly," Barth sighed as he toyed with the man's comb. A few strands of brown hair still clung to it—Barth said that sort of thing made it easier to divine things about the object's owner.

"Spy," Kerok shook his head. If he weren't so weary, he'd be angrier than he was.

"We know that, now," Kage pointed out. "I imagine plenty of people come and go outside the gate. We can't label all of them spies."

"We can keep a better eye on them," Barth huffed. "Beginning now. Who knows whether Narvin and Willa were waiting outside to transport them away? I find that the most likely scenario."

"I worry that Kaakos will restore their power," I said, rubbing my forehead. A tension headache had formed behind my eyes, and now threatened to become debilitating.

"That would be most unfortunate," Kage breathed.

"I'll have to reset the shields everywhere, to prevent those two from walking into an unsuspecting village," I told Kerok. "They could burn something to the ground if they're not stopped."

"Start with the shields around the domes here," Kerok said, his mouth settling into a grim frown. "I don't want them back inside any part of the domes."

"I'll do it now," I said and rose from my chair in Kerok's study.

"Will you need assistance? I can send for Colonel Armon," Hunter offered. Until now, he'd been busy scribbling notes for the official records, and hadn't spoken.

"No, I'll get this done tonight, and worry about the villages tomorrow. Looks like my plans to supervise training have been changed."

"Take Cole and Caral with you tomorrow," Kerok said. "You know why."

"I will."

~

*J*UBAL

Sly little bitches, both of them. I wasn't about to give up my bed for them, either. Those two younglings that Narvin and Willa dragged into my house could sleep on the floor. I didn't care what the voice wanted to do with them; I wanted *nothing* to do with them.

The way Willa fawned on them turned my stomach, too. Like they were *her* kids instead of somebody else's.

Girls? *Faugh.*

All her fault. All of this. I should still be in the army, blasting the enemy.

*Except now, I was working* for *the enemy, wasn't I?*

All her fault.

∾

*Sherra*

"You think Kaakos will give their power back?" Caral grimaced. She and I knew what power in the hands of those who'd misuse it meant.

"I hope not, but I think that hope is useless," I muttered.

Cole's slight nod confirmed my words. He thought the same as I—that Kaakos had a definite goal in mind when he took those two.

We stood inside my study, mapping out a plan of which villages to visit first to adjust the shields.

"We just got word that the man who escaped with Jeen and Ferni was found dead outside a small village, fifty miles south of the dome he left behind," Hunter poked his head in the door. "Thorn wants you to investigate, and he's asked Levi and Misten to go with you."

"How did he die? Do you know?" Cole asked.

"Burned to death," Hunter said. "Narvin's work, no doubt. Alf probably had no idea that he'd become useless, once he got those girls away. His status as a spy was revealed, and Kaakos knew we'd be looking for him."

"Another body to add to the pile," Caral grumped. She and I were in agreement in this—that Kaakos' demise, if it were possible to achieve that goal, couldn't come soon enough. Neither of us would mourn the passing of someone who'd sold himself to the enemy, but the trouble it caused us made things that much worse.

151

"We're here," Misten said as she and Levi walked past Hunter to join the rest of us.

"I hear the spy's body was found," Levi nodded to us.

"Yes. We're going to the villagers who found him, to ask questions. Then, we'll have to adjust shields to keep those two miscreants out of the villages. I figure they'll burn whatever they can if they get their power back," I said.

"I don't understand how that's possible," Misten breathed.

"Kaakos is more than powerful," Cole told her. "Don't discount any improbability, where he is concerned."

"How did he become so powerful?" Misten asked. "This just seems strange, that somebody would not only live through his childhood without being caught there, but then develop so much power he takes it over—that just doesn't seem possible."

"He had help much of that time from Ruarke," Cole pointed out. "A powerful right hand is important, when you have a nation to subject to your murderous whims."

"I have trouble believing that he's confounded an entire nation into thinking that the power he displays comes to him through their Prophet, and by permission granted by a god nobody ever talks about," Levi observed.

"We should get going—we have a long day, today," I said. I didn't want to go. I wanted to train Anari and the others. That would have to wait.

"Let's go down to the garden to *step* away," Levi gestured toward the door. We followed him out of my study and down the hall toward the stairs.

~

"WE THOUGHT it was lightning last night," the village headman told us. "The flash of light and the boom—it happens now and then. When we saw no evidence of a fire afterward, we left it until this morning, before going to look."

The man was old, with a wrinkled face and wispy, gray hair

floating in the morning breeze outside his village. All of us stared at the charred remains of a man who'd died unsuspecting, I think.

"There's no telling where Narvin took those girls after this," Levi shook his head. "They could be anywhere. If the enemy has any sense, this is misdirection."

"I agree," Cole nodded. "They got this far on foot, before Narvin and Willa *stepped* in to take the girls and kill the witness."

"Senseless," the headman muttered.

"I think that's a recurring theme," Levi said.

"These spies are getting paid?" Misten asked.

"Yes," I said, lifting my head to look at her.

"Then why don't we look for people who have more than they should—and recently, maybe."

"Follow the gold?" The headman blinked at her. "That's something I'd look for, too. I think I'd know if anybody in my village started eating or dressing better."

"We may be onto something," Levi patted Misten's shoulder. "Good work, Corporal."

"I just got a promotion," Misten breathed.

CHAPTER 11

*K*erok

"I've got the task force leaders in place, and they now have instructions to investigate anyone who displays wealth above their means," Hunter laid papers on my desk. "The names of each and the villages where they're stationed in all four quadrants," he added.

It was only mid-morning and Hunter had been running most of that time, ever since Sherra sent mindspeak about, as she put it, *following the gold.*

"Good. Did you tell them to be discreet?"

"I did. These are people we can trust," he tapped the papers with a forefinger. "Barth approved of them, before they were offered the job."

"All of them former messengers, I see," I shuffled through the sheets looking at names.

"Yes. And military before that. All more than reliable. They can *step* here with messages if anything needs our attention right away."

"I think I'll ask my Queen to see if there's latent mindspeaking talent in any of them," I said, squaring the sheets and handing them back to Hunter. "Good work."

"Mindspeaking would be helpful."

"It would."

"King Thorn," Adahi appeared in my study as Hunter turned to leave.

"Adahi?"

"I am currently searching for those two girls, but, like Narvin and Willa, they have disappeared from my sensing skills."

"Then we know for sure that the enemy wants them for his evil purposes," I sighed.

"Yes. I'm surprised he chose two females, considering his immense hatred for them. These two must be especially appealing in some way—their power, when he gives it back to them, will no doubt be an asset to him."

"He could be attempting to confuse us," Hunter suggested.

"True. He has managed to do that, recently."

"I never thought I'd say this, but I wish we were back to armies fighting on a battlefront. This espionage and terrorism infuriates me," I said.

"Better the enemy you can see," Adahi concurred.

"We hired four task force supervisors to look into unusual behavior, and we just asked them to look for an increase of funds where there shouldn't be," Hunter offered the papers to Adahi.

Adahi lifted an eyebrow as he accepted the sheets and scanned through them before giving them back.

"A sound idea," he said. "Something we should have done sooner, perhaps, but I am just as remiss as anyone else in this."

"We're not used to dealing with this," Hunter said. "It's all new. We're building our responses from the floor up."

"Whereas Kaakos has had centuries to plot and plan. We have to catch up quickly, if we are to deal with this effectively."

"I wish I could do more in the field," I said. "It angers me to be sitting behind this desk so much of the time. I'd rather be standing next to my Queen as she asks questions. She could be siphoning my energy to help adjust shields around villages."

"This has been a conundrum faced by the monarchy for eons,"

Adahi reminded me. "I think you might get out now and then for a bit of fresh air, though."

"I can clear your schedule one day a week," Hunter offered.

"Then do it," I waved a hand. Was I the King, or wasn't I?

~

*Ny-nes*

*North*

"Leave the city," I advised as I worked to heal the burns on the man's leg. Kaakos' raver wasn't particular in who he harmed, if anyone stood in his way. That thing—he was no longer human—wanted information on me, and he'd do anything to get it.

Even when those he questioned said what they knew, he burned them anyway. The only positive thing to come of this was that citizens were crossing the river in droves at night, while Kaakos' warrior-priest babysitters locked the raver up so they could rest.

"Is it true—the Supreme Leader lies to us?" The man grunted as I worked on his burns.

"Yes. He has lied to you from the beginning. Know the truth, now. He has no care for the people the Prophet said to protect, feed and clothe. He only has room in his heart for his own ambitions."

"I leave tonight," the man said as I took my hands away.

"Good. Convince as many as you can to go with you. Take his targets away. He, his warrior-priests and his army are not true ambassadors of the Prophet, who would be ashamed that they do these things in his name."

"Wish I read book," he turned his head away.

"I know. This is something else he has done—to take the Prophet's words away from you, so he might be the sole interpreter of them. He lies."

"I see. Now."

"Good. Escape. Live in peace."

"Thank." He nodded before rising from the dirt floor of his lean-to. "I get ready, now."

"I'll go to the others who need help, then."

He watched me walk away, wondering, no doubt, how and why I'd come to them now. It was something I didn't wish to explain to anyone; the answer was more complicated than most of them would ever understand.

"Healer, come," the small girl appeared from between hovels, gripping my hand tightly. I went with her.

~

*Sherra*

By the time we reached Secondary Camp long after nightfall, I only wanted to lay my head on the dining table and sleep. I'd sent Cole home, after inviting him to stay and eat with us. He'd declined and disappeared quickly.

Caral's sister and two others had stayed in the dining hall, to serve us a cold meal before we collapsed on our beds. I worried I wouldn't be able to return to the palace after eating.

Therefore, Kerok had come to join us, bringing two bottles of wine with him. He'd eaten hours earlier, so he had a glass of wine while the rest of us ate cold fowl with vegetables.

We needed baths, too, but that could wait until after the meal. I only wanted to fall in bed, once I was clean.

"All done?" Kerok asked, pouring glasses of wine for us.

"Mmmm," Levi grunted around a mouthful of food.

*Yes*, I sent weary mindspeak. I'd had to pull energy from my associates, but it got done in a day. If those two troublemakers attempted to cross my shield barrier, from inside or outside, well, I'd prepared for that possibility—for them and for Willa and Narvin.

Perhaps soon, I'd see whether my hastily prepared spell would work. Yes, I was calling it a spell for lack of a better term, since I was too tired to name it otherwise.

I had ideas, too, regarding the spies Kaakos had sent against us, but that would require more thought and a great deal of energy.

I'd need a few days or weeks to consider it, while my strength returned.

"Come," Kerok folded one of my hands in his. "I think you're finished with your food."

I was—I'd been staring at nothing while my thoughts chased one another inside my exhausted mind. The moment Kerok pulled me up from my seat at the table, he *stepped* us away.

~

I WOKE while Kerok dried my skin with a soft towel. He'd joined me in the shower, carefully washing the day's dirt and sweat off me. I'd fallen asleep during the bathing.

"Let's get you to bed," Kerok murmured against my ear. As he carried me in that direction, I fell asleep again.

~

*Ny-nes*

*North*

The raver was awake and burning everything around him early that morning. Flames sprouted in his hands, as he flung fireball after fireball in a drunken fashion at shacks, lean-tos and hovels.

That section of the city had been vacated the night before, and Kaakos had wakened early to that fact. As a result, smoke and cinders from the raver's burning billowed high into the sky, to join the soot-and-sludge-filled atmosphere in Kaakos' city.

Even the warrior-priests cowered far behind the raver as he set fire to anything that would burn. From a distance, past smoldering piles of ash and debris, I watched the conflagration.

At least these had heeded my warning to get away under cover of darkness. Kaakos likely believed his citizens harbored me somewhere, and that perhaps I'd gotten away, running with them when they escaped.

"Stop there." A new voice made me jerk my head in the raver's direction. Who would shout at a raver, thinking he would listen? Someone who didn't care if he died perhaps? It was a male's voice, that was certain. When the smoke cleared enough that I could see, I blinked in disbelief.

A mountain of a man stood before the raver, untouched, as the raver tossed fireballs at him, one after another.

He'd shielded himself, this one. How that was possible, I had no idea. I had no doubt that his shield would fall and fall soon, when Kaakos got wind that someone stood in his way.

"Who are you?" A warrior-priest strode forward, demanding an answer from the one who blocked the raver's efforts.

"You don't need to know, worm," the man hissed.

"No!" A woman's voice shouted as a light appeared not far away.

Too late; the one who'd shielded himself sent a massive fireball at the raver and his attending warrior-priests.

All but the raver died a fiery death, because the raver could *step* away and did so, leaving his priests to scream and burn to ash behind him. Another flash of light occurred, then, and the one who'd destroyed the priests also disappeared, leaving me more puzzled than I'd been earlier.

Until the voice came in my mind.

Her voice. She'd remained behind, and hidden herself behind a shield, much as I had.

*He'll get himself killed, if he's not careful,* she spat. *Next time, do me a favor and get him away before this happens again.*

*How did you know?* I fumbled for a reply.

*Just as I saw your light, you can see mine.*

*Who?* I thought to ask.

*Arresh,* her answer echoed in my head.



≈



*Sherra*

"Are you all right?" Kerok set a cup of tea and the familiar, small folded paper filled with marching draught on my bedside table. I sat

159

up in bed, my head in my hands. My dreamwalker had broken the law, and I hadn't known about it until now.

"Kerok?" My voice sounded small. Guilty.

"What is it, my love?" He sat on the side of the bed before handing the tea to me, his fingers gently wrapping mine around the cup. I felt chilled—the warmth of the mug was more than welcome.

"I ah, well, my ah, dreamwalker broke the law," I mumbled, my admission filled with shame and remorse. I set the tea on the bedside table before covering my eyes with both hands, which now trembled. I was such a fool, and a terrified fool on top of that.

"Tell me." He pulled my hands away from my face.

"I—she—sent Garkus to Ny-nes. He fried six warrior-priests early this morning, before I could send him back to his work in the palace. I don't think that's why we sent him there."

Kerok ducked his head while he rolled his shoulders to keep knots from forming there. "We didn't know how he got there, but we knew he was there," Kerok lifted his head to search my eyes with his. "Adahi heard it from Kyri. For now, only Hunter, Barth, Adahi, Doret, you and I know this. I'd prefer it stay that way."

"You're not mad?"

"I am. A little," he dropped his gaze. "I don't know why your dreamwalker wanted it kept a secret, but we'll keep that secret for now. Love, drink your tea. Use the marching draught if it's necessary. We have to catch up on yesterday's duties that went undone."

"I know." Lifting the cup, I sipped my tea and wondered how in the first escort's name my dreamwalker could keep such secrets from me. A part of me was terrified she'd do it again. Another part worried that she'd kept something from me this time, too. All I recalled was the attempt to stop Garkus, before sending him back to the palace.

Kerok likely felt the same as I—that my dreamwalker would do this again. I worried I'd lose his trust, and that was the last thing I wanted.

"I'll take this with me, in case I need it later," I shoved the envelope of marching draught in a pocket after breakfast.

Kerok nodded; he and I left the suite together, to begin our day.

~

*Ny-nes*

*Kaakos*

Six warrior-priests, including my mindspeaker, dead. This healer was stronger than I imagined. It infuriated me that he'd somehow built shields to hold off my raver's fireblasts. I'd have to give better instructions to the raver next time, before leaving his mind to attend to other things.

I needed another mindspeaker, and there weren't any.

*There is one in Az-ca,* I recalled. Perhaps I should leave things in the hands of Narvin, his escort and the two new ones from now on. Yes, I would give that serious thought while I sent more warrior-priests and my raver into the city again.

I hadn't killed servants this time; I'd only blasted furniture to cinders. Perhaps I was becoming more patient as my adversary revealed himself. It left my mind clearer, to make plans to destroy him.

My raver, sitting in a corner of my study, growled as he shifted his position. "Quiet," I ordered amiably. "You'll bring justice to me soon enough."

~

*Kyri*

*What the fuck were you thinking?* I nearly blasted Garkus' brain cells with mindspeak as we carried out our duties in Kaakos' kitchen. He'd been forced to tell me what he'd done, because he wanted to know who or what had tried to stop him from killing the raver.

He'd only heard the voice and seen the flash of light nearby, just before he'd leveled a blast against the raver and six warrior-priests. The priests died—the raver escaped by *stepping* away.

Garkus thought it could be the healer's voice he'd heard. I had a different idea. The fact that Garkus could have been seen only ramped up my worries. *Were you the one who killed Aspe?* I demanded as that thought came to me.

He refused to reply.

*Fucking hell,* I shouted at him mentally. *You'll kill us and Az-ca too.*

*I didn't kill him,* he finally mumbled. *I wanted to, but even I know not to send a note with the body.*

My shoulders sagged as I considered his words.

*We have one mission here,* I hissed at him. *We kill Kaakos. Until that opportunity presents itself, we stay away from his notice. And the notice of anyone else, is that clear? If it isn't, I'll send mindspeak to Arresh myself, and ask her to remove you from Ny-nes. I imagine your jail cell is still waiting in the King's City, don't you?*

*Fine,* he acquiesced. He still sounded belligerent, however.

*Remember, it's follow my rules or go back to the King's judgment,* I told him.

He didn't reply, but I could hear the increased whacks of his cleaver as he tore into a haunch of meat across the kitchen.

∼

*SHERRA*

Armon and Misten joined me at Cole's cabin, before training with the young ones began.

Both were fresh; I was more than weary.

*Doret tells me the young ones have been sneaking into Kyri's library, to find books to read. They're returning them and exchanging what they've read for others,* a brief smile touched Cole's mouth while he sent mindspeak.

*I don't want them to get in trouble for that,* I began.

*Don't worry, neither Doret nor Kyri care, as long as the books are returned. Reading is learning. I recall how eager I was when Kyri taught me to read when I was young.*

*It's an escape,* I admitted. *I read every book of fiction available in my village. I wish I'd had access to Kyri's library back then.*

*Doret is most fortunate, to have watched you grow up and into your power*, he told me. *Most fortunate, indeed.*

I didn't tell him that I'd grown up lonely, with Pottles being my only friend. At times, I envied Anari, Laren and Kyal. They had one another, and were so close in age and friendship, too.

"Here," Cole placed a cup of tea in my hands. "Take this to the training grounds. I think you'll need it."

"Wait," I pulled the marching draught from my pocket and looked at it for a moment before stuffing it back in my pocket. I didn't want it unless it were absolutely necessary. "I'm ready," I said, downing a few swallows of hot tea.

~

*ARMON*

Sherra drank her second cup of tea while Caral and I worked with the three young ones. They built their combined shield again, while I sent blasts against it.

They held, against the most powerful blasts I was willing to send against them. Sherra finished her tea while she watched us perform.

"How did they do with their blasts yesterday?" I asked. Cole would have a report from the other instructors; I was sure of it.

"Very well," Cole said. "Anari is beginning to demonstrate her talent in that area."

"Can you show me?" I asked the teens. By their smiles, they were more than willing to show me what they could do.

"I had stones moved in for their next practice," Cole said, leading us along a sandy strip of beach moments later. I'd trained by firing blasts at brick walls; Cole trained his people using large rocks of various sizes and densities.

"You want us to destroy that pile of rocks?" Laren was daunted by the first pile we came upon.

"I do, but only when you combine your blasts," Cole told him. "Until that time, we'll work on the pile farthest away—it's sandstone, and not so difficult to blast."

"So we'll be working our way closer to the village with each successful blasting?" Caral observed. "Smart."

"It's logical," Cole said. "You'll be weariest after you finish the closest pile."

*I think Cole should train the boys in Az-ca,* Sherra sent mindspeak. *He has much more patience and a better rapport with his students, compared to that piece of spiteful misogyny Kerok removed recently.*

*While I agree with you, it will take acceptance from the other instructors. Cole is an outsider, remember?*

*Fucking hell.*

*Exactly.*

*Too bad we can't mix common sense and tolerance into their morning tea,* Sherra added.

*That would be a blessing, and therefore is never likely to happen.*

*I'm constantly amazed at how right you are all the time,* she teased.

*Tell that to Levi. He thinks I'm wrong more than half the time.*

*You sound like an old married couple.*

*We* are *an old married couple.*

I got a chuckle and a hug from her.

"Are we ready to combine blasts?" Cole asked our three eager students.

"Yes," Laren grinned.

"All right. Want to try it on your own, or do you want Sherra to connect you, first?"

Laren looked from Anari to Kyal before turning back to Cole. "We remember how to do it," he said.

"Then proceed," Cole swept a hand toward the hasty construction on the beach.

All three gripped each other's hands, with Kyal in the middle, Anari on one end and Laren on the other. Anari and Laren raised their free hands, where I could see a blast forming.

"Release," Cole commanded.

I will remember what that looked like for the rest of my life; those three, obliterating a roughly-constructed pile of rock, and blasting a wide hole in the sand beneath it. I doubted any building made of brick or stone could have held firm against them. They'd have blasted a hole in those structures, at the very least.

"Well done," Cole breathed when the young ones opened their eyes to see. Immediately they were hugging and laughing at their success. Misten's hands were over her mouth—to keep from giggling, I'm sure.

"We have two competent pods," Sherra smiled. She was right.

❀

*KEROK*

"Lift it and bring it to you." Adahi's eyes were slits as he watched my feeble attempts to lift a tea mug from a tray across my study. The objective was to float the cup across the room and deposit it on my desk.

The cup lifted on one side before dropping onto the tray again, sloshing tea. "This is harder than I thought," I grumbled, frowning at the cup.

"Think of it this way," Adahi philosophized. "You *step* yourself. You can also *step* others. This is no different from that; you're merely a few feet away from it, now."

"You told me once to move a truck," I reminded him. He didn't miss the sarcasm in my words.

"You thought I was joking. I wasn't," Adahi snorted.

"Can you move a truck? Really?"

"Once I could, as could the one you were named after."

"Why can't you do it now?" I demanded, still staring at the cup.

"I have to collect energy to do the things I do," Adahi replied stiffly. "You replenish your energy through eating and sleeping. I must take what I can from suitable sources."

That made me go still for a moment. "What—do you do?" I croaked.

"I siphon energy from others," he shrugged. "I hoard what I collect, to use it when it becomes necessary."

"Who?" Much depended on his answer.

165

"Those in the lockup. Those sentenced to labor in the fields for wrongdoing. I take from them, rather than innocents."

I didn't realize how stiff my body had become before my shoulders sagged and a ragged breath escaped my lungs.

"I understand the logic in this now," I said, taking a seat behind my desk. "I just never thought that a—spirit would need to replenish his energy."

"That's why I needed Sherra's help in dealing with Ruarke," Adahi said. "The ah, method I used to obtain that help was from pure desperation, I assure you. Had I been alive and whole, I could have dealt with him myself—until Kaakos intervened, that is." The bitterness in his voice was palpable.

"I see I still have much to learn," I said, expressing some bitterness of my own.

"This is why I allowed venomous snakes to kill targets at times—it means I don't have to expend the energy to do it a different way."

How many times had I wondered about that? It made sense, but I'd never have figured it out on my own.

"You're saying you could pull energy from me, if you wanted?"

"I believe you could stop me, if you were aware," Adahi replied. "You're powerful enough to do it, as are Sherra and a few others, if they are so minded."

"Curious—and strange at the same time." I needed tea. Badly. Holding out my hand, I concentrated on *stepping* the cup to my desk. It disappeared from the tray and dropped onto my desk, with only a few drops spilled.

"Excellent," Adahi chuckled. "Perfect," he added. "Next, we move a boulder."

~

*SHERRA*

"Long day?" Pottles watched me as I sat wearily on a guest chair in her office.

"Yes. I'd like to go home and go straight to bed, but Kerok wants to have a dinner meeting with me, Armon, Barth and Hunter."

"What does he want to discuss?"

"I think you have a good guess," I said, leaning back in the chair and closing my eyes for a moment.

"How long it will be before we're in a position to attack Ny-nes?"

I didn't answer verbally; I gave her a nod, then a hand-covered yawn, my jaws almost cracking with the wideness of it.

"I suggest a marching draught," Pottles slid a cup of tea in my direction.

"I have one in my pocket," I blinked my eyes open to look at her. She was worried; I could see that easily.

"Then use it," she said. "You need to be alert for this. Never has a King of Az-ca considered going to the source of the problem to shut it down. The Queen must be awake and contributing to this discussion, instead of nodding and half-asleep."

"Fine." Pulling the draft from my pocket, I dumped it into the cup of tea before I could change my mind. My hand shook as I lifted the cup to my lips and drank, not stopping until it was all gone.

"There. Done. I hope I can sleep afterward."

"Then go to the palace. The sooner the meeting starts, the sooner it's over."

*I took the marching draft when I went to see Pottles,* I told Kerok, whose forehead was creased with concern as I sat beside him at the table. Besides Armon, Barth and Hunter, Kage had also come.

I suppose Kerok thought it time to bring his royal assassin on board with our plans, too.

"Good," Kerok replied as plates were set in front of us by servants, one of whom was Briar.

When she and the others withdrew, closing the door behind them, Kerok cleared his throat before speaking. "Eat," he urged. "While we're doing that, we can discuss the best possible ways to attack Ny-nes."

Kage's head jerked up at Kerok's words. The rest of us weren't as surprised as he, because we'd been expecting some sort of announcement. After a moment's consideration, Kage nodded his approval and lifted his wineglass to Kerok.

❧

"I HESITATE to involve those younglings in any type of battle, but they certainly can form a pod easily," Armon said when Kerok asked about it. Barth and Hunter were only now learning about our experiment, while a light had grown in Kage's eyes; he wanted to see this for himself.

As a former warrior and a Colonel who'd commanded the warrior training post in the King's City, Kage recognized the potential in our newest experiments. I imagined he wanted to participate, too, if I read the signs correctly.

"I'm hoping to receive information from Kyri, who is in Ny-nes, now," Kerok went on. "With someone on the inside, perhaps we will know better how to deal with what we'll find when we go."

"Will she cooperate?" Barth asked the obvious question.

"I hope so. She sends mindspeak to Adahi often, and Doret, too. If she won't reply to us, perhaps one of those two can carry our messages to her."

*Don't forget Garkus*, I sent to Kerok, who dipped his head for a moment in acknowledgment. Garkus was what Pottles called a loose cannon, and could be unpredictable.

"I will be happy to act as a messenger to Kyri, as I am somewhat familiar with Ny-nes, too," Adahi appeared inside the small dining room.

"Is it possible to send and receive images?" Kerok pointed his question at Adahi, who'd moved to an empty chair to sit.

"If the sender and receiver are talented enough," Adahi said.

"Are you?" Kerok's next question was direct.

Adahi's answer was unflinching. "Yes."

"Good. Are you skilled at drawing those images, or should we find someone who can translate your words to drawings?"

"I can give you an approximation," Adahi shrugged. "Along with the written descriptions, of course."

"What about their weapons and war machines?" Barth asked.

"I can ask Kyri about those, too," Adahi said. "I understand the importance of the information, Diviner."

"If we do this, we have to get it right the first time," Hunter said. "I doubt Kaakos will take kindly to an attack on his home soil, and he'll turn everything he has against us afterward, if our army dies in Ny-nes."

"He has no care for anyone other than himself," Adahi nodded to Hunter. "He will sacrifice all of them if necessary, just to make us pay."

"This information stays in this room," Kerok ordered.

"There is something else," Adahi said.

"What's that?" Kerok turned to the ghost.

"If Kyri is revealed before you attack, Kaakos may turn everything he has against you anyway."

"Why does he hate her so much?" My question burst from me unbidden.

"I cannot tell that story," Adahi's eyes became mere slits.

I wanted to push him further on the subject, as I felt he was holding something back. That's when the frantic mindspeak came, forcing my dreamwalker to roar to the surface. I didn't recall what came after; others had to explain it to me later.

# CHAPTER 12

*K*erok

Anyone with mindspeaking ability in the dining room heard the cry for help, but only Sherra's dreamwalker located the source of it. With a shriek of anger, her dreamwalker *stepped* all of us away, with no idea where we were headed.

The moment we landed in the small shack outside the far northern village of Gaull, we were too late to hold back the one Kaakos had taken.

Instead, we were forced into an immediate battle with Narvin, Willa and the two missing girls. Narvin was faster and better prepared than we were, as he'd watched the shack's inhabitant disappear while screaming for help.

He fired a blast the moment Sherra's dreamwalker set us down inside the small home; the repercussions of it were so powerful as it bounced off Sherra's shield that it blew the home apart around us, flinging burning boards and splintered furniture far into the night.

Both girls were now screaming inside Willa's shield. Narvin had only seconds to react as Armon fired a tremendous blast in return. Willa's shield broke, leaving her bleeding, weeping and writhing on what was left of the floor.

Narvin and the girls had *stepped* away in the tiny amount of time it had taken to break Willa's shield.

"Tell me what happened," Barth demanded, standing over Willa. "Whose house is this? Answer me, or I put my hands on you and you'll wish you'd told me everything already."

"Jubal. He screamed before he was taken," Willa wept. "I think my leg is broken."

"Bloody fuck," Adahi muttered.

"Who is Jubal?" I demanded.

"I know that name," Hunter said. "Was injured in his first battle, several years before you took over the army. His escort's shield failed. She died, as I recall. The reason I remember this is because he petitioned the King, your father, to return to the battlefield, as he had mindspeaking ability."

"And I advised against it," Barth drew away from Willa. "Because of the reading I got from him. He wanted revenge—against his escort and any woman who got in his way. The Crown still sends him a stipend as a disabled warrior, unless I am badly mistaken."

"He has gold. Plenty of it," Willa's voice sounded pitiful. "I wondered why he hated me and the girls."

"Payment from Kaakos, no doubt," Armon growled.

"Be careful of your words, he may be listening," Sherra's dreamwalker stated flatly.

"Fucking hell," I snapped.

*Kill her*, Barth's voice sounded in my head.

*No*, came from Sherra's dreamwalker. *We will keep her—for a short time. Let Kaakos worry that she knows things and will tell us all. We must keep her strongly shielded, so he won't pull her away too, before we use her to our advantage.*

"I will take her to the lockup," Kage said. "She can be tended for her injuries by the training camp physicians."

"Very well," I said. "Report to me when her injuries are tended. Who will take us back to the palace?"

"I will," Armon volunteered. "Kage, I'll meet you at the lockup afterward."

"Good," Kage agreed. "Perhaps we will learn something together from this one—such as where Narvin may have gone with those two girls."

Kage grasped Willa's arm and *stepped* her away; Armon pulled the rest of us together and *stepped* us to the King's garden.

~

*SHERRA*

"You're back?" It was a weighted question when I stalked into our shared bedroom. Kerok's gaze was troubled as he watched me walk toward the bathroom.

"It's me," I sighed, turning toward him. "I had some thinking to do."

"Must have been serious; you've been gone four hours."

"You shouldn't have waited up," I said, guilt saturating my voice.

"I couldn't sleep," he countered. "I was worried," he added.

"I know. I don't think she cares about things like that."

"What does she care about?"

"You. Everyone else in Az-ca—who hasn't sold themselves to the enemy. She found this," I pulled a leather pouch from my uniform pocket and tossed it to Kerok. "Jubal's gold, from Ny-nes."

"This is heavy," a frown creased his forehead as he pulled the strings loose to look inside. His eyes met mine after studying the gold in the pouch. "Enough here to make someone's life easy until they die of old age; even an old warrior." He pulled the strings to close the bag before setting it on his nightstand.

"Hunter says Jubal was in his seventies," Kerok said. "Sold himself to the devil he wanted to fight so hard against in the past."

"I imagine he thought it an easy job, providing the enemy's requests to spies and receiving their information, before sending mindspeak to his overlord," I pointed out. "I doubt he considered the actual lives involved."

"What will Kaakos do without his pet mindspeaker in Az-ca?" Kerok asked.

That question had concerned me, too, in addition to my

dreamwalker. It was foremost on my mind the second I came back to myself. "There's something else, too," I confessed.

"What's that?"

"For now, only a theory," I said.

"Tell me." He rose from his chair to walk toward me.

"Every time the dreamwalker has come while I'm awake?"

"Yes?"

"It's after I've taken a marching draught."

Kerok stopped halfway between me and the bed. "That's an interesting theory," he whispered.

"So far, it has held true," I said. "Kerok, that terrifies me in ways I can't explain."

"I think we should explore this theory," he moved toward me again, until he was close enough to pull me against him. "My love, do you recall anything from your dreamwalker, whenever a marching draught was involved?"

"Not much," I confessed. "So far, I recall very little of what went on earlier. I know she ransacked what was left of Jubal's home to find that pouch. It was hidden beneath a burned floorboard in his bedroom. She may have learned other things about Jubal, but I can't say what they are."

Kerok pulled me into a tighter embrace. "I am terrified for any warrior or escort who can mindspeak," he mumbled against my hair. "They could all become targets for Kaakos."

"I know, and there are three names that I am very concerned about," I said.

"We will keep a close watch on those young ones. I'm hoping they are outside Kaakos' reach where they are."

"As do I."

"I'm very concerned about the mindspeakers that Narvin and Willa knew about."

I drew my head away from his shoulder to blink at him. "Armon," Kerok and I said together.

❧

"It isn't just Armon," Hunter observed at breakfast the following morning. "They knew about three others, too, I think."

"Two of those died in the last battle," Kerok said before sipping his tea.

"I'll look into it." Hunter pulled a folded scrap of paper from his pocket to scribble notes. "I'm making a note to ask Barth to do a second divination on the remaining mindspeakers' census papers."

"Good idea," Kerok agreed. "Ask him to add that question to anyone's census papers—perhaps we've missed someone with latent talent. Sherra found several when she went looking for them before. That's why Caral and a few others can mindspeak now."

"True." Hunter added to his notes.

"I think we should send someone to Gaull, to ask questions about Jubal," I said. "What his capabilities are—what exactly he might do for the enemy in Ny-nes—that sort of thing."

"He's blind in one eye and walks with a limp; we got that from Willa last night," Hunter said. "She hated him, because he hated women in general. Said she ended up doing all his cooking and house-work, because that was her place, in his opinion."

"Have Barth do a divination on the leather pouch," Kerok said.

"What leather pouch?" Hunter lifted his eyes from the notes he scribbled to ask.

"The one my dreamwalker found last night," I admitted. "If she discovered anything about it, she didn't let me know."

"Where is it now?" Hunter asked.

"Here," Kerok held out a hand and seconds later, the leather pouched slapped against his palm before dropping onto the table with a loud chink.

"I'm still working out the bugs, as Adahi calls them," he said, lifting the pouch and handing it to Hunter. "This is the gold found beneath Jubal's floorboards—paid by the enemy, I'm sure, for gathering infor-mation and harboring fugitives."

"How did you do that?" I asked, staring at the bag as wild specula-tion saturated my mind.

"It's like *stepping* something—either to you or away from you,"

Kerok said. "Adahi seems to think I can move trucks eventually, but I'm a long way from that, I believe."

"*Stepping* something. That's—I want to try it, too."

"Feel free when you're working with the others," Kerok grinned. "Maybe they'll try it with you."

"I will," I said, yawning.

"You both look like you need a marching draught," Hunter said.

"No!" My response was immediate.

"Aren't you joining us for training today?" Pottles frowned at me when I told her I was heading to Secondary Camp instead. "Caral and Misten are here," she continued, as if I didn't already see them on the training ground, working with trainees.

"I want to work with Armon and Levi today," I said. "You don't need me—Caral and Misten know what to do."

"Hmmph." Pottles didn't like my attempt at an explanation.

"Look, I want to try something new," I whispered next to her ear. "At least let me try it, to get it out of my system."

"Fine. If you're successful, I expect a report."

"Hmmph. What if it's secret?"

"Hmmph."

"I love you, too," I hugged her and *stepped* away.

"I watched him do it," I told Armon. "Now, I want to try it with you and Levi first, then move on to Caral and Misten if we're successful."

"Just *stepping* something from me to somewhere else?" Levi shook his head at me. "It just doesn't sound possible."

"You go first," Armon jerked his head at me. "When you do it, then you touch us and show us how."

"No pressure," I shook my head.

"No pressure," Armon's smile was wry.

"Fine. What should I try to move? It needs to be something that I know exactly where it is, I think."

"How about the papers on your desk? Caral says you're working on updating other laws."

"Those would be light enough," I said. "Hold on, let me visualize them," I closed my eyes, hoping to recreate the image of my desk in my mind.

"*Step*," Armon whispered.

I shrieked when the papers hit my outstretched hand so hard, some of them ripped. My eyes popped open fast enough to see bits of paper floating to the ground around me.

"Fucking hells," Levi said, wonder in his voice. "Fucking, bloody hells."

"Show us," Armon demanded, taking the paper fragments from my hands.

"Can we try this together? Like combining shields?" Levi asked.

"Wait, what?" I turned to Levi.

"It was only a thought," he shrugged.

"No, hold onto that," I held up a hand. "Armon, do you know where a truck is?"

"Yes, but why?"

"Because we're going to try and move it," I said.

"I don't know," Armon sounded reluctant.

"Come on. If you don't want to try it here, then let's *step* elsewhere to try it."

"Fine. We need privacy," he pointed out.

"How about North Camp—or what's left of it?" Levi suggested.

"Let's go—we can't be gone long," Armon growled.

～

*KEROK*

*What do you mean, I need to be near the truck at the training camp storage building? Its solar collector is fried,* I told Armon.

*Sherra has this insane notion that she, Levi and I can move it. I need a witness. This is your fault, you know, for putting that crazy idea in her head to begin with.*

When I bent over with laughter in my study, Hunter, who sat across from me, asked what the problem was.

"Come on, Hunt," I said, rising from my chair. "Let's take a break."

"Where are we going?" he stood, too.

"To the storage shed at the training camp. There's an old truck there that we need to see."

"That thing? It doesn't work," Hunter grumbled.

"I know that. It's not the reason we need to see it."

"All right." He turned toward the door.

"Nah," I said. "Let's *step* from here."

Moments later, we stood perhaps ten feet away from the old vehicle, which hadn't been moved in years. Many times, it had been scavenged for parts, which meant doors, the hood, tires and a myriad of other things were missing.

"They're going to try to move it?" Hunter's arms were crossed over his chest, while an expression of pure skepticism enveloped his features.

"Together. I don't know why I didn't consider it before," I grinned.

"What if they fail?"

"We keep trying," I shrugged. "You have to admit it's a good idea."

"Plenty of good ideas never work."

*We're ready on this end*, I sent to Armon.

*Good.* We're connected, he replied. *Give us a moment.*

*Take as much time*, I began when the truck shook for a moment before disappearing in front of us.

Hunter was in shock, I believe, when I grabbed his arm and *stepped* to the burned ruin of North Camp.

*Sherra*

Armon was swinging Levi around like a rag doll, while both laughed. When Kerok arrived with Hunter, he whooped and ran toward me. I jumped into his arms and wrapped my legs around his waist, before kissing him, over and over.

"We're really going to attack Ny-nes," Hunter breathed.

"You bet your ass we are," Armon let Levi go and went to clasp hands with Hunter.

"I want to send it back, now—with you," Kerok said when I stopped kissing him after a while.

"Yes. I want to work with you on this," I breathed, overjoyed at the light in his dark eyes.

"Then let's do it," he grinned and set me on my feet.

"I'll keep my eyes open this time," I said, bumping his shoulder with mine before clasping his hand and reaching for his power, to combine with mine.

"Is that all?" He turned to blink at me before the truck disappeared, going right back where it came from only minutes earlier.

❧

*KEROK*

Not only did I move the truck on my own inside the shed, but convinced Hunter to try it, too. He moved it with me, grinning like a fool the entire time. Adahi appeared while we were playing with our new-found power.

"Fascinating," he said, leaning against a tower of crates to watch. "I suppose you connected with Sherra the first time?"

"Yes," I grunted, moving the truck again without Hunter's help.

"The next step is moving it to Ny-nes," Adahi said.

"It doesn't work—it's a rust bucket," I countered.

"All the more reason to drop it on Kaakos' palace—from very high above it. That may do the most damage, don't you think?"

"Maybe we ought to send boulders, instead," Hunter joined the conversation. "We have plenty of those."

"I'd prefer to send lightning," I moved the truck back to its original place with a sigh.

"Sounds good to me," Adahi replied. "I suggest you work on that, next."

~

*Ny-nes*

*Kaakos*

How the hell was I to know he couldn't walk more than a few yards? Glaring at Jubal did no good; he couldn't drag his useless leg much farther than that. I considered blasting him to get him out of my sight, but reflected on the energy expended to get him here and reconsidered.

I had plenty of warrior-priests, and only one half-blind, crippled mindspeaker. It occurred to me that he could be carried, pushed or rolled along in a conveyance.

Liam, my chief of technical sciences, hadn't brought me up to date recently on his progress; perhaps it was time to call him in to address this situation, too.

"Sit down before I blast you," I snapped at Jubal. He hid his anger and watched me carefully as I strode toward the door to summon a messenger.

~

*Jubal*

All. Her. Fault.

~

*Kyri*

*What the bloody hell?* Garkus' mindspeak made me lift my head from staring at the dishes in the sink where I worked.

Turning, I watched as a technician walked past the kitchen door, followed by several workers carrying ledgers, and two at the end, pushing a wheeled conveyance. *What do you suppose that's for?* Garkus went on.

*No idea,* I said, turning back to my work.

*I don't like this,* he informed me.

*Do you think I'm having the best of times?* I retorted. *Keep working. We'll find out what it is eventually.*

We didn't have to wait long, as it turned out. An hour later, the conveyance was back, only this time it bore a man, pushed by warrior-priests.

*Fuck,* Garkus said. I was about to tell him to mind his business, when his next words chilled me. *That's Jubal,* Garkus said. *Wounded in his first battle when his escort died. He's a mindspeaker.*

*Why does Kaakos need a crippled mindspeaker?*

*You tell me.*

*How the hell did he get here?*

*How did Merrin get here?*

*Point taken. Adahi, Doret,* I sent mindspeak. *We have a new development.*

*We discovered Jubal was a spy, albeit too late,* Adahi replied after I gave my information. *We are now attempting to determine why he was required by the enemy.*

*My guess is Kaakos wants a mindspeaker. Maybe that's what he was useful for in Az-ca—sending and receiving messages,* Doret weighed in. *Why else would he bring in a cripple? Kaakos hates that.*

*I know,* I told her. *I imagine he couldn't wait to remove Jubal from his sight. Two warrior-priests pushed him out the back door.*

*Ah,* Adahi said. *Kaakos wants regular reports on the raver's doings, no doubt.*

*That's the best explanation,* I agreed. *What does the King say? Or Sherra?*

*They're working diligently on plans to thwart Kaakos, I believe,* Adahi replied. I understood his reluctance to tell me what they were doing; if Kaakos discovered me, I'd have no knowledge to be tortured away.

*Will they be able to help Kyri?* Doret asked.

*For now, I cannot guarantee anything. I can only say I hold hope,* Adahi answered.

*I'll settle for hope, then. Will you let me know if things—begin?*

*Of course. I urge you to wait until Sherra arrives, however.*

*Will she come, or will it be her dreamwalker?*

*I cannot say—in my visions, they are difficult to differentiate.*

*Then I'll hope,* I said. *And hope that it won't be a hopeless hope.*

~

*North*

The raver waited beneath a leaking tin roof in an alley, while a heavy rain drummed around him and his crew. His eyes were completely mad, his movements jerky and impatient. Kaakos had halted him and the others for some unknown reason.

Hidden from their sight, I watched and waited with them.

Shock can best describe my reaction when I discovered what they waited for—or in this case, whom.

Kaakos had little patience for anyone less than perfect. This one would be far less than perfect to Kaakos, yet he'd commanded him to join the raver, while two warrior-priests pushed the open, high-wheeled cart he rode upon.

*Who are you?* I sent to this poor, soaked soul, not expecting any sort of reply.

*Jubal,* he responded promptly, his eyes filling with terror as his head turned this way and that, searching for another mindspeaker. *Please help me,* he begged.

~

*Kerok*

"Kyri told me she saw Jubal. Her opinion is that he's being used to keep Kaakos advised of the raver's movements and actions, so Kaakos can turn his mind to other things. We suspected he wanted him as a mindspeaker, but had no idea why."

Doret and Adahi had both come to see Sherra and me, once they'd received messages from Kyri in Ny-nes. Hunter, as usual, scribbled notes as he listened to our conversation, while Barth attended the conversation closely from a chair nearby.

We'd chosen the garden table as our meeting place this time, once I received mindspeak from Doret. Adahi had arrived shortly after she did, a grim look on his face. This turn of events had surprised and angered him, although he didn't say it.

"What is the raver after?" Sherra asked.

"Kyri says he's hunting the healer who arrived in Kaakos' city. Kaakos doesn't want another power wielder, unless the power wielder is under his thumb and serves his purposes," Adahi said. "Anyone who might lead the people to rebel against him dies quickly, as you may have guessed."

"Except this one appears to still be alive," Doret sniffed. "Kyri says rumors come to the palace servants, that many are moving across the river and away from Kaakos and the raver's reach. From that point, the population can scatter in many directions, and it would be next to impossible to find the healer in such a massive relocation. I'm sure Kaakos has considered all this; he wants a mindspeaker to stay in contact, as the raver and his warrior-priests question those who remain in the city. If the healer has crossed the river, Kaakos will consider sending his minions there, too."

"What will it mean if all the people desert the city? Other than it being empty?" I said.

"Kaakos will lose his ready supply of soldiers, servants and victims. It's much harder to track those born with power, if they're scattering everywhere," Adahi pointed out.

"I think the healer has the right idea, then, if he's encouraging the people to leave," Sherra observed. "They may not fully understand his purposes, but it's still a good thing to get children out of that bastard's reach."

"Amen to that," Doret said.

"Adahi?" I turned to him, then.

"King Thorn?" An eyebrow lifted as I addressed him.

"Is there a way to get in contact with the healer? That you know of?"

"That could be dangerous," Adahi said after considering my question. "We do not know whether he holds us as much in contempt as he does Kaakos. This is a delicate situation; you must understand that."

"Damn. I wish there was a way to feel him out—provided we could find him," I shook my head. "Kaakos is certainly having a difficult time tracking him, if I understand things correctly. If we could work with him in this," I left the sentence unfinished.

"His name?" Sherra asked. "Does anyone know?"

"He calls himself North," Doret said. "Kyri says several palace servants have been healed by him, and they swear by his ability."

"An unusual name," Sherra said, a frown tugging at a corner of her mouth. "Do you think he named himself that?"

"No idea. Kyri hasn't seen him. She only hears the tales."

"Has she spoken to anyone who's had direct contact with him? The healer?" I asked.

"She says that a kitchen worker was healed by him, before she was commanded to come to the palace to work. The story is that the healing made the conscription possible, but she holds no grudge for that part of it," Doret replied.

"Kyri finds this one believable?"

"Yes. I asked her about that, too. The woman is quite reliable."

"I never thought to hear that about anyone in Ny-nes," Barth observed.

"Generally, they're not evil," Adahi said. "Their leader lies to them daily and they follow his lead blindly—until this healer came along. I'm glad he's convincing them to vacate the city. The raver is helping in their decisions, no doubt, but it's a good thing. The air across the river is better for them anyway. All the manufacturing plants are in the city, under Kaakos' thumb. That means the soot, ash and anything else they expel is covering the city in filth and filling children's lungs."

"Does that reduce the life expectancy?" I asked.

"Greatly. To find an inhabitant of the city more than fifty years of age is remarkable."

"This almost makes me rethink attacking Ny-nes," I grumbled.

"Lungs can clear after only a brief exposure," Adahi quelled my fears. "It's living in that filth every day of your life that will kill you."

"There's only so much a body can take of poisoned air and unclean water," Doret agreed with Adahi's assessment. "Here, at least we don't pump that filth into the air, further contaminating what we have. The bombs and waste that created the poisoned lands will take forever to leave that ground."

"Waste?" I turned to her. "What are you talking about?"

"There is a by-product of past methods of energy creation," Adahi explained. "It will remain poisonous for many thousands of years. The answer back then was to bury it. Of course, unless the containers lasted as long as the poison, or if someone managed to breach the underground storage facility where it was kept, it was only a matter of time before it began leaking into the ground around it."

"Which of those things happened?" Sherra asked.

"Both, although the attack leveled upon it at the last sealed the land's fate and any who lived around it—until nothing was left except poisoned land."

"Disturbing," Barth shook his head.

"Extremely," I nodded at Barth. Frightening, too, but I kept that to myself. I'd carried prisoners twice to the poisoned lands myself. How much danger had I put myself in?

"Those with power have a better immunity to it than those who do not." Adahi must have read my expression. "Brief exposures aren't harmful, normally."

"I should have removed Merrin's power myself." As long as I lived, I would castigate myself over that.

"We all have a list of should-haves," Doret sniffed. "Don't drown in them, Thorn. You'll see that the longer we live, the larger the list grows. The best we can do is to do better next time."

"Well said," Adahi dipped his head to Doret.

"On another note," I began, "Have we heard anything from anyone regarding Narvin and the two he has with him?"

"Nothing as yet," Hunter replied. "But they have to eat, and their supply of food and shelter has disappeared. They'll be forced to find something else. They currently have no mindspeaker for Kaakos to command."

"So he'll be looking for someone else here," I growled. Every time I considered that Kaakos could move so easily among Az-ca's population, picking and choosing his spies, it burned my heart.

"He'll be dependent on Merrin's knowledge of Az-ca," Adahi said. "This means that we'll have to watch those Merrin knew, in case Kaakos decides to take them."

"Did either of those girls have mindspeak?" I turned to Doret.

"No, thank the stars," she said. "Deaf as posts in that way—Sherra checked all of them."

"Will a strong shield keep Kaakos out?" Sherra asked.

"In some cases, perhaps. It depends upon how much energy he is willing to expend to take someone."

"Did Jubal still have the ability to *step*?" Sherra turned to me.

"I don't know. Hunt?" I asked him.

"All his abilities were affected by his injuries," Hunter responded. He'd gone through the records to check, I'm sure. "*Stepping* was out of the question for him, because it was unreliable and likely to go awry more times than not. Same with his fireblasts—the physician's report is with his discharge records. Only his mindspeaking was left unharmed."

"No wonder they wouldn't let him stay, then. Those things, combined with his frame of mind, warranted his removal," I said. "Under battle conditions, he'd become a liability rather than an asset, if he couldn't move freely or protect himself."

"Well, that's moot now—he's under Kaakos' thumb, and I figure he's regretting his treason already," Doret said. "Kaakos isn't kind to anyone, and holds in contempt those he sees as not whole in any way."

"That's disturbing," Sherra observed. "You mean he has no compassion at all?"

"Only for himself," Doret snapped.

"He has no capacity for such," Adahi confirmed. "No empathy, either. Born without, as you may imagine. His view of the world is narrowed to himself and how things affect him."

"He's angry all the time, and he takes that anger out on every hapless person standing in his way. He has the ultimate hate for Az-ca, however, and it burns his soul that it remains and thrives." Doret turned her head away to hide her disgust.

What I couldn't determine, was what caused that hatred to begin with. Did we have something he desired, or was it another reason that made us a target? I considered asking Doret and Adahi if they knew the underlying reason, only to think better of it. How would they know such things? Their experience must lie in what they'd seen from him through the centuries.

"Something just happened," Sherra stood, a look of alarm and hope in her eyes.

"What?" I stood with her.

"I think Narvin just walked into my trap," she whispered.

# CHAPTER 13

*S*herra

"How did you figure out how to do this?" Adahi stood next to Kerok; the others were nearby after landing in North Camp's remains.

There, floating several feet above the ground in a bubble shield, was Narvin. He'd attempted to blast himself out—once.

His clothes were charred as a result, and there were burns on parts of his body, from the strength of his blast.

He hadn't leveled most of his power against the bubble shield, or he'd have fried himself. Perhaps he wished that had happened anyway, as Kerok glared at him from below.

"It was a desperate idea," I answered Adahi's question. "I had no idea whether it would work."

"It worked—quite well," Kerok growled. "I want this taught to anyone talented enough to learn it."

"I was hoping to catch the other two as well," I said. "I suppose they're hiding elsewhere so they wouldn't be caught together."

"I imagine they were hoping to find something to eat left here in the ruins," Adahi said. "That means those girls may go looking for the same thing elsewhere. How many villages have this protection, daughter?"

"All of them that I know," I shrugged.

"Can we take him to the lockup?" Kerok turned to me. "I'd like to ask questions after his power is burned away and the physician tends his wounds."

"Of course," I agreed. "I'll bring him inside the shield and release it, once he's at the lockup. Who's going to burn his power away?"

"I'll have Kage waiting," Kerok said. "He took care of Willa, too."

That's when Narvin began to shout at us, his voice muted by the heavy shield around him. "She better be alive, you heathen," he yelled.

"He's calling us heathen?" Adahi's eyebrows rose.

"Looks that way," Kerok said dryly. "Come, my love, we have plans for this treasonous bastard."

"I'll be right behind you," I said, indicating Doret and the others. Adahi could get himself back if he wanted to go.

Narvin shouted again when they disappeared. "Stop yelling," I told him. "Willa's alive and in the lockup. You'll likely be punished together, now." I *stepped* to the lockup, the bubble shield in tow as Narvin unhappily considered his fate.

∼

Ny-*nes*

*Kaakos*

The fool had gotten himself caught, and I couldn't get a good image of what happened the moment he was trapped. Therefore, I had no idea whether he lived, still. The two young ones were still alive, but they possessed a child's logic and I found that less than satisfactory.

The only reason they survived was they'd heard Narvin's yelp before he disappeared from their sight. They'd *stepped* away, then, too terrified to stay and find out what happened.

North Camp was now a trap; I filed that information away after correcting what I'd learned from Merrin. He'd burned it to the ground in the past—it sounded like a logical place to look for food and shelter among the ruins.

Someone had gotten there ahead of us, and that angered me. *The entire neighborhood is deserted,* Jubal's shaky mindspeak informed me. *Zis says they have taken their belongings and crossed the river.*

*Then I shall send troops across the river to drive them back. You and the raver will go with them; I'll send someone to guide you when they are ready.*

*Yes, Supreme Leader.* He hated calling me that. At my earliest convenience, I'd teach him better manners. Servants such as this one never appreciated what they had until it was taken away. I looked forward to seeing his reaction when neither of his legs worked.

Until then, I'd send others into the city to take stock of the missing. A true headcount was impossible, because nobody kept records. Until now, it hadn't been a problem.

"Send for a messenger," I shouted at the door. A guard's hurried footsteps echoed across marble floors to answer my call.

～

"THEY MUST BE USING whatever they can find to float across," General Tern informed me when he arrived in my study. "None of the military transports have been used for such."

"You're sure of this?" I toyed with a piece of fruit left over from the midday meal. Citizens outside my palace would give much to have a scrap of it. I crushed it in my fist while considering that.

"Yes, Supreme Leader. I have kept watch, as have my officers. You know those transports are kept at the eastern docks. Word has come that many escapees are floating across on bits of their own homes— they've torn them down to gain access to the opposite shore."

"How many are gone, do you think?"

"Perhaps a third? Maybe more; I'd have to visit the districts to make a better determination."

"Towel," I held out my hand to a cringing servant. He came quickly to wipe the squashed fruit from my fingers before stepping away and bowing to me at the same time.

I considered that all should bow to me in exactly the same manner. *Especially those in Az-ca.*

"Good enough," I waved my now-clean hand. "Gather troops and cross the river, General. I wish to know where my citizens think to escape."

"It will be as you say, Supreme Leader." The General bowed and stepped backward, much like the servant had.

*Good.*

~

*KEROK*

Willa cast nervous glances at Narvin, as we questioned him inside an adjoining cell. Sherra kept her shield about him while we did so; I had no idea why she was nervous about dropping the shield, but didn't want to question her judgment.

"Who have you contacted?" I demanded, staring Narvin down. "I want names." He turned his head, ashamed to be dressed down like this by his former commander. He'd followed Merrin, away from his vows and duty, and was now reduced to this cringing shadow of his former self.

Had he believed Merrin would raise him up? I'd ask that question later, but for now, I wanted to know what treasonous acts he'd committed for Kaakos. With his head still turned away from me, Narvin refused to answer.

"I can kill you now," I said. "And still have the same information I had before we found you."

"No," Willa leapt from her bunk to plead with me, her splinted leg causing her to fall back onto the blankets.

*Add your shield to Sherra's,* Adahi arrived and nodded to me. *As will I,* he went on.

*Why?* I kept my eyes on Narvin, rather than turning to face Adahi with my question. Without further argument, I allowed Adahi access to my shield. "Names," I snapped at Narvin, while Adahi pulled my shield inside his before slipping both behind the one Sherra held about Narvin.

Adahi held my shield steady; if he hadn't, I'd have drawn back in alarm when Narvin turned to face me. His eyes were red, and the voice that came through him was terrifying. "Shut up," he snarled. "You die, now."

If we hadn't had so many shields around Narvin, he could have killed us when he exploded with Kaakos' wrath.

$\sim$

*Sherra*

Willa wept. I felt ill as we stood outside Narvin's cell, the bloodied shield containing his remains floating inside. We'd have to dispose of it somewhere; we couldn't leave it hanging inside a cell for anyone to see.

I worked to contain my nausea while Adahi gazed grimly upon Narvin's sacrifice; Kerok was angry and repulsed at the same time. His anger, no doubt, was pointed at Kaakos for his ability to do this to anyone he'd taken as his own.

"Did you mean to ally yourself with such evil?" I turned to Willa.

"I followed Narvin," she sobbed. "He made the decisions."

"Well, you see now what those decisions got him," Kerok snapped at her. "Adahi, can you get rid of that?" He waved at the bloody shield.

"It will be as you say," Adahi nodded before disappearing with the carnage. *Drop your shields now*, he mindspoke Kerok and me several moments later.

I released mine with a sigh.

"Come," Kerok took my elbow to lead me out of the lockup. "We have other things to do."

*Kage*, he included me in his mindspeak. *Willa's execution should happen now. Make sure she's unaware it's coming.*

*It will be so*, Kage responded.

$\sim$

"AND THUS END two lives that could have been better spent," Hunter set glasses on Kerok's desk minutes later, before pouring whiskey into them. He included himself and Barth in the serving of spirits; we needed a stiff drink to deal with recent events.

"We'll discuss this later," Kerok growled as he lifted his glass and drank the contents in one swallow, then held his glass out to Hunter for a refill.

My mind was crowded with questions, however. Sipping the potent whiskey, I considered that those questions were disjointed and chaotic. I needed Cole or Caral—perhaps both—to help me put them in order.

All my questions ended with the largest of them all.

*How?*

*How had Kaakos done this? How had he taken Narvin over, to attempt to kill us while we questioned his minion?*

Perhaps Adahi would know. I added him to my list of people to consult about this. How much power did it require? Was it more than we had? What would we face when we attacked him?

I wanted those answers before we laid our plan of attack. I had no intention of committing suicide, merely by transporting myself and my colleagues to Ny-nes.

"Contact Armon," Kerok downed his second glass of whiskey. "I need to consult with him, Doret, Adahi and everyone else pertinent to the situation."

"I'll see to it," Hunter agreed and wrote himself a note.

~

"THOSE TWO GIRLS are still out there," I told Cole. I'd joined him for tea in his small kitchen, while I informed him about the method of Narvin's demise.

"You worry that Kaakos will take them the same way, don't you?"

"Yes."

"You also worry your shield-trap won't hold them, if that's the case."

"Yes."

"It held Narvin—until he was questioned by the King."

"You mean he was waiting for the right moment, to cause damage?"

"Either that, or he didn't want Narvin to release information. I can't help but believe that what he did took a great deal of power."

"Then Narvin must have possessed vital information."

"I think so, too."

"What could it be? Should we have kept Willa alive longer, in case she knew?"

"I doubt she knew much, if I know Kaakos at all. My guess is that Narvin had names of spies. Kaakos didn't kill Narvin until Thorn demanded names of collaborators. Now that Narvin's dead, Kaakos may intend to use those two girls the same way he used Narvin. Therefore, we need to find them quickly."

"They'll have to show up somewhere, or they'll starve," I said.

"I concur."

"Perhaps it's time to pay Jubal's neighbors a visit—to see if they noticed anything."

"I'll come with you, if you like."

"Let's go."

∼

"TAKEN BY THE ENEMY?" Stave, Jubal's closest neighbor, asked. "I thought he'd finally had enough and blew his own house down around him."

"You thought he killed himself?" Cole asked.

"That's what I thought." Stave spat on the ground—it was something to do while he considered the new set of facts surrounding Jubal, and whether he'd be held accountable by the Crown for having anything to do with him.

"You're not a suspect," Cole read Stave as easily as I did. "We only want as much information as you can give us—for the official record."

"Is he—alive?" I'd have asked the same question, if I were Stave.

"The last information we had said so, but that could change—the enemy is unreliable and capricious."

I wasn't sure Stave had ever heard the term *capricious*, but he didn't say anything. "Never woulda thought," Stave shook his head and spat again. "I carried Jubal's census papers back to the village myself—never saw any sign that somebody else was here."

Cole and I exchanged troubled glances.

~

"DID YOU GET ANYTHING?" Kerok asked as I sat wearily at the small dining table inside our suite.

"The neighbor only told us what we already knew—that Jubal was bitter over his injuries and forced retirement, and didn't like women at all. Stave thought Jubal killed himself after he saw the state of Jubal's cabin after the explosion."

"He never saw anyone else there—staying with Jubal?"

"He says he didn't, and it wouldn't be difficult to hide somebody—Jubal always talked to Stave on the front porch when he visited."

"Then my question is where did he get enough food for them? It had to come from somewhere."

"Any reports of raided gardens in outlying homesteads?" I asked. "Have the quadrant leaders said anything?"

"Nothing so far, but I can ask Hunter to relay the question."

"I think we should—somebody was feeding them, that's for sure. Jubal was probably paying for it, too. The question is, who could it be, and how were they producing enough food to feed them? I really want to talk to whoever did that."

"I can see that," Kerok dipped his head in a nod. "I want to question them, too, as long as they were born without power. What else?" His brows drew together. He knew there was something else, just by watching my face. "Out with it," he sighed.

"Jubal filled out census papers," I blew out a breath. "I already talked to Barth. Neither he nor the other diviners got a single thing off Jubal's papers. Not even a twinge. Kaakos did that—I know he did.

The census was long overdue, and it may lead us to other things, but Kaakos' spies aren't included in that list."

"Fuck me." Kerok raked fingers through his hair in frustration. "Well, there's nothing to be done about it, now. Let's eat and get the taste of this day out of our mouths."

"I'm ready," I said and lifted my fork.

~

*Ny-nes*

*Kaakos*

Someone had built a shield powerful enough to hold me back, but only at a great distance and certainly not at my full power. I wasn't foolish enough to expend that much energy to save a worm such as Narvin.

If he'd had mindspeak, he'd be here instead of Jubal, who had to be carried throughout the city behind my raver.

Besides, the two young ones were still alive. I'd ponder the takeover of their minds later, when I felt less angry. If I were to attempt it now, I'd likely blast their few brain cells by accident, just from the bleed-through of my fury.

Too bad my father wasn't alive to see what I'd become; he'd commit suicide rather than look upon me at full power.

"Father," I mumbled to an empty room, "I'd have helped you on your road to oblivion if I could. I still hate you, too—after all these years."

It made me think of the bitch, who told me that hate destroyed the soul. As if that were a thing. Let the masses believe that tripe; I had no use for it, other than to control their tiny minds.

"Look at me, getting maudlin now, of all times," I considered. "Guards," I shouted. "Send for Liam."

The planes were almost ready. I wanted an update. Az-ca had taken something from me. I would take more back.

~

*North*

Kaakos was sending troops across the river. I stood far down the bank to watch them cross the bridge reserved for the military.

Many of the escaping citizens had built rafts of boards from their shacks to float across; it was a good idea, as they were taking their building materials with them when they went.

I'd gone across myself a few times, urging the refugees to move southward, away from the city's filthy air. Besides, some would be injured in the crossing—they weren't experienced navigators and the river was wide.

A healer was much sought-after, once they knew of my talents.

Reports had reached me, too, regarding work in Kaakos' factories. Planes would be finished and ready to send soon. Decisions had to be made regarding that information.

Most of those decisions involved whom to approach with that information, and my concern as to whether they'd believe me.

If I knew how to reach the shining woman—but that could spell danger. Much danger. Too many fates balanced on the head of a pin. One thing going awry could topple all, and my work would be for naught.

All those I could depend upon—dead. Far in the past, too. For now, I felt more alone than I'd ever been, and just as troubled.

Except—perhaps there was someone to approach after all. He'd asked for my help. That help could be offered—*for a price.*

~

*Sherra*

"I've been thinking," I said, when Caral and Cole arrived in my study to work. Caral turned to Cole, as a smile spread across her face. Cole answered with one of his own.

"Why are you smiling?" I asked.

"It's just that whenever you've been thinking, amazing things happen afterward," Caral turned toward me, then. "I never hear Armon say you've been thinking too much anymore."

"That's true," I grinned.

"So, what is it?" Cole asked.

"Well, actually, Misten deserves credit for this."

Caral's eyes widened. "How?"

"She's the one who said follow the gold. We're looking for evidence of it now. What I thought, though, is this. All that gold has to come directly from Kaakos, don't you think? He doesn't want anyone else to know he can get it from Ny-nes to here, unless I'm very mistaken."

"That makes sense," Cole nodded. "Since power is frowned upon except in the rarest of cases there, and Kaakos has those talented ones directly under his thumb." He didn't add that we both knew the census was now useless in identifying Kaakos' spies. We needed another way to find them.

"The gold comes from Kaakos. What does that knowledge do for us?" Caral asked.

"Well, I may have to consult with Barth, but I'm really hoping that we can perform a long-distance divination."

"You've lost me," Caral grimaced.

"Oh. I'm thinking ahead of my mouth," I admitted. "I know Kaakos' power signature. Don't ask how," I held up a hand as Cole prepared to do exactly that. "I just do. Now, I need to find a way to project that information across miles, to look for places where that power signature may be hiding."

"We find the gold, we find his spies," Caral breathed.

"We haven't tried it, yet, so don't get your hopes up," I cautioned as a light appeared in Cole's eyes. "We don't know it's possible, yet."

"Is Barth available?" Caral said. "How long will this take?"

"I don't know. I haven't determined whether that kind of divination is even possible. Barth has to touch something, remember? I was just thinking about how we could focus on something—like a truck, and *step* it somewhere else. I want to do that with divination—*step* it somewhere else."

"I need tea while I consider this," Cole sat heavily on a nearby chair and gazed out my window. His mind was whirling with possibilities, provided we could get this idea to work.

"I'll send for tea," Caral headed for the door.

~

"Whatʼs this?" I didn't know Barth was meeting with Kerok and Hunter when I sent mindspeak to him. They all showed up in my study.

"It's just an idea," I said.

"She wants to send divination out, like sending a truck to North Camp," Caral smiled at Kerok.

"That's an interesting idea, but why?" Barth queried.

"We want to follow Kaakos' gold," Cole said. "If we can divine from a distance, perhaps we can focus that divination on a single thing."

Kerok blinked at me before turning to Cole, then Caral, and finally to Barth. "It sounds impossible," he sighed. "And I'll keep my hopes alive that it's not. Make this work, my love. Please."

He'd seen the possibilities, just as I had. If I could locate Kaakos' gold, who knew what else we might focus on?

"I need time to consider this," Barth said. "I'm not sure how to begin, even."

"Tomorrow, then?" I asked him. "I think we may need to be in contact to attempt it. We'll start with something nearby, but not touching either of us."

"I'll do this for the King," Barth released a sigh. I understood he thought it a foolish notion, but we had to try. If we failed, then we failed. There was no shame in that; the shame would lie in not making the attempt.

*Thank you,* I sent mindspeak to Kerok.

*He's balking because he doesn't like to fail at anything,* Kerok responded. *Give him room to doubt, then show him the way.*

*I don't know that it'll work, either,* I admitted. *But I have to try.*

*My love, I pray for your success,* he said. "We'll go, now," he said aloud, leading Barth and Hunter from my study.

"Want your tea warmed?" Caral asked once the three of us were alone again. "Armon showed me how."

"Kerok usually does it for me," I said, pushing my cup toward Caral. "I need hot tea after all that."

~

*North*

*Jubal?* I sent mindspeak. I could see his wheeled conveyance ahead as two warrior-priests heaved his cart through cluttered, narrow trails between empty shacks and lean-tos.

The boards easiest to carry had been stripped away, leaving a wretched monument of rubble to lives lived in squalor for centuries.

*Who?* He was too frightened to turn his head, now.

*North. You asked for help. Tell me why I should give it.*

*He took me from my home and forced me to do this,* his mental voice wobbled.

*Kaakos? How did he find you? I assume you were hidden from his sight for a very long time—he doesn't take kindly to those less than whole, and neither do his warrior-priests.*

*I came from Az-ca.* I watched him hunch his shoulders in the distance.

*How did you come to Kaakos' attention?* Suddenly, I knew, without his excuse of a reply. *You were a spy for him. Weren't you? Tell me it isn't so, and don't lie—I can tell if you do.*

*I'm sorry I ever fell in with him. I swear.*

*And I'm sorry, too—sorry that I ever considered helping you. You are on your own, Jubal, and I sincerely hope your demise is less painful than most I've seen at Kaakos' hands.*

*No—please,* he begged.

I didn't answer. I was done with this one.

I had one more to call upon, once night fell and he was in his bed. He was also from Az-ca, and no doubt had an interesting tale to tell concerning his arrival in Ny-nes.

I knew Kaakos hadn't pulled him here. He'd arrived in a different manner, and that he'd never spied in his life for the one who named himself Supreme Leader of this grace-forsaken land.

I didn't know his name.

*Yet.*

He was responsible for sending Kaakos after me, though, and for the countless deaths of citizens who stood in the raver's way afterward.

Yes. He would serve or he'd be exposed.

The choice would be his to make.

# CHAPTER 14

*y-nes*
*North*

A sound sleeper.

Who snored.

*Wake,* I tapped his forehead, never suspecting such a large man could move so swiftly. He was awake with his back against the wall before I had time to register his movement.

Until it dawned on me—he'd *stepped,* albeit a short distance, to get far enough away to protect himself. His fists, clenched, glowed dimly in the night; he was prepared to level blasts against me.

*Stop that and listen to me,* I snapped at him in mindspeak.

*Who?* He demanded to know.

*I'm North. You know—the one you goaded Kaakos into hunting down? The one that too many citizens to count have lost their lives over—when you decided to kill off seven of Kaakos' pet warrior-priests?*

His eyes widened. Nobody knew about the first one; he'd killed the other six who'd been with the raver. He'd killed Aspe first, and hadn't owned up to it, yet.

*What do you want?* he silently growled.

*I want you,* I said amiably. *Now, you can come quietly, or I can make so much racket, the guards will come running and the entire servants' quarters will be wakened. Is that what you want?*

*I can't go. I'm here with someone else,* he grumbled. *I have to protect her.*

*Who? The name, or I'll turn you over to the guards myself.*

*Kyri.* He turned his head away at the admission.

I went still. Never did I think—well, it no longer mattered. I suspected Doret would be the one, and that was—well.

*Where?* I gripped the collar of his tunic.

*Women's quarters,* he responded, as if any dolt would have known it.

*Come.* I jerked him toward me, while the breath whooshed out of him in surprise. Then, I *stepped* both of us to the women's quarters, to collect the one called Kyri.

❧

*KYRI*

"Let me go." I fought with Garkus. Somehow, he'd gotten me out of the women's quarters without waking me or any of the others.

Except Garkus wasn't the one whose arms were holding me against him, telling me to shut up and not bite him again.

That's when I went still, my face pressed against a hard shoulder. Slowly, and with deliberate movement, I disentangled myself from my captor's clutches and stood back to look at his face.

A lop-sided grin met my angry gaze.

I hauled off and slapped him.

Hard.

❧

*NORTH*

"I'm not the only one lying to you. Who's lied to you," I amended as Kyri glowered in my direction. I'd *stepped* us to an ancient bunker that nobody remembered, now, Kaakos included.

"Hmmph." Her response wasn't a word. It was a one-syllable dressing-down.

Garkus, arms folded across his wide chest, was almost as displeased as Kyri. I'd get to him in a moment. "He lied to you, too," I flung out an arm in Garkus' direction. "He killed Aspe, then complicated the killing with an asinine note that resulted in the deaths of many."

At least she'd turned to glare at Garkus, now. His arms dropped, as did his head—an admission of his guilt in anyone's eyes. Kyri was furious, now.

"What, in the name of the first fucking warrior are you doing here, alive?"

Now it was my turn to drop my eyes. "I could ask you the same thing. Kaakos locked you out, last I checked."

"Why didn't you help me, then?" she demanded, her teeth clenched, her words hissed.

"The time wasn't right."

"And it is, now?"

"Yes. I was waiting for a sign. Not long ago, the sign came. I came out of hiding and began weaning the population away from Kaakos and his lies."

"Is that what this is?"

"It's my plan, yes."

"Who the hell is this?" Garkus decided to speak, a finger pointing an accusation in my direction.

"Shut up." Kyri and I shouted him down simultaneously.

*DORET*

*I have no idea how it's possible, and I'm really not speaking to him right now to find out. Truly, I doubt I want the answer anyway,* Kyri said.

*You know we can't tell anyone about this,* I warned. *This is impossible,* I added, almost to myself.

*You think you're telling me something I don't already know?*

*No. I just—I don't know what to think,* I admitted. *Will you let Adahi know?* That had just occurred to me.

*He could have helped us last time—Adahi and me—if we'd only known he was here instead of, well, that's water under the bridge, as they say. Adahi gave his life to get me out, then. What do you think he'll say if he discovers this?*

*Nothing good,* I huffed. *What do you think will happen if the bastard finds out who North really is?*

*No idea. It's not a pleasant thing to consider, you know.*

*Do you trust him?*

*I didn't trust him before. You know why.*

*I do.* I thought about commenting on what might have been, but Kyri and I had argued too many times about that already. It all boiled down to poor choices and distasteful things ignored or left undone.

*You know Sherra and Thorn are planning to attack Ny-nes, don't you?* Now that Kyri was away from Kaakos and his palace, I felt safer allowing her to have the information.

*Fuck,* Kyri's reply was swift. *He said he was waiting for a sign, and that it had come to him recently. I suppose that's what it was.*

*Then I hope he also sees a successful outcome in this,* I said. *Or we'll all be screwed.*

*We may be screwed anyway,* Kyri informed me. *Kaakos' Chief of Technical Sciences has been seen at the palace quite often, lately. That spells new disasters for Az-ca, if I know anything at all.*

*Fuck.* It was my turn to say it, I suppose, so I said it again—*fuck.*

Bloody, fucking hellfire.

History had turned upside down and it could work to our detriment in too many ways. Kyri said she'd slapped him.

I wanted to slap him, too.

*Fuck.*

~



"I thought Cole was supposed to be here today. Sherra, too," Kyal kicked a small piece of driftwood toward the water. The beach was shadowed by the cliff above us as we walked toward a new set of blasting targets.

"They're busy," Laren draped an arm over Kyal's shoulders.

"I think they're worried," I said.

Kyal's head lifted. Now he looked worried. "About what?" he whispered.

"You know—Ny-nes." Laren was also whispering. He let his arm drop back to his side as Kyal turned to face him.

Cole and the others generally didn't answer our questions about Ny-nes, and I wondered why that was. We'd stopped asking about it after a while, because we never received a satisfactory answer.

"I think we should look for stuff on Ny-nes in Kyri's library," I said, before clamping a hand over my mouth.

"It's probably in all that stuff we can't read," Kyal said, sounding gloomy. He hated that there were books he couldn't read. He really wanted to know what was in them.

I did, too, but I didn't tell him that. We were sneaking around in Kyri's library when we shouldn't, and if we were caught, I had no idea what the punishment might be.

"We'll go tonight, if you want," Laren said. "We'll look around. Here come Liri and Giles—they're probably wondering why we're taking so long to get to lessons."

I turned; Liri had stopped a distance away—Giles was still walking toward us, nodding when he saw we'd noticed them. Kyal, Laren and I began our trek down the beach again. Giles and Liri were good teachers and patient, but we never moved so fast in our lessons as we did when Cole and Sherra were here.

~

*Sherra*

I'd asked Cole to hide a small bag of Jubal's gold. He'd hidden it somewhere in my study, and neither Barth nor I had any clue where it was. What we did have was a single, small nugget from Jubal's stash, to link with the other.

*If we could.*

Barth fingered the nugget we had, his eyes closed as he worked his divination. I saw his mouth tighten after a few moments, before I saw anger passing over his features.

He'd seen a part of Kaakos, no doubt.

"I only see the intent," Barth set the nugget down on my desk. "I couldn't get past that, to see anything else."

"It's probably just as well," I told him. "It may be the same as reading a coiled rattlesnake."

"That concerns me," Barth said. "Very much."

"Now that you have a feel for the intent," I said, "let's join hands and send out a search for the same elsewhere."

My hope was that my usual talent for amplifying Barth's divination would come into play, and we could locate the hidden gold. I'd handled the nugget, just as Barth did, and Kaakos' malevolence was very apparent in it.

When I gripped Barth's fingers in mine, I could tell he was working to recall the feel of the nugget.

"Barth," I said, closing my eyes, "Lift the nugget in your free hand."

His fingers tightened around mine the moment he lifted the nugget to connect with Kaakos' intent.

With the two of us touching, in my mind, I saw the nugget throbbing in a purplish, black color. I saw what Barth was seeing in it. Casting about my study, I searched mentally for the same vibrating colors.

*There!* Barth's mindspeak was sudden and almost made me jump.

He'd found the answering signal from the other gold—hidden behind a vase on a corner shelf.

"I'll be damned," Barth mumbled, letting go of my hand and stalking toward the vase. He lifted the bag of gold seconds later, as if it were a trophy to display. "You know we have to do this together, don't you?" He added after a moment. "There's no way I can do this on my own."

"Maybe it's time to test it with other diviners—pooling your talents, like we've been pooling our shields and blasts," I pointed a finger at him. "And this is only across a room. We have to try it longer distances, too."

"I'm willing, anytime," Barth said. "I'm sorry I doubted you in this. Truly."

"Then I'll ask Cole to hide this again," I said. "I really want to find those spies."

"There's something else to consider in this," Barth said. "We need to search for much of it together, rather than a single nugget here and there—we may be pulling innocents into our trap, when they only accepted the gold in payment for goods or services."

"True," I said. "We'll look for larger amounts, then, but failing that, we can ask questions as to where the gold came from—if the spy has spent all of it."

"Yes," Barth said after considering my suggestion. "Follow the gold," a reluctant smile lifted the corners of his mouth. "Just as Misten said."

*Cole, Kerok,* I sent mindspeak. *We found the gold. Now we need to hide it farther away.*

*On my way,* Cole said.

*I'm coming, too,* Kerok replied. *I want to see this for myself.*

Moments later, they walked through the door of my study, Cole grinning, Kerok giving me a sly wink and a nod at Barth.

"We found it so quickly, after I held the nugget I'd divined," Barth said, handing the bag of gold to Cole. "Hide it well. We'll test this to the limit."

"I'll stay with these two," Kerok nodded at Cole. "I'll connect with both, to see if I can tell how they're doing this."

"I'll let you know when it's hidden," Cole said, striding out the door.

"You went straight to it?" Kerok asked Barth.

"When Sherra told me to pick up the nugget, to connect with it," Barth replied. "I was struggling to recall the exact divination, when I really didn't have to—we had the actual thing here." He set the nugget in Kerok's hand.

"Like a bloodhound, with a scent?" Kerok lifted an eyebrow at Barth.

"Very much like that. Why didn't we think of this before?"

Kerok shrugged at Barth, then turned and winked at me again.

*It's hidden*, Cole's mindspeak reached us.

*We're on it*, I told him.

~

NY-NES

*Kaakos*

"Their chains, my Lord." The warrior-priest set the wrist chains from two escaped minions on the floor next to my feet. He then backed away slowly.

"They were taken from the servants' quarters?"

"Yes. Both the men's and women's quarters." He didn't add that it had happened right under my nose and I'd slept through it.

"Then the healer has to be behind this. He has abilities I did not suspect," I said. My vision had gone red with my anger; I struggled not to blast the foolish warrior-priest before me to assuage it.

"He is evil, my Lord." The warrior-priest's words were cautious. He had no idea whether he'd survive the next few minutes.

"Yes. An evil, to be sure. We must renew our efforts to exterminate this evil." I nudged the items with a foot, the chains making a metallic chink as they slid across marble. How had I not felt the spell being compromised?

Unless it wasn't compromised.

If not, how the hell had they come off? I was the only one who could remove them and leave the spell intact.

"Hand them to me," I snapped at the warrior-priest. The chains were snatched up and settled in my palm in a blink.

How had this happened? *The spell was intact.* "How did this happen?" I roared, flinging the chains across the room. The warrior-priest and two guards cowered before my wrath.

~

*Kyri*

*You still haven't told me who he is,* Garkus accused as we followed our liberator through narrow alleys and warrens on the western edge of the city. We were wrapped in a mirror shield as we went, to keep anyone from seeing us.

*Call him North,* I cut off Garkus' inquiry. *That's all you need to know.*

*Where are we going, then?*

*I have no idea. We're stuck with him, now. You called his attention to us by murdering warrior-priests. Live with it.*

*Why can't we just* step away? *We don't have to stay with him.*

*Trust me—we're better off if we can keep him in our sights.*

*It's rude to have a conversation about me while I'm right here,* North's mindspeak interrupted.

*Fuck,* Garkus growled.

*We'll be healing—and giving warnings against Kaakos,* North added. *I know you're curious—there's your answer.*

*How do you know where to go?* Garkus demanded.

*Garkus, this I will tell you,* I said. *There are few better at divination than North. Now shut up and keep walking.*

*So you've decided to call me North, eh?* His message was for me only.

*Better than your real name.*

*Debatable.*

*Not from where I'm standing.*

*You hate me that much? I thought absence made the heart grow fonder.*

*Not your absence.*

*Ah. Here we are.* He turned down a side alley that almost looked clean, compared to those closer to the factories.

"What's this?" He spoke aloud to a man sitting outside the small shack when we arrived. I could smell the putrid odor of infection the moment the man rose and led us inside.

"Who?" The woman, lying on a pile of filthy rags inside the hovel, demanded of North. She'd expected the healer, but not two helpers. She was naturally suspicious.

"This one," North pointed in my direction. "She can heal as well or better than I can."

"Show." She pulled a filthy piece of cloth away from her leg. There it was—the source of the stench.

"This needs to be removed," North told her, kneeling to examine the spreading gangrene. "If we don't, you'll die. It's your choice, but my advice is to remove it as quickly as possible. She and I," he nodded again in my direction, "can make this less painful than it sounds. You'll be forced to walk with a crutch, but you'll live."

"Take. Hurts," the woman grimaced.

"All right. Garkus, keep watch outside. Let her husband hold her hands while Kyri and I work."

Garkus grumbled, but did as he was bid.

*Shield my power from sight*, North sent.

I wanted to grumble, too, but did as he said anyway.

When the woman's husband sat behind his wife, pulling her head into his lap and her hands into his, North began. I shielded his hands when they began to glow with his fire, and using both, gripped the woman's leg just above the knee and burned through her flesh in less than two seconds, leaving a seared stump behind.

I watched as he turned the leg to harmless ash inside a bubble shield, then went to work on the burn left behind.

It had happened so quickly that the woman didn't have time to scream or register the pain. Joining my power with North's, I worked to keep the ensuing pain at bay while he did repairs.

"How we cross now?" The husband asked later, while the woman slept. North had told him to flee to the other side of the river. The man was right—Kaakos' military was spread out along the river bank, watching for escapees.

*We can take them*, I said.

*But*, North argued, his dark eyes clouded with disagreement.

*We'll tell them the Prophet wants it*, I countered.

*I don't want the Prophet brought into this.*

*That body lying in Kaakos' chapel is Adahi's and you know it*, I said. *He'd want them taken to the other side.*

*Fine.* "Garkus, lift the woman. We'll take them to the other side."

∽

I SHOULD HAVE KNOWN he'd find the exact spot to set down across the river, so he'd be greeted by an adoring crowd. Garkus, carrying the woman, received his own share of adulation. Few had seen anyone so tall and robust in their lives.

So many reached out to touch North as he passed through the throng—he'd either healed many of them, or word had spread.

"Come," a man walked forward to motion us farther along. "Have room."

He did—an extra space in his lean-to, so Garkus could set the woman down and make her comfortable.

The husband fussed about, covering his wife with a scrap of blanket offered by the owner.

"Soldiers farther up," our host spoke softly. "Come looking." He pointed at North. "Safe?" He then pointed to Garkus and me.

"Safe," North inclined his head. "Healer," he pointed to me. "Protector," he pointed at Garkus.

"Yes," the man nodded. "Go. Be safe. We see nothing."

That was certainly different. These same people would have handed their children to Kaakos' priests in the past, knowing they'd die a horrible death. North had accomplished something, at least.

He'd planted doubts in their minds, along with the idea that not all with power were bad. Part of his plan was working—I granted and begrudged him that much.

*We'll give them a show*, North sent as we walked out of the lean-to. He caused our images to fade away instead of disappearing abruptly when he *stepped* us back to the eastern side of the river.

"What now?" Garkus demanded the moment we landed in yet another crowded alley.

"Find the next one to heal, what else?" North squared his shoulders and began walking the narrow lane. We had little choice except to follow.

∽

*KEROK*

"Rise for the King," Armon shouted to the mess hall. Everyone rose quickly as Sherra, Barth, Cole and I made our way to Armon's table to have a midday meal with the troops.

"So, what have you been up to?" Levi grinned once we and the rest of the hall were seated.

"This," Cole plopped the small bag of gold on the center of the table, making a soft chink as the nuggets settled inside it.

"Did it work?" Caral sounded breathless.

"We found it—six times," Barth was proud of his accomplishment. I'd not seen Barth that happy before. It made me think of how pleased Hunter was, when he and I moved an old truck around a storage shed.

"We'll try it on other—sources—tomorrow," Sherra said. Plates of food were set in front of us by Caral's sister, Darissa, and two other servers, who couldn't help smiling at us.

"I miss this," Misten sighed, lifting her fork. "Having meals with all of you," she clarified.

"I hear you received a promotion, Corporal," I smiled at her. "About time, too."

"We ah, were wondering when we could approach the likely candidates for ah," Armon considered how to word his question.

*You're asking about combining shields and blasts?* I sent mindspeak.

*Yes.*

*Give me two days to consult with Barth and Hunter. You'll have the list of names, then. I'd suggest taking them to North Camp, but that place has left a bad taste in my mouth recently. South Supply Camp will be good enough. I'll attend the meeting with Sherra.*

*Thank you,* Armon visibly relaxed.

"This looks good," I cut into the chops we'd been served.

"It is good," Sherra said. She'd expended plenty of energy—now it was time to replenish. I also hadn't seen Barth this hungry in a while.

*Taxing work,* I sent to Barth.

*Very true,* he replied while stuffing another chunk of meat in his mouth. *It would be more fun if it weren't so deadly serious at the same time.*

*You have that right,* I said. We were about to take the information supplied by the quadrant leaders, and point our divinations in those directions. I hoped we'd begin finding Kaakos' spies quickly.

~

*HUNTER*

"You're sure of this?" Claude brought me the news himself, rather than trusting it to one of his assigned messengers.

"I'm sure. The hand and footprints belong to either older girls or young women. I'm grateful for the small amount of rainfall before those two hunters were killed."

"By blasts." I shook my head as I made notes. "This means the enemy certainly restored their power."

"I don't understand how that can be, but I've seen the results myself. They waited outside the shield area, for hunters or whoever to step outside it. Then, they waited for a successful hunt before killing the two men and stealing the deer they'd killed to provide the village with meat."

"Did you warn the villagers to stay inside the shielded area?"

"Yes, but they rely on sending their hunters out twice a week."

"Leaving those two an easy way to feed themselves."

"Yes."

"The King is away right now. I'll hand this information to him. I'm sure he'll send troops to look for those two girls."

"That deer will last them for a few days, if they know how to keep the meat from spoiling. I have no idea whether that's something they know," Claude said.

"They'll have to build a fire to cook it, unless they want to blast it crisp," I pointed out.

"Blasting something is always delicate business, if you want to eat it afterward."

"Hunt? Claude?" Thorn walked in, followed by Barth and Sherra. "What's going on?"

"Those two girls murdered two hunters, looks like," I reported. "In Claude's quadrant."

Thorn turned toward Sherra and Barth. "We'll go with Claude now," Thorn said immediately. "We have ah, a new technique to try."

"With what?"

"I'm sure there's something of the deer left at the scene," Thorn said.

"Please let this work," I said, begging Thorn with my eyes.

"Hold that thought," Thorn replied. "Claude, will you *step* us to the murder site?"

"Of course, my King."

~

*Sherra*

A bloodied leather strap and a clump of fur—that's what we found. The strap had been used to carry the deer between two men, but had fallen off when two girls awkwardly *stepped* the dead animal away—after murdering two hunters, of course. The hunters' charred bodies lay nearby. The rest of the villagers stood inside the outer edge of the shield I'd erected, watching us. I couldn't hear their words, but no doubt they were talking among themselves about the King himself coming to investigate.

"Barth?" Kerok handed the strap to his Chief Diviner, while I moved closer to Barth and reached for his free hand.

We both closed our eyes, while Barth began the divination. Wherever those two murdering teens were, the deer would also be.

Kerok's hand gripped mine. Barth and I had located the glow related to the items he held. We *stepped* in that direction, before repeating the process again.

That's how we'd accomplished what we had earlier—to keep *stepping* toward the glow until it was so bright we could see our target with eyes open.

Less than fifteen minutes later, we found the girls roasting a deer over a hastily-built fire.

Flinging a heavy shield about them, I prepared to haul them to the lockup, only to witness a second time what happened to Narvin. An explosion of red bloomed inside the shield I'd constructed. There'd been no time for either girl to scream, it happened so fast.

That's when I learned that Kerok had *stepped* Claude with us. He shouted his anger to the skies while Barth and Kerok cursed.

I wanted to retch as I blinked at the bloodied shield I'd built around two troublemakers. Kaakos had killed again.


*POTTLES*, I sent. *Ferni and Jeen are dead. Kaakos killed them so we couldn't ask questions.*

*Fucking hells,* she said. *How did you find them?*

*It's a long story. I'll tell you later. Right now, I have to throw up.*

# CHAPTER 15

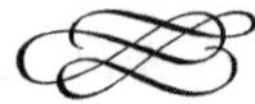

*D*oret

*She tracked them down—with help from Barth, after Kaakos made them unseeable,* I repeated. Kyri had trouble believing what I'd told her. After all, Adahi hadn't been able to find them, and he was the best tracker I'd ever seen.

*How? Did she tell you?*

*I only have sketchy information,* I said. *The same thing happened to those two as happened to Narvin. Exploded inside a shield. The blood and guts of two girls was too much for Sherra's stomach.*

*If you find out how she did it, let me know. I want to recreate it if I can.*

*How are things going with ah,* I didn't finish my question.

*Call him North. He's named himself that. I don't speak to him if I don't have to.*

*What are you doing, then?*

*Healing people. We've healed eleven today already.*

*Well, at least you're accomplishing something.*

*I don't know how long I can do this,* she admitted.

*You mean without putting a knife in his back?*

*Something like that. I think he was expecting to find you here, instead of me.*

*Ruarke's dead. He should know better.*

*Agreed. I think he didn't expect that to happen, somehow—that Ruarke would die in Az-ca.*

*He wouldn't have if Sherra hadn't helped Adahi.*

*Sherra's an unseeable,* Kyri mulled that information between us.

*So he may not have foreseen any part of that, then?*

*It's possible—and the only explanation I have for now.*

*I don't feel good about withholding this information—from Adahi or Sherra,* I said. *How do you suppose Adahi will react if you tell him?*

*He won't be happy.*

*I think that's a mild assessment. Adahi will find out eventually, and then you may never see or hear from him again.*

*That may happen anyway, if he finds out we're following North around like lost puppies.*

*I don't think you have a choice,* I said. *You certainly can't go back to the palace—Kaakos will kill you.*

*Yes, I'm sure the death sentence has already been declared. I'd worry that some of the citizens would turn us in for the reward, but there aren't many left in the city, now. The ones staying behind know they're marked just as much as Garkus and I are; they just haven't made up their minds to flee.*

*Has he sent the military after them yet—the ones who've gotten away?*

*Yes. We heard that this morning—that troops are watching the river now, looking for any who attempt to cross.*

*What are they doing to feed themselves? The refugees?*

*There's better farming land to the south; I think many are going that way already. They haven't built a massive camp across the river, so more and more are traveling farther south at night, to avoid being tracked so easily. There are villages everywhere, once you get away from the city. Not all of those are held in a death grip by Kaakos—he hasn't been out of the palace in years.*

*Are some of his overseers accepting bribes to look the other way?*

*Of course they are.*

*I'm not surprised.*

*I learned a few things on my journey to the city, you know. I had to eat along the way. A few coins will buy necessities, and conversation will provide information. I believe that part of North's plan is working, though.*

*Which part? There's more than one?*

*He's slowly turning the people away from Kaakos and his pretend religion.*

*How is he doing that?*

*By healing those who need it, and telling them the truth when he heals.*

*That's something Kaakos never did—and never will do, I considered. Healing. Never would have thought.*

*The North I knew seldom thought about it.*

*You think his philosophy has changed?*

*No idea. He may have seen a way to get what he ultimately wanted, and that was through healing.*

*I'll reserve my judgment, then, until we know for sure. Does he look at you like he wants something?*

*I think he's avoiding that—since I slapped him so hard.*

*He never liked to admit his mistakes.*

*Tell me about it.*

~

Jʊʙᴀʟ

I knew who he was. The bastards calling themselves warrior-priests said his name was Vengeance. I knew better.

I considered calling him Merrin, just to see whether there was any recognition in his eyes. He had full power—enough to get us away from here. He didn't have enough sense to use it for anything other than what Kaakos wanted.

I'd already seen what Merrin could—and would—do for Kaakos. When the warrior-priests asked questions about a mythical healer, Merrin would blast them if the warrior-priests weren't satisfied with the answer.

Already, I'd seen men, women and little ones left behind in a burning, charred heap. The stench unsettled my stomach. I wanted to reach out to the one who'd refused to give me help, once he'd discovered I was a spy for the enemy in Az-ca.

I swore to myself if I were ever able to get away from this wretched existence, I'd never do anything else wrong in my life.

Still, it was *her* fault, though, that brought me to this.

Fire bloomed ahead; Merrin had killed another. I cringed and huddled in my chair from the blast of heat that wafted backward, followed by the sickening stench of burned hair and flesh.

I had no doubt what would happen to me should I attempt to hobble away while the others slept. I wore a chain on my left wrist, proclaiming me the property of Kaakos.

Slaves in chains—that's what all his servants were. Slaves who couldn't escape, except for two who'd ran away two days earlier.

I'd overheard the warrior-priests talking about it while they ate—separately from me and from Merrin, who ate by himself in an opposite corner to mine.

We regrouped every day at the same place—a barracks at the warrior-priests' compound. At night, after the evening meal, Merrin would be locked inside a tiny room at one end; that room was reinforced with metal. Should he fire a blast, he'd regret it.

The warrior-priests assumed Kaakos' and Merrin's power came from their Prophet. I wanted to laugh at how stupid and misinformed they were. They were born with it. How Kaakos managed to survive in Ny-nes puzzled me.

I wasn't surprised that he'd come to power afterward. He was inclined to kill anyone who stood against him. I'd learned so much in the short time I'd been his captive. I envied the escaped servants—nobody could figure out how they'd slipped their chains.

Those chains were meant to stay in place until the wearer died. The warrior-priests didn't know how they worked.

Kaakos' power is how they worked, and it angered him that two had thwarted his power.

I wanted to know how they'd done it, because I wanted to do the same.

"Where is the one called North?" The warrior-priest in charge demanded of his next victim. I waited for the inevitable, fiery ending of this one, too.

~

*SHERRA*

"We have suspects, and their villages are marked," Claude unrolled a roughly-drawn map on a table.

Kerok, Barth, Hunter and I examined the map inside the meeting room, the door closed tightly and shielded against intrusion.

No servants would see or hear about this new venture; we'd already seen how Kaakos could infiltrate the palace. Barth and I, following our evening meal the night before, had done our divination, searching for more of Kaakos' gold inside the palace itself.

We hadn't found any.

Kerok breathed a relieved sigh afterward.

"Let's look here, first," Barth pointed out the village closest to the King's City.

"I can take you," Claude offered.

Kerok dipped his head, giving Claude permission. The King wanted to come, too.

*Armon, will you or Caral come to the palace?* I sent. I didn't want the King anywhere near a potential spy without enough guards around him. If Kaakos had supplied weapons along with his gold, we ought to be prepared.

"We'll wait for Armon," I held up a hand as Barth turned toward the door. Hunter, who'd be staying behind, soundlessly agreed with my assessment. Kerok appeared only mildly annoyed.

Less than ten minutes passed before Armon, Misten and two warrior-escort pairs walked in. Kerok recognized the newcomers and spoke to them by name. Caral and Levi stayed at Secondary Camp, to ensure a mindspeaker was left in a position of authority.

"Claude will take us to our first destination," Kerok announced, giving Claude permission to *step* us from where we were.

In moments, we were at the edge of a small village, near the headman's house. Barth pulled the gold nugget into his palm before taking one of my hands. We began our search from there. I closed my eyes as Barth did, to hone in on the signals we were getting.

More than one signal appeared. More than three, then, all shining with purplish malice. Kerok's sudden, indrawn breath let us know that someone was approaching. My eyes flew open to see several men running toward us from a distance.

Misten and I formed stronger shields quickly, when small bombs were flung in our direction by the running men. If we stayed where we were, we ran the risk of getting hurt. I'd dealt with one of those bombs before.

Seven were now flying in our direction.

Forming a bubble shield around all the others, and encompassing their shields with it, I desperately lifted it far above the ground with all of us inside.

*Where did they get those weapons?* Kerok's mindspeak blew into my brain with the force of a storm as the ground exploded beneath us, the reverberation of it battering my bubble shield.

A small shriek escaped one of the escorts as we were flung from one side to the other inside my outer shield; I fought to steady the bubble and hold it in place, so we wouldn't be flung into the distance in a swiftly rotating ball.

The devices flung toward us were so powerful, that had we stayed on the ground, a huge crater would have buried the shields surrounding us.

Kaakos was sending more—and worse—weapons, in his attempts to destroy us.

"Fire," Kerok shouted at Armon. He'd kept enough of his head to realize we needed to kill those tossing bombs at us. Together, they released blasts at seven men on the ground, who were now attempting to toss more weapons into the air at our floating shield.

One such device bounced off my shield after making contact, before exploding on the way back down. Our attackers knew how far to stand back so they wouldn't be affected, and could throw their bombs from quite a distance.

Kaakos had chosen these well.

Seven men scattered as Kerok and Armon fired more blasts.

Three died in that volley.

"Move your shield. Fucking hells, chase them, Sherra," Kerok yelled, as if I didn't realize it needed to be done.

I did chase them, forcing the bubble forward with power and will, attempting to pace the men below. In their haste to get away from us, they left rough sacks holding more bombs on the ground behind them before running faster.

"Hold steady," Armon shouted as the sacks exploded, one after another, their explosions unsettling the air about us and rocking my bubble shield, forcing it upward and making it wobble. Kerok cursed again as he almost fell against Armon.

"Steady it," he snapped at me, anger in his voice as he struggled to stand upright.

Steadying the bubble while flying it was harder than I anticipated, due to the violent air currents created by exploding bombs.

"Draw from me," Misten called out. Connecting to her power, I desperately employed it to steady the bubble while juggling its forward movement with the veering and doubling back of running men who'd reached the end of the explosives they'd carried.

We were now flying over the village itself, and all around us, villagers were coming out of their homes to watch the chase, not realizing they could be in danger.

"Fire," Kerok snapped, the moment the bubble steadied after yet another, sharp turn. He and Armon released blasts against running men.

"Give up," Barth shouted at the spies. That was useless; they understood that if caught, they'd be questioned and then put to death for treason.

Two more died, leaving only two—the youngest and fastest, still running ahead of us, before making another turn to the right. They were running toward a cluster of houses, hoping to keep us from firing blasts into their midst.

"Get us closer," Kerok snapped at me.

Taking a breath, I expended more power to speed up after the turn. I'd never transported more than myself inside a bubble shield, so it was unwieldy at best, and the two pairs of warrior-escorts had no idea how they were being held aloft. Mostly, they huddled against one side of the shield and tried not to get in anyone else's way.

That meant I was forced to fight their movements inside the bubble, in addition to increasing my speed and holding the shield walls steady and impenetrable in an attempt to reach the last two spies before they made it to the cluster of homes.

They'd almost reached the two outermost houses, when Kerok shouted again.

"Fire," Kerok commanded.

Both traitors died in that last effort, one of them continuing to run for a few more feet before he fell and perished in a fiery heap.

~

*Kerok*

"Seven, under your nose, headman." I wasn't complimentary as I paced before a terrified village head. We'd found gold inside his house; Kaakos' gold.

He'd been bribed. Barth verified it by divining the headman's belongings and confirming it in mindspeak between us.

Sherra, Claude, Armon and the extra troops searched seven other houses, finding gold in all of them. This had turned into a proper nest of spies; there were only sixty-seven villagers living here.

Unfortunately, the headman didn't care where the gold came from, and didn't ask. He was going to die for treason, and had no idea that's what he'd done.

"Take him to the lockup," I waved a hand in dismissal at his bluster. "Charge him with accepting bribes and consorting with the enemy."

"Claude and I will see to it," Armon said. "Misten, go back to the palace with Sherra, to help with the report. I'll join you soon. The rest of you, report back to Levi."

Misten nodded; we watched as the warrior and escort pairs *stepped* away, followed by Armon and Claude, who held the headman between them.

"Barth, is there anything else we need to do here?" I turned to my Chief Diviner.

"Unless you want to witness the election of a new headman, we're finished," he said.

"Then we're finished. Sherra?" I turned to her.

"I'm ready." She looked tired—and upset. That wasn't a surprise. I realized I'd yelled at her, forcing her to do things she'd never done before, and was impatient when she didn't get all of it perfect on the first try.

I'd cursed at her, too, when she was doing her best to fly an unsteady ship behind running men.

A ghost of an idea was forming in my mind, however. Something that would certainly bear further consideration—when I had time to think about it. For now, I needed to see to my Queen's comfort and make things better between us.

"I'll get us back," I said, raising a hand before Misten or Sherra could offer. I'd only fired a few blasts, and nothing significant at that, to keep the entire village from burning to the ground.

*Hunter, we're on our way back; we only had time for one village today,* I reported to him, and in my mind, I could envision him taking the scrap of paper from his pocket to make notes.

~

NY-NES

*Kaakos*

They couldn't track my minions in Az-ca, so they'd found a way around it, but how? That puzzle would keep me awake, and that was something I didn't like.

Perhaps—then.

For now, I'd have to find a way to keep my spies out of their hands. Liam said the planes were ready for a trial run. I intended to make that trial run count.

And, while Az-ca's army was busy trying to deal with the aftermath of that attack, I'd tend to other business.

Yes. Attack on two fronts, only on one of them, they'd never see it coming.

I liked that. Very much. It would almost compensate for my sleepless night. "Clean up the mess," I shouted at wary servants, who'd been called into my meeting hall to clear out the remains of four guards and one advisor, whose bloodied bits littered the floor.

I so enjoyed watching them scurry. If I weren't so angry, it would be the highlight of my evening.

∾

*North*

"Here." I set the bag of food on Kyri's lap. She'd settled in a corner of our hideout, her back to the wall as if she expected Kaakos' troops to come running in at any moment.

"Where did this come from?" she demanded, opening the bag to peer inside.

"The vegetables were paid for, from one of the southernmost farms. The meat is alligator, caught in the nearby swamps. I usually take two young ones; the family living nearby will cook both and keep the meat of one in exchange for what I catch. They think I live in the swamp, actually," I shrugged.

"Of course they do." She didn't add that I'd told far too many lies for her liking, and didn't know whether to believe me now. I didn't want to argue about it, because lies were a convenience, at times. I also didn't want her to point out the magnitude of some of my lies and deceptions.

At least I knew they were lies, unlike the delusions that Kaakos fed the people of Ny-nes. Unschooled and ignorant for centuries, they'd been programmed to accept his words as truth.

"Stop rationalizing everything," Kyri snapped at me, forcing Garkus to raise his head.

*You always could read those things in me,* I admitted.

225

*I should have seen what you were long ago, rather than deluding myself,* she countered.

*Yet here we are.* "Shall we eat, or are you going to spar with me all night?" I asked.

"Garkus, there's more than enough for all of us," Kyri began laying out what I'd brought for us.

"I wish Sherra would send us food from Az-ca again," Garkus rose from his place on the floor and approached Kyri and me.

"Someone sent you food?" I blinked. "Someone can come and go at will—and send things through?"

"Hmmph. How do you think I got in here?" Kyri snorted. "I'd have died if I attempted to get through the barrier on my own. I thought I could do it, but when it actually came to it, I knew I was doomed if I tried it on my own."

"Tell me it's the shining woman—the one who tried to stop Garkus from killing Kaakos' warrior-priest."

"That was Arresh," Garkus spoke now.

"Arresh?" I'd never heard that name anywhere.

"Sherra's dreamwalker," Kyri sighed.

"There's another dreamwalker?"

"I see you're a bit behind on the news, then." Kyri's sarcasm was deadly and aimed in my direction.

"She spoke to me—the dreamwalker," I admitted. "I was hidden behind a mirror shield. She saw me anyway."

"Too bad she doesn't know everything about you," Kyri pointed an accusing finger. "She'd probably come back and make you as dead as you pretended to be."

"You're saying she could take me on?" I argued in disbelief.

"Nobody knows what she's capable of doing. Not really." Kyri's words made me go still. "I got a message from Doret earlier. Not only did Sherra transport herself and nine others in a floating shield, but she managed to sail it along like a flying ship so two warriors could fire at fleeing spies who attempted to run away. Those spies were tossing amplified grenades at them, too, and she kept the shield steady and strong while the warriors fired their blasts."

"You're lying. She'd have to drop her shield to get the blasts through," I said.

"Like I said, behind on the news," Kyri tossed out a hand, as if she found me hopeless.

"It's true. I've seen it myself," Garkus shook his head. "If the escort is talented enough, she can get the feel of her warrior's power, so his blasts will go through her shield while it stays up and strong."

"That's—that bears consideration," I rubbed my chin while working through the logistics of it. "Can you contact Sherra?"

"She's not exactly pleased with me for wanting to come here." Kyri turned her head away, as if the admission shamed her.

"She took me out of a jail cell—at least her dreamwalker did—and brought me here to protect Kyri." Garkus didn't like his admission, either.

"She changed his skin color," Kyri pointed at Garkus. "So he wouldn't be marked from the beginning."

"That's not a simple spell," I said. "Who taught her?"

"Nobody taught her that. Her dreamwalker knows things that Sherra doesn't, I think."

"Is she teaching others how to do the shielding spells and such?"

"She's teaching people as fast as she can, but some of them are opposed to the training. There was an attempted coup in Az-ca," Kyri frowned at me. "Ruarke tried to kill all of us. He'd have succeeded without Sherra and Adahi standing against him."

The moment she said Adahi's name, she wished to take it back. I saw it in her eyes and the stiffening of her body.

She and I knew Adahi's body lay in Kaakos' palace. I went still. "His dreamwalker survives." My words were flat.

"Yes. I will never tell him that you survive. I cannot begin to imagine his anger if he learns of it."

I turned away this time. Adahi's death shamed me and Kyri knew it. At least a part of him lived, still, but he could never come to Ny-nes again. If he did so, his dreamwalker would be pulled toward his moldering body and all of him would die.

The other thing I knew was something Kyri would never say—not

227

in front of Garkus. Adahi's life meant more to her than mine ever did. A deep chasm lay between us and betrayal washed through the bottom of it, creating an ever-widening gulf.

She had her goals and was willing to give her life to achieve them, just as Adahi had a goal of helping her and keeping her alive.

He'd kept his oaths; I'd failed in mine.

That was in the past. Now was the time I'd foreseen—to complete my self-appointed mission of destroying Kaakos.

"An uneasy truce, then," I dipped my head to Kyri. "It's your choice whether you tell Adahi or not."

"You know you're safe enough here," she spat at me. "He comes to you now, all of him perishes. Convenient, don't you think?"

"So you're not going to tell him."

"No. Unless there is no other way, and I greatly dislike not being honest with him."

"As do I."

"You can take your dislike and shove it up your ass," she said and *stepped* away.

"Is she going back to Az-ca?" There was longing in Garkus' voice.

"No. If either of you attempt to *step* past Kaakos' power grid, you'll fry in it."

"Good to know," Garkus rumbled and bit into a chunk of alligator meat.

~

*KEROK*

"Tell me how you did it—for the records," Hunter said as Sherra and I had our evening meal with him and Barth.

"It would be easier to write it out for you—tomorrow," she said. She'd refused a marching draught when we returned to the palace. Armon and Misten had given their reports to Hunter already, before going back to Secondary Camp.

Barth had written his own accounting and given it to Hunter. I'd also scribbled notes, so I could make my report as accurate as I could when I gave it to Hunt.

I'd attempted to coddle Sherra upon our return, but she'd brushed off my gestures and set about making sure the gold was sealed and shielded inside a heavy metal box in the treasury. Then, she sat with Armon and Misten while they gave their reports to Hunter. She barely glanced my way during the meal.

*What did you do?* Hunter sent mindspeak. He'd certainly noticed the silence between Sherra and me.

*I yelled, when I didn't have to,* I said.

*Then it's your fault.*

*It would seem so.*

Grae had never shut me out like this, but I considered that perhaps she was afraid to stand up for herself. She'd go quiet at times, but never refused to speak with me or turned away my advances.

I felt guilt, too, because Grae's birthday had come and gone, and I hadn't laid flowers.

After all, you don't rip out parts of your life, just for the convenience of other people. Yes, I knew I was being petty, but I'd been Commander of the army far too long to change old habits.

*I see the look of belligerence on your face,* Hunter pointed out. *Your father would get the same look, at times.*

*Did my father deal incessantly with the distraction of every underling's needs and wants?*

*Constantly.*

"I'm done. I have work and thinking to do," I rose, tossing my napkin on my chair and stalking toward the door.

⁓

SHERRA

"I'm tired. My apologies, Hunter, Barth," I nodded to both before rising from the table. Kerok had shown his anger and impatience. I wasn't willing to make it worse by snapping at his closest advisors.

Kerok's shouting earlier in the day had come back to haunt me more and more as the day progressed. He didn't need to yell; I was already trying to do what he wanted. No, he didn't know that, but he'd chosen to vent his frustrations anyway.

He was angry; I was angry. We were angry together. That meant I wanted to sleep apart. Heading toward our suite, I intended to snatch up clothing and make my way toward my mostly unused personal suite.

*Sherra?*

A new voice. I realized my dreamwalker had heard it before, however.

North.

*Well, well,* I snapped at him. *What do you want?* I wasn't in the mood to be charitable to any man. Not tonight.

*I just wanted to see if you remembered me.*

*My dreamwalker does.*

*Ah.*

*Is there an emergency?* I asked.

*No. I just wanted to let you know that Kyri and Garkus are with me, now.*

*Good. I hated that she'd gone to the palace. That was suicide, in my opinion.*

*Mine as well.*

*How did you survive in Ny-nes with power?* I demanded.

*Gets right to the point. I can't tell you that,* he countered. *It's—inconvenient.*

*Then why did you contact me? Other than to see if I'd answer?*

*I was wondering if you'd take Kyri out of here if I asked.*

*Just like every other man I know,* I flung at him. *Only civil when it suits them. Only speaking when they want something.*

*I don't want it right now—I meant if it became necessary to get her away to save her life.*

*I'll consider it,* I said. *And not because you asked, but because she's important to me.*

*And I'm not.*

*I have no idea who you are. I owe you nothing, including a proper conversation. Go away. I have things to do.*

*Very well.*

I wanted to tell him to fuck off, but I didn't. Instead, I strode into the King's suite, pulled clothing from drawers and the wardrobe, then *stepped* to my private suite. Let Kerok complain about my flaunting the law to an empty room.

~

KYRI

At least they'd left me a portion of alligator meat. I found it when I finally returned to North's hideaway.

I'd come to the realization that whether I liked it or not, we were probably safer together, rather than apart. I longed to send mindspeak to Adahi, to consult with him on recent developments, but that would require that I tell him about North.

It made me ill to contemplate it.

I'd spoken to Doret, though. She suggested I launch a fireblast at North when he'd least expect it. The worm kept a shield about himself at all time, however, so it wouldn't do much good.

I didn't tell Doret that North expected her to come, rather than me. He should have remembered that Doret's first target was Ruarke, with Kaakos a close second. At least that was one less weapon in Kaakos' arsenal.

A part of me wanted to point out that it had taken Sherra and Adahi to take down Ruarke. Shoving that thought away, I lifted a piece of alligator meat and bit off a healthy chunk of it.

*erok*

I'd laid lilies on Grae's resting place before breakfast. I'd spent the night alone; Sherra had gone to her personal suite to sleep.

"Sherra went to Secondary Camp for breakfast," Hunter informed me when I took a seat at the table. Briar poured tea while frowning.

*Was every woman in the palace against me, now?*

"She wrote her report last night. She gave it to me before she left this morning," Hunter added.

Then she was sleep deprived, just as I was. A part of me felt vindication. Another part felt shame.

Today, of all days, I missed my father a great deal. I wanted to talk to him about this. He'd give good advice, too. Perhaps it would have been advice I didn't want to hear, but needed anyway.

General Weren, another good source of advice, was also gone. "How did we lose so many good men?" I asked aloud.

"What?" Hunter was surprised by my sudden change of subject.

"My father. General Weren. Too many others to count. All lost—either to disease or the enemy."

"Are you deliberately leaving out the women who've died—from disease and by the enemy's hand?"

"No. Fuck no," I moaned and covered my face with both hands. "I just," I dropped my hands to blink at Hunter. "I need advice from a married man."

"That makes sense." Hunter pulled the butter dish toward him. If Sherra had been here, she'd have taken half of what was on that small plate already.

Neither of us would have begrudged her that. "Did she say anything else to you—other than she was going to breakfast with Armon and Caral?"

"Nothing. It isn't like her to talk about—those things. Not with me."

Without Hunter's admission, I knew she wouldn't discuss those things with others, either. She'd sworn a vow—to keep my secrets, as I kept hers.

I wondered how well I was doing in that department. "What else is on her calendar, today?" I loaded bacon onto my plate.

"Supervising the young ones in Cole's village."

"Ah." That meant she'd be gone all day, and likely come home exhausted.

Again.

"I was hoping to go out with her and Barth—to another village, looking for spies," I said.

"If you think Kaakos' other spies haven't heard rumors on the events of yesterday, then I think you're fooling yourself," Hunter pointed his fork at me. "I've already asked Claude to watch for people leaving villages abruptly, once the news is spread that spies were killed yesterday."

"Good thinking." I crunched into a slice of bacon. "Give any information collected to Barth and me. I'll make sure someone is sent to look into it. Let Barth know that we'll go to another quadrant tomorrow."

"Done," Hunter said after his eyes unfocused for a few moments. "Do you, ah, want me to let Sherra know, too?"

"Please."

"I will."

"Claude is here to see you, my King," a guard tapped on the open door. "Three others are here with him."

"Send them in," I said. We were going to receive verification on Hunter's speculation; I had no doubt on the matter.

Claude stepped in, followed by the other quadrant leaders.

They'd all come. My skin began to prickle—this didn't look good.

"We all have the same report," Claude sighed. "Last night or early this morning, reports of deaths have come to us. Deaths of otherwise healthy men—in violent ways. All appear to have exploded. A search in only a few of their houses produced the same thing." He pulled a small leather pouch from a pocket.

I'd seen too many of those in the past few days.

*Kaakos' gold.*

"He killed his spies?" I almost choked on the words.

"Once he learned we could find them, I think. I have no idea whether he left any alive. I think you'll have to determine that, my King."

While I gaped at Claude and my mind went numb, Hunter took over. "I'd like names of the spies and their villages," he told Claude and the others. "For the official records. Collect the gold; we'll distribute it to the villages as fairly as we can afterward."

"We'll see to it," Claude dipped his head to me and then to Hunter, before he and the others left the room.

~

*Sherra*

"Do you think things feel off because you're tired?" Caral asked. Armon didn't speak, but I didn't miss the tightening of his mouth, either, when I said I didn't sleep the night before. I'd spent the time writing a report for Hunter, instead.

"I'm not sure," I said. "But something definitely feels off to me." I didn't tell them that Kerok and I were having an angry standoff, although I think Armon knew it anyway.

"When? When did this feeling start?" Levi asked.

"About an hour before sunrise, I think. I just felt—anxious, for some reason."

Without a word, Armon drew something from a pocket and pushed it toward me. I knew what it was without asking. He'd gotten it for himself, most likely, but offered it to me, instead.

A part of me studied the paper-wrapped marching draught with revulsion. Another part wondered whether my dreamwalker might handle things better than I could—if the uneasy feeling I had turned into an actual event.

"I'll take it," I made up my mind quickly, before I had second thoughts. Once it was dumped in my tea, I drank the draught-laced brew.

"I'm sending Levi and Caral with you today," Armon said after I set my empty cup on the table. He and Misten were supposed to go; it was their turn.

He was weary from yesterday, too, and I only realized that now. Not from physical exertion, but from the stress of it. We'd all been thrown into a new, nerve-wracking experience, and had come out somewhat worse for wear.

Kerok's shouting hadn't helped, either.

Armon was used to being as competent and confident as any warrior could be on the battlefield.

Flying above a village while chasing bomb-tossing spies hadn't gone smoothly—to put it in mildly-acceptable terms.

The process needed work—in a practice setting, rather than perfecting it on the fly.

"What are your plans for the day, then?" I asked Armon.

"The King wants to meet with the chosen candidates."

Here was the real reason Armon wasn't going to Cole's village with me. "Good luck, then," I said.

"Are you intending to let the young ones try what we did yesterday?"

"Maybe. We'll see. You know they'd be excited about it."

"Young ones usually are, if handed an opportunity to try new things."

"Armon, make sure they're the right choices—the ones you're meeting with. We don't need to be chasing after spies who can send fireblasts against us from beneath," I floundered for the proper words.

"Understood." Armon's eyes were hooded. Neither of us wanted to say too much, in case we were overheard.

"Are you taking the four who went with us yesterday?"

"Yes."

"Good. They didn't cause trouble in a tenuous situation."

*His words upset you, didn't they?* Armon sent.

*Armon, don't ask me about that.*

*You did an amazing job with what you had to work with,* he told me. *Thorn will recall that soon enough, I think. If he hasn't already.*

*Right.*

*This has bothered him greatly—the fact that the enemy has too many spies among our own people. People willing to sell us out for a bit of gold, when the army has been risking—and giving—our lives for years to keep them from harm. It isn't a good way to show your appreciation, you know.*

*I know. Do you think it doesn't trouble me just as much? We've only just developed a way to track those traitors. Now they're likely hiding in the deepest holes they can find, after learning what we did to the ones we found yesterday. That doesn't include the heads-up that Kaakos has gotten. You know he'll retaliate in some way.*

*I expect so,* Armon dipped his head in a slight nod.

*We just heard from the Quadrant Leaders,* the unexpected mindspeak came from Hunter. *They're reporting dead spies everywhere, and the search for more exploded bodies continues. Thorn may want you and Barth to help in that search.*

*I'll be ready,* I replied. No need to take my anger out on Hunter, who was the messenger. Kerok, on the other hand, was a coward for not telling me himself.

Well, coward might be too strong a term. He didn't want to get into a shouting match with me, no doubt, so he'd elected to tell Hunter what he wanted from me instead.

"Levi, Caral, are you ready?" I asked both aloud. "We have a lot of work to do, today."

"We're with you." Levi stood quickly, followed by Caral.

"Thank you," I told them. Squaring my shoulders, I gathered power to *step* them to Cole's village.

~

*ARMON*

Misten and I stood guard behind Thorn, as he informed the small group of troops chosen for training. Any who declined would be noted and watched, I knew, but that couldn't be helped. Wend and Marc, sitting on the front row, gave us nods of encouragement. They'd stand with us, even if nobody else would.

"You're saying that this has already been successful?" A captain raised his hand when Thorn opened the floor to questions.

"In a limited experiment," Thorn replied. "Quite successful."

It wouldn't take much for the troops to make the leap to Sherra and her hand in all this. I waited, my breaths shallow, to see if any blowback would come from that realization.

"You say this will enable us to attack Ny-nes?"

"Yes—that is the plan," Thorn said. "I realize that can be a frightening concept, but we have spies there, now, who can relay information regarding locations, installations, and numbers of enemy troops. That information must be guarded with your lives," he added.

Several nodded at the King's words. He'd warned them about the sensitive nature of the information he would give them, and offered them the opportunity to leave right away if they felt they couldn't keep secrets.

Nobody left.

"Who did you send?" Someone else raised a hand.

"I can't tell you that—for their safety and yours," Thorn said. "In addition to the combining of shields and blasts, there are other—

things to experiment with. Yesterday, two warrior-escort pairs experienced it first-hand. I hope they see the potential in it, just as I do."

"May I speak freely, my King?"

Captain Indus, one of the warriors with us the day before, rose from his seat. My breath caught. Whatever he said could make or break us, here and now, should Thorn allow it.

"Speak your mind, Captain Indus," Thorn nodded.

"I witnessed the downfall of Ny-nes, yesterday," Indus turned to face those gathered about him. "Not the actual downfall—that is yet to come. What I saw—a rounded shield, carrying us aloft and keeping us safe from bombs while we chased treasonous spies on the ground, is no doubt what can make us victorious against the enemy. You all know he sent a flying machine against us. If we are successful in the things the King asks us to do, we will also fly in the face of the enemy, and show him what we are truly made of."

For a moment, everything was so still I could hear Misten breathing beside me. Until the troops rose as one and cheered.

~

*KEROK*

I never realized how frustrated the troops had been all those years, fighting back the enemy on our own soil.

*And only on our soil.*

After determining that all present wanted to learn whatever they could to make an attack against Ny-nes possible, we invited them to gather their things at Secondary Camp and meet us at one of the empty training grounds in the King's City.

Armon would let the others know that these were on special assignment. They were more than pleased to be training in the King's City, too.

"Better chow," Armon grinned after witnessing their excitement at the newly assigned location.

"No," I replied. Armon understood I was teasing.

"You know this training depends on Sherra," he said, his words sober.

"I know." I scuffed the heel of my boot against the concrete floor of the abandoned mess hall where we'd met. "Did she talk to you about yesterday?"

"She refused to talk about it. I guessed it, though. She will never do anything or say anything that will paint you in a bad light, Thorn. You should know that already."

A part of me did know that. "Armon, you know as well as I do that every relationship has its ups and downs."

"I do." His words were dry.

After a moment's reflection, I considered how foolish it was to say that to someone who'd been bonded for sixteen years.

"I'm sorry—that was stupid." With a thumb, I rubbed a throbbing area above my left eyebrow, where a headache was forming.

"I think it would be better if you said the same thing to Sherra. Not that I'm offering advice or anything."

"I suppose I should say it soon; I need her to start training them tomorrow. I'll have to ask Cole and some of his to come, to help her."

"I wish I could get away to do it, too. I suppose I'll have to rely on her teaching me after hours or a couple of days a week," Armon sounded wistful.

"You'll take to it faster," I said. "You have since the beginning. You, Levi and your escorts. I'm sure Sherra will give you special attention, too. Without yelling at you or making you feel like an idiot."

"Coming around, then?"

"I see a very deep, contrite apology in my future," I said.

∽

*SHERRA*

"Like ducks to water," Cole laughed as we watched Anari, Laren and Kyal floating above us in their own bubble shields.

"We'll have to raise turbulence beneath them when they're more comfortable—so they'll learn how to make adjustments," I said. I'd gotten the worst version of the same lesson the day before, and it still left me in a sour mood.

"They can take turns holding the shield and combining blasts," Cole sighed. "I can't wait to see that happen."

"Call them down, and ask them to do it now," I suggested.

～

*ANARI*

I never thought I'd be able to fly through the air like a bird. Laren and Kyal thought it was the best thing we'd ever learned, and we'd learned a lot.

When Cole called us back to the ground so we could practice flying together, Sherra taught us something else, too.

Something that everyone with power needed to know.

"This is your line," she'd said, while we closed our eyes at her bidding. She'd looked inside each of us, showed us our power, and then the line that we shouldn't allow our power level to drop past, or we could die.

"If you ever wanted to know how power is burned out of someone, this is how it's done," Cole explained, once our eyes were open again and we were staring at Sherra in shock.

"Most warriors and escorts who die on the battlefield, die because the escort's power has been drained past that point," Cole said. "When that happens, and the enemy bombs are still dropping, it's easy to see how they'd die—unless the warrior is able to get himself away in time. Until recently, the escorts weren't trained to *step*. Or fire blasts, or several other things."

One of Kyal's hands gripped mine as he stared at Cole. "We're not letting that happen to Ani," Laren declared.

Sherra ducked her head. I realized after a moment that she was hiding a smile. Not because she found it funny, but because she agreed with Laren.

"So, when they burn the power out of someone," I began.

"Then they're just like anyone else—who doesn't have power," Cole said. "Most of the time, that happens before a sentence is levied against wrongdoers."

"Can their power be restored?" Kyal asked.

We knew the power had been muted in Jeen and Ferni. We also knew, because Cole told us, that they'd sided with the enemy. The enemy killed them himself, because he didn't want to let them answer the King's questions.

He said Sherra saw what the enemy did to them. Even though they'd broken the law, she still didn't like what happened to them. Cole wouldn't tell us how they'd died, only that they had.

"The power has been restored to many who washed out of the army in the past," Sherra said. I could tell she held something back, though. I wondered what it was, or whether she'd ever tell us.

"Now, since you all have mindspeak," Cole said, going back to our lessons, "It's up to you to tell each other when your power levels are low. You can make adjustments if that happens, or break away from the battle or whatever, if need be. You can all *step*. If you are all nearly drained, I suggest combining your remaining power and *stepping* away together."

"I think we can do that," Laren agreed.

~

*Sherra*

*I didn't want to tell them that Kaakos managed to restore power to criminals in Az-ca—from his palace in Ny-nes, I told Cole when he asked. That's frightening enough for adults to know.*

"I agree with your assessment," Cole's response was soft. After Anari, Kyal and Laren successfully floated a shield together, and fired a few blasts at piles of rocks on the beach, we'd let Caral and Levi practice floating their own bubble shields with the young ones. As I imagined, both found it easy enough, once I'd touched them to show them how.

"Even if you were to walk from here to Ny-nes, these shields will allow you to cross the wide river," Cole said. We watched Caral laugh as she moved her shield this way and that, playing bubble-shield tag with Anari.

Levi was grinning like a fool, swiftly moving his shield along the shoreline while Kyal and Laren chased after him.

"We'll have to teach those floating into Ny-nes how to get past his barrier," I said.

"I think a few may be up to that challenge. I doubt all will be able to accomplish that feat," Cole advised. "You may have to set a separate shield around the ones they construct, just to get them inside."

"Excellent idea," I said. "Sounds tiring," I added.

"I would imagine so, depending upon how many times you're forced to do it. I hope some of mine will be able to learn from you—well enough to help."

"I think they're planning to start training the troops tomorrow," I said. "I'd like for you to help with that. If you want, choose a few others to bring with you. They can help us teach what they already know. On some things, though, we'll all be learning at the same time."

"What time do you want us there?"

"Meet me for breakfast. I think I can manage a few extra spaces at a table, somewhere."

"Perhaps in the garden? We don't see those types of flowers often."

"I'll set it up. Let me know how many are coming."

"I can tell you now—I'll bring five others with me."

"I think Armon and Misten will be there, too, so we'll have at least nine at breakfast. That means another table. I'll ask Hunter to make the arrangements."

"Anything else?" Cole asked.

"I think," I said. "Yes. I probably should have considered this long ago. I keep worrying about Ani and the boys. Will you mind if I put up another, special shield around your village?"

"Not if it's for the purpose I imagine."

"I'm hoping I know enough about Kaakos to keep him away from here—and away from all of you, if he thinks to target Laren or Kyal. He failed with those two girls, so I hope he'll forget Anari exists. Merrin never knew the extent of her abilities anyway. He likely assumed it was one of the boys who *stepped* them away. Unless I'm very wrong, much of Kaakos' information came from Merrin."

"I think the same," Cole agreed. "If Kaakos invades a mind, he can strip away every thought and action, if he so chooses. It requires direct contact, I think, but he is capable."

"Is something wrong?" Cole's eyes narrowed as my hand went to the collar of my uniform, attempting to loosen it. Suddenly, I'd felt warm, and then hot.

Hunter didn't have time to call for help; my dreamwalker streaked to the surface of my consciousness and *stepped* to the palace in a blink.

*KEROK*

"Get back," I shouted at the guards, while facing a raving lunatic that had once been Hunter.

"You will die," Hunter hissed at me, his words spitting saliva in my direction. It wasn't his voice.

This was deeper. Menacing. Hunter's transformation had happened between one breath and the next. My heart raced as I considered what needed to be done—the necessary thing that would snuff out the life of perhaps my closest friend and ally.

"No," Sherra screamed as she landed near Hunter. He turned toward her, Kaakos' eyes peering through Hunter's pupils.

"Ah. The putrid Queen of Az-ca," Hunter's face contorted into an ugly grin. "Come closer. I wish to kill you myself."

"Sherra, no," I launched myself in her direction, as her hand reached out. Before I could stop her, her hand had connected with Hunter's forehead.

I will never forget the screams as long as I live—hers and Hunter's.

"WE'VE MADE THEM COMFORTABLE—AS comfortable as we can, inside the lockup," Barth set a glass before me, then poured a generous dollop of whiskey into it.

Neither had awakened after Sherra touched Hunter and both had screamed as if their lives were ending.

Cole had followed Sherra here; he paced in the garden, waiting for news that could be good or bad.

I doubted it would be good, and we'd be forced to kill both of them.

"I have word from Kyri," Adahi appeared inside my study, where I sat, fingering the glass of whiskey.

"What word is that?" I asked, my question little more than a growl.

"Planes are missing from the manufacturing facility in Ny-nes," he said. "I think they have been sent in our direction."

"It could take days to get them close enough to fly them into Az-ca," I mumbled. Lifting the glass of whiskey, I drank it in three swallows.

"Not if Kaakos expended his power to get them very close," Adahi warned. "He thinks to attack us on two or more fronts, at the very least. He killed his spies, then attacked Hunter. That is one front. As for the other; those planes could be in the sky now, flying toward us, if they aren't here already."

"Barth, get Armon in here. Cole, too."

"Right away."

~

*ARMON*

We'd been so full of ourselves, thinking our plan to attack Ny-nes was a good one. Solid. Until Kaakos attacked us, first.

We thought to surprise him. He'd surprised us, instead. I had little doubt that our killing a few spies the day before had somehow shoved his plans forward. Killing his spies after we'd found a way to locate them? It was prudent enough—if you were Kaakos.

We were moving too fast for him, and the only way to deal with that was to level his arsenal of attacks first. No doubt, he'd read in

Hunter's mind exactly what our plans were, and there'd be no surprise coming from Az-ca, now.

Cole told me what Sherra said to him earlier—that Merrin had supplied information to Kaakos, willfully or not.

Hunter was Merrin's uncle. Kin. Merrin knew too much about Hunter, making him a target for the filth sitting in the seat of power in Ny-nes.

Why hadn't we realized this before?

*Colonel Armon, the King wishes to see you.* The message came from Barth.

*On my way,* I replied.

When I arrived in Thorn's study, I found Cole and Barth also there. As was Kage, Thorn's assassin.

"No," I said aloud, focusing on Kage. He'd been called for one reason only; *in case two we loved had to be destroyed.*

"Armon," Thorn said, holding up a hand to stop my protests. "I need you to take the troops now in the city and deploy them around the eastern and northern borders. We believe Ny-nes is sending planes packed with bombs against us. Cole, will you bring some of yours, too?"

"How do you know this?" I demanded of Thorn, my heart thumping a painful, irregular beat in my chest.

"The spies we have in Ny-nes," he replied, lowering his eyes. The King looked worn. Defeated. Barth poured more whiskey into a glass for Thorn.

"What about?" I couldn't say their names. Couldn't. Fear gripped me—more so than it had in years.

"We wait—for a little while. If the worst becomes known to us, well." He shrugged.

"Fuck." The word escaped my lips before I could stop it.

"Did Caral and Levi learn how to make the flying bubble shields?" Thorn went on, still refusing to meet my eyes.

"Yes, my King." Caral had been overjoyed by it, as had Levi. That joy was very short-lived.

"Good. We may need to train quickly. You understand why."

"I do."

"Go. Spread your troops. Look for signs and sounds of an attack. If you see or hear anything, report it to me immediately."

"It will be done, my King." My standard reply sounded angry.

"Go, then," Thorn sounded just as angry. "Do your duty, as my Commander of the army. And I will do my duty, as the King of Az-ca."

Without thinking I dipped my head to the King, then turned and stalked toward the door. My job was difficult. I wouldn't trade it for Thorn's, no matter what was offered. Depending on the outcome of this night, my respect for him could crumble.

~

*DORET*

"Let me see her, you oaf." I attempted to shove my way past a guard burly enough to be a sumo wrestler. Not that anyone living in Az-ca at the moment would know what a sumo wrestler was.

Except for Adahi—and he couldn't be counted among the living anyway.

"Let her through," the chief guard barked at the blockade masquerading as a sentry. Brushing past him, I walked the few remaining feet to Sherra's cell. It was located beside Hunter's—they'd kept them together, in case, well, in case.

*Kyri, they're both unconscious,* I reported, once I stood outside Sherra's cell.

*Tell me Thorn is waiting until they wake to do anything drastic.*

*That's what Adahi says, too. He's with Thorn, now, but he says the King's assassin is in the King's study with them.*

*Fuck.*

*I'm worried Kaakos will take them,* I said.

*Like he took Jubal?*

*Yes. And we know what he did to Merrin.*

*I think Jubal is still in his right mind, although that isn't saying much. I'm sure Kaakos couldn't wait to get him out of his sight.*

*What does North say?*

*I haven't told him.*

*Kyri, this is Sherra we're talking about. And Hunter. If he knows anything useful.*

*I'll tell him when he's done healing this woman.*

*Kyri, you can send mindspeak. Tell him.* Now.

∿

*KYRI*

*I hate to interrupt, but there's been a development in Az-ca,* I sent. I almost used his real name, too, and that would be a mistake.

*The planes can't have gotten there yet,* he grunted, pulling the leg to settle the bone back in place, while Garkus knelt behind the woman to hold her still, both arms wrapped around her waist.

*That's not the problem. Kaakos took Hunter over, and Sherra tried to stop it. They're both in the lockup now, and unconscious.*

I watched as light glowed around his hands, bonding the pieces of bone together.

*Unconscious, you say?* He stood, patting the woman's shoulder and nodding to Garkus to let her go.

*Yes.*

*That's not the worst news, I suppose. They could both be awake and raving, right now.*

*Doret wants to know if you have any ideas or suggestions. We can't lose Sherra.*

*Yes, you can. You've known that all along—that none of us are invulnerable. Adahi fell, and he was powerful. Kaakos made short work of him, I think.*

*He was protecting me.*

*As you say.* "The leg will be fine in three days," he said aloud to the woman and her family, who now crowded about her. "Try not to walk on it until then."

*You're telling me there's nothing we can do?*

*I'm saying that in order to intervene, someone would have to connect with one or the other of them, and help fight Kaakos' power with their own. Even long distance, his mind is powerful. I have no hope for your friends.*

*Fuck you,* I snapped. Turning away, I broke into a run to get away from him and his vile, insufferable logic.

∾

*ARMON*

"We don't have any idea where those planes could be coming from?" Caral studied my face as if she were looking for clues. She, Misten, Levi and I were in the training camp commander's office in the King's City. In the barracks nearby, every elite warrior and escort waited for my command.

"There aren't enough troops in the entire army to cover the perimeter of Az-ca." Levi pointed out what I already knew.

"Then what's your suggestion?" I barked at him, before reeling in my temper.

Levi knew I was upset. He also knew why I was upset, because my fears were his, too. "I think," he began, "that Kaakos targeted Balsom for a reason. It's flat there. Might be a good place to land a plane if he had too."

I went still as I considered Levi's words. "Levi," I breathed after a moment, "You're a genius." I kissed him without thinking about it, then shouted mindspeak to Claude.

*I'm sending warriors to Balsom,* I informed the Quadrant Leader. *Get those people out of there, and from any other villages close by. The enemy is on his way.*

*On it,* came Claude's reply.

"Gather the elite troops," I snapped at Caral. "We're going on a special mission."

∾

*KEROK*

"The bodies are jerking. I think they're having seizures," the physician reported. Adahi's eyes narrowed as he sat across from my desk, as if assessing my reaction to this news. One glimpse of Barth showed

248

me a stone-faced Chief Diviner. He disagreed with my assessment—but wouldn't speak it aloud.

Kage stood near the door, waiting for me to give the word.

Perhaps I'd dallied long enough. Kaakos had my rose and my Crown Prince in his grasp. Neither would wish for the fate Kaakos intended. If this happened to me, I hoped someone would grant me the same mercy of a quick death.

"Let's go," I said, abruptly rising from my chair.

Adahi cast a dark look in my direction before disappearing in front of me.

"We'll walk out of the palace," I said, choosing to ignore Adahi's exit. "Then *step* from the courtyard to the lockup."

# CHAPTER 17

*erok*

When we arrived at the lockup, I found Doret there already, staring at Sherra through the bars of her cage. Sherra writhed as if in pain upon her bunk, while Hunter, in the adjoining cell, only jerked now and then.

Kaakos had turned his full power against my Queen. I was forced to make a decision I never wanted to make.

"Be ready," I nodded to Kage, who lifted his hands to form blasts.

"No," Adahi appeared before me.

Why had he disappeared for a short time, if he were planning to be here at the last anyway? It no longer mattered. "Stand out of the way, Adahi. We have to do this and you know it."

*ARRESH*

Had anyone ever gotten this intimate with Kaakos—and survived? I worried I wouldn't, and that meant Hunter was lost as well.

Kaakos' mind was a roiling mass of poisonous, murdering snakes. The pull exerted against me was like a vortex, sucking me toward dark, evil waters. Already, I'd seen parts of his psyche as he struggled to control me; repulsive was too mild a term. If my body had been conscious, perhaps I'd have vomited my revulsion.

"She's suffering," I heard a voice in the distance. "Get out of the way."

"Thorn, I disagree with this course of action," someone else argued.

"You will wait," another voice said.

I knew those voices. No time to be concerned about their intent; Kaakos required all my strength to struggle and maintain against him.

"Stop," a third voice. A woman's voice. "You'll die."

A laugh.

*Daughter*, one of the voices connected with me, then. I felt his energy sliding alongside mine. *Connect with me*, he coaxed.

Adahi. My energy welcomed him. He'd help us. We—he and I—had stood against Ruarke, with Kaakos coming in to take over at the end.

Adahi would stand with me, to remove this evil. Somewhere, behind us, Hunter's energy languished inside a shield I'd built around him—I'd barely forced Kaakos away from Hunter before he turned his attention on me.

To Kaakos, Hunter was inconsequential, next to the Black Rose Queen of Az-ca. I was almost as good a prize to him as Kerok would be.

Killing or taking me would harm Kerok, too, and that was another of Kaakos' desires—to hurt Az-ca as much as he could before destroying it.

I heard Kaakos' voice, then.

He knew. *Adahi, old friend, come to die entirely? At long last?* Kaakos sent.

Adahi didn't respond.

Had I known what he planned, would I have stopped him? Like the blinding blast of the bomb that almost destroyed me in the past, Adahi burst his energy between Kaakos and me, throwing my spirit back and sending Hunter with me.

I recall screaming, I think, before losing consciousness again, only this time, no enemy waited there for me; only blackness.

~

*Kerok*

"Adahi sacrificed himself. Just as he did years ago, to save Kyri in Ny-nes." Doret sat on a chair on the other side of the bed. Sherra lay between us, unconscious again, but whole, according to Doret. The former queen had flung the rest of us aside and touched Sherra after Adahi released his final blast of energy.

Hunter had been saved, too.

Doret said Hunter was the worst off, as Kaakos had infiltrated his mind and attempted to force him to do unspeakable things, once he had control.

It could take a while for Hunter to recover.

*If* he recovered.

"You're saying that Kaakos killed a ghost?" I demanded.

"Shh. Not so loud. She'll wake on her own, or should, if you'll keep your voice down."

*Kaakos killed a ghost?* I repeated in mindspeak.

*Kaakos didn't have anything to do with that. Adahi expended the whole of his energy in a single surge. He chose it. It's like suicide for a dreamwalker, I think. He did it to shove Sherra and Hunter away from Kaakos' grasp.*

She turned away from me; her hand reached up to touch her face. She wept, and didn't want me to see.

Adahi was truly gone. A part of me felt empty. Another part was grateful. The last part was furious.

Furious that Kaakos had done this.

I still hadn't heard from Armon, either, regarding the planes Kaakos was sending. "Nobody can take on Kaakos single-handedly and defeat him," Doret whispered. "Adahi attempted it. As have—others. All have failed. It will take more than one, and a great deal of power to bring him down."

*We're flying bubble shields, to watch for the planes,* Armon sent mindspeak at last. *It took a bit to get some of ours on board, but they're floating quickly across the skies on the eastern edge of Balsom, now, keeping watch.*

*Armon, you are a genius,* I replied. He'd figured this out, when I couldn't.

*How is Sherra?* He sounded afraid to hear the answer.

*Alive and sleeping. Adahi sacrificed himself to save her—and Hunter. Doret says Hunter may be damaged because Kaakos held him longer, and he couldn't fight that darkness as well as Sherra could.*

*That is—that is terrible news,* Armon replied. *About Adahi, and Hunter. My heart feels joy for Sherra, however.*

*Mine too, and it's not the most comfortable place to be—joyful and mourning at the same time.*

*I'm getting a report,* Armon interrupted. *Levi's the actual genius. He had a feeling they might head for Balsom. It's clear there, and yes—we can now see the planes in the distance. I think they intend to land in that flat area, recharge batteries and then attack tomorrow.*

*Take them down tonight,* I hissed.

*We'll do as much damage as we can, my King. Cole brought in the three young ones from his village, too. They are better-trained in this than the others. Unless the enemy suspects somehow that we're here, they won't know what hit them.*

*Do it. Keep your people alive, Armon. We need all the troops we have when we attack Ny-nes.*

*It will be as you say, my King.*

~

*Anari*

Cole was inside our bubble shield as Armon directed us toward the flying machines. Somewhere, on the opposite side, Armon, Levi, Caral and Misten did the same.

Other troops were behind us as backup; they didn't have the training we did in flying a bubble shield or combining their blasts.

*Young ones,* Cole informed us in mindspeak, *we need to fire from a safe distance. Those planes carry bombs; I'm sure of it. Once the blasts are fired, we must* step away. *We can always* step back *in to fire other blasts if needed.*

*Do Armon and Caral know that?*

*I have informed them,* Cole said. *Armon is waving the other troops back, and telling them to step away, once blasts are fired. My hope is that one successful hit will make all three planes explode, since they're close together.*

*Wait, Armon is sending the others away,* Cole reported. *He says that one plane caused the enormous blast last time. There are three here. Young ones, I will step us away the moment we fire our blasts. I think I know where to take us, to watch from a distance and return if need be to deliver another blast. Armon is doing the same. He will let us know when to fire. Concentrate on uniting your power. Anari, hold the shield and make it stronger if you can.*

*I will,* I said. It meant Kyal and Laren would have to combine their blasts with Cole's. I would hold the shield alone, with only a thin connection to Cole, so he could get us away together.

The planes had almost arrived between our bubble and Armon's in the distance; Cole reported it.

*Fire,* he snapped.

The combined fireblast burst away from our bubble, while Cole *stepped* us far away.

❧

ARMON

We weren't far behind Cole and the young ones, landing in the burned remains of Jubal's cabin. Far in the distance, we watched the enormous fireball as it mushroomed high into the night sky.

I hoped the nearest inhabited villages were safe; we hadn't had time to evacuate all of them—only Balsom and a few others that were too close.

*They've been destroyed, my King,* I sent mindspeak.

*Thank you, Armon.* Thorn's words held a grateful sigh of relief.

❧

NY-NES

*Kaakos*

"We only have one more plane ready, Supreme Leader," Liam bowed to me. "It is in the northeastern facility. We'll have to bring it here to install batteries and load the last three bombs we have."

"Then you will do that," I said. My head throbbed with pain from wrestling with the black rose and then being thrown back by Adahi's last expenditure of power. I'd have had the bitch queen, too, if that fool Adahi had stayed out of it.

I had no idea how they'd learned of the planes we sent, and managed to bring them down before they could land and recharge.

No matter; they wouldn't expect this one—I'd see to it myself. Shield it myself. Make sure it reached its destination myself. I wouldn't be satisfied until it dropped its bombs over the King's City of Az-ca.

I'd seen the bomb crater left by the previous bomb we sent— through Ruarke's eyes. A plane with three bombs would not only destroy the King's City, but everything around it, too.

"Make it ready," I growled at Liam. He bowed again and walked away. "Bring my physician," I shouted at the guards. Running footsteps sounded immediately.

∼

*North*

"They have one more plane and three more bombs." I flung myself to the floor of our hideout, weary from a night of reconnaissance.

"I suppose it was a foolish hope that those three were all he had," Kyri whispered. "We should know by now that he always has a backup plan. Where did you find it?"

"There is a small facility far to the northeast. I found the plane there, after almost deciding it wasn't worth the trip. The bombs and the batteries are in the city."

"He'll have to bring the two together," Kyri observed.

"I need time to think about that," I said. "Admit it—if we destroy it here, he'll know for sure there are spies and not just a rogue healer and two escaped servants."

"I'll let Doret and Adahi know."

"You do that. I need sleep."

~

*KYRI*

Had I known what news Doret would tell me when I contacted her, perhaps I'd have chosen to wait.

Forever.

Adahi—gone from us for all time, his dreamwalker sacrificed to protect Sherra and Hunter.

North lay nearby, his breathing even as he slept. He wouldn't see the silent tears I wept for an old friend, who'd given one life for me and another for the Black Rose Queen of Az-ca.

*We'll keep watch on the last plane,* I finally sent to her. *North says if we try to destroy it, Kaakos will know there are spies in his city.*

*I'll inform the King,* Doret's mental voice sounded weary and troubled. Neither of us said it, but we both knew Kaakos wouldn't stop until we were all dead.

~

*ANARI*

Cole told us to rest after the night before. He was doing the same. That's how Kyal, Laren and I came to be sitting together beneath a tree, staring westward toward the ocean.

"He said there were two men in each plane, and that they weren't normal men. He said the enemy was controlling them in some way, and their job was to kill us." Kyal shivered against me as he repeated Cole's answer to his question.

"Do we know whether any villagers got killed in the blast?" Laren asked.

"I didn't ask him that—he shooed me out of his house and told me to get some rest."

"I sent mindspeak to Sherra, but I didn't get a reply," I admitted. "So I tried Doret. She said Sherra was sleeping and couldn't get back to me. The sound of her voice made me worry that there's something wrong."

"We fought the enemy last night, and they're still keeping stuff from us," Laren grumbled.

"I know." I leaned my head against his shoulder. In moments, he laid his cheek against my hair. Kyal scooted closer on my other side, and eventually, we fell asleep like that.

∾

*KEROK*

Late afternoon, Sherra opened her eyes. Hunter woke mid-morning, but his words were jumbled. Briar fed him by hand; he ate and fell asleep again.

*Similar to those with stroke symptoms*, the physician said. He'd been called the moment Hunter awoke, only to watch jerky movements and slurred, incomprehensible speech.

Had Adahi sacrificed himself, only to bring Sherra and Hunter back like this? Almost too afraid to speak, I opened my mouth to ask how she felt.

Doret beat me to it.

"How are you feeling?" Doret asked.

"Adahi's dead." Sherra closed her eyes again, while a tear coursed down her right cheek.

"We know, sweetums," Doret soothed, brushing tangled hair away from Sherra's forehead. She knew not to tell Sherra that I'd asked Kage to end her life—and Hunter's.

"Hunter?" Sherra refused to open her eyes again.

"He's not perfect yet. We'll do our best to get him back to full strength. We fed him; he's sleeping again. We'll feed you, too, if you'll open your eyes and stop blaming yourself for this mess."

257

"I feel sick."

"Because you haven't eaten," Doret countered. "Thorn, make your-self useful and get one of those servants of yours to bring a meal—something easy to digest."

"Kerok?" Sherra's eyes opened and blinked to bring me into focus. I stood behind Doret. The look my Queen gave me was a hard one.

*She knew.* I had too many things to feel guilty about, not least of those that Adahi had done what I should have at the beginning—connected with her and added my strength to hers to get them both away.

I hadn't done that, or even considered it.

"I'll send someone to the kitchen right away," I said, and like a coward, I walked out of our suite.

~

LATER, Barth sat with me at the garden table, while we had tea and talked about the night before.

I needed advice from Hunter and Adahi. One was certainly lost to me; the other could be, too. Only time would tell on that quarter, and I'd have to search for another heir.

"You need another assistant—a good record keeper—while Hunter recovers," Barth interrupted my thoughts. He didn't add that the job could become permanent, if Hunter's mind was compromised. "Sherra is all right?" he added.

"I believe so. She sounded like herself when she woke."

"Good. Very good."

Again, Barth didn't voice his thoughts—that I'd ordered Kage to kill her the night before. Hunter, too. Adahi had refused to accept that sentence for them, and intervened. "I feel like a failure," I said.

"Most of us do, at one time or another," Barth replied. He rose, stretched, and then *stepped* away. I had no idea where he'd go, but figured he had thinking to do.

~

*DORET*

I sat in Cole's tiny kitchen, at his table, drinking tea. This time, I'd brought a box of tea to him, to replenish his supplies.

"I should have known what his reaction would be," Cole said, turning his cup in his hands. "A request for a volunteer or perhaps more than one—someone could have connected their power to Sherra's. I know Caral and Misten would have provided extra energy, with no questions asked."

"He's the King."

It was the only reply I had for the situation, lest I turn my thoughts and accompanying profanity loose. "The young ones were asking for Sherra. They don't know anything—yet." I turned to a different subject.

"I'd like to keep it that way, but you know how curiosity works. We'll have to explain things to them—in the least vile way possible."

"I should have connected with Adahi before he went in. We all may have survived that way." I voiced my version of guilt in the matter.

"It happened too quickly," Cole said. "Adahi didn't ask for help, and someone had to hold off the King's assassin."

"I should ask Sherra about her battle with Kaakos, when she's better," I said. "We don't know whether either of them had the upper hand, and I'm sure Sherra was using part of her strength to shield Hunter."

"I believe he'd have died as those others did, had she not protected him."

"Like Jeen and Ferni, you mean."

"Yes."

"That would be horrible."

"That means she was fighting Kaakos on two fronts rather than one, dividing her strength. Adahi's intervention was appropriate and timely, I believe."

"I told Kyri about Adahi. She didn't take it well."

"Neither do we. Shall we go find the young ones, now, and explain things as best we can?"

"I'll come," I said. "This is going to be hard."

~

*ANARI*

Laren's arms were wrapped about me, and Kyal was very close to both of us as Doret and Cole told us what happened—or almost happened—to Sherra.

"Hunter—what will happen to him?" Kyal asked. We'd liked the Crown Prince very much. To hear he might never be whole again was frightening.

We didn't know much about Adahi, and had only seen him a few times. He was dead, now. He'd died to save Sherra and Hunter.

They'd carefully left out what the King—Sherra's husband—was doing during this time. That worried me.

"Hunter will be given all the care necessary to recover. If things aren't exactly the same as before, then he will still be cared for, as the brave man he is," Cole said gently.

"Do you think we can do something? To make the enemy know we stand against him?" Laren's chest rumbled against my back as he spoke.

"I think he knows that already—he knew when we destroyed his planes last night," Cole gave us a rare smile. "And we will do the same again, if it is required. I will be going to the King's City tomorrow, to train others to do what you three did last night. In this, you are far ahead of them."

"Will we still be able to practice?" I asked.

"Not only that, but I think you can help the others here in learning the same thing. We need to be prepared, do we not?"

"We get to teach?" Kyal sat up straighter.

"I think I just said that," Cole laughed. "You know what to do—practice tomorrow, and then train others after that."

Our joy was shared in near-mindspeak—we'd discovered that we could share our emotions as well as our words.

"Thank you," Kyal sounded breathless. "We won't let you down."

"You haven't yet," Cole said, reaching out to tousle his hair. "Keep working hard. Everything you've done until now has certainly paid off."

~

*SHERRA*

I was exhausted and only wanted to sleep more. Pottles forced me to eat something. Kerok hadn't come back once he'd left to order food.

I had mixed emotions about that. I knew what he'd done the night before—he'd told Kage to kill Hunter and me. Hadn't waited until he knew for sure we were beyond his reach, just arbitrarily gave the order.

If Adahi hadn't stepped in to help, we'd have died at Kerok's hand before I had a chance to turn my full attention to Kaakos. If Hunter hadn't required my strongest shield after forcing Kaakos out of his head, I may have put up a better fighting front.

"You have that look on your face," Pottles said when I stopped eating.

"What look is that?" I dropped my eyes to stare at the scrambled eggs on my plate.

"The one that says you're furious about something."

"I heard him, Pottles. What do you think I should feel about that?"

"Heard who?"

"Kerok. Last night, when he ordered Kage to kill Hunter and me."

"Ah."

"You were there; I heard you arguing with Adahi."

"I see." It was her turn to drop her eyes. "Your body was convulsing, Sherra. As if you were having a seizure. We didn't know what to think of that, other than to assume that Kaakos had taken both of you."

"Trust me—if he'd been able, I'd have died last night. I can't say I was winning, but we were deadlocked. Adahi's connection to me forced us apart. Now Adahi's dead, because nobody else thought to help."

"I doubt any of us would have known how to help." Pottles sounded regretful. "How did you force Kaakos away from Hunter?"

"My dreamwalker did that. He didn't expect us to fly into Hunter's mind like that, and knock him away. Of course, he corrected for that immediately after, and grabbed onto me while my dreamwalker was building a shield around Hunter's mind."

"Deadlocked, you say?"

"We were certainly at an impasse. I felt and saw the vile, black evilness that is Kaakos. His mind was a writhing nest of poisonous snakes, to me."

"You saw his mind and you're sitting here, talking to me?" She sounded incredulous.

"Yes. When Adahi connected his power to mine, I thought we were going to extricate ourselves together. Adahi had a different idea." I felt like crying when I spoke about his sacrifice. He called me daughter. No other man had done that, not even my own father.

"Thorn wants to train the special troops beginning tomorrow," Pottles sighed. "He wanted to do it today, but other things have prevented it."

"You mean he wants me to teach them," I said.

"Yes. I understand he hasn't approached you on the matter. He did ask me to send a message to Cole, however, and he will certainly be here tomorrow."

"Then Cole and I will handle it. Feel free to pass that message to Kerok."

"You don't want to tell him yourself—and yell at him at the same time?"

"That will take energy that I'm unwilling to spend on him."

"Ah."

"I want to see Hunter, too. When he's awake again."

"I'll see what I can do."

"Make it happen, Pottles."

"I'll make it happen."

～

*KEROK*

*I need to see you*, Doret sent mindspeak.

*I'm available now—in my study.*

Ten minutes later, she let herself in after a brief knock.

"Please sit," I offered a chair. "Would you like tea?"

"I'd take tea," she agreed and settled on one of the chairs opposite me. "I also have news on Sherra. First off, she heard you order Kage to take her life, last night."

"I figured that out." I busied myself with moving things on my desk that didn't require it.

"Then she took me to task for arguing with Adahi when he came to help."

That surprised me; I jerked my head up to stare at her. "What did she say? Exactly?"

"That we should have thought to help her, and we didn't."

"But Kaakos," I said, feeling angry.

"Her dreamwalker didn't hesitate to thrust herself between Kaakos and Hunter's mind—she said that she surprised him by jumping in like that. And she said that she had to expend power to keep a shield around Hunter's mind, while she managed to wrestle Kaakos to an impasse. I have no idea which of them would have ended up on top, but Adahi turned the tide in our favor."

"By making the ultimate sacrifice."

"She said that she thought he was only going to add his power to hers, allowing them to get away from Kaakos. Instead, he forced them apart by exploding the last of his energy."

"Do you feel as if you've lost an important battle?" I baldly asked Doret.

"Yes. I was already feeling guilty. This makes it worse."

"As bad as it is for you, mine is a hundred times worse. You didn't order her death. I did."

"I should have thought to help, and I didn't."

"Same here."

Tea was brought in, so we watched while it was poured and sipped in silence for a while.

"She wants to see Hunter when he's awake."

"I need to see him, too. So far, only Barth and the physician has seen him."

"Then let me know—I'll be the one standing beside you, in case he finds us guilty, too."

"There may not be enough of him there to level blame against anyone."

"I heard about that."

I didn't tell her that Barth was barely speaking to me. My fears kept me from asking if Sherra would see me—or talk to me. I owed her an apology before this happened. Now, things were so much worse.

*Armon, I need to see you,* I sent. *And Levi. Come for dinner. We'll talk.*

*Is Sherra well enough to see visitors? I and a few others would like to see her.*

*I'm sure she'll want to see you, although she may still be tired. Come anyway. I need advice from an old married couple.*

~

Secondary Camp

*Armon*

"I don't know exactly what happened," I said. "I'm afraid to ask anyone else." Levi had asked me why Thorn needed advice now—from a married couple. I'd already told Levi everything I knew, but I still didn't know what happened during Sherra's struggle against Kaakos. If Thorn wanted to discuss that, I had no idea how to respond.

I only knew that somehow, Adahi had stepped in to help her break away from that evil bastard. Adahi was dead—for all time, I suppose. "I'll leave Captain Neele in charge and we'll go to the palace as requested. I'm hoping Sherra will be awake so we can talk with her."

Marc and Wend would normally be left in charge, but they awaited training in the King's City. I had to depend on another backup in the meantime.

"Sherra could have died." Levi leaned his head on my shoulder.

"I know." I rubbed his back. "She's still with us, though. I'm grateful."

"I don't know if I can take any more of this."

His words shocked me. "Levi, what are you saying?" I gripped his arms and pulled him around to face me.

"Things are so different than before. Back then, we had a known enemy, and we lost friends, I admit that. But this—I don't know how to keep doing this, Armon. Without going crazy with it."

"Because we've never been this involved with others? Is that what you're saying?" I pulled him into a hard embrace.

"Some. Yes." His answer was muffled against my chest. "There's just no end to it, and it keeps getting worse."

"My love, stay the course with me through the attack on Ny-nes. I don't know how fast we can make that happen, but Thorn is more than determined, now."

"What if we don't survive it?"

"I wondered the same thing every time we fought a battle with the enemy. We'll either get through it or we won't."

"What if we don't?" Levi whispered.

"We stand or fall together, as it has always been," I told him. "If it comes to that. In the meantime, I think I'd like to meet your family."

"Really?" He pulled away to look at me.

"Really."

*Ny-nes*
*Kyri*

"Does he know how much he resembles?" Garkus didn't say the name. He meant North, who'd left to gather more food.

"I have no idea if he knows, and I'm not about to tell him," I said.

"It's uncanny," Garkus mumbled while walking away. *Uncanny.* To someone who didn't fully understand, it was a good description. I still hadn't told North about Adahi. I held back because I didn't want to see the indifferent censure in his eyes. He wouldn't care. Hadn't cared the last time either, that was obvious.

Adahi. So many times, I'd leaned on his judgment. Gone seeking his advice. I'd shared mindspeak with him often, during my imprisonment inside Kaakos' boundary around Ny-nes.

If I ever made my way back to Az-ca, and that was a big if, I would celebrate Adahi's long life and erect a memorial in his name. I promised him—and myself—that much.

Sherra and I—we needed to talk about Adahi, too. I wanted her to know things that he'd held back. Things he never wanted her to know, but that she deserved to know.

"Food." North set the bag down nearby. "We even have some bread, this time."

Bread. It was almost magical, that word. Wheat didn't grow well in many parts of Ny-nes. Kaakos kept a close watch on its production, and the biggest part of it went to the palace to serve him and his warrior-priest flunkies.

"The raver crossed the river last night," North went on as he settled, cross-legged, on the floor to divide the food in three portions. "If the people weren't already scattering, they started when that news reached them."

"There are too few of them left in the city, and most of those are thieves and cutthroats," Garkus rumbled as he took a seat on the floor opposite North. "If the King of Az-ca ever thought to attack Kaakos, then now would be a good time."

"Welcome to the second stage of my plan," North grinned at Garkus, before pushing his share of food toward him.

"What was the first stage?" Garkus asked before biting into the small loaf of bread he'd been given.

"Getting the people to trust him by healing them, and then sending them out of the city," I said, taking an empty space on the floor between Garkus and North.

"What's the next stage, then?" Garkus spoke around a mouthful of bread.

"That should be obvious," North shrugged. "Confront Kaakos and destroy him. Of course, I'm waiting for Az-ca's troops to arrive to distract his army, first."

"An army without power won't last long, unless they have a stock-pile of bombs and weapons," Garkus said.

"They do have those things."

"Where?"

"Don't get any ideas," I snapped at Garkus. "If we destroy that stockpile, it needs to happen just before those troops arrive, and not a second before. Doing it now will turn Kaakos' attention back to us. It's likely he already suspects we're here, after he took over Hunter."

Garkus stopped chewing. North's small loaf dropped to his lap. Both blinked at me in shock.

"I guess you didn't see that, then," I said, lowering my eyes.

"Tell me," North commanded.

"Kaakos invaded Hunter's mind," I began, staring at my hands and the cracked concrete floor below them. "Sherra was the only one who tried to stop it. I don't know the full story on that, but Adahi came to lend his power to Sherra's, to get them away from Kaakos' grip. Adahi blasted the entirety of his power between them, killing himself for all time, to release Sherra and Hunter."

North closed his eyes as if that news pained him. I didn't believe it for a moment. He no longer had that sort of emotion left for old friends and acquaintances. He only had his self-appointed mission, and that was all there was to him, now.

"Are Sherra and Hunter still alive?" Garkus asked.

"Yes, although Hunter's mind may never be whole again. I have that news from Doret."

"Does Kaakos now know everything Hunter did? Did he occupy his mind long enough to see that?" North demanded.

"I don't know. Doret said it was only moments, as she understands it, before Sherra's dreamwalker came to help Hunter. Before that, he was threatening the King."

"Fuck." North stood and walked to a far corner of the room.

"Does this mean we can't surprise Kaakos with an attack? Does he know for sure who we are and that we're here?" Garkus was worried, too.

"I don't know," I confessed. "I'm hoping Sherra will connect with Hunter soon, to learn what it is Kaakos took from him—if she can."

"How much damage did he do to her? Does anyone know?"

"Garkus, you surprise me. I'd almost think you've come from being a misogynist to a believer in a woman's power," I said.

"I've been thinking about what it took to get us here," he admitted, hanging his head. "And the mistakes I've made, and the fact that she showed up the last time, trying to stop me from making another. And," he went on, "I've watched you and North heal people. I had no idea that was possible. I thought the power was only used to fight others."

I didn't ask him to fully explain his change of heart. I didn't want to hear it. Adahi's death still weighed heavy, and I blamed North for holding his help back in Adahi's first death.

Sherra was probably blaming herself for Adahi's second death. I considered that I should contact her in mindspeak soon, to tell her that Adahi always made his own choices, and she had no part in it.

"Eat," North was back, dropping onto the floor again next to his pile of food. "We have things to do tonight."

"What things?" Garkus asked.

"We have a raver to kill," North growled and stuffed food in his mouth.

~

*J*UBAL

I was sick to death of all the killing, and even sicker of the stench of burned bodies. Most of those we found had no acquaintance with personal hygiene, and that made it worse.

My terror at being killed overrode my desire to get away—that and the fact that my new overlord had placed limits on what little power I had left. I'd learned that only recently, after trying to start a fire beneath a canopy while more rain poured down.

There'd never been a time when I couldn't form a few sparks to make a fire. That small act was now beyond my capability. If I'd ever wanted to murder anyone, outside my worthless escort, anyway, it was the one who'd snatched me away from Az-ca.

I was forced to include one other in my murderous desires; the raver who now stalked narrow tracks between temporary homes across the river. Maybe I ought to include the warrior-priests who held the raver's leash, too—more than once, they'd told him to kill the children of the adults already burned to death—because nobody wanted to take care of the orphans they'd created.

We had to rely on the army for our food, here. There wasn't an easy way to transport provisions from the storerooms that supplied the palace and the other warrior-priests under Kaakos' thumb.

At least we'd gotten regular meals before. Here, we relied on an army, in which we were an afterthought—they were too entangled in an attempt to stop the mass exodus away from Kaakos' city.

We didn't have a comfortable place to sleep, either, and often relied on what was abandoned by fleeing families, or were forced to ask for a place on one of the large boats the army used to cross the river.

A large dock, built from logs, extended into the water from the far side of the river; the warrior-priests led us over it, toward the huge boat anchored there. The two who pushed my cart heaved its wheels over the uneven surface toward the vessel, jarring me and making my bones ache.

I knew not to hope for a comfortable bed at the end of this; the beds on the boats were hard surfaces with perhaps a blanket laid atop. I hated myself for ever believing that what I'd had in Az-ca were unlivable conditions.

"Get that thing to the back of the boat," a commanding officer shouted at the warrior-priests. He'd caught sight of the raver and wanted nothing to do with him. "Take the rest of yours with you; I'll have someone bring your meal. You can sleep on the deck, too. I'll see if there are extra blankets."

If Merrin were still in charge of his senses, he'd probably have turned the officer to cinders for being disrespectful. Instead, he was herded past the man with barely a glance in his direction.

How had Kaakos done that—reduced a powerful warrior to nothing more than an animal that only acted upon command? All my life, I'd imagined an enemy much like us, who was afraid of us.

This one—I had no idea whether he was afraid of anything. His ability was formidable, and I doubted whether anyone in Az-ca really knew what they'd fought against for centuries.

"Get out." My cart stopped next to the back rail of the boat. They never helped me, either; they expected me to crawl out of the contraption on my own, which I found difficult and generally painful.

On this end of the boat, too, the reek of what they called fuel offended my nose. I was used to cleaner air, and I'd had trouble breathing from the moment I'd been set down in Kaakos' palace.

Once I'd disentangled myself from the cart, I limped to the back rail to stare at the water. As one might expect, it was filthy, filled as it was with soot, leaking fuel, debris and the occasional floating body.

No wonder nobody bathed—the lack of clean water was a real problem in Ny-nes, if all their streams and rivers were like this.

When the boat was hit the first time, it jarred me from my thoughts. It felt as if it had been hit by a fireblast, and shuddered in the water as the noise of the explosion almost deafened me. When smoke and flames billowed high on the other end, I realized that's exactly what had happened.

*Someone had fired a blast at us.*

Who else in Ny-nes could do that, other than Kaakos? Another blast hit the front of the boat, causing men to scream and many of them to run—I could hear shouting and the echoes of scrambling feet as they ran toward the dock and an escape from the boat.

"Bring him," a warrior-priest commanded my cart-pushers. They rushed toward me, ready to heave me away from the rail and into my cart so we could also flee the burning hulk.

That's when three appeared before us, blocking our way. I blinked. One of them could have been mistaken for Garkus, except for his skin color, which was as pale as mine. Another, he looked—no. That was only my imagination, hoping that someone thought to help me.

The other—the woman? I had no idea, and wondered why she'd come with the men, as she'd likely be useless.

"Kill them," the chief warrior-priest shouted at the raver, who lifted his hands to perform his duty.

Before Merrin could form massive fireballs, the three who'd come fired blasts at all of us.

It took six tries before the raver's shield was broken, but it broke, and he died a fiery death, just as the warrior-priests around him did.

I was the only one left standing, and that didn't last long. My useless leg dropped from under me first, and I hit what remained of the deck—hard.

"Come on," the one built like Garkus snapped, lifting me from the deck and flinging me over his shoulder. "He said to bring your sorry ass, so I'm bringing it."

❧

*Kyri*

"That's the healer?" Jubal asked in disbelief, after Garkus set him down in our hideout. Jubal's chain had been removed earlier, and dropped into the river not far from the burning remains of the boat.

"Yes, I'm the healer." North approached Jubal, placing an even stronger shield about him than Garkus had. "I've shielded you from detection—that means Kaakos' mindspeak cannot reach you and he cannot use other talents to locate you. He'll assume you perished with the others on the boat. I blasted it and the dock before we left. If any went into the water, they'll likely die in a few days, it's so filthy."

"Thank you for saving me," Jubal's eyes were on the floor.

"Oh, don't thank me. You're a traitor to your people, and I won't hesitate to fry you myself if you don't prove useful, or if you alert the enemy to our location."

"Here is food," I took what I hadn't eaten earlier to Jubal. "Eat. We have clean water, too, but that's all we have to drink."

"Thank you." Jubal wasn't used to saying those words, I could tell.

"I'd prefer to kill you now," Garkus hissed at Jubal, whose head jerked up to meet Garkus' dark gaze. "Filthy spy."

"Calm down, Garkus," North held up a hand. "We need to ask Jubal some questions about Kaakos."

Jubal's mouth worked, but no sound came out. It was obvious he recognized Garkus' name, if not his face.

❧

*Sherra*

"I don't like this," Kerok grumbled as he paced at the foot of Hunter's bed. I hadn't asked his permission to touch Hunter; whether he said yes or no, I intended to do it anyway.

"She has him shielded," Pottles sniffed at Kerok. He wasn't in her good graces at the moment, either.

"But she's weak," he tossed out a hand.

Weak or not, Hunter was more so. His eyes bore the blankness of someone who failed to recognize his surroundings. I wanted Hunter back. The Hunter I'd known and come to love.

Kerok and I needed to talk, but I was still too angry with him to have that conversation. I had no idea when I'd be calm and rational enough to have it. "Hunter?" I reached out to touch his hand, searching for his power.

I'd connected with him before, to show him how to shield and several other things. I felt it after a few moments had passed, but it was so weak and fragile, it terrified me. It was as if he'd been emptied —more than any drudge or washout had been emptied. This— Hunter's power had been scoured from him, leaving barely a trace of it to tell anyone that he'd ever had it to begin with.

I could attempt to restore his power—when mine was at full strength again. I didn't want to do that unless Hunter regained his mental stability.

Kaakos had sucked the power away from Hunter—I understood that, now, to assist him in his attempt to fight off Adahi and me.

Adahi may have understood that. I didn't until now. I'd shielded Hunter's mind against Kaakos, thinking that's all that was needed. Kaakos had resorted to draining Hunter's power instead.

*Bastard.*

"I think I'd like to blast the person who came up with the idea of pulling power away from someone else," I said, letting go of Hunter's hand. "Along with the one who came up with the idea of invading another's mind to control them."

"What did you find?" Pottles asked.

"His power is completely drained, and he doesn't recognize any of us right now."

"Fuck." Kerok rubbed the back of his neck.

"Do you think he'll recover?" Pottles looked worried.

"I don't know. When I'm better, I could try to restore his power, but I don't want to do that if he's still having other problems."

"I command that you not restore it until he's whole," Kerok said.

I rose when he spoke, and turned to look at him. "Fuck you," I said and *stepped* away.

～

I FELT weak as I stood next to Cole on the training ground, watching hand-selected troops form and fly bubble shields. It was a good exercise to get them proficient. After that, they'd work on combining shields and blasts. It was no surprise that Marc and Wend were leading the pack in perfecting what they'd learned.

"You really shouldn't be here today," Cole pointed out. He and I watched and listened as Levi, Misten and Caral shouted instructions to floating troops.

"Probably, but I just said *fuck you* to the King, so I had to go somewhere."

"Then your exit was the best solution, I'm sure."

"I'm glad you agree with me."

"I do. Will he know to come looking for you?"

"I don't care whether he does or not."

"You love him," he stated flatly. "Don't you?"

"Maybe not today."

"I think he's worried."

"He tried to kill me."

"I know." Cole shook his head. "I think it came from the right place, but we'd all be lost if he'd gone through with it."

"Came from the right place?"

"He didn't want you to suffer. Just as he didn't want Hunter to suffer. Kaakos is an evil, and nobody with a kind heart should be subjected to that."

"I came in contact with a part of that evil," I admitted. "It was horrible."

"And if the King had all of his sense with him, instead of allowing his fear to rule his head right now, he'd be here, telling you everything would be all right."

"I shouldn't be talking about this," I sighed.

"Yes, you should. To someone you trust. I hope I've earned that from you."

"You have. I just hate discussing personal matters."

"It will never leave my mouth," he said. "Your secrets are safe here."

"I'm grateful. I just feel—like I'm adrift on the wind," I said. "That everything that tethers me to those I love has been cut away, and I can't make a connection again. Like they've deserted me, somehow."

"They're afraid," Cole said softly. "For you and of you—for now."

"That's not comforting."

"I know."

"Thank you for speaking the truth," I told him. "Even though it's not the easiest thing for me to hear right now."

"I have news from Kyri," he said, surprising me. "She says that Merrin is now dead and they've captured Jubal. They're holding the spy for questioning. She says they may execute him for his crimes after they learn everything he knows about Kaakos."

"What would he know?" I was puzzled by Cole's words.

"He has been a spy for years—and has mindspoken with the enemy on uncounted occasions. Something useful could have been revealed in that time—or in the time he was taken from here to serve Kaakos directly."

"That sounds logical, I guess. I'm just so angry about his treason against us. Who knows what he's told them over the years? How many deaths he's caused, because he provided information?"

"I feel the same way. Had he known where to find my village, it could also be in peril."

"That's too awful to consider," I said. "Did Kyri say how Merrin died?"

"She says that North, Garkus and she went after him, killing him, the warrior-priests who guarded him, and sinking a boat filled with enemy troops. They snatched Jubal away at the last moment, to make Kaakos believe he perished with the others. He is now so heavily shielded, even mindspeak cannot pass through to him."

"Are they trying to turn Kaakos' attention away from Az-ca?" I asked.

"It could be. Or, perhaps it is in retaliation for Adahi's death. Kyri cared deeply for him, as you know."

"I know. So did I. Did she say that? That she wanted to retaliate? It could place her in danger."

"She said North chose the action, and she and Garkus agreed with it."

"Strange."

"True."

"Sherra. Cole." Barth appeared nearby.

"Barth?" I turned toward him.

"Thorn insisted that I be the one to come looking for you."

"Oh."

"While we are here, outside his presence, I want it known that I disagreed with him the entire time."

"I know. I heard you," I said. "Thank you for that."

"You heard us talking?"

"Yes. I heard it all. Clearly."

"If I were prone to using profanity, I believe now would be a good time for it."

"What does the King want? Other than for you to find me?" I asked.

"He asks that you come and have dinner with him. So you can talk."

"Right now, I don't know that I have any kind words to say."

"I understand. Tell him that."

"You want me to tell him that?"

"Sometimes it helps to speak the truth."

"He's the King, Barth. He holds the power in Az-ca."

"He also listens to reason. When you tell him the truth, make it as reasonable as you can. In other words, instead of calling him a pig, tell him he hurt you. I believe Armon and Levi are also coming, to offer advice."

"That won't be uncomfortable," I said.

"Ah, sarcasm. It makes the world turn, does it not?" Barth dipped his head to me and disappeared.

~

*ARMON*

I had no idea we'd be walking into a near-standoff between Sherra and Thorn. Yet there she was, sitting on the opposite side of the King, while there were places laid between them for Levi and me.

This would be uncomfortable, I think, for all of us. I wanted to tell Thorn that this was a mistake.

Instead, I nodded to Levi to take his seat, while I pulled mine out and settled on it. "Thank you for coming," Thorn told me. "I think I'd like to talk about our attack against Ny-nes, and whether you think Kaakos now knows that we plan to come against him."

Levi visibly relaxed, then. We could talk about the army's involvement. Neither of us felt comfortable giving relationship advice while both parties glared at one another from opposite ends of the table.

Servants walked in to set plates of food in front of us. Once they were dismissed, Thorn began to speak again. "Earlier today," he said while cutting into the pork on his plate, "Sherra connected with Hunter. His power has been drained, he doesn't recognize anyone, and there's no way to tell whether Kaakos pulled important information away from him before Adahi intervened."

"Even so, Hunter didn't have the date of an attack, because we hadn't made a decision, yet," I said.

"And that gives me some hope," Thorn said. "I worry that he'll find a way to keep us out of Ny-nes when we go—some way to trap or kill us when we attempt to cross the boundary."

"I can get past his boundary—now," Sherra said, refusing to look at Thorn.

"And I worry that he'll change something, to prevent it," he countered. He also refused to look at Sherra, concentrating on spearing green beans with his fork in grim determination.

*Your food isn't the enemy*, I sent to Thorn. *Neither is your Queen.*

"I think we should have a conversation with those in Ny-nes—our spies," Levi suggested. "They'll probably know such things before we will."

"I don't have direct contact with any of them," Thorn admitted. "Sherra may have access."

"I can reach them." Her voice was a low grumble—she didn't like being pulled into this conversation, which had turned into a strategy meeting. "Doret would be a better choice to talk with them."

She wasn't pleased with Doret at the moment, either.

"Will you go get her? Tell her the King needs her services," Thorn said.

"Be happy to." Sherra rose and dropped her napkin over the plate of food she hadn't touched, before stalking out of the small dining room.

"She's so mad she could spit," Thorn sighed when enough time had passed. He rolled his shoulders; an indication of how stressful this was. "She heard me telling Kage to destroy her and Hunter," he admitted. "I thought they were suffering and in Kaakos' grip, so I did what I felt I had to. Adahi was the one to shove me aside and do what needed doing."

"I think your heart was in the right place," Levi said cautiously. "It was a judgment call."

"Which turned out to be the worst sort of judgment," Thorn wiped his face with a hand. "I confess, if I were in the middle of a power battle with that evil filth, and overheard somebody talking about killing me as if they were discussing the weather, well."

"It likely didn't help that it was the one person she loves more than anyone else," I said.

"Yes, although that probably isn't the case any longer."

"You don't know that." Levi tore his roll in half to butter it.

"No. I don't think I know much at all at the moment. What I do know is this; if he'd come for me instead of Hunter, she'd have done the same thing—come tearing in to help me."

"You're the King; you have a position that is larger than any single life, no matter how dear it is," I told him.

"This is where it gets shameful," he admitted. He'd stopped toying with his food and sat there, clenching and unclenching his hands.

"What's that?" I asked.

"I'd have done whatever it took to get Grae back—including fighting Kaakos at the time."

"You weren't King, then."

"I don't feel like a King, now."

"You're saying you'd rather have Grae?" Levi lifted an eyebrow as he leveled his gaze at Thorn.

"I—don't know. I don't know anything anymore. Grae would never shut me out like this."

"Because that made things simpler for you." Levi bit into his bread.

"Grae never had the power or intellect that Sherra does. I'm sorry to say that, because I cared for Grae, too," I said.

"Then what's your advice, Armon?" Thorn sounded bitter.

"If you desire the lightning, you must also prepare for the storm."

*NY-NES*

*Kaakos*

"We do not know how the boat sank—we only saw lightning about it—from this side of the river," the warrior-priest messenger reported. He'd walked through heavy rainfall to reach the palace, and now dripped on the marble floor beneath my high seat.

I already suspected something had happened—I couldn't reach Jubal in mindspeak, and my connection with Vengeance had been broken.

My raver was dead, along with the warrior-priests around him, and an entire boat had been destroyed.

Of all those things, the loss of my raver and the boat made me the angriest. Neither would be easy to replace—if they could be replaced.

"You don't suspect an attack?" I battered the warrior-priest with the force of my question.

"We could not tell from our position across the river." He kept his head bowed before me while his hair continued to drip water on the floor.

"Then go find out," I said. "Send someone in to clean up this mess," I thundered as he turned to leave.

"Supreme Leader?" Someone else had arrived while servants ran around him like rushing water around a rock to clean the floor.

"What is it?" I wasn't pleased that he'd come unannounced, and looked almost as wet as the last one.

"You received another message—like the one before, my Lord."

"What message? Why didn't you bring it to me?" I considered what his brains would look like if they were smeared across the floor. After all, servants were already here, cleaning. They could clean that up, too.

"It's ah, quite bloody," he replied, bowing his head.

"Fuck me." I flung myself off the chair and stomped down the steps to the floor, kicking sharp squeals from a servant or two on the way.

Without another word, the guard led me out of the room, down two flights of steps and out the back door, which led to the gate.

*And the message waiting there for me.*

A knife, stabbed into one of my warrior-priests, held the paper in place, surprisingly dry in the rain that continued to fall.

Ripping the paper away, it began to absorb raindrops as I read it. Like before, it was written in the language from Az-ca, and only I was able to read that, after Ruarke's death.

*Your enemy is at your gate, Kaakos,* it read. *Too bad you've been looking in another country for it all along.*

*North.*

"Find the healer," I shrieked to anyone listening. "Find him now and bloody kill him. Tear the city apart if you have to. I and the Prophet command it!"

# CHAPTER 19

I didn't particularly want to speak with Pottles. I did anyway. Thorn, Armon and Levi waited at the palace, because they wanted a regular channel to Kyri, Garkus and the healer in Ny-nes.

Pottles cut her eyes toward me after I told her what Kerok said. She didn't snap at me, telling me that I could speak with Kyri as well as she could, though, because she still felt guilty. She also knew we weren't back to a comfortable level in our relationship, either.

"May as well come; I haven't eaten yet. I assume Thorn can lay another plate on the table." She gathered a jacket from the back of a chair in her study.

"I'll see to it."

"Fine. Let's go."

I *stepped* us to the garden, and walked toward the side door of the palace. Guards moved aside to let us in. It had taken longer than I'd thought it would to get back, but I'd taken a detour—to the rock in the small lake outside North Camp.

A part of me wanted to clear the air with Kerok and Pottles. Another part wanted to yell at both of them. The best I could do was set that self-argument aside for later, after it had taken far too long to come to any sort of resolution.

Then, I'd gone to fetch Pottles, holding my anger in check the whole time.

"Thank you for coming, Doret," Kerok said when we walked in. I hadn't expected him to say anything to me—I'd taken too long to come back, after all.

"Briar, will you bring another plate of food?" I asked, after finding her in the room, refilling glasses of beer and wine.

"Of course." She hurried out of the room to bring Pottles' dinner.

"Did Sherra tell you what we need?" Kerok turned to Pottles.

"She says you want a regular channel of communication between Kyri and the others," she said.

I pushed my glass of red wine in her direction—it was still full, since I didn't touch it earlier.

"We need that connection," Kerok said. "Kaakos may have information from Hunter, as you know, that we're planning an attack. What Hunter didn't know, because we hadn't decided, was a time for it. I want regular updates on what is happening in Ny-nes, and whether Kaakos strengthens or changes the barriers around the country."

While Pottles and Kerok talked, North decided to contact me again in mindspeak. *I just baited Kaakos,* he informed me. *He's screaming his palace down, and demanding that somebody bring him my head on a pole.*

*Why are you telling me this?* I asked.

*Because you appear to be a rational person, and I don't want to contact anyone else there,* he replied.

*You're with Kyri and Garkus,* I fired back. *Why not tell them?*

*I dislike arguments.*

*You sound like an old married couple—with an extra,* I jabbed at him.

The humor he sent back was wry. *I think it's worse than that,* he said. *The reason I wanted to contact you is this; Kaakos is now somewhat distracted. If you intend to invade Ny-nes, then it should be soon.*

*I'll pass that along,* I sniped back. *I'm not the King, you know.*

*I hear you're the Queen.*

*As if that means anything. How is Kyri? The last time we spoke, you asked if I'd be willing to take her away from Ny-nes if you thought she was in danger.*

*I still hold that in reserve,* he said. *For now, she is safe enough, I think.*

*Are any of you safe enough from Kaakos?* Hunter wasn't in the best shape, because he hadn't been safe from Kaakos, even from a great distance. Somehow, North understood my meaning.

*Kaakos was able to get to Hunter as he did because of Merrin's blood, you know. It's a part of his sorcery—blood spells. Merrin was closely related to Hunter, so Kaakos undoubtedly took some of his blood. Then, after casting a specific blood spell, he could slip past the barriers erected around the palace and go straight to Hunter.*

*Blood spells? I only thought he was evil before. This sounds a thousand times worse. Did Kyri know these things?*

*She did.*

*And she didn't tell us?*

*It isn't something to drop into a casual conversation.*

*Great.*

*Blood spells are also required to create a raver. In case you haven't heard, Merrin is now completely, irrevocably, and in every other way, dead. That's the message I sent to Kaakos, and why he's calling for my head.*

*Why did you do that?* I didn't understand why he'd make himself a target.

*The answer is too deep to discuss in mindspeak. Perhaps in the future, if we both survive, I'll tell you.*

*You do that,* I said.

*Tell the King the attack should come soon. I'm sure Kyri will have the same advice, when Doret contacts her.*

*Do you know everything?*

*Not everything. Almost everything. I find I live longer, that way.*

*Right.*

"Sherra?" Pottles snapped her fingers at me. Who knew how long she'd attempted to get my attention?

"Sorry," I apologized. "I was just having a conversation with North."

~

*KEROK*

If a bomb had dropped in our midst, it may have had less of an impact. "North?" Armon asked.

"The healer. From Ny-nes," Sherra shrugged.

"You've spoken to him before?" I wanted to tear into him with my bare hands.

"My dreamwalker spoke to him first," she hedged.

"And how many times have you spoken to him?" I demanded.

"Twice. Don't get tied in a knot, Kerok," she mumbled. "I've been rude both times, and still he feels like it's necessary to give me information."

"What information?"

"He says that he killed Merrin, to send a message to Kaakos and keep him away from Az-ca. He says that we should attack Ny-nes soon, while Kaakos is distracted with hunting him."

"Thorn, settle down," Doret held out a hand to stop my interrogation. "Kyri just told me the same thing."

"Did you know about the blood spells?" Sherra flung at Doret.

Doret's eyes widened. She hadn't expected that. Frankly, I was interested to hear her answer.

"What are blood spells?" Levi asked.

"North said that the way Kaakos got past all my shields around the palace, to invade Hunter's mind, was because Hunter was a close blood relative to Merrin, and he got blood from Merrin to do the spell. He said it takes a blood spell to make a raver, too."

"It's how he was able to take over Ruarke, when Ruarke was powerful in his own right," Doret admitted, lowering her eyes. "The power he uses to take over his spies is different, and those bonds aren't nearly as strong. That's why he'll kill them rather than let us question them. If they were part of a blood spell, they'd never tell us anything."

"Is that how he was able to drain Hunter's power?" Sherra continued her onslaught.

"Yes," Doret sighed.

"Why has this information been withheld from us?" I asked, attempting to remain civil while waiting for an answer.

"I told you it will take more than one to take Kaakos down. It has to do with the way he creates those spells," Doret said. "Every warrior-priest has given him blood. He can drain their energy at a moment's notice, if he wants. It isn't the same as draining someone with real power, but it's energy, just the same."

"Fuck." Armon pinched the bridge of his nose. No doubt he was just as dismayed as I by this information. Armon wasn't as angry as I was, however.

"Does this mean that our planned attack is a suicide mission?" I hissed at Doret.

"No. I think combining fireblasts and shields is the best idea and the best way we've ever devised to combat the threat that Kaakos represents."

"Sherra, you were with Cole, today," I turned to her, now. "How long until those troops are ready to go? Minimum?"

"At least three days, to get the fundamentals worked out and to become accustomed to combining their efforts," she said stiffly.

"Armon, prepare the rest of the army to protect Az-ca in our absence," I directed. "Make sure our special troops are ready to invade Ny-nes. Barring changes or difficulties, we attack in four days."

"I'll make it happen, Commander." Armon rose from his seat and dipped his head to me.

Levi also rose and bowed, although he didn't speak. "You're all dismissed," I waved a hand. "Doret, I want regular reports from Ny-nes."

"I'll see to it," she agreed.

"Sherra, stay," I motioned for her to sit again, after she'd stood with the others.

Lowering her chin to hide a deep frown, she did as I said.

Doret was the last one out, and she closed the door behind her.

Drawing a shaky breath, I focused on Sherra's face and considered what to say.

~

*SHERRA*

I had to force myself to meet his gaze—perhaps the most difficult thing I'd ever done. He didn't speak for several moments, which made it worse.

"I had twelve escorts before you," he scooted his chair back so he could stand, shoving its legs across the stone floor in a jarring, wince-inducing scrape.

If he thought that information was a good opening, then he was quite mistaken. Yes, I'd wondered about that in the past, but had put it out of my mind. Now, he thought to bludgeon me with it—that I was only another in a long line of women.

*He'd killed them, too, draining their power away to fight Kaakos' armies.*

"None of them ever argued with me," he went on, turning his back toward me to stare out the window. "I was always in charge, and they understood that. If they had arguments, they bit back their words and bowed to my position and my commands."

At that moment, I was grateful to Adahi—and Barth—for disagreeing with him where my life and Hunter's were concerned. I considered standing, flinging insults at his back and *stepping* away.

I didn't. If he wanted to destroy our relationship for all time, I'd hear him out and hold the words tight inside me. That way, I'd remember how he'd broken my heart and remind myself never to love like that again.

"None of them," Kerok bowed his head and crossed arms over his chest, "Not one of them could do even a quarter of what you can, Sherra. I never wanted to be King." I watched his back move as he drew a deep breath.

"I thought I could live with the eventual rule of my brother," he went on. "That I could work around his pettiness and greedy, self-serving ways. I intended to command the army and continue the fight to keep Az-ca whole. I had no idea that Az-ca was cracking all around me, and that everything would change so swiftly I'd have no way of dealing with it."

He turned toward me, then. "Without you, not only would I have died at my brother's hand, but Az-ca would be destroyed." Dark eyes searched my face. "Even if all my previous escorts were alive and holding shields around me for protection, Az-ca would still be destroyed. Of all those women, I truly loved only Grae—until you came along. Grae calmed the fire within me. You—you build that fire so hot it could destroy the planet."

"What are you saying, Kerok? I thought this would end in my leaving you for all time." My voice cracked on the words.

"If you leave me, I will be destroyed. I've lost Hunter—he doesn't recognize me, now. I can't lose you, too, and I almost made that happen."

The anguish in his voice weakened my knees and made my breath tremble. If I'd been standing, I probably would have fallen. When he *stepped* to my side, I struggled to rise.

Instead, he pulled me up and into his arms, before *stepping* us to our bed and showing me how hot the fire within him really was.

∾

*Doret*

"Tea, Hunter." I wrapped his hand around the cup while he blinked at the warmth invading his fingers from the pottery mug. "Lift it up, like this," I helped him lift the cup to his mouth.

"Smell the tea? You remember that, don't you?" I asked gently. "Sip," I begged. "Taste the tea and remember."

The scent made his brows draw together and a frown crossed his face—something in him knew it, but he couldn't connect it to its name. "Sip," I said again, making smacking noises with my lips, then helping him get the cup closer to his mouth.

He drank—and blinked. Then drank again. He remembered the taste of it. "Tea," I said. "Tea."

When I pulled the mug away, I watched as his hand dropped, and then went to his chest, as if fumbling for something.

"He's looking for his scrap of paper," Sherra breathed. Somehow, she'd come into Hunter's room and I hadn't noticed, I'd been so focused on getting him to drink.

*Please tell me you think he'll get better*, she sent mindspeak while sitting next to me on the side of Hunter's bed.

*I don't know*, I replied, and pulled her into a hug.

*SHERRA*

"Briar, will you take these things and leave them on the table beside Hunter's bed?" I handed several scraps of paper and two pens to her.

"You think he'll remember writing?" Briar looked hopeful.

"I hope so." Without thinking, I pulled her into a hug. Her eyes were round with surprise when I let her go.

"You're like family," I struggled to find words. "All of you here," I gestured with a hand.

"That's the kindest thing I've ever heard," Briar whispered.

"It's only the truth," I said. "And, if you can find the time, then sit and have a cup of tea with Hunter, or just talk to him. If there's a way to bring him back, I think that's the way to do it."

"I hope you kill the one who did this to him," Briar mumbled.

"I hope the same thing," I agreed. "And we're working on that."

"I'll go now. Is there anything you'd like me to bring you on the way back?"

"I have to go to one of the training camps," I told her. "Cole and I are working with the troops today."

"What about the King? Will he need anything?"

"He and Barth are meeting with Armon and a few others in the garden this morning. I figure they'll want tea after a while."

"I'll see they get it."

I waited until she walked out of my study before *stepping* to the training camp in the King's City. Cole and I had three days to get troops ready to attack Kaakos.

~

*KEROK*

"Are you still mad at me?" I asked Sherra. She'd just walked out of the shower, dripping wet after a long day training troops.

"I don't think so. Should I be?" Her mouth tugged into a slight frown. I wanted to kiss it away.

"In all that happened last night, I never said I was sorry. And I am." I moved forward and took her face in my hands before leaning in to kiss her. "I've driven myself crazy all day because of it," I admitted when I pulled away.

Dark eyes searched my face, before she leaned her forehead against my shoulder. "I'm getting you wet," she sighed, but didn't move.

"I don't give a fuck," I said.

"The towel is behind you—on the sink."

"Still don't give a fuck."

"You intend to dry me off with your clothes?"

"Yes." I pulled her tighter against me. "There's something you should know before I let you pull my damp clothing off. Slowly, please."

"What's that?" Her head tilted so she could kiss my cheek.

"I chose my heir today, to fill in while Hunter is incapacitated."

"Who? Armon? Someone else?"

"It's you," I told her. "You have a good working relationship with everyone that matters, and as for the Council, they're too afraid of you to do anything stupid. I signed the decree this afternoon, with Barth, Armon and a few others witnessing. It's locked in the vault, now, and Barth has a set of keys."

"Nothing is going to happen to you." She tried to pull away. I didn't let her.

"You don't know that," I said, resting my cheek against her hair.

"I won't let it," she said. "Don't even think about it. Hunter will get well, too, and then we can tear up that decree."

"When that happens, I'll let you tear it up yourself."

"Fine."

"Fine." I kissed her, then, and she did remove my clothing. Slowly, as requested.

~

*N*Y-*NES*

*Kyri*

"They're coming in two days. Doret says so," I told North and Garkus the following morning. North barely dipped his head in acknowledgment; a light appeared in Garkus' eyes. He wanted to blast someone, that was easy enough to see.

"I think they're almost ready to send the last plane to Az-ca," North's feet shuffled on dusty, rough concrete as he turned toward the high, narrow window. He'd created that window, I knew—the original bunker had been completely buried and needed no windows.

"I think we should take our friend Garkus, here, to the facility and let him destroy it. To work off excess energy, you understand," North went on.

"When?" Garkus rose from his usual seat on the floor against the wall, dusting off his trousers afterward. He'd cleaned the spot earlier before sitting. For such a large man, he was surprisingly fastidious.

"Tomorrow evening," North said. "Before the troops from Az-ca arrive the next day. Kaakos will be furious—especially after I send him another note, saying I'm responsible. All his efforts will be pointed inward, then, and he'll not be watching his borders so carefully."

"His troops are scattered across the river, looking for you now," I pointed out.

"And that's exactly what I wanted to happen."

"I'm so pleased everything is working according to your plan, then." He hadn't bothered to tell either Garkus or me just what his plan entailed, and it made me angry.

At least Merrin was dead; the people fleeing from Kaakos' troops were singing North's praises for eliminating the raver and his warrior-priests. At least the regular army couldn't fry them where they stood if they weren't cooperative.

"Kyri. Her words always seasoned with sarcasm." North actually turned and smiled at me. There was a time when that smile may have melted my heart. I'd never trust that again.

He'd lied and tricked his way to where and when he was, now, and then refused to help when it was needed most. That brought Adahi's final death to mind, and I was the one to turn away this time.

*You're thinking about him, aren't you?*

*You think I'd tell you?*

*It cost us before.*

*It cost* me *before, remember. Adahi was my friend. I can't say the same about you.*

*If he hadn't told you,* he began.

*I'd have found out another way. We both know that.*

*Adahi was my friend, too.*

*You had a fine way of showing it.*

*Don't throw that in my face. I made my plans. You took it upon yourself and attacked too early.*

*Because I thought you were dead. How's that for an excuse?*

*Fuck.*

*Yes, fuck. Fuck for all time. Fuck to the universe, and especially to you.*

*Not all the mistakes are mine, you know. You thought you could do something with—well. Only it all turned out badly, didn't it?*

*Yes. I fucked up. Rub that in a little harder, all right?*

I'd turned away from him. I hadn't realized he'd come up behind me until his hands gripped my shoulders. I jumped.

"We own this—you and I," he said softly, his breath fanning tendrils of hair at my temple.

"And it is as bitter as hell," I replied.

∽

*ANARI*

"Ready to go again, young ones?" Cole asked as we ate breakfast in his small kitchen. "Most of my people will be coming with us, today, to train with the others. They may be chosen to go to Ny-nes when the time comes."

"I love training," Kyal grinned before stuffing half a sausage in his mouth. "Do you think the King will let us go with them, when they attack Ny-nes?"

"I can't say," Cole shook his head. "I'll ask Sherra. Perhaps she'll know the answer. You must understand that war is not pretty," he went on. "Terrible things happen."

"Like when Merrin took us and killed our parents?" Laren growled, his words bitter. "We saw villagers die, when things didn't go his way. Those kinds of terrible things?"

"Yes, and some may be worse. I will tell you what Kyri told me many years ago, when I began training," Cole said. "Never let revenge cloud your mind. A clouded mind can get you killed."

Laren blinked at Cole for a moment before turning to me. I dipped my head in a slight nod. What Cole said made sense. We had to stay focused, because our lives depended on it.

"You wanted revenge?" Kyal asked.

"Yes, young one, for many, many things. I learned to set it aside and tend to my duties. Afterward, you can determine whether revenge was taken, and never during the moment. Does that make sense?"

"Yes, I suppose."

"Good. Now, finish your food, clean your teeth and we'll go to the King's City."

~

*SHERRA*

Armon, Levi, Caral and Misten came to help with training. Only a few clouds trailed across the western sky; those hung over the ocean in the distance, I think, and kept their moisture far away from those of us who'd appreciate it the most.

Not that it would fall through the domes anyway.

I missed rain—although so little of it fell on Az-ca. In Cole's village, it was a more regular occurrence. There, boughs of evergreens hung heavy after a rain, and a shoulder brushing against them would send a flurry of drops onto unsuspecting heads. I liked it.

"You're lost in thought today," Cole said, placing a cup of tea in my hands. He'd brought the cup from home; I recognized the scent of the tea he used.

"I was just thinking about the rain in your village," I said. "It's so —peaceful."

"I agree."

"We have to get everyone on board with combining their blasts today, because I want to take them outside the King's City tomorrow."

"To do target practice?"

"Yes."

"Good idea."

"Things are—better, now, with Kerok."

"I'm pleased to hear it. He isn't the type who won't admit to his mistakes—when his head clears."

"You're right." I sipped my tea—it was good.

"Do you think we'll be ready when the time comes?" he asked.

"I hope so. Pottles says Kyri and her bunch are planning some sort of raid tomorrow, to distract Kaakos. I hope it works."

"Did she say what it was?"

"No. It's better that way, I think. Kaakos can't stop an attack if he can't suck the information away from someone else."

"How is Hunter?" Cole's voice was low and troubled.

"No better, no worse. I asked Briar to talk to him whenever she can. I'm hoping it helps."

I didn't add that if Hunter could see himself like this, he may have chosen not to survive. A part of me felt guilty about it, but I'd taken him back from Kaakos. At least he wouldn't die at the bastard's hand. Not if I could help it.

"So many times, I watch them learning," Cole nodded to the exercises on the training field. "And I can't help but wonder whether any of them will survive."

"I didn't think I'd survive, when my bus rolled into North Camp that day," I admitted. "The odds were against me lasting more than two or three years past that point. I felt that I and everyone on the bus with me were already dead—we just hadn't realized it."

"Kyri always said that Ruarke had much to answer for, although I didn't hear the full tale of it until he'd returned here to cause trouble."

"You mean the changing of the laws, because of his treason?"

"Yes—and the murders and betrayals, never forget that."

"Pottles still misses her sister, and it's been centuries," I blew out a breath.

"Love seldom gets turned on and off, like a piece of machinery."

"I've discovered that for myself."

"I doubt anyone saw one such as you coming," Cole laughed. "Kyri only learned of you from Adahi."

"Adahi?" This was something new. "He told her about me? When?"

"When you were born, I believe."

"Why would he do that?"

"Ah, well. I doubt any of them wanted you to know," Cole dipped his chin and studied his boots.

"Wanted me to know what?"

"That he was your many, many times great-grandfather. Do not make me regret telling you this secret, by confronting either Kyri or Doret about it. Since Adahi's final death, I felt you ought to know."

"But," I was confused and floundered for words. Only questions crowded my mind, and there wasn't anyone to answer them.

"Kyri told me that only three dreamwalkers have been known to exist. You, Adahi, and Adahi's great-grandfather, who died when Adahi was young. All of them come from that lineage, Sherra. I think Adahi was hoping that a son would be born eventually, who'd carry a dreamwalker within him. He got a daughter, instead. Your great-grandfather's bones lie in Ny-nes, now. He gave that life to save Kyri. He gave his dreamwalker's life to save you."

"Cole, I have deaths to avenge," I hissed. Everything made more sense, now. Adahi had called me daughter, because in a sense, that's what I was to him.

"Only this morning, I warned the young ones about revenge clouding their minds. Focus on the battle to come, dear one, and worry about revenge when it is over," Cole said.

I'd do that, and there'd be no mercy in any of it.

*y-nes*
    *Kaakos*

"There have been no new sightings, and we've found no evidence that he's healed anyone recently," my General's messenger offered a written note while he bowed.

"Anything else?" I fingered the folded paper.

"Only that after a lengthy torture, an escapee said that the healer has two who help him."

"Two?"

"A man and a woman."

"Did you get descriptions?"

"The informant died before we could extract that information."

"Too bad for us, then."

"As you say, my Lord."

I had an idea who those two could be, however. North had taken them from my palace, right under my nose.

Just as he'd killed my raver, Jubal and my warrior-priests. This prick had to be found, before he stung me again.

"I want all my troops to focus on finding this heretic," I snapped at the messenger. "Empty the barracks. Make sure they're all focused on this, or the Prophet will see them die."

"I will carry that message, my Lord."

"Go. Report to General Tern right away. I want those troops across the river before the day's over."

"It will be done." He dipped his head before turning smartly and marching out of the room.

"You're damned right it will be done. Fucking incompetents," I spat. "Guard," I shouted for someone standing outside my audience chamber. One scuttled in quickly. "Send for Liam," I said. "I wish to see him right away."

"Of course, my Lord." He ran out faster than the messenger did.

∼

*JUBAL*

Except at mealtimes, I was treated as if I were invisible. Nobody wanted to talk to me, and I felt isolated.

"It's your own fault, traitor," North set a mug of fish stew in front of me. He'd read my mind, too, and provided an answer I didn't want to hear.

Where he'd come by the crockery, I had no idea. It didn't matter, it would disappear with him the next time he went out for food.

Who cooked our meals I had no idea, although they were competent, at least. I'd never found bones in any of the fish we'd eaten.

"If you hadn't blamed others all your life for what you perceive as your mistreatment, your life would have been different," North went on. "Eat, before it gets cold."

He walked away from me then, to join the other two across the bare, concrete bunker.

That's what North called it, once—a bunker. I thought bunkers were underground, and told him so. He laughed and said time had partially uncovered this one. I caught the scent of the stew, finally, and my stomach rumbled.

"You can't make me forget the injuries I've suffered at others' hands," I mumbled at North's back. He laughed, letting me know he'd heard.

~



Kerok joined us in the afternoon; he wanted to practice with Armon and the others. They welcomed him into their group, although I'd told him already that he should stay in Az-ca while the rest of us went.

He planned to go out with us on the final day, too, for target practice.

Then, I'd join the group, and together we'd see how much fire-power we had, and how strong our shielding was.

We'd make judgment calls on the others, too, and make a final determination on who would go and who, if any, would stay behind.

Cole told me Anari, Kyal and Laren wanted to go. I relayed that message to Kerok, who said he'd watch them during practice, and decide afterward.

He considered them warriors, now. They'd helped take down the planes Kaakos sent against us, which was more than many of our current troops had done. There was no disagreement that they could outfly almost anyone in their bubble shield, and could turn it on the head of a pin, almost, if needed. Those three had bonded with each other, far earlier in age than the rest of us had.

It worked to their advantage. Someday, if we survived, I would be compelled to have a conversation with Cole, as the Queen-heir of Az-ca. Someday, those three young ones wouldn't be satisfied with a bonding of one male to one female, or one male to one male. It would be all three together or they could walk away from us. I hoped Cole's village would accept such an arrangement, as those in Az-ca could take a dimmer view of such things.

*Queen-heir of Az-ca.* That's what Kerok said my title was, and I wanted nothing more than to unload it as soon as I could. With Hunter's condition, it could take some time.

"This is fun," Kerok walked toward me, a huge grin on his face. "I think we can blast half of Ny-nes at once, if you're with us."

"I don't want to blast half of it. I only want to blast a small portion —the one containing Kaakos, his army and his flunkies. The rest of the people don't deserve to be blasted, most likely."

"True, but stop thwarting my joy, woman."

"I'll stop thwarting your joy," I laughed.

"All right. Now, who do you think we can employ to drop rocks in Ny-nes?" he asked, sounding more serious.

"I think that would require transporting rocks, or finding a rocky place there. I'd prefer to find the places where he stores his trucks and such, and lob those at him from nearby."

"Good idea. I'll talk it over with Armon, after I get information from our spies."

"It's funny how they've become our spies. What do you intend to do with Garkus, if he survives?"

"I'll take that under advisement for now and decide afterward, if necessary."

"And North? Whoever he is?"

"You know more about him that I do."

"Just because he sends mindspeak, which I don't appreciate, by the way, it doesn't mean I know anything at all about him."

"Then I'll wait and speak with Kyri or Garkus."

"That sounds like a good idea. When do you intend to leave here?" I asked. "To facilitate the attack?"

"We'll make those decisions tonight, over dinner. Armon will let his people know shortly before we leave. He's already warned them to be ready on a moment's notice. This is no different from the days when the enemy attacked unawares."

*Sherra?* Armon's voice sounded in my mind.

*Armon?* I replied, holding up a hand so Kerok would know I was engaged in mindspeak.

*I'm authorized to perform a bonding ceremony,* he said. *Caral and Misten want to do this tonight, before we ah,* he didn't finish.

"Can we have Caral and Misten's bonding ceremony in the King's garden?" I turned to Kerok.

"Yes. Tell them to come, and we'll have dinner afterward."

*Armon, come to the King's garden after training today,* I sent. *Kerok will perform the ceremony, and we'll have dinner afterward.*

*I'll let them know. Tell the King I'm grateful.*

"Armon says thank you," I told Kerok.

"Their ceremony will be the first of its kind in centuries, and it's long overdue," Kerok agreed. "Tell Armon he is more than welcome, and that Caral and Misten are deserving."

BRIAR HERDED servants around and had several more tables brought to the King's garden, then decorated them with flowers after laying out cloths and beautiful dishes.

Kerok and I saw it first; Armon and the others hadn't arrived, yet. Food would be brought for all attending after the ceremony was performed.

Candles, rarely used for any purpose except emergencies, were waiting to be lit on the tables, too.

"It looks like something from a tale," I hugged Kerok's left arm as we took in the preparations.

"It'll be even more like that when it's darker and the candles are lit."

Sighing, I laid my cheek against his shoulder. He turned his head to kiss my hair. *I wish I'd given you something like this,* he sent mindspeak.

*We were in a war,* I reminded him.

*We still are—but the rules have changed. Instead of allowing Ruarke to toss bombs in our direction, Kaakos took a direct interest the moment Ruarke died.*

*I don't regret Ruarke's death,* I said.

*Neither do I. He deserved it, just as Merrin deserved his final fate. Let's hope Kaakos finds his death, too, on the other side of our attack.*

I didn't add that I hoped we survived the attack ourselves, but that was a morbid thought. Tonight, I wanted to celebrate Caral and Misten's love-bonding, and set my fears aside.

"We'll have the meeting indoors after our meal," Kerok spoke aloud. "Doret is bringing a map with her, and we'll talk target points when we see it."

"She has a map?" I pulled away from Kerok.

"Drawn from images and instructions sent by Kyri. She told me earlier that she'd spent most of the day yesterday on it."

"I hope she has the locations where they keep their bombs and trucks," I said. Kerok frowned and nodded, the scar on his face becoming more noticeable. I reached out to touch it.

"I wish you'd stay here," I told him.

"This is my fight, and my country. I want that bastard to know that even Az-ca's King is willing to come against him. I'll just hold that information back from the spies, in case they're captured before we get there to unleash hell against Kaakos."

I didn't tell him that his leaving Az-ca frightened me in ways I couldn't explain—especially since Hunter wasn't himself.

"Who will you leave in charge?" I asked.

"Barth and the quadrant leaders," he said. "With Claude being chief among the quadrant leaders, under Barth. I've already met with them, and Kage will be standing by, in case anyone decides to take their authority too far."

"Good. We don't need an uprising while we're gone."

"Most people don't know about Hunter's condition," Kerok pulled me into a tight embrace. "Barth and the others are acting on his behalf while I'm gone, with Kage standing behind them. They have the power to mobilize the military left behind, if it becomes necessary."

*Necessary.* I drew a shaky breath. What he meant but hadn't said was this; if we failed absolutely in Ny-nes, then Barth, Claude and the others would have to fight against what was coming as best they could.

*Necessary.*

Because Kaakos would see Az-ca die if he won the battle we

carried against him. Things had come to that, as I should have known they would.

~

*Ny-nes*

*North*

*They've come to move the plane already,* Kyri's voice hissed in my mind. I didn't need the information; I could see it for myself.

We were high in the rafters of the ancient hangar, while a unit of Kaakos' troops and a pod of six warrior-priests crawled about the aircraft like ants collecting a grasshopper's carcass.

Garkus was so angry, I imagined he'd snort fire if he could.

*What should we do?* Kyri asked.

*What we came to do,* I said. *Only now, we're going to bring down the entire hangar instead of destroying the plane and letting it burn itself out.*

*He may guess that there are more than one with power if we do that,* she snapped at me.

*He has no idea what kind of power we have—together or separately.*

*But.* She wanted to argue.

*On my command,* I said, *Garkus, you blast the plane. I'll blast the front of the hangar. Kyri, you take the back. We don't want any of the ants escaping, now do we?*

~

*Kerok*

A love-bonding was far different that a warrior-escort bonding. As it should be. "Misten, do you take Caral as your bonded partner in love, and pledge to her all that you are, from this day forward?" I smiled at Misten, who blushed as she lifted her eyes to Caral's.

Caral's hands squeezed Misten's, lending her support to answer.

"I pledge to do so," Misten's voice wobbled.

"Do you, Caral, take Misten as your bonded partner in love, and pledge to her all that you are, from this day forward?"

"I pledge to do so," Caral breathed. A tear coursed down Misten's cheek at the love in Caral's voice.

"As the King of Az-ca, I announce to all the country that I rule, that you are now bonded, and any who come against your bonding will answer to me."

Misten laughed through her tears and flung her arms about Caral's neck. They shared a kiss to a great deal of applause from attendees.

*The last plane has been destroyed, along with the building that housed it. A few of Kaakos' minions may have perished with it*, Doret sent mind-speak. *Kyri just informed me of this.*

*Then thank her for me, and for Az-ca*, I replied.

"Let's eat," I held out my hands to a general cheer.

⌒

*SHERRA*

Kerok, Armon, Levi and I sat at Caral and Misten's table. Both wore their dress uniforms, as was befitting a couple in the military. Besides, we'd had no time to find formal clothing for either of them.

I think they were more than grateful that they could have a ceremony. Having the ceremony in the King's garden, with their close friends and Caral's sister in attendance was the sweetest frosting on the best cake ever.

Darissa chose to sit at a nearby table, filled with drudges from Secondary Camp. Caral and Misten wanted them to come, and they were more than excited to do so. Some had never been to the King's City, let alone allowed into his garden.

*I'd like to call them something other than drudges—it's demeaning*, I sent to Kerok.

*Where did that come from?* He lifted an eyebrow at me. *This is supposed to be a celebration, and not work. That comes later.*

*I just don't want to call them that*, I argued.

*Then come up with a more suitable title, and I'll consider it. Now, drink your wine—you only get one glass. We have a battle to plan after this.*

*Cooks, cook's assistants and retainers*, I said.

*What?*

*I read it somewhere—servants were sometimes called retainers. I like that better.*

*I suggest you approach them with it; they may have never heard the word retainer. I'm fine with the other titles.*

*I think you're selling them short,* I countered. *They all know how to read. Some do it whenever they have time and access to reading material. I also suggest a library at Secondary Camp.*

*Sherra,* he sounded weary. *We have a battle to plan, remember? When you return, as Queen-heir, you can collect as many books as you can find and place them in an empty space at Secondary Camp.*

*I will.*

*I know how stubborn you are. Of course you will.*

*We don't have anyone writing new fiction,* I said. *It's all as old as Kyri, I suspect. We need writers. I know there have to be people in Az-ca who want to do that.*

*Most of them are engaged in the daily task of finding food and water for their family,* he frowned. *If you find someone with the will and imagination, I'll provide writing supplies.*

*Thank you.*

*Drink your wine. Battle. Remember?*

*I do.*

*Good.*

⁓

Nʏ-ɴᴇs

*Kaakos*

I'd have to restrain my anger in the future; I'd killed twenty this time—guards and servants. With most of the population scattering across the river, my warrior-priests would have to be sent out farther to fetch suitable replacements.

Not only did I curse the healer—again—for destroying the last plane I had, he'd destroyed the hangar with it.

It wasn't my fault that I'd been turned away from collecting information from Merrin's Uncle Hunter, when the bitch Queen of Az-ca interfered and placed herself between us.

If North had come from Az-ca, there'd been no report from anyone about it. Even Jubal hadn't known anything, and that meant it was likely the healer had somehow escaped my notice—and Ruarke's —for years.

Information from one or two informants—before they'd died— said the healer came from the far south of Ny-nes.

*Nothing ever shows up from there—it's all swamp and alligators,* Ruarke often said. Perhaps he'd just preferred not to search the area for power holders.

One had certainly escaped our notice, and now ran amuck in my country, flaunting what he had under my nose.

"Blast you, Ruarke," I hissed. "Damn you to the hells, Merrin," I added. Both had gotten themselves killed, when they should still be in my service and advancing my agenda.

As for Narvin—he'd been a weaker version of Merrin. He was also Merrin's half-brother, although Narvin never realized it. Narvin hadn't known who his father was. Merrin's father was much like Merrin in that regard, and too fond of sex with anything possessing female parts. He'd told Merrin he suspected Narvin was his after Narvin was taken to the training camps to become a warrior.

I'd wanted to rape Hunter's mind like I had Merrin's—to learn everything he knew to further my cause.

*After he'd killed the King of Az-ca for me.*

I'd spent the last of Merrin's collected blood to do it, too, thinking I could always go back to the source. The effort I spent on Hunter had come to naught, thanks to the Queen's intervention.

Merrin was now beyond reach, and the source of that blood gone. How had things come to this? Ruarke had seen to it long ago that a queen in Az-ca would never again have power, and women would only be allowed training as escorts in the army. He'd also manipulated everything, so that no escort would receive proper training. No matter how good they were, no escort would last longer than five years of continuous battle.

I'd planned this—to kill the power gene in Az-ca, with my goal to destroy it completely, allowing me to walk into Az-ca one day and have them bow to me—before I killed all of them.

Somehow, all those new rules and traditions had been cast aside, and things had gone back to the way they were before, and right in front of our eyes, too. The bitch Queen had much to answer for, and I wanted her throat in my hands as I watched her die.

~

*KEROK*

"Here's the palace," Doret pointed to the oddly-shaped outline of it. "Over here, two miles away, is the factory and storage facility for their trucks." She tapped two large rectangles.

"Now," she continued, "This is where the three planes came from that were sent recently. The word I have is that they're still empty, but it could be used as a mustering position for our troops."

"We need an image or an icon to focus on to *step* there, once we cross the barrier," I said.

"I can provide that." She slid a photograph over the selected rectangles, covering those lines.

"What the hell is that?" Armon breathed.

"It's an ancient plane—one of the first ever built, long before the End-War," Doret explained. "It was originally covered in cloth, but you see it's only the frame, now."

"I don't understand how it could fly, but then flying something made of metal escapes me, too," Barth said.

"The first ones to arrive need to *step* in next to this. The next wave need to *step* in near the first ones, and so on. We don't need troops landing atop one another."

"You mean the first wave focuses on this," I tapped the image. "The next wave focuses on the ones who went before?"

"It's an old trick, and it works," Doret sniffed. "It's described in the history I'm writing. It's almost the same when you *step* to a dining hall

—a designated corner is where you step, and then you get the hell out of the way for the next one."

"Interesting. I want to read that history when I return."

"It's almost finished."

"I suggest *stepping* bubble shields there, one at a time," Sherra said. "And lay out the order now, so that everyone knows when they're supposed to go and who or what they're supposed to focus on."

"Good plan," I said. Doret nodded her agreement.

"Once all the troops are gathered, then those chosen beforehand will create the strongest mirror shields they can, and *step* to the truck facility. The second wave will head toward the barracks containing the troops remaining in the city, and the third wave will fly their shields toward the warrior-priests' temple. A mindspeaker will go with each wave, to signal my commands."

"It's important to kill the warrior-priests especially, so I suggest their temple be fired upon first," Doret said.

"We'll take them out first, then," I agreed. "In addition to the blasts we level against them, we'll toss trucks at their buildings. That should take them out quickly enough. Now, our second target is Kaakos's troops. Once their barracks are destroyed using the same method, those sent to take out the warrior-priests and the troops will gather near the palace. We've been told the shield around it extends to here," I pointed to a circular line drawn around the building.

"Kaakos' quarters are here," Doret indicated a wing of the palace. "His meeting room and audience chamber are close by, here." She tapped a secondary wing. "Those who've gone to the truck facility should begin throwing the remaining vehicles at the palace, as hard and fast as they can. If the shield is breached, both by lobbing blasts by the two designated groups and by the trucks hitting it, then Kaakos' likely hiding places should be targeted simultaneously," she tapped the two wings again. "This will ensure the best chance of forcing him into the open, if you don't kill him outright in the initial attack, once the shield is down."

"That may be too much to hope for," Sherra frowned. "He has power we haven't seen yet, I think."

"He's never had combined blasts leveled against him, either. We have that ability, now, and you, Sherra, may be able to get past the palace shield anyway. Should that happen, then get other bubble shields inside as quickly as possible."

"If we can do that, I may call in the troops from the truck facility," I said. "To join our efforts at attacking him directly."

"Yes—but only if you breach the shield," Doret said. "Now, all of you listen carefully to what I say next. Never forget that every cell in Kaakos' body is evil. Show no mercy, ever. Remember that. Don't wait for him to attack first, as you've done in the past. Destroy him quickly, before he has the opportunity to kill you first."

❧

NY-NES

*Kyri*

"You can do it—you've done it before," I glared at North.

"She's just a kitchen drudge."

"And a friend," I argued. "You can get past the shield around the palace and bring her out of there. Besides, we need someone to keep an eye on Jubal, just in case."

Jubal grunted his displeasure from his usual seat on the floor. The hard concrete pained his hip, but North refused to give him any sort of comfort by healing misshapen bones.

As a traitor to Az-ca, he deserved worse, but it still pained me to look at him. "You healed her before she was taken for the kitchens," I pointed out maliciously. "So it's your fault she's in there to begin with."

"Fine." North replied before stepping away. Jubal moved uncomfortably on the concrete, once North disappeared. Like a true male, he didn't want to show weakness.

"Garkus, stand by and fry Jubal if he tries anything," I said as I moved toward our captive. I intended to fix a few things in North's absence.

"Just give me the chance, please," Garkus' gleaming, dark eyes held a threat for Jubal, who attempted to make himself smaller.

~

*NORTH*

Soobi's eyes were round with fright and wonder, while my hand clamped tightly over her mouth to keep her quiet.

"We have to remove your chain, first, before I can take you out of here," I whispered.

A slight nod told me she understood. Grabbing her chain-encircled wrist so there'd be no sound when I removed it, I cast the spell to deactivate it for only a blink. Certainly not long enough for Kaakos to notice—not that he'd be able to, anyway.

I wanted to laugh at his ignorance in the matter, but held it back.

Setting the chain on the edge of Soobi's bed, I helped her rise, before lifting her over my shoulder and stepping away from the palace. In my haste to get away, one of Soobi's swinging hands behind my back knocked the chain onto the stone floor.

My heart pounding and the escaping servant alarm sounding, I *stepped* through the shield before Kaakos had a chance to strengthen it.

~

*KYRI*

*I made things worse*, North snapped at me. He'd set Soobi down near me, so she'd know there was nothing to fear.

His anger was directed at me, however, and me only.

*How?* I shot back.

*When her chain accidentally dropped to the floor, it set off the alarm*, he said. *I barely got out before Kaakos had a chance to increase the power of the shield. When the attack comes, they'll have a harder time breaching it, now.*

*Fuck*, I replied. I didn't want to lay blame—he'd done what I'd asked him to do and knew he'd never have set off the alarm intentionally.

He'd just made it harder to attack the palace. No, *we'd* made it harder to attack the palace.

Soobi was alive, though. I was grateful for that much, anyway. Jubal, too, sat easier on the floor, once I'd readjusted an ancient hip injury, employing power to align and curve bone to fit easier in the socket.

I doubt Jubal had experienced this much relief since before his initial injury. If North noticed what I'd done, he didn't say anything. We'd had too many arguments lately, and neither of us had the strength or the liking for another.

*We may have made things more difficult for you,* I sent to Doret. *Kaakos increased the power of the shield around his palace tonight, after we rescued a servant.*

*Kyri, we've discussed this failing of yours in the past.* She already knew the whole thing was at my request. *I hope her life is worth it,* she added.

*I hope that too, and I already feel shame,* I admitted. *I just couldn't leave her there to die.*

*Right. We could lose many more lives than that one as a result, and more important ones, on top of that, because you couldn't leave her there to die.*

*I know.*

*You know, and you'll remember—until the next time. And the time after that.*

*I know.*

# CHAPTER 21

*Kerok*

"Let your troops sleep late," I told Armon before he left for the training camp. They wouldn't go back to Secondary Camp until after we attacked Ny-nes. Caral and Misten were invited to spend their bonding night at the palace, in Sherra's private suite.

"We're going tomorrow night, aren't we?" Armon asked.

"Yes. Doret says Ny-nes—the part we're attacking, anyway, is three hours earlier according to the clock. If we leave at midnight our time, then it'll be very early morning, and most of Kaakos' palace should be asleep. I prefer to catch them unaware, if we can."

"I agree with that assessment."

"I just received mindspeak from Kyri," Doret touched my arm. "She says Kaakos just increased the shield around the palace."

"Does he know we're coming?" I breathed, suddenly fearful that all our plans were falling apart.

"No—it was something boneheaded that Kyri did, and we'll pay for it in the long term," Doret replied. "Let's hope combined blasts and shields will hold sway over what Kaakos can do."

"We leave at midnight tomorrow," I told her.

"Good. It'll be deep in the night in Ny-nes. Kaakos sleeps soundly when he sleeps," she said. I didn't think to ask her how she knew that until later, and she'd already gone home to find her own bed.

Sherra had already taken Caral and Misten to their suite for the night, so she wasn't there to ask questions, either.

Armon shrugged and walked out the door, with Levi close behind. Only Barth was left in the room with me.

"I expect you to watch over everyone, Claude and Kage included," I told him. "I've left a signed document in the vault, if anyone questions your authority. The other person who will help you if needed, is Doret. She won't be going with us, and she was once Queen of Az-ca."

"I was hoping you wouldn't leave it all to me—I'd like more firepower to stand with me if necessary," Barth remarked dryly.

"I'll let Doret know before we leave, that she's your backup, should the need arise."

"You won't be gone that long—or you shouldn't be," Barth said, his words and voice tight with emotion.

"Barth, don't worry unless it's warranted," I clapped a hand against his shoulder.

"Then don't do anything foolish. You, and Sherra, too. I've gotten used to having you here at the palace."

He was concerned for Hunter—and the condition the former heir was in. Hunter had been his closest friend for years uncounted, and now—Hunter couldn't speak, didn't recognize anyone, and was learning how to feed himself again.

"I don't know how you did it, all those years in the army," Barth said softly. "Losing friends. Losing escorts—losing Grae, too. It didn't register until recently."

"I know. It never gets easier, Barth. Come, now, our beds are waiting and it's late. We need sleep if we're to do battle."

～

*Sherra*

Misten and Caral asked if I wanted to stay and share the bottle of wine delivered to the suite I'd lent them.

"No," I held up a hand. "This is your private celebration, not mine."
I stood at the door, ready to leave.

"Thank you, then—for this," Caral pulled Misten against her.
"Without you—we wouldn't be here or bonded."

"Stop," I said. "It's right and it's fair, and I think somebody would
have realized it eventually. Enjoy your stay at the palace. Tomorrow
will be hard work—but we'll sleep late." I grinned at them.

Misten giggled and pulled Caral's head down for a kiss. I shut the
door softly behind me and headed for the royal suite.

$\sim$

KEROK'S SHIRT WAS OFF, as were his boots, but he still wore his pants as
he gazed out the wide window of our suite.

I could see the scar that began at his lower back, before curving
around and down a leg.

It wasn't as deep as those he bore on the front, but it could have
killed him, had the physicians not worked so hard to save his life.

"Kerok?" I moved behind him and placed my arms about his waist.

"Just thinking," he said.

"I know." Likely we were thinking the same—*what would happen if
we failed?* If we spent our best and strongest resources against Ny-nes,
and it wasn't enough—well.

Laying my cheek against the hard muscle of his back, I closed my
eyes and breathed in the scent of him. Touching him like that, if I
wanted, I could reach out with my power to see the fire within. For
me, he'd always had the strongest of any I'd felt. I never told anyone
else, for fear they'd feel less capable.

And, as I couldn't gauge my own fire, I had no idea how it looked
to anyone else.

"I'm going to let those three young ones go with us—Cole will be
with them, as he was when they helped destroy those planes. I'll give
him instructions to get them away if things aren't going well."

"Thank you. I think they'd have seen themselves as failures if you
left them behind."

"What if they're killed?" His voice sounded anguished.

"They understand the risks, Kerok. They have ever since they watched Merrin burn their neighbors to death in front of them."

"Fucking Merrin." Kerok's chin dipped with a weighted sigh. "How much of this is his fault? That Kaakos could take whatever he wanted from that weak-minded fool and use it as a weapon against us?"

The bitterness over Hunter's condition lay heavy on Kerok's heart, and he was letting it out, now. "Merrin may as well have stood on a mountaintop and waved a white flag at the enemy, begging him to come and take him."

I didn't argue. Merrin wasn't the only one in this, though. Drenn had put many things in Merrin's mind—promised him many things, including Kerok's position at the head of the army.

Would Drenn have done the same, if he'd know what the ultimate result would be? That Merrin could have a hand in the final destruction of Az-ca?

Drenn had effectively taken himself out of the equation, whether he intended it or not. Everything that happened afterward was strictly Merrin's fault.

And now he was dead—killed by the one who called himself North, with help from Kyri and Garkus. A sudden, unexpected end to a life lived far beneath its potential.

Was Kaakos the same? Had he gone another way, he could have accomplished much. Ny-nes could be a stronger nation if he'd built it up, rather than spending all his time and energy to tear it down.

Merrin wanted power.

Kaakos had power. Why, then would he keep throwing his armies and technologies against a country so far away, that, until now, never thought to attack him where he was? What did he want? I didn't believe him to be so zealously religious that we offended him this much. Especially since he held power much the same as ours.

*Much the same.*

My heartbeat thumped hard in my chest, as speculation began to form. My dreamwalker had known something perhaps, and had diverted my attention away from it.

For now, though, my fears kept me from going straight to Doret for answers. For good or bad, we were going against Kaakos the following night.

Should I survive, I'd be sure to ask questions.

"My love," Kerok turned in my arms. "You're wearing too much clothing," he murmured as his lips grazed my neck. "Let's take it off."

*N*y-*nes*

*Kyri*

Soobi slept nearby, her breathing soft and regular. Across the room, Garkus did the same.

North, like me, lay awake. Jubal was the one to snore—his rough breathing a by-product of injuries sustained long ago in a bomb blast.

I'd heard from Doret, after she attended a meeting with Thorn and the others in the King's City.

*They're coming at midnight tomorrow, their time,* I sent to North.

*Good. That will serve to roust everyone here from their beds, and they'll be disoriented at first. Heavy blows tossed against Ny-nes' army may not be answered.*

*Will we meet them at the empty hangar in the city?*

*You can meet them—you and Garkus. I have another plan.*

*What plan is that?*

*A plan to trip Kaakos just a little, making it easier to breach his shields.*

*That sounds like a fool's errand to me.*

*I knew you'd say that. It's why I didn't tell you until you asked.*

*Fine. Do whatever you want. It's what you've always done,* I accused.

*Thank you. I will.*

*I was being sarcastic.*

*My dear, you are the most adept practitioner of that particular talent I've ever met.*

*Don't try to mollify me with sweet words, asshole.*

*I find your willingness to fight with me charming.*

*Only because you're perverse about everything.*

*Will you come over and sit with me, while I think?*

*What?*

*I mean it.*

I could have said no. I could have called him names again. What I realized was this; this time tomorrow, we could be dead or dying. How many of us would refuse arms about us, when faced with that prospect?

Without a reply, I *stepped* to him, and making as little noise as possible, I sat beside him as requested.

His arms came around me as I knew they would; he kissed my hair and leaned his cheek on my head. I sighed and closed my eyes.

~

DORET

*Doret?* I blinked—the mindspeak came from Barth.

*What is it, Barth?*

*Apparently, Thorn signed a decree leaving me in charge of the quadrant leaders and everyone else, if the need arises. He also decreed that you act as my ah, backup, I believe is the term he used, in case I need help.*

*I'll be happy to back you up,* I replied. *If you need it.*

*I think I'd like you to come to the palace when they leave tomorrow night,* he said. *Because this is going to be difficult.*

I didn't argue with him. When a Chief Diviner is worried, then there's generally something to worry about.

*I'll be there,* I promised. *Let me know if you want me to get there sooner.*

*I will, and thank you, Doret. Having you with me will ease my mind.*

His mindspeak cut off, then, leaving me blinking in the dim light of my bedroom. *Barth.* Who would have thought?

~

SHERRA

I woke earlier than I intended and left Kerok sleeping in our bed while I went to my study to consider plans for the day. We'd practice at North Camp until mid-afternoon, then send everyone away to rest and eat.

Armon was in charge of letting the troops know how and when to coordinate, and I planned to place a specially-designed shield of my own around every bubble shield before we left for Ny-nes, so they could *step* past the barrier.

Everyone had seen the image of the plane's ancient, skeletal frame by now; Armon and Cole had seen to it. Cole would bring his troops in for training, and they'd spend the rest of their day at the training camp in the King's City.

"Tea, Queen Sherra." Briar set a cup on my desk. "Would you like breakfast in here, too?"

"Yes," I said. "Thank you."

"I know something is going on," she said. "I don't need to know what it is," she held up a hand. "Just know that I and the others here in the palace stand with you, no matter what."

"Things are different now, aren't they?" I asked. "Different from before, when Kerok's father was King."

"And when his brother was the Crown Prince," Briar spoke Drenn's title with contempt. It appeared none of the palace staff had been fond of him. "It's more evident, now, to us—what King Thorn, you and the others have done for us all this time. We never saw any of it before—not like this. We had no idea how much danger we were in, we were so far away from the battlefield."

"I know. And that's how we wanted it," I told her. "To keep you all safe and away from that awfulness. Now, it's trying to attack us every-where, and we're fighting it as best we can."

"You have my gratitude," Briar said. "For that—and for other things. Now, do you want eggs with your sausages? Cooked the way you like?"

"That sounds wonderful."

"Good. I'll have it here soon."

"Sherra?" Kerok walked in, with Cole, Armon and Caral right behind him.

"I see I'm not the only one who couldn't sleep late," I said, taking in Kerok's damp hair. He'd showered before coming to find me.

*I feel excited—and scared at the same time,* Caral sent. *Misten went to the training camp to meet with Levi, Wend and Marc. You have a nice bed,* she added.

"I just asked for breakfast. I'll tell Briar to bring extra plates."

That's how we came to have our morning meal in my study, and we talked while we ate—about inconsequential things.

Time enough for seriousness later.

*KEROK*

When Sherra joined our group inside Caral's floating, mirror-shielded bubble, I couldn't believe the firepower we wielded.

A distance away from North Camp's lake lay a deep, massive crater, now. Doret, standing back from our war games, relayed our success before we could see it for ourselves.

*Level that against Kaakos and see what he does,* she sent mirth with her mindspeak.

*Just what we intend to do,* I told her, as we moved our bubble out of the way to make room for the next bubble to fire.

*After this round, tell them to stand down and return to the King's City,* I sent to Armon.

*Yes, Commander. Did you ever think we'd attack the enemy from the air?* He added.

*Not in my lifetime—or in any other lifetime,* I admitted. *Until the enemy flew one of their infernal planes at us, I didn't think it possible. Now, I know it's old technology that they've revived, but we've found a new way to combat it, using our power.*

Neither of us said what we knew, however. Had Sherra not thought this possible, we'd never have tried it on our own.

She'd looked inside all of us at one time or another, I think, and told us how strong we were—how capable we were. Until then, we hadn't been using what we had to its fullest potential.

*When we return*, I sent another message to Armon, *remind me to outlaw some of the things Kaakos does—those things should be forbidden to anyone with power, and a heavy price will be levied against anyone who attempts it.*

*With pleasure, my King.*

I never wanted to hear of anyone taking over another's mind as Kaakos could, and then using that person for their own nefarious gain. No matter how bad Merrin had become, he didn't deserve the fate Kaakos forced upon him.

*Let's go back*, I told the crew inside our shared bubble. *It's time to rest and eat.*

~

ARMON

Levi and I had other plans for an evening meal. It required some assistance from the training camp mess, but it was put together without much fuss. Then I allowed Levi to transport us to his home village.

We stood outside a modest home, the porch posts made of cedar that had been carefully sanded in years past. Those posts bore the patina of too many hands to count, and parts of them gleamed in the late afternoon light.

The door opened before we had a chance to knock, and an elderly, dark-skinned man hobbled out to see who'd come. His entire life was mapped in the wrinkles of his face, and in his younger days, I imagined he'd looked much like Levi.

A younger woman peered around him, her eyes wide with concern; she didn't recognize either of us.

"Pap?" Levi said softly.

The old man, whose eyes had dimmed with age, stopped still. "Only one man ever called me that," he said. "Levi, is that you?"

"It's me, Pap. I brought my bonded with me—and dinner, if you'll share it with us."

"Levi?" the woman came from behind the old man. "Levi?" The

timbre of her voice rose, and before she could be called back, she'd flung herself into Levi's arms with a happy shriek.

"Rosie, I'm glad to see you, too," Levi sounded muffled and emotional as they hugged.

"Come in, come in," Levi's father invited. "We're just about to put our own supper on the table."

That's how we ended up having a feast of sorts—and a reunion—with Levi's parents, his sister, her husband and two children. All of them couldn't stop grinning at both of us, and told us about every relative still living, and a few who weren't.

As a meal before going to fight an enemy far away, it was perfect and ended far too soon.

~

*SHERRA*

Both of us wore battle uniforms as we stood on opposite sides of our bed.

We'd shared the bed earlier—to take our minds off the coming attack. Now, after another light meal, we'd dressed and made ourselves ready to join the troops at the training camp.

"Ready, my love?"

"Yes."

"Then come kiss me again, before we go."

I was happy to oblige.

~

*KEROK*

The troops, escorts and warriors stood at attention in the largest mess hall, where all tables and benches had been removed to make room.

"You know why we're here," I said, standing before them. "For the first time in Az-ca's history, we are taking the war to the enemy, instead of waiting here for their next attack. May good fortune travel with all of us tonight. Focus on your skills. Perform to the level I know you can—all of you. You are Az-ca's elite troops. Never forget that."

"Pods, gather. Form your bubble shields. Sherra will come to each of you and place another shield to get you through Ny-nes' barrier. We move on my signal. Never forget who you are, and what you fight for. We stand or fall together."

"As it has always been," they chorused back to me.

I watched as bubble shields were formed by the first row. Sherra went to them and placed her shield before they *stepped* outside the mess hall. The same procedure was repeated forty times before they were all aloft outside.

"Time for us to lead," I spoke to Armon, Sherra and the others.

Caral formed the bubble shield. Sherra added hers to the mix, and *stepped* us outside, to the others.

"Sherra, tell them the signal is given," I told her, my eyes focused eastward, where the enemy waited.

Her mindspeak sounded in all our heads; *Proceed to Ny-nes. The King commands it.*

We *stepped*.

*y-nes*
*Kyri*

I will never forget the sight of bubble shield after bubble shield appearing inside the hangar, in an elaborate dance of fitting into a confined space. The first had focused on the ancient plane. The others focused on the bubble previous to theirs. It was an old trick of getting an entire army from one place to another, without *stepping* on each other.

In all, forty-one appeared. Sherra *stepped* out of the one she was in, with Thorn at her side.

Garkus, waiting beside me, fidgeted. Here was his King, and he had no idea what Thorn would say to him. King and Queen of Az-ca walked toward us. I hated that North hadn't decided to stay to meet them, but too many explanations could have come from that.

"Where is North?" Sherra asked when they reached us.

"He said he had other things to do—to trip up Kaakos—or that's the excuse he gave."

"King Thorn," Garkus bowed to the King.

"Ah, Garkus. I almost didn't recognize you," Thorn lifted an eyebrow at Garkus' current skin tone.

"I erred," Garkus bowed again.

"And that will be addressed when we return to Az-ca," Thorn said. "Tonight, we fight together."

"It will be my honor," Garkus assured him.

"Good. Kyri, what are your plans?"

"We will join you when you attack the palace," I said. "I have hope that North will add his talents to ours when we arrive."

"Excellent. We are ready to commence our attacks on Kaakos' troops and his warrior-priests. I thank you for the images you sent—they have been more than helpful."

"Then let's proceed," I indicated the floating bubble shields about us.

"Sherra?" Thorn turned toward her. She closed her eyes to send mindspeak to everyone. I blinked, as every bubble shield went invisible, after employing a mirror shield.

"I never thought I'd see this day," Garkus breathed beside me.

"You're seeing it now," I said, as Sherra and Thorn *stepped* back to their bubble, which disappeared last of all. "Come, we have our positions mapped outside the palace. Let's go."

"I'm ready," Garkus growled.

~

*Anari*

Our pod had been one of several assigned to attack the warrior-priests. I saw a gleam in Cole's eyes as we followed other bubble shields in that direction. We'd be high above it, to allow those who were selected to lob trucks to hit the building without damaging our shields.

When the first truck hit, we were to level blasts against the warren of barracks, mess halls and other buildings in the compound.

Kyal practiced his breathing exercises—aimed at calming his heart and sharpening his focus. Laren nodded to me over Kyal's head. I saw his face in the dim light of the moon. The shining orb hung halfway to the horizon in the west, where Az-ca lay—across a distance that we never thought to travel.

The first truck hit below us, crushing half of a building beneath it.

"Fire," Cole said, his voice calm and measured.

We fired, and in the light created by at least five massive fires blooming at once, I saw warrior-priests running like insects to escape us, only to be hit by our next fireblasts.

*Kill them before they kill us*, Colonel Armon had instructed. And so we did.

~

*KAAKOS*

Had I a mindspeaker, news would have traveled swifter than the alarms did. I didn't wake immediately; I'd incorporated the alarms into a dream I had. A dream where I attacked Az-ca while flying high above it. Their alarms were sounding as a result of my efforts.

When I did awaken, after a guard pounded on my chamber door, I discovered it was our alarms sounding. Az-ca had come to Ny-nes, as it turned out, and thought themselves wise to attack the troops and warrior-priests, first.

*Send more troops*, I flung mindspeak to my Generals, knowing they'd hear my voice inside their heads, although they couldn't reply. We'd trap the fools on the ground between burning buildings and the vehicles and bombs I sent against them.

*They're not attacking on the ground*, the voice came to me, then.

Drawing in a breath, I returned mindspeak. *Come to me, you worthless piece of excrement*, I shouted back at him. *Die before me, like the dog you are.*

It had to be the healer, and how would he know the way we were being attacked?

*See for yourself*, the voice came again, and this time, it held laughter.

My mind was bombarded by the images, then, of fireblasts raining from the sky, far above the warrior-priests' compound, and upon the troops' barracks. When a heavy vehicle was flung into the burning mess of the compound, it launched a storm of sparks skyward, which would in turn fall upon anything flammable around it.

They intended to set the city ablaze.

Cursing, I shut off the images and placed a shield to keep more from coming in; I had a battle to plan, to take them all when they attacked my palace.

"Get past my shields if you can, you devils," I hissed aloud. While shouting for my guards, I flung on a dressing robe and stalked out of my suite, heading for my audience chamber.

*Fire the weapons*, I commanded my Generals in mindspeak. They could hear my mental commands, some of them for the first time. I held that much power, and more. If any of them guessed I held power not given by the Prophet, it no longer mattered. They weren't going to survive, anyway.

As for the attack I commanded against the enemy, I no longer cared that bombs would be lobbed at my city. I cared not that it could be destroyed in the process. It was already burning—let the devils of Az-ca deal with our returning firepower—for now.

Their delight at destroying two compounds would end quickly enough, when they had to contend with my first round of opposition.

Reaching out while chanting the spell under my breath, I called in the power from every warrior-priest still alive. It turned out to be more than I thought, too, and I reveled in the energy of their lives pouring into mine.

Less than half were at their compound when they were hit; many were across the river looking for the healer, just as my troops were.

How fortuitous was that?

The first puny blasts the enemy leveled against the palace shield were only heard and not felt. They'd have to do better than that to get anywhere near me. The moment my warrior-priests were drained and dead, I turned to the power within my troops.

Had the enemy thought me alone and helpless? I had thousands to draw from, and the capacity to hold all the power of their life-force, until I chose to unleash it.

*Against them.*

~

*KYRI*

Fire and move. Fire and move. We'd begun our attack against Kaakos' palace, Garkus and I, as puny as those efforts were.

Let him think we were insufficient—that more than one group was firing at him from different locations, with no results.

Let him believe that. We fired again, watching the flames bloom against an impenetrable shield—with only two of us working. We weren't combining blasts—we hadn't attempted it.

We'd see soon enough what the others could do.

*We're being fired upon,* Sherra sent to me. *They've wakened their war machines and are lobbing bombs. We're in the process of capturing them and sending them back, but it's taking time away from our other efforts. Two of our pods have been destroyed.*

*Then come to the palace. Let them hurl bombs at Kaakos' shield and see how he likes it.* A few moments passed; I imagined she was having a rushed conversation with Thorn.

*On our way,* she replied.

*Our backup is coming,* I informed Garkus, who leveled another blast from our current position before I *stepped* us away.

~

*SHERRA*

*What just happened?* I sent to Kerok and the others inside our shield.

The war machines had stopped—almost at once, and we now flew through the eerie quiet that descended upon Kaakos' city.

No bombs or blasts were fired at us as we raced toward the palace. Were they waiting for us to get there, before opening fire again?

*Has he commanded them to stop firing?* Armon asked a question of his own.

*I don't know,* Kerok replied.

*Something's wrong,* I hissed into Kerok's mind.

*I think you're right*, he agreed, his mindspeak revealing deep concern. There was no mistaking the bombardment of ill will hurled at us. Something else lay within it—perhaps it was our nearness to Kaakos, but I couldn't be sure.

*There's the palace—we're almost at the shield line*, Caral drew us back to the business at hand.

*Tell the troops to take their positions*, Kerok barked. I relayed the message. We intended to form a ring around Kaakos' shield wall, and the first blasts would be released in unison.

I still couldn't shake the feeling that something was terribly wrong —and it was increasing, rather than decreasing.

*Focus*, I reminded myself sternly. We had a job to do, and a tyrant to kill.

~

NORTH

Servants cowered in every dark corner of the lower level. Heavily shielded, they didn't see me as I walked past them, my footsteps muffled with power.

It wouldn't do for Kaakos to realize I'd come. Let him think I was outside with the others, although he should have known better.

Perhaps, in his delusional egotism, he didn't think I had enough strength to go against him alone.

He was right.

*Mostly.*

The steps to the upper levels were before me, now, as the first concerted blasts from Az-ca's army hit Kaakos' outer shield.

He hadn't expected them to rock the palace, sending loose ceiling ornaments crashing to the polished marble floors.

Some of the debris bounced off my shield before shattering in a massive, laborious series of clanks—with plaster and stone dust clouding about me.

Grateful that the servants were likely cowering more than they were before, I began my journey up the first flights of steps, heading toward Kaakos' audience room. No doubt he was orchestrating his counterattack from there, against an enemy he hadn't expected to arrive so soon.

*Keep him occupied*, I silently begged the outside forces. I needn't have worried; the second round of blasts knocked even more plaster and stone down, and cracks began threading their way through the walls.

Kaakos' shields held, but they didn't hold far underground. He'd never expected to get attacked with this much force, and the need for a full bubble shield around the palace, threaded through the rock and soil beneath it, had never crossed his mind.

The combined blasts hitting his shield now didn't break it, but they were certainly breaking into the earth beneath the palace.

I was now on the second flight of steps. "Keep him occupied," I breathed aloud. None were on the steps with me—they either cringed from the blows leveled against the palace, or were in the audience room with Kaakos, awaiting his orders.

No doubt they were terrified—as they should be. They had no way to escape.

Only Kaakos could do that, and I intended that he stay right where he was, and receive his long-overdue death.

Now on the third level of steps, I heard a crash and groan behind me; the second level of steps I'd just climbed had collapsed, cutting off any who thought to follow.

Only Kaakos and those closest to him would be on the third level. Another jolt rocked the palace, and I was forced to leap toward the landing at the top of the third-level steps before they crashed into a pile of rubble below.

So much for the ancient building Kaakos called his palace. It, like many others had before it, would fall soon enough.

*I must hurry*, I chastised myself as I ran a lengthy hallway to reach the audience chamber. If the palace fell before I could get near enough, all would be lost.

～

*ANARI*

The outer wall surrounding the palace fell with a deafening roar, and once one part caved, the rest followed, like gaming tiles set on end in rows.

*He didn't make his shields round,* Kyal snickered in mindspeak. *The ground is caving beneath his palace.*

We'd been firing blasts for what felt like forever, although dawn hadn't arrived in Ny-nes, yet.

Perhaps a rosy glow in the east indicated it, or maybe it was the glow from a city that burned all around us, now.

We hadn't been sent away, as Cole said we might, if we appeared tired or the task too much for us.

We still had energy—the four of us.

*The shield is still holding against our attacks,* Cole reminded us. He knew, just as we did, that the enemy inside the crumbling palace could *step* away, and we'd be back where we started. I was hoping we'd breach it by now; with Az-ca's elite troops all around us, anyone else's shield would have been destroyed already.

Not this one.

*Fire,* Cole commanded. It was our turn, so we fired another blast.

～

*SHERRA*

*Lay a shield around the palace,* Kerok commanded. *One he can't cross, if you can. I don't want the bastard to* step *away from us.*

*I'm ahead of you,* I informed him. *I laid the shield before we fired the first blasts. It goes below the lowest point of his and forms a bubble,* I added. *It should block him if he tries to escape.*

*Good. Excellent. Do we have anyone asking to pull back? I think dawn is coming.*

*None have asked to pull back,* I reported. We didn't have a large number of mindspeakers, but we'd devised a signal, if anyone had spent themselves and needed to *step* away.

I worried that what Kerok thought of as dawn was only the city burning farther east, but I didn't say that.

Daylight would be welcome, but I didn't want to give myself false hope. With all the smoke and fire billowing around Kaakos' shield, we couldn't get a good reckoning of the damage to the palace.

I worried that servants were dead inside, but I shoved that thought away. He'd have killed them anyway, eventually.

*Hold steady*, Kerok commanded as our bubble wobbled slightly. He and I stood shoulder-to-shoulder, our power combined with that of Armon, Levi, Caral and Misten. Our pod was powerful, although not a crack had appeared in Kaakos' shield as yet.

*Keep firing*, Kerok snapped. I relayed that message to the others.

~

*KAAKOS*

I wasn't ready to *step* away—not yet. I hadn't fired a single blast against the enemy, and they'd grown confident that they'd kill me inside a crumbling palace.

They should know better. I wasn't done with them—not by a long way. Gathering power about me, I frightened the guards standing in a ring around my body. Some of them ran, while the others backed away.

Let them know I was powerful. I wanted to laugh at their fear as those remaining backed away faster, before turning to follow the first wave of runners. At any other time, I would have killed them immediately, but the enemy required my attention, now.

Leveling that first blast against the enemy blew past my outer shield, then unexpectedly ricocheted against another. In a rush, I was forced to absorb rebounding power into myself, to keep the palace from exploding around me.

As I struggled to assimilate my own blast, I felt the hands about my throat.

*Someone had breached my personal shield.*

~

*NORTH*

I didn't waste time on words, although I'd dreamed often of what I'd say when this moment came.

Instead, I focused on the ring on my left hand, and pulled power through it—enough power to kill the one whose throat was in my hands.

The palace shuddered beneath our feet, almost making me fall. I could not—would not—remove my hands, however. Pulling more power through my ring, I tightened my fingers on Kaakos flesh, cutting off the air he fought to draw into his lungs.

~

*SHERRA*

I hadn't noticed his distress—until the drain on Kerok's power became a drain on my own, causing me to shriek in pain and rage. My connection to Armon and the others ensured that they felt the drain too, and that only served to terrify me. Their connection was severed first—by Armon.

"Disconnect from Thorn," Armon shouted at me, then, his words ringing dimly in my ears, as if they were encased in cotton wool.

Kaakos had found a way to tap us—through Kerok. I screamed as more power was sucked away, before I was forced by the others to disconnect from Kerok. Once my power was no longer being leeched away, Kerok dropped to the floor of our bubble, unconscious.

"He's dying," I wept as I dropped beside him and held Kerok's limp body against mine. "My shield has been destroyed," I wailed.

"Sherra," Armon shouted, "Focus." When I continued to weep, Caral slapped me hard across the face.

That forced me back to the battle, whether I wanted it or not.

*What's happening?* Cole's voice sounded in my head.

*I think Kaakos has taken Kerok,* I sobbed, attempting to reset my shield.

~

*KYRI*

Kaakos' shield wavered. I'd explored it often enough since my arrival in Ny-nes to recognize that fact.

*Let's go,* I snapped at Garkus, and waiting for the next weakening of Kaakos' shield, I *stepped* to his audience chamber.

The sight that met my eyes I will never forget.

~

*KAAKOS*

I couldn't breathe. Every time I flung power against my attacker, it was absorbed or deflected.

*How was that possible?*

My vision began to darken, and the grip on my throat never lessened.

I only had one last attempt to make, and it wouldn't be enough to get past the shield surrounding mine.

*Until I felt it fall.*

With the last bit of strength I held, I drew power from every servant still wearing my chains.

My blood had been used to create the spells within the chains, and those who wore them were a final source of energy for a desperate attempt at escape.

Sucking their power into myself, I *stepped.*

Before I left my palace behind, I leveled a blast against the area where fire still rained upon the building.

My joy at seeing enemy bodies hurled through the air, I'd recall and savor later. I *stepped* farther away, to save myself. Perhaps there was a roar of anger behind me—it no longer mattered.

*I was free.*

~

*Armon*

Thorn was unconscious and barely alive as dawn revealed the still-burning, smoking ruin of a city.

The only thing that hadn't burned was the palace, and it would have if Kyri hadn't sent mindspeak to anyone who could hear to stand down.

Kaakos had escaped, and he shouldn't have. In all, we'd lost twelve pods—most of those at the last, as Kaakos fired at them before escaping.

Had Sherra's attention and some of her power not been diverted, he'd have died at our hands.

Kyri told us to wait, and to bring Sherra with us to the wing that held Kaakos' audience chamber.

As far as we knew, Kaakos had found a way to extract power from Thorn—even through the bubble shield and the other layers of shields around our pod. How he'd managed that, I still couldn't fathom.

I hoped Kyri had answers, because I had plenty of questions.

Sherra sat on the ground not far away, with Thorn's head in her lap. She'd cried herself out, I think, at the empty husk in her arms.

It was bad enough that this had happened to Hunter.

Now, we were forced to deal with the same malady in our King.

I'd sent most of our remaining troops back to Az-ca, Cole and the young ones included, for food and much-needed rest.

In the city and across the river, not a single troop nor warrior-priest still lived. Kaakos had somehow emptied all of them, before grasping at Thorn's power.

I wanted to curse, and found myself too weary and disheartened to do it.

*Come now*, Kyri sent. *I want to explain what I know.*

～

*Sherra*

Armon offered to carry Kerok in his arms. Instead, I used power to form a bubble about Kerok's unconscious body, and, unwilling to let it out of my sight, *stepped* it with me to the audience chamber, where Kyri waited for us.

She and Garkus stood next to the high seat that had been Kaakos' throne.

Upon that seat, and in Kaakos' place, another man sat, his head bowed, shaggy, dark hair falling about his face. With Kerok's bubble floating beside me, I approached Kyri, and the one I assumed was North.

He lifted his head, causing me to gasp.

Kerok hadn't looked much like his father, but Drenn did.

This one—I wouldn't have been surprised if he'd been Kerok's father, they looked so much alike.

My eyes fell to his hands, which gripped the arms of the chair so tightly, his knuckles were white.

There, I saw it—on his left hand. An identical ring to the one Kerok wore—the one he'd said had come from his namesake ancestor.

Kaakos hadn't emptied Kerok of power.

*This one had.*

With a scream of anger, I launched myself at him.

## CHAPTER 23

*Kyri*

"I wish it were otherwise," I told Sherra. "If you kill him, you kill your Thorn, too. They're connected, now. One fate is tied to the other."

"If they're connected, then why is Kerok emptied of power?" she demanded. She was angry, now. Later, she'd empty herself with weeping again. I knew that cycle all too well.

"I don't have a good answer," I replied. "I only know their lives are intertwined. "North says that ah, if you attempt to restore Thorn's power with your own, that the power will only drain through the ring your Thorn wears, and come to him. It's the spell he created, and once it's activated, it only goes one way."

"Fuck him. Fuck you. Fuck everybody for not telling me this," she hissed. Her power was returning—Garkus had found food in the kitchen and made sure everyone ate.

Except Sherra's Thorn.

Thorn the First, who'd called himself North to hide himself from Kaakos and anyone else who might recognize that name, was busy pacing and blaming himself for letting Kaakos get away.

Who knew where the bastard was, now?

That was another tale that Sherra would have to be told, and North and I had to take that blame, too.

As for Ny-nes, someone needed to rebuild it, and teach the people to govern themselves. I didn't know whether North would take that task, or find a quiet place somewhere to begin looking for Kaakos again.

I'd sent mindspeak to Doret, so she and Barth knew of Thorn's condition, and that Sherra would be in charge upon her return, until Thorn recovered.

*If* he recovered.

North was also nursing a broken nose, after Sherra punched him in the face. I decided not to help with that. Let him feel pain for what he'd inadvertently done. Kaakos wouldn't be surprised again; I'd lay the entire resources of Ny-nes and Az-ca on it.

"He's Kaakos' father, isn't he?" Sherra demanded. "North. I refuse to call him Thorn. Kerok is a thousand times the man he could ever be."

"He isn't the only one to blame in all this mess," I confessed.

"Oh, I know you attempted to train Kaakos when he was young. I saw it. At the time, I thought you'd rescued him from Ny-nes, and he'd gone back after you'd failed with him. That's how I got through his shield, you know—I saw him in your past and got a feel for his power. But for anyone else to get through, they have to be tied to his blood in some way, don't they?"

Sherra's assessment was more than shrewd.

"Yes." It was how North had gotten close enough to put his hands on Kaakos.

"I'm going home, and the others are coming with me," Sherra snapped. "I don't give a fuck what happens to you from now on."

Her words were like blows and made me cringe. "What about North?" My voice wasn't steady.

"I wish I could say the same to him, but his life means Kerok's life, now. Try not to let him die, or I'll blame you for that, too."

I wanted to apologize. To say how sorry I was that my past mistakes had harmed her so much. She was gone before I could open my mouth.

~

*KING'S PALACE, Az-ca*

*Sherra*

"Lay him down carefully," I said, as Levi and Armon lowered Kerok's body onto our bed.

A moan escaped Kerok's lips. It was the first sound he'd made since his power had been drained away by the filth who was once King of Az-ca.

"I'll get broth," Briar whispered. She'd followed us inside the suite, her eyes wide with fear.

"I hope he wakes enough to swallow," I sighed.

"Sherra," Barth walked into the room.

"Barth?" I turned toward him. He looked gray, and the lines in his face told a tale of no sleep. Pottles peered around his wide shoulders. She was afraid to say anything, I'm sure, lest I accuse her, just as I'd accused Kyri.

"My Queen, the rule of Az-ca is now in your hands," Barth bowed to me. "I will accompany you to the Council tomorrow, where it will be announced to all, and messages will be carried to the villages. For now, what is your command?"

"Bring Colonel Armon to me in twelve hours, after he's rested," I nodded to Armon so he'd know he and Levi were allowed to leave. "We have plans to make, to keep the bastard son of Thorn I out of our country."

~

*NY-NES*

*North*

"Adahi, old friend, I had his throat in my hands. I was so close," I spoke to the remains inside the glass case. "I didn't realize Thorn was connected to his Queen, and that I'd drain some of her power with his. Her shield fell, which was keeping Kaakos from *stepping* away. I owe you—and her—an apology. I owe Thorn II more than that. What was it you always told me? That I was too full of myself? That has come home to roost, as Kyri would say."

Kyri had told me afterward, because I hadn't guessed it, that Queen Sherra was Adahi's many-times great-granddaughter. His child worked to save Az-ca, while mine had done his best to destroy it.

Now that I was connected to my descendant, neither of us could remove the rings we wore, or we'd die. It was the first blood spell I'd cast in the distant past, thinking I'd made it as perfect as possible.

Again, I'd been too full of myself. I'd simulated my death shortly afterward, begging Adahi in my last written request that he or someone he trusted ensure that the ring in the catacombs would come to my namesake in the future. The body in the catacombs was some poor soul whose likeness I'd spelled to resemble mine.

The book I'd left for a future King Thorn was another miscalculation, enveloped in a hurried spell not fully thought out. Thorn's brother had carried the book away. If he'd found the ring, however, it would have killed him the moment he attempted to remove it.

For better or worse, Adahi had done as I'd asked, never suspecting what would come of it. He'd died honorably, too.

*Twice.*

By saving Kyri the first time, and saving his descendant's life the last.

"You, my friend, are the noble one," I said, dipping my chin to Adahi's corpse. "While I have brought evil to everything I've touched."

# EPILOGUE

## SHERRA

erok woke the following morning; I found him sitting up in bed, shivering violently when I walked out of the bathroom. After mentally shouting for Barth to fetch the physician, I ran to his side.

"S-so cold," he mumbled, while I struggled to pull blankets about him. "W-what happened?"

"I'll tell you after the physician comes, all right?" I held him in my arms, terrified by what was happening.

Az-ca still had a King.

*A King without his power.*

I had no idea how that would eventually play out, especially if North went looking for Kaakos and managed to die in the attempt. If North died, Kerok would die, too. I didn't want to tell Kerok that, but if his mind were whole, he'd want to know.

*Fuck you, North,* I sent mindspeak. *Fuck you to a thousand hells.*

The End

Sherra and Kerok's story will continue in *Queen of Thorns and Roses.*
*Estimated release: Spring, 2018*

~

## Names of Characters and Places Appearing in this Book:

**Adahi:** AKA the phantom; well acquainted with former King Thorn. Dreamwalker, who has a long history with Kyri and events in Ny-nes

**Alf:** Worker in the berry farms under Az-ca's southern domes. Spy for Ruarke and then Kaakos.

**Alun:** New hire for the King's palace in Az-ca. Spy for Kaakos, sent to kill Thorn II

**Ana:** North Camp Instructor, Second Cohort

**Anari:** 17-year-old black rose girl with mindspeaking and stepping talent

**Armon:** Colonel in Az-ca's army, currently serves as First advisor to Prince Commander. Chosen by Caral

**Arresh:** The name chosen by Sherra's dreamwalker

**Aspe:** Warrior-priest and favorite of Kaakos

**Az-ca:** Desert country ruled by King Wulf; always at war with barbarians from Ny-nes

**Balsom:** Village in eastern Az-ca, roughly twenty miles south of Sa'wann. There, the terrain is relatively flat

**Barth:** King's Chief Diviner

**Beckley:** Warrior, chosen by Reena

**Beels:** Warrior-priest; mindspeaker and spy among warrior-priests for Kaakos

**Bela:** Former washout

**Barney:** (Barna) escort trainee and former washout

**Blane Grove:** former Council member and Merrin's ally

**Bones of the Prophet:** a drug given to those in Ny-nes' army and its clerics, to ensure their compliance

**Book of the Rose (The):** A book in the King's library, describing talents and duties of Black Rose escorts

**Bray:** Barth's secondary Diviner

**Briar:** Servant in King's palace, Az-ca

**Bulldog:** a nickname used by Yasa, North Camp Instructor, Sixth Cohort

**Calli:** escort who, with her warrior, deserted the army and joined with Merrin

**Captain Indus:** Officer in Az-ca's army; chosen as one of the King's elite troops

**Captain Neele:** Ranking officer often left in charge of Secondary Camp

**Caral:** Fourth Cohort trainee at North Camp

**Claude:** Former sergeant in Az-ca's army. Mindspeaker who worked as a messenger after his retirement

**Cole:** a refugee from Ny-nes. Born with power, he was tortured as a child until he escaped by stepping to Kyri's City at her invitation

**Colonel Kage:** Training Instructor for warrior trainees in the King's City—becomes a King's assassin

**Colonel Weren:** Training Instructor for warrior trainees in the King's City; becomes General of the Army

**Commander Alden:** Post Commander for Secondary Camp

**Dar-den:** Caral's former village

**Daria:** Doret's sister, killed by Ruarke

**Derissa:** Caral's older sister, from Dar-den

**Dayl:** General Linel's personal messenger

**Derk Beadl:** former Council member and ally of Merrin

**Doret:** Former Queen of Az-ca; more than 200 years old

**Drenn Wulfson Meris Rex:** Crown Prince of Az-ca (deceased)

**East Camp:** one of four training camps for black rose trainees

**End-War:** crippling event that changed and destroyed nearly everything on the planet

**Falia:** Instructor at North Camp

**Ferni:** One of two young troublemakers at the training camp for girls

**F'nexscot:** AKA the King's City

**Gale:** Armon's former escort

**Garkus:** Drill instructor at Secondary Camp—became a King's assassin

**Garth:** Outpost Commander

**Gaull:** Far northeastern village in Az-ca. Jubal lives outside the village

**Geb:** retired warrior—now works as a traveling instructor for all trainees

**General Linel:** Chief Commander of the army in the Prince Commander's absence

**General Tern:** Officer in Ny-nes' army

**Giles:** Instructor from Cole's village

**Grae:** Kerok's deceased escort

**Gram Plicton:** former Council member, who became Merrin's ally after Drenn's death

**Harel:** messenger who was burned by Merrin's warrior allies before escaping to take the news of Merrin's location to the Crown Prince (deceased)

**Hari:** escort abandoned by her warrior (Narris)

**Harnn:** Bela's warrior

**Hayla:** black rose trainee

**High Commander Finn:** Supreme Commander of Ny-nes' army

**Hunter Lattham:** King's advisor, Uncle to Merrin, Drenn and Kerok

**Jacob:** Council member for Dar-den, Caral's former village

**Jae:** black rose trainee—Sixth Cohort, North Camp (deceased)

**Jeen:** One of two young troublemakers at girls' training camp

**Jerr:** Council member from Wildtree Village

**Jubal Raime:** Disabled warrior and mindspeaker, who became a spy for Ruarke and then Kaakos

**Kaakos:** the name taken by the Sovereign Leader of the Free Nation of Ny-nes.

**Kage:** see Colonel Kage

**Kerok:** AKA Thorn Wulfson Kerok Rex, King Wulf's youngest son and Prince Commander of the army—becomes Crown Prince upon Drenn's death, and then King upon his father's death

**Ketchi:** the village where Cole and many other refugees from Ny-nes live. All were born with power and were sentenced to death by Ruarke

**King Wulf Carlson Alexander Rex:** King of Az-ca (deceased)

**Kyal:** 11-year-old warrior boy with mindspeaking talent

**Kyri:** Female Diviner—believed to be a legend or myth

**Laren:** 16-year-old warrior boy with mindspeaking talent

**Lera:** escort abandoned by her warrior

**Levi:** Captain, serves as Secondary Advisor to Prince Commander. Chosen by Misten

**Lewus:** Council member for Merthis and five other villages

**Liam:** Kaakos' Chief of Technical Sciences

**Lieutenant Marc:** Chosen by Wend; promoted to Captain

**Lilya:** North Camp Instructor, Fourth Cohort

**Liri:** Chief instructor from Cole's village

**Marc:** See Lieutenant Marc

**Mari:** black rose girl; Romma's daughter

**Marra:** Daria's chosen warrior

**Marta:** General Weren's wife

**Mendacium:** Ny-nes' capital city, renamed after Kaakos took over rule of the country. He named it that in a private jest

**Merrin:** Nephew of Hunter and King Wulf; cousin to Drenn and Kerok (on mother's side)

**Merthis:** small village where Sherra was born

**Miri:** North Camp Instructor, Fifth Cohort

**Misten:** North Camp trainee, Sixth Cohort

**Narris:** warrior-turned-traitor who left his escort behind (Hari) before deserting army

**Narvin:** deserter who, with his escort Willa, chose to follow Merrin

**Neka:** North Camp trainee, First Cohort

**Nguyen-Mei:** resident of Kyri's City—caretaker for Mari, a black rose girl

**Niles:** cleric who became Ruarke's second-in-command upon Ward's death

**Nina:** North Camp Instructor, First Cohort

**North:** Healer in Ny-nes—has changed his name to hide a past identity

**North Camp:** One of four camps where black rose trainees are taught

**Ny-nes:** Land of barbarian enemies

**Nyra:** Levi's deceased escort

**Olan:** Chief Diviner for the army

**Oren:** Messenger for Crown Prince Thorn

**Pa-sen:** small village in southwestern Az-ca

**Phantom:** see Adahi

**Pottles:** Blind pot seller and friend to Sherra (see Doret)

**Poul:** Assassin for King Wulf (deceased)

**Querl:** Army deserter and Merrin's chief ally

**Reena:** Former washout

**Reva:** escort who, with her warrior, deserted the army and joined with Merrin

**Romma:** Resident of Dar-den, mother of Mari, a black rose girl

**Ruarke:** Chief Cleric of Ny-nes, and Kaakos' second-in-command

**Sa'wann:** Village in eastern Az-ca, nestled in a hilly area prone to predator attacks

**Secondary Camp:** Location for final escort training after warriors are chosen

**Sherra:** Black Rose trainee from Merthis. Bonded to Thorn Wulfson Kerok Rex; Doret considers her an adopted daughter

**Soobi:** Kitchen servant in Kaakos' palace

**Stave:** Resident of the far northeastern village of Gaull in Az-ca; Jubal's closest neighbor

**Tera:** North Camp trainee—Sixth Cohort

**The Rose Mark:** a forbidden book. That decision was overturned by Crown Prince Thorn, and copies were provided to all trainees.

**Thorn's Book of Advanced Divination Techniques:** a forbidden book

**Ura:** North Camp trainee and one of the Bulldog's pets

**Vale:** Northernmost supply village for Az-ca's army

**Varnon:** village elder in Merthis

**Venge:** Top General in Kaakos' army

**Vengeance:** Raver created by Kaakos, after taking over Merrin's mind

**Veri:** North Camp trainee and one of the Bulldog's pets

**Ward:** cleric and Ruarke's second-in-command (deceased)

**Welton:** Chief Physician, military post

**Wend:** North Camp Trainee, Sixth Cohort

**Wendal:** Assassin for King Wulf (deceased)

**Weren:** Former Colonel and warrior trainee instructor. Becomes General of the army

**West Cana:** area where Kyri's City is located

**Willa:** escort bonded to warrior Narvin. She and her warrior deserted the army to follow Merrin

**Wulf Tadson Ruarke Rex:** see Ruarke

**Yasa:** AKA Bulldog, or the Bulldog

**Zis:** Warrior-priest in Raver/Merrin's entourage

# ACKNOWLEDGMENTS

As always, this book is the result of collaboration. If not for the support of my family, my editor, my cover artist and my beta readers, it would be less than it is. All mistakes, as usual, are mine and no other's.

# ABOUT THE AUTHOR

Connie Suttle lives in Oklahoma with her husband and a small army of cats. They'd wear uniforms, but they can't agree on anything, let alone clothing designs or who will actually be in charge.*

*This is why Cats don't rule the world, although they have taken over the Internet.

*Find Connie in the following ways:*
www.subtledemon.com

Blood Destiny Series:

Blood Wager

Blood Passage

Blood Sense

Blood Domination

Blood Royal

Blood Queen

Blood Rebellion

Blood War

Blood Redemption

Blood Reunion

Legend of the Ir'Indicti Series:

Bumble

Shadowed

Target

Vendetta

Destroyer

High Demon Series:

Demon Lost

Demon Revealed

Demon's King

Demon's Quest

Demon's Revenge

Demon's Dream

~

God Wars Series:

Blood Double

Blood Trouble

Blood Revolution

Blood Love

Blood Finale

~

Saa Thalarr Series:

Hope and Vengeance

Wyvern and Company

Observe and Protect*

~

First Ordinance Series:

Finder

Keeper

BlackWing

SpellBreaker

WhiteWing

~

R-D Series:

Cloud Dust

Cloud Invasion

Cloud Rebel

∼

Latter Day Demons Series:

Hot Demon in the City

A Demon's Work is Never Done

A Demon's Due

∼

Seattle Elementals Series:

Your Money's Worth

Worth Your While*

∼

BlackWing Pirates Series:

MindSighted

MindMage

MindRogue*

∼

Black Rose Sorceress Series:

The Rose Mark

Rose and Thorn

Black Rose Queen

Queen of Thorns and Roses*

~

Anthologies:
Other Worldly Ways


*Forthcoming